Praise for MARY DAHEIM and her hilarious BED-AND-BREAKFAST MYSTERIES!

"The reigning queen of the cozies."
Portland Oregonian

"A joyous series. A visit with Judith and Renie
is comfort food for the mind."
Romantic Times

"Mary Daheim is one of the brightest stars."
Seattle Times

"Delightful mysteries."
Kansas City Star

"Like Joan Hess' Maggody series,
Daheim's bed-and-breakfast mysteries show
a funny and often stinging insight into
people's relationships and behavior."
Houston Chronicle

"Daheim writes with wit, wisdom, and a big heart."
Carolyn Hart

"She is really good at what she does."
Statesman Journal (OR)

Bed-and-Breakfast Mysteries by Mary Daheim

ALL THE PRETTY HEARSES • LOCO MOTIVE
VI AGRA FALLS • SCOTS ON THE ROCKS
SAKS & VIOLINS • DEAD MAN DOCKING
THIS OLD SOUSE • HOCUS CROAKUS
SILVER SCREAM • SUTURE SELF
A STREETCAR NAMED EXPIRE • CREEPS SUZETTE
LEGS BENEDICT • SNOW PLACE TO DIE
WED AND BURIED • SEPTEMBER MOURN
NUTTY AS A FRUITCAKE • AUNTIE MAYHEM
MURDER, MY SUITE • MAJOR VICES
A FIT OF TEMPERA • BANTAM OF THE OPERA
DUNE TO DEATH • HOLY TERRORS
FOWL PREY • JUST DESSERTS

Coming Soon in Hardcover

THE WURST IS YET TO COME

MARY DAHEIM

ALL THE PRETTY HEARSES

A BED-AND-BREAKFAST MYSTERY

AVON

An Imprint of HarperCollinsPublishers

AVON BOOKS
An Imprint of HarperCollins*Publishers*
195 Broadway
New York, NY 10007

Copyright © 2011 by Mary Daheim
Excerpt from *The Wurst Is Yet to Come* copyright © 2012 by Mary Daheim
ISBN 978-0-06-135159-4
www.avonmystery.com

First Avon Books mass market printing: June 2012
First William Morrow hardcover printing: August 2011

Avon Trademark Reg. U.S. Pat. Off. and in Other Countries, Marca Registrada, Hecho en U.S.A.
HarperCollins® is a registered trademark of HarperCollins Publishers.

Printed in the U.S.A.

10 9 8 7 6 5 4

To all my children,
who return the love I've given them with interest

Author's Note

The action of this book takes place in early 2005.

ALL
THE PRETTY
HEARSES

Chapter One

Judith McMonigle Flynn flinched, winced, and wondered why Cousin Renie was screaming her head off while trying to batter down the back door of Hillside Manor.

"What's wrong with you?" Judith demanded, opening the door. "Are you insane or being chased by ravenous wolves?"

Renie virtually fell across the threshold. "Both," she gasped, leaning against the wall next to the pantry. "That's the last time I ever stop by the parish school office to drop off my Campbell's Soup labels."

Judith gestured for Renie to follow her into the kitchen. "I didn't realize you still saved them after all these years. You haven't had a kid at Our Lady, Star of the Sea School for twenty-five years." She pulled out a kitchen chair for her cousin. "Sit. Stop hyperventilating. Coffee?"

Renie shook her head as she flopped into the chair. "Old habits die hard. Old SOTS just die," she went on, using the acronym for her fellow parishioners, "but not before they can avoid falling into the clutches of younger parents who are active school fund-raisers."

"Oh." Judith sat down across from Renie. "I managed to avoid some of that by going into exile out on Thurlow Street with Dan. My son's tenure at SOTS was all too brief before he had to attend public school. Since I held down two jobs, I was rarely an active parent except when I'd try to find where he'd hidden his latest report card."

"Count your blessings," Renie murmured. She twisted around to look at the old schoolhouse clock. "Almost noon. I could've sworn it was five o'clock. The last twenty minutes seemed like hours." She reached for the sheep-shaped cookie jar on the table. "I'm hungry. They're having hamburger lunch today at school. I was tempted to wait for the delivery from Doc's Burgers and steal one." She tapped the cookie jar's lid. "What's in here?"

"Stale Christmas cookies," Judith responded. "I vowed not to bake again until January tenth. Between running the B&B and all the holiday goodies, I'm tapped."

"Hmm." Renie's brown eyes twinkled. "You, too, will be dragooned into this charitable work. You're a parishioner. Contributors aren't limited to school parents. In fact, you don't even have to be a SOT."

"If you told me what it is," Judith said, "I'd know how to avoid it."

"Martha Morelli has the last of her five kids in eighth grade this year," Renie said. "You know what a demon she is for fund-raising. It's not enough to have the annual auction, the crab dinner, the St. Patrick's Day dinner, the Italian dinner, the sauerkraut dinner, the First Martyrs of the Church of Rome dinner . . ."

Judith held up a hand. "Whoa. We don't have a . . . what did you just say?"

"Oh." Renie held her head. "That's right. Bridget McDonough suggested that event a couple of years ago, but Father Hoyle pointed out that the First Martyrs in Rome *were* dinner. For the lions, that is. Nero's Circus Maximus was short on clowns and trained seals."

"Not all the fund-raisers are for the school, though," Judith remarked. "Yes, they had the Christmas wreath and poinsettia sale in early December, but the spring auction is the major source of school funding. It's been enormously successful."

Renie nodded. "We lucked out with some of the city's high-profile athletes moving to Heraldsgate Hill and joining the parish. But now they've either retired or been traded. That's part of the problem, so they're looking at additional revenue producers. Martha wants to put a cookbook together. Guess who she wants to design it."

Judith laughed. "That's logical. You *are* a graphic designer."

"Yes," Renie conceded with a longing look at the cookie jar. "But I'm trying to scale down. This year I'm only taking on the gas company's annual report, but my deadline is late January. Plus I'm doing a brochure for Key Largo Bank and reworking somebody's in-house botched newsletter for retired city lighting employees. Both are due in mid-February, the same as the cookbook. Martha should've asked me sooner, like in the fall."

"Why didn't she?"

"She insists she tried to get hold of me in early November, but we'd all gone on our Boston trip," Renie explained. "By the time you and I got back, it was mid-November, and Martha was caught up with Thanksgiving and Christmas. So were we, for that matter."

Judith got up from the chair. "I've got to start making Mother's lunch. If you're hungry enough to eat the sheep's head on the cookie jar, I'll make you a sandwich, too."

"No, thanks," Renie said. "I should go home. Oh—by the way, we're all supposed to contribute cookbook recipes. That includes you."

"I can do that," Judith said. "What are you going to offer?"

Renie was on her feet, rummaging in the new—and huge—handbag Bill had given her for Christmas. "Shrimp Dump."

Judith almost dropped the mustard jar she'd taken out of the fridge. "I hope you're kidding."

"No. Hey, I like it."

"Nobody else does."

"You mean like you and the rest of my family?"

"More like the rest of the world. Why not offer your Bean Glop and Clam Doodoo, too? The names alone would make most people gag."

"Hey—have you forgotten that at one of my bridal showers the guests were asked to bring their two favorite recipes and your contributions were Pottsfield Pickles and How to Can a Tuna Fish?"

"That was over forty years ago," Judith said, placing two ham slices on the cutting block in the middle of the kitchen. "Well . . . you knew I was joking. You aren't."

"That's right." Renie clutched her key ring and slung the handbag over her shoulder. "Oh—there's another new parish event on the schedule for next fall. This one you'll love."

Judith regarded her cousin warily. "What?"

"Alicia and Reggie Beard-Smythe want to sponsor a hunt-club outing. Shall I sign you up now?"

"Very funny," Judith said drily. "Will my horse have an artificial hip like mine?"

"I'm sure that could be arranged." Renie headed through the hallway to the back door. "See ya."

"Wait," Judith called. "Is this hunt-club thing serious?"

Renie turned around. "Yes. There's a new hunt club over on the Eastside. The Beard-Smythes are avid hunters. For a mere three hundred bucks apiece, parishioners can take part in a hunt. Horse provided, bad riding habits optional. The money goes to SOTS."

"It's a good thing all those dot-com zillionaires have moved to Heraldsgate Hill in recent years," Judith said.

"The Beard-Smythes might get some of them to sign up. I assume you won't be one of them."

"Correct. As you may recall, I was the first person to ride a horse on the I-5 Interstate before it was completed. I did not want to do that, but my horse did. I never got on a horse again and don't intend to."

"Good thinking," Judith said.

"Which reminds me," Renie said, "when do the guests arrive for their free overnight?"

Judith clapped a hand to her cheek. "Oh my God! I forgot about them. Let me check my schedule."

Renie followed her cousin back into the kitchen. "The auction was in May," Judith said, sitting down at her computer on the counter. "I completely forgot I'd offered that overnight during the slow January season." She paused, scrolling through Hillside Manor's January confirmations. "This Friday, January seventh. Norma and Wilbur Paine bought it for their children and grandchildren. I can't believe they have grandchildren old enough to stay at a B&B."

"I could never believe they had children," Renie remarked. "Nobody as homely as the Paines should've been allowed to procreate."

Judith pointed at the names with her cursor. "Andrew and Paulina Paine, Walter and Sonya Paine, Sarah and Dennis Blair, Hannah and Zachary Conrad, Chad and Chase Paine, Zoë Paine and Octavia Blair. Does that sound right to you?"

Renie shrugged. "The Paines had kids in the school, but they were older than ours. I vaguely recall that Hannah was a year ahead of Tony—or was it Tom?"

"So Chad and Chase—I assume they're both boys— must belong to either Andrew or Walter Paine," Judith said. "Oh— Zoë, too. Octavia has to be Sarah's daughter."

"Was dinner included?"

"I'm afraid it was," Judith replied. "I must've had a weak moment."

"Does it say where these Paines live? If I've seen them at Mass, I haven't recognized them."

"No," Judith said, turning away from the monitor. "The only contact information is for Norma and Wilbur. I don't recall running into any of their offspring at church. Maybe they all moved away."

"Good thinking on their part," Renie remarked, once again heading for the back door. "I'd move, too, if Norma was my mother." She stopped suddenly, a stunned expression on her round face. "My God—do you think that's why all three of our kids live so far away?"

"Probably. If I were you, I'd blame it on the Shrimp Dump."

Renie glowered at Judith. "Right. I now formally withdraw my offer to help you with the dinner Friday night."

"You didn't volunteer."

"I didn't?" Renie shrugged. "It crossed my mind. Say, maybe the Paines would like Shrimp Dump for dinner."

"I'm not that desperate."

"Let me know if you change your mind." Renie made her exit.

"Not a chance," Judith murmured under her breath, keeping an eye on Sweetums, the orange-and-white feline whose legal human and kindred spirit was Judith's mother. The cat had entered the house before Renie closed the door behind her.

Ten minutes later, Judith went out to the converted tool-shed that served as her mother's apartment. Gertrude Grover peered suspiciously at the sandwich her daughter set on the cluttered card table. "You call this ham?" the old lady rasped. "It looks like linoleum to me."

"It's the ham we had for New Year's Day dinner," Judith informed her mother.

"Which New Year's?" Gertrude snapped. "How about 1995?"

"The New Year's dinner we had Saturday," Judith said patiently. "It's Tuesday. You're the one who kept ham until it turned blue."

Gertrude poked a gnarled finger at the newspaper in front of her. "You see this? Elder abuse, that's what. This is part two of a series on how children torture their aging parents. Spoiled pork must be one of the ways they do it. It gives old folks like me trigonomosis."

"You mean trichinosis," Judith said.

Gertrude glared at her daughter. "Isn't that what I just told you? You must be going deaf, too. You're already daffy."

"Do you want me to take a bite first?"

Gertrude snatched up the plate. "Aha! Now you want to starve me! By the time I get through to the last part of this series on Friday, I may be dead. And where's the rest of that cheesecake you bought at Begelman's Bakery for New Year's Eve?"

"We ate it," Judith replied. "Do you want some of Kristin's Fattigmann Bakkels?"

"I don't like bagels," Gertrude declared. "Especially fat ones. They're too hard to chew with my dentures."

"They're not bagels," Judith said. "They're Norwegian Christmas . . . never mind." The old lady was chomping away at the ham sandwich. Kristin's colossal output of holiday foodstuffs was probably past its pull date. Judith never ceased to be awed by her daughter-in-law's prodigious domestic enterprises. "If you want a sweet, Mother, you must've gotten ten pounds of Granny Goodness chocolates for Christmas. I assume you haven't eaten all of them in ten days."

"Ten days of what?" Gertrude asked, stabbing a fork into one of the gherkins on her plate. "I thought there were twelve days of Christmas. Or have the lunkheads in the Vatican changed that with everything else, too? And whatever happened to those two old saps, the Ringos?"

"They died," Judith said. "They were almost as old as you are. Your new Eucharistic minister is Kate Duffy, remember? She's been coming by every week for the past two years."

"I wish I could forget Kate Duffy," Gertrude muttered. "She's as bad as the Ringos. She always wants to pray with me. The last time, I told her I'd been praying for her not to come. All that phony-baloney pious claptrap is as bad as your screwball cleaning lady, but in the other direction. 'Born again,' huh? Once was enough for Phyliss Rackley."

Judith sighed. "I know Phyliss can be a trial, but she's a good cleaning woman. And Kate means well. She's sincere, if misguided. Our family managed to keep our feet planted firmly on the ground."

"That's because us old folks went to the School of Hard Knocks," Gertrude asserted. "Common sense, that's what it is, not Satan hiding behind every bush like Phyliss says, or hearing the Holy Ghost whisper in Kate's ear. When she came by after Christmas, she told me the Holy Ghost wanted her to go to Nordquist's designer clearance."

"Ah . . . well . . . I hope the Holy Ghost gave Kate an increase in her credit limit," Judith said, edging toward the converted toolshed's door. "If I have time tomorrow, I'll bake some gingersnaps."

"Then snap to it," Gertrude said, spearing another gherkin.

Judith promised she'd try. Halfway down the walk to the house, Arlene Rankers popped out of the massive laurel hedge that separated the two properties.

"Is Serena still here?" she asked, calling Renie by her given name.

"No," Judith replied. "She's probably home by now. Did you want to talk to her?"

Arlene didn't answer right away. In fact, her pretty face looked troubled. "I don't really know."

Judith couldn't keep from smiling. "In that case, you probably should wait until you remember why you wanted to see her."

"I didn't," Arlene said. "That is, I just got a call from Mary Lou Daniels at the school." She nodded in the direction of the hill behind the Flynns' garden. The church and school were three steep blocks away, but out of sight. "She called to tell me Brooks was sick and she couldn't get hold of Meagan or Noah at work, so Carl just left to pick him up."

Judith knew that two of the Rankerses' grandchildren attended the parish school. Brooks and his younger sister, Jade, had been enrolled in the fall after Meagan and her husband, Noah, had moved from Eugene, Oregon, to Heraldsgate Hill the previous summer. But she couldn't make any connection between Renie and the sick grandson. Unless, she mused, Renie had already donated her recipe for Shrimp Dump to the school. "What's wrong with Brooks?" she asked.

"A bad stomachache," Arlene replied. "Three other children are sick, too. I wondered . . . oh!" She brightened. "I remember what I wanted to ask Serena. Mary Lou mentioned that your cousin had stopped by with a bag of soup labels. I thought Serena might've heard if the sick kids had the same symptoms. It'd be a shame to have a flu epidemic at the start of a new semester."

Judith understood Arlene's concern. The Rankerses' daughter, Meagan, was a teacher at a nearby public school. Her husband, Noah, had been transferred from Oregon by the pharmaceutical company he worked for. Finding a sitter for their two children had been easy. Carl and Arlene had been eager to take on that role, not having spent much time with Brooks and Jade until the family moved north.

"Renie was there before noon," Judith said. "If anybody was waiting to be picked up in the office, she didn't tell me. I suppose the flu is going around. It usually is this time of year."

"True," Arlene said, suddenly on the alert. "I'd better go back home. Carl and Brooks will be back any minute."

Judith paused at the foot of the porch stairs. It had rained on New Year's Day, but the sun had been out ever since. The thermometer on one of the porch pillars registered forty degrees. She looked at a clump of tiny snowdrops in the flower bed next to the steps. Judith smiled. Her mother always called them "Christmas roses" because they usually bloomed the last week of December. Next to the snowdrops, she noticed that several daffodil shoots had emerged above the ground. *Brave,* she thought to herself. *It could still snow.*

"That's it!" Phyliss Rackley announced, storming out onto the porch and waving a dust mop. "Satan's familiar just shredded the lace curtains in Room Five. If you don't put him to sleep, I'll do it for you."

"Why," Judith asked mildly, "did you let him into Room Five?"

"Let him?" Phyliss's gray sausage curls seemed to dance in outrage. "He can go through walls, can't he? Just like the Archfiend himself." She lowered her voice. "The Powers of Darkness."

Judith joined the cleaning woman at the door. "How much real damage is there?"

"See for yourself," Phyliss snapped. "I've got a dust mop to shake."

Judith carefully went up the back stairs, ever mindful of her artificial hip. Room Five was the second door on her right. Sweetums was asleep on the freshly made bed. Sure enough, almost a foot of lace fabric was ripped beyond repair. Judith pummeled the mattress. "Get out, you little stinker!" she cried. "You're not allowed upstairs."

Sweetums' plush fur bristled as he regarded Judith with malevolent golden eyes. He yawned widely, then started to resettle himself.

"Out!" Judith yelled, scooping up the cat and carrying him into the hallway. He struggled in her grasp, but when she set him down, he merely gazed indifferently at her pitiful human displeasure before he began his grooming process.

Judith took the ruined curtains off the rod. Fortunately— though not so fortunate in terms of income—Room Five was vacant until the weekend. She had extra curtains stored in the cupboard area down the hall. Looking out through the window with its western exposure, Judith could see the wan winter sun glinting off the bay. The mountains over on the peninsula seemed to sparkle. A barge laden with green, blue, and rust-colored cargo containers moved smoothly southward to the city's industrial area while a superferry pulled into the downtown slip just beyond the viaduct. Judith smiled again. *Strange,* she thought, *how seldom I take time out to enjoy the scenery that others travel thousands of miles and spend thousands of dollars to see, while I can look at it from my house.* It occurred to her that Parisians no doubt passed the Arc de Triomphe and the Louvre without paying much attention, while Romans no doubt ignored the Colosseum and the Pantheon.

What Judith couldn't ignore was the phone. Unfortunately, it wasn't the guest phone that was on a table near the top of the main staircase. The ringing was coming from the kitchen, barely audible, but insistent. Judith wasn't going to risk a fall by dashing downstairs. After four rings, the call switched over to her message service. After reaching the kitchen and tossing the curtains into the garbage can under the sink, she finally picked up the receiver. There was no *click-click-click* sound indicating an unheard message. Judith checked her caller ID screen. Norma Paine's name and number appeared. Either Norma had decided to call back later or—more likely—she was leaving one of her typical long-winded messages.

Phyliss was running the vacuum in the front parlor. Judith walked through the dining room and the entry hall to the parlor door. The cleaning woman had her back turned and was singing—or squawking—a hymn. Cringing at the third "Go Down Moses," Judith waited to be acknowledged.

"What?" Phyliss demanded, silencing the vacuum. "I haven't gotten to 'bold Moses' and the 'smite' verse." She patted the vacuum bag. "That's when Moses here does his best work at deep cleaning."

Judith was used to her cleaning woman's biblical nicknames for various appliances. The washer and dryer were Noah and Jonah. The floor polisher was Jezebel because, Phyliss insisted, it was wayward, wanton, and woefully ignorant of God's word.

"You're right about the curtains," Judith said. "They're ruined. I've got new ones on the top shelf in the guest room storage cabinet."

Phyliss's eyes narrowed. "Did you kill Beelzebub's evil tool?"

"You know," Judith said firmly, "that Sweetums rarely goes upstairs. When we found him as a kitten shortly before I finished converting the family home into a B&B, I trained him not to go beyond the basement and the first floor."

"You can't train cats," Phyliss asserted. "They're sinister beasts."

"They're the last domestic animal to become . . . domesticated," Judith countered. "They've only been tame for five thousand years."

"Then they're slow learners," Phyliss said. "Those Egyptians thought cats were some kind of god. False idols, just like you Catholics, worshipping graven images and statues of people holding flowers or books or a bunch of house keys, which, now that I think about it, it's no wonder that statue in the backyard has got a flock of birds hanging on to him. Whoever he is, he must not have liked cats."

Judith's shoulders slumped. She'd long ago given up trying to convince Phyliss that Catholics didn't worship statues. They were like photographs or snapshots, a reminder of someone who had lived a holy life. Phyliss remained unconvinced. Not even explaining how the Lincoln Memorial served as an inspiration to other Americans had swayed her. "I've seen pictures," she'd argued. "Abe's just sitting there, staring off into nowhere. What's inspiring about that? He could be watching TV."

Thus Judith kept her mouth shut and went back into the kitchen. Maybe Norma Paine had finished her message. She sat down by the computer, picked up the phone, and dialed in her code.

"This," Norma said in her braying voice, "is Norma Paine. I'm calling about Friday night and your generous offer of Hillside Manor to my children and their children. Very kind of you, as I've always wondered why you hadn't done this before." Slight pause. "Well, better late than never. I'm pleased that you included dinner instead of just an overnight and breakfast. After all, Wilbur and I ended up paying fourteen hundred dollars for your item, and he insists that's going to set him back a year in retiring from his law practice." Another pause. "Not that I wonder if he won't feel lost without going to the office every day. In fact, I hope he doesn't expect me to entertain him constantly. I keep reminding him, 'Wilbur,' I say, 'I have a life of my own, and it keeps me very busy.' I don't think men understand what their wives do when they're gone all day earning a living. But I digress. I'm calling because some of our family members have food allergies. Now let me get this right."

A much longer pause. Judith had picked up a pen and was tapping it on the counter. "Andrew is lactose intolerant. Hannah should avoid leafy green vegetables. Dennis insists he doesn't have diabetes, but I disagree. He's glucose-intolerant, and as you no doubt realize, that's an early stage of diabetes. I'm very careful when I cook for him, I can tell you that. Zoë is vegetarian. Zachary has a severe seafood allergy. Now let me think . . ." The next pause was so long that Judith's elbow slipped off the counter and she dropped the pen. Retrieving it was impossible without bending over and risking dislocation of her artificial hip. Instead, she took another pen out of the drawer. And waited. "I may've omitted something important," Norma finally said. "I'll call you later. It's so kind of you to offer your very expensive hospitality."

"Aaargh . . ." Judith groaned, turning off the phone as Joe Flynn entered the hallway from the back door.

"What's wrong?" he asked before taking off the winter jacket Judith had given him for Christmas.

"I have a Paine," Judith said. "A whole houseful of Paines. Remember last year's school auction?"

Joe's round face looked momentarily puzzled. "Oh—you mean that auction and dinner fund-raiser when Bill and I tended bar?" He shook his head. "I recall very little about it, except I tried to auction off Oscar, but Bill told me if I did that, we could take it outside."

"Oh God!" Judith gasped. "I forgot that part!"

"Yeah," Joe agreed, "it got kind of ugly there for a minute. And Oscar didn't even come to the auction."

Judith jumped up, grabbing Joe by his jacket sleeves. "Do not buy into that Oscar fantasy! He's a stuffed monkey, he's not real." She stared into her husband's green eyes. "You and Bill weren't *that* drunk."

"Maybe. Maybe not." For once, the magical gold flecks

weren't dancing. "Besides, he's not a monkey, he's a dwarf ape."

Judith dropped her hands. "Skip it. I'm talking about Norma and Wilbur Paine. They bought the dinner and overnight for their children and grandchildren. It's this Friday."

Joe removed his jacket and hung it on a peg in the hallway. "So?"

"So Norma just left a message with a laundry list of allergies and other prohibitions for her brood. I need to hire a dietician."

"Do a buffet," Joe suggested. "They can pick and choose."

Judith thought for a minute. "You're right. That's a good idea." She smiled at Joe. "What would I do without you?"

"You had nineteen years to figure it out." He put an arm around his wife. "So did I. Happily, we managed to finally get it right."

Judith leaned against Joe. "Sometimes when I think of the years I spent with Dan while you were with Herself, I feel cheated. All that wasted time coping with a pair of drunks. I marvel your ex is still alive."

"She's not," Joe said. "She's pickled, preserved forever in the Florida sunshine."

"Let's hope she stays that way. I mean," Judith added quickly, "Vivian stays in Florida. I don't know why she doesn't sell the house here in the cul-de-sac instead of renting it. She's never been happy living in this part of the world."

"That's because liquor stores around here don't deliver," Joe said. "Now that she owns the house on the corner as well, she might make more money renting instead of selling. The Briscoes seem like a nice couple, and that Fairfax fellow travels a lot in his job as an auctioneer. All three newcomers seem like decent people. Quiet. Pleasant. Dull."

"Dull is good," Judith murmured. "I'd like a few months of dull." She suddenly remembered where Joe had spent the morning. "Why are you home so early? Isn't your surveillance job an eight-hour gig?"

"It was." Joe moved away from Judith, a sheepish look on his face. "Mr. Insurance Fraud is no longer able to bilk SANECO out of six million dollars for being semiparalyzed."

Judith grinned at Joe. "You caught him walking?"

Joe shook his head. "No. Somebody else caught him—with a .38 Smith & Wesson. He's dead."

Chapter Two

You're serious?" Judith said after the first shock wave receded. "The guy was really murdered?"

"I'm afraid so." Joe had taken an orange-flavored energy drink out of the fridge. "I was hoping you wouldn't ask."

"I always ask about your work," Judith said. "I'll admit you haven't told me much about this current job, but you just started yesterday. I don't even know who this insurance cheat is. Or was."

Joe sat down at the kitchen table. "I don't know either."

Judith sat down, too. "What do you mean? You told me he was a civil servant who'd been involved in an accident that left him paralyzed from the waist down. His name was . . ." She grimaced. "I forget. It was James something-or-other."

"James Edward Towne," Joe said, after sipping from his drink. "He lived in a condo on Lake Concord near the ship canal, first floor, decent view for Mr. Towne, not so good for me having to set up in a vacant houseboat owned by a SANECO vice president, Charles Knowles. His daughter and her husband live there, but they spent Christmas in Hawaii and are touring Australia and New Zealand until later this month. Age of deceased between forty-five and fifty-five, unmarried, had two live-in caregivers, who spelled each other every third day. One was a man, the other was a woman. I saw her yesterday—blond, but no bimbo. The male caregiver was supposed to come Thursday morning, but won't, given that Mr. Towne doesn't need him."

"Are you implying that Mr. Towne was shot while you were on surveillance?"

"Yes, I am." Joe looked disgusted. "He was shot on my watch, and I didn't see a damned thing." He glanced at the schoolhouse clock. "Approximate time of death, eleven A.M., Tuesday, January fourth."

"Did you see him get shot?"

"I not only didn't see it, I didn't hear it. I was too far away." He shook his head. "Some cop, huh? It's a good thing I retired from the force before I blew a few official homicide cases."

Judith was confused. "I'm not tracking. If you didn't see or hear anything, how did you know the guy was shot?"

Joe gazed up at the kitchen's high ceiling. "Gosh, I guess it was all those emergency vehicles and flashing lights and loud sirens. As a former law enforcement officer, I immediately realized that something was amiss. For all I know, it may've happened when I was in the can."

"Would you have seen it if you hadn't been away from your post?"

Joe gave Judith a sardonic look. "Maybe. The condo has big view windows in the living room, dining area, and kitchen. But when Mr. so-called Towne rolled his wheelchair into what I assumed was one of two bedrooms or the bathroom, I couldn't see him."

"Where did they find his body?"

"The living room." He grimaced. "That I could've seen, but I didn't. It's possible that he wasn't shot there, though. I didn't get details."

"How do you know he wasn't using his real name? Wouldn't SANECO Insurance know who he was?"

"Not if he was a fraud," Joe said impatiently. "The real James Edward Towne may be alive and well, except for being partially paralyzed. The cops couldn't find any ID. Or hadn't by the time they got through talking to me."

Judith frowned. "Talking—or interrogating?"

"Both," Joe said, "until I told the homicide 'tec who showed up that I used to work the same job."

"Do you know him?"

Joe shook his head. "Recently promoted," he said after another swig of his drink and leaned forward, eyeing his wife suspiciously. "You're the one who seems to be interrogating me now. Why don't you just play wife for a while?"

"Sorry," Judith said, and meant it. "I just wondered."

Joe leaned back in the chair. "His name is Keith Delemetrios. He joined the force just before I retired, but worked out north. No partner. The police budget is frozen while the mayor tries to figure out which streets are sinking into the ground, which bridges are about to collapse, which way is up."

"Did this newbie ask for your help?"

Joe laughed—or grunted. Judith wasn't sure. "Del, as he prefers to be called—more citizen-friendly—thought I might be a suspect. The only reason I'm not still being interrogated downtown is because I insisted he call Woody and have him vouch for me."

Judith grimaced. "I'd like to think you're kidding, but . . ." She let the words trail off.

Joe nodded. "Exactly. I had to turn over my Smith & Wesson so they could tell it hadn't been fired."

"Oh, Joe! That's ridiculous."

"No, it's not," Joe said. "Del's young, barely thirty, in over his head, and no partner assigned to him."

"Who called in about the shooting?"

"Whoever lives next door. He—a single guy who works at home—was in the hall on his way back from somewhere when he heard the shot. He knew something about the vic and thought he might be sufficiently depressed from being paralyzed to off himself. The female caregiver was running errands, but of course her alibi will be checked. Woody told me that when I called to give him a heads-up on my involvement. Did you know he's the acting precinct captain for this part of town?"

Judith was surprised. "When did that happen?"

"As of January first," Joe replied. "He took over for Jack Plummer, who suddenly announced his retirement in early December. When we went to the cocktail party at Woody's a week before Christmas, he had no idea he'd be reassigned from Homicide. It's a promotion, but Woody isn't sure he wants the job. Too many headaches with staff and budget cuts. I don't blame him. He's not going to be happy tied to a desk."

"So Woody is Delemetrios' boss," Judith murmured. "I assume you're no longer a suspect as the shooter."

"Woody has to jump through the hoops," Joe said, "but I should be cleared once my weapon is tested. Meanwhile, I'm out of a job."

"Well . . . that's not all bad," Judith said.

Joe leaned closer to Judith. "What do you mean?"

"I was thinking . . ." She shrugged. "You wouldn't get paid, but maybe you could help Woody by offering to mentor his rookie detective."

Joe chuckled. "Right. And you could help me help him help Woody." He shook his head. "No, this is none of our business. I didn't see anything, I didn't do anything, I can only give a statement, which I've already done." He leaned back in the chair. "Over and out."

Judith stood up. "It was a thought. I assume you've got some other irons in the fire. January is always the worst month for the B&B."

Joe's gaze seemed fixed on the green-and-white-striped tablecloth. "Oh . . . sure, but I'll have to make some calls."

Judith stood with her fists on her hips. "In other words, you don't have a job lined up."

Meeting her dark-eyed stare, Joe first looked sheepish, then abruptly turned defensive. "Hey—you know that these insurance fraud jobs are usually good for a couple of weeks. How could I schedule anything until I knew for sure that I'd nailed this guy?"

"He got nailed permanently," Judith snapped. "You'd better make those calls or we'll be eating Sweetums' Bluefin Buffet for dinner."

Joe, who was seldom cowed by anyone, least of all his usually good-natured, compassionate wife, pushed his chair away from the table and got to his feet. "Fine. I'll go up to the third floor and see if I can get a job working security for one of the lap-dance dumps."

"Don't mention 'dump' to me!" Judith shouted as he stomped down the hall to the back stairs. "I've had enough of that already with Renie!" Frustrated, she watched her husband disappear off the hallway to head up to his office in the family quarters.

Ten minutes later, Judith was deciding what to serve her Tuesday-night guests as appetizers for the six o'clock social hour. Maybe she'd keep it simple. Smoked oysters and clams, an assortment of crackers, some of Falstaff Grocery's expensive if exclusive foreign cheeses. In her current mood, she felt like tossing some pretzels and Ritz crackers in a bowl, opening a can of Cheez Whiz, and calling it done. The phone rang before she could make up her mind.

"Judith?" a high-pitched female voice said at the other

end. "Is this Judith?" the caller asked again without allowing for an answer.

"Yes!" Judith replied, and winced at her sharp tone. "Yes, it's me," she added more kindly.

"Oh, good!" the woman said. And went silent.

"How can I help you?" Judith inquired after a lengthy pause.

"What? Oh! I got distracted," the caller said. "What have you got for us?"

Judith slumped in the chair by her computer. "What do you want?"

"A recipe, of course." The woman paused, but more briefly. "It's me, Martha Morelli. Your cousin Serena told me about your wonderful Pottsfield Pickles."

Fleetingly, Judith thought about strangling Renie. "Gosh, Martha, I haven't made those in years." *As in never.*

"Oh." More silence. Judith checked her e-mail while waiting for Martha to speak again. Maybe someone wanted to make a reservation. That might lift her flagging spirits.

"Serena also mentioned canned tuna fish," Martha finally said, and broke into earsplitting laughter. "I'm having trouble reading my notes. I need new glasses."

How about a new brain? "Sorry—that's another one I haven't used in ages." *But maybe I should, if we get relegated to eating cat food.* "I do have other recipes, including my husband's version of Joe's Special."

"Oh." Shorter pause while Judith didn't find any guest requests. "Did he invent that?"

"Joe took the original and altered it slightly."

"Well . . . if it isn't original, I don't think we can use it," Martha said. "There might be a trademark problem. I'd so hoped you could help us."

"Sorry," Judith replied without enthusiasm. "I guess I can't."

"Yes . . . well, no. You can, actually," Martha went on, her voice brightening. "Do you have a Thursday-night vacancy?"

Judith grew wary. "Uh . . . I might. Why do you ask?"

"It . . . that is . . . I just spoke to Alicia Beard-Smythe. Their furnace has gone out and the gas company can't come until Friday. So many outages and problems, even in a mild winter like this one. They considered spending the night at a downtown hotel, but hated to leave their dog. They live only two blocks from your B&B—I'm sure you know that— and I suggested that perhaps you'd have a vacancy for the night. I don't mean to seem presumptuous, of course, but the idea just flew into my head, probably because I was about to call you anyway, and so naturally it occurred to me that you might . . ."

Judith held the phone away from her ear. For a slow starter, Martha apparently couldn't stop once she got up to speed. Hillside Manor did have a vacancy on Thursday. She didn't know Alicia and Reggie Beard-Smythe very well, but they seemed like decent, if wealthy, people. Generally, Judith found that The Rich were definitely different, and not just because they had more money.

Martha finally ran out of steam. Judith put the phone back to her ear. "Yes, I can give them the big bedroom or a smaller one. That's their decision. Of course," she added quickly, "if I get a request for the big room, I'll have to renege on that part of the deal."

"Understandable," Martha said. "I'll call Alicia and let her know."

With that, she abruptly rang off. Judith shrugged, set the phone back in its cradle, and typed in Beard-Smythe for Thursday, January 6, Room Three. That was two hundred dollars, enough to raise her spirits a notch. Especially in January, every booking counted.

She would later remember the old saying "Don't count your chickens before they're hatched."

Chapter Three

Joe was in a better mood that evening. Renie's husband, Bill, had stopped by during one of his long walks on Heraldsgate Hill's south slope. Like Joe, Bill Jones was semiretired, but still saw some of his longtime patients in his capacity as a psychologist. He also occasionally guest-lectured at the University, where he'd taught for many years.

"What did Bill have to say?" Judith asked during dinner. "Would I be wrong to guess it has something to do with winter steelheading?"

"Yes, you would," Joe replied, ladling more pot roast gravy onto his potatoes. "Or do you already have some things you want me to do around the house like cleaning out the basement or fixing the broken garage window?"

"Well . . . that window should be replaced. The pigeons fly in there sometimes."

"Why did anyone ever put a window that high up? It's useless."

"Grandpa Grover did that because of the chickens they kept there during the Second World War. They nested in the loft. He could check on them through the window."

"Why would he do that?" Joe suddenly waved a hand in

dismissal. "I don't actually want to know. Besides, Bill has a real job for me."

Judith almost choked on a carrot. "You . . . mean . . ." she sputtered, "a . . . paying job?"

Joe nodded. "Indeed."

Judith narrowed her eyes. "It better not involve Oscar."

"It doesn't," he asserted. "It's a former patient who believes he's being stalked."

Judith was still leery. "In other words, Bill didn't cure this patient."

"I don't think that's true," Joe said, looking serious. "This guy has physical proof that there's some kind of harassment if not actual stalking going on. Whoever is pestering him leaves souvenirs at his residence or sends them through the mail."

"Why doesn't he call the cops?"

"For the same reason I mentioned earlier," Joe explained. "He did call, but this sort of nuisance stuff isn't a high priority with limited resources. Admittedly, it sounds a little goofy, but that doesn't mean whoever is doing it might not escalate the situation."

Judith considered taking a second helping of pot roast but changed her mind. Joe was already forking more onto his plate and Gertrude would want the leftovers for sandwiches. Judith was watching her weight as she always did, especially after the holidays. "Dare I ask who's on the receiving end of this harassment?"

Joe shook his head. "Doctor/client/PI privileges."

"Then you're taking on this job?"

"Sure." Joe's cheerful expression changed to puzzlement. "I thought you wanted me to get out there and earn."

"I do," she assured him. "It just sounds a little . . . strange."

"Bill's patients usually are a little strange," Joe said drily. "Otherwise, they wouldn't be his patients."

"You told me this person was . . . healed."

Joe made a face. "Nobody's ever 'healed'—as you of all people know. This kind of thing could cause a relapse, or whatever shrinks term backsliding behavior."

"Bill usually refers to such conditions as 'going off his or her nut.'"

Joe nodded absently. "Bill speaks laymanese to the rest of us."

"Can you tell me what sort of things his patient is getting from the alleged would-be stalker?"

"Innocuous stuff," Joe replied, dishing yet more pot roast onto his plate. "A leather belt. Little restaurant cups of mustard and ketchup. A Serpentine Downs program from last summer." He paused. "Oh—a wilted carnation bouquet."

Judith stared at Joe. "That's a very eclectic, not to mention bland bunch of items. What does Bill—or his patient—make of it?"

"They don't, which is why the ex-patient is concerned." Joe eyed Judith warily. "I can see the wheels turning in your head. Let it go. The client's agreed to pay my usual fee. That should satisfy you."

Judith didn't say anything for a moment. Finally she shrugged. "Okay. It's not my problem. I'll dismiss it from my mind."

Both Flynns knew better than to believe her words. But neither of them said so out loud.

By Thursday afternoon, there had been no other requests for Room Three, though Judith had added one more guest, a single woman for Room Two. Rooms One and Five remained vacant, but at least the B&B was over half full.

By the time her four Wednesday-night guests had checked out and the remaining middle-aged couple in Room Six had left for the day, Judith headed up to Falstaff's Grocery to check out the weekly specials. She brought along the notes she'd taken for the Paine family's complicated dietary requests as well as some lactose- and gluten-free recipes she'd printed out from the Internet.

The first stop was the produce section. She wondered if broccoli counted as a leafy green vegetable. Spinach would, but not carrots, green beans, or peas. Judith bagged two pounds of green beans and the same amount of carrots. Salad was problematical. If one of the Paines couldn't eat leafy greens, she'd make something with fruit or serve raw vegetables. She was still mulling when someone bumped her from behind. "Move it, lady," Renie barked. "I have to get to the oyster mushrooms."

"Coz!" Judith exclaimed, turning around. "I need mushrooms, too. I'm trying to figure out what to feed those Paines."

"Try poison," Renie suggested, bringing her cart alongside Judith's.

"Don't say that!" Judith exclaimed in a hushed voice. "Have you forgotten that the first time I encountered a murder, it was at my dining room table?"

"So?" Renie said as they moved on to broccolini. "Didn't that first corpse reunite you with Joe?"

"Well . . ." Judith paused to reflect on her reaction when, after a twenty-year absence, the love of her life had walked through Hillside Manor's front door. Detective Joe Flynn had been the primary assigned to the apparent murder of a fortune-teller. The victim's death had set a new life in motion for Judith—and Joe. "Everything has its upside."

"I can still help tomorrow night if you want me," Renie said.

Judith studied the broccolini. "Leafy or not leafy?"

"What?"

"One of the Paines can't eat leafy green vegetables."

"Oh." Renie thought for a moment. "Some think it's a cross between broccoli and asparagus, but it's not. The broccoli is paired with a more obscure vegetable related to cabbage. Stick to the asparagus."

"Good idea," Judith murmured, backing up to the asparagus bin. "But," she asked after rejoining Renie, "what about Bill?"

"He's going to the University's basketball game with Uncle Al. Freebies, of course."

The cousins had reached the diverse mushroom section. "Has Uncle Al ever actually paid for a ticket? I've never figured out how he's so connected to every political, athletic, labor union, and entertainment segment in the city without getting arrested. Several of his close friends, including a former sheriff, have done prison time."

Renie shrugged before putting her oyster mushrooms into a produce bag. "Uncle Al's a bit of a con artist and he's always been lucky, even when he gambles in Nevada. He also has enough moxie for three people. Say," she said suddenly, "would Joe like to go with Bill and Uncle Al? Surely he doesn't want to be home while the Paines are there."

"I'll ask," Judith said, finding the freshest button mushrooms.

"Okay." Renie picked up two packages of udon noodles. "Did you know that Uncle Al already won a grand at Santa Anita since the track opened the day after Christmas?"

"Via his bookie?"

Renie nodded. "He calls the guy his stockbroker. Maybe he's that, too. Who knows with Uncle Al."

"Not me," Judith said as they moved on to the meat-and-seafood department. "So what's with this patient who's being harassed?"

"Oh . . ." Renie paused where turkey parts were on sale. "Wings, drumsticks. Good. I'll freeze them until Bill and I stop gobbling from Christmas and Thanksgiving." She moved on past chicken and duck.

"Wait, coz," Judith said. "I think I'll do something that clucks. Tell me about the patient Joe is supposed to take on as a client."

Renie shot her cousin a disparaging look. "You know Bill never talks to me about his patients, except in vague generalities. The only time I hear specifics is if his practice has an impact on our private lives, like the time he couldn't go to San Francisco because a patient was threatening to jump off a window ledge. You had to fill in for him, as I'm sure you recall."

"Oh, I couldn't forget that," Judith admitted, putting a dozen skinless, boneless chicken breasts into her cart. "Not so much about the patient, as about the body in the piano."

"Right." Renie had picked up some baby back spareribs and a couple of Cornish game hens. "Bill wouldn't have liked that part. I assume Joe is equally discreet."

"Yes." Judith studied the four different kinds of shish kebab skewers. She chose six of the teriyaki beef variety, despite knowing Gertrude would complain about being served wooden sticks for dinner. "What did you think of the story in the paper about Joe's surveillance subject getting whacked?"

"I haven't had time to read the paper the last two days," Renie admitted. "You know I never watch TV news unless I'm with you and you're going to be part of the latest homicide case. I've got too many projects that keep me from reading more than sports scores in the paper. I assume Joe's been cleared of suspicion?"

"You mean officially?" Judith shook her head. "I don't think the bullet and weapon tests have come back yet. The police department is in a serious budget bind."

"The whole city's in a budget crunch," Renie remarked. "Yum . . . yearling oysters." She picked up two jars. "They're on sale. That doesn't happen very often. You'd better get some."

"Oysters are one of the few *fruits de mer* I don't like," Judith reminded her cousin. "I can't serve them to the guests because one of the Paines has a bad shellfish allergy."

Renie nodded. "Prudent. You know what happens to me with nuts and peanuts. Certain death with the latter, slower death with the former. But I thought Joe liked them."

"He does," Judith said. "My father used to go oyster hunting on the peninsula and slurp them right out of the shell. Mother never cared for them, but she was a sport about it." She shook her head. "I always wonder what she'd be like if my father hadn't died so young."

Renie's expression was wry. "Maybe not so different. Aunt Gert would just take out her venom on Uncle Donald instead of you." She smiled. "I remember being with you and your folks on the peninsula in search of oysters. That was fun. As a midwesterner, it's taken Bill years to eat different kinds of seafood. The only oysters he'll eat is if we're out to dinner and somebody orders an appetizer tray on the half shell with a side of vodka shooters."

"Ah, yes," Judith said. "Dan used to do that, too. Except he'd eat them all himself and his idea of a shooter was a pint. It's a wonder I didn't shoot him."

"You should have," Renie remarked. "Don't you remember Cousin Sue always told you if you did kill Dan, she'd swear in court that she was with you the whole time? The rest of the family would've done the same."

Judith shook her head. "I didn't have to kill him. He did that to himself between the food and the booze."

"You still didn't get off cheap," Renie murmured. "Nineteen years is a long prison sentence."

"And hard labor at that," Judith said. "Holding down two jobs was no picnic with Dan rarely holding any."

When Judith and Renie reached the dairy section, they

parted company. Realizing that it was already past the noon hour, Judith hurriedly polished off her list and checked out. Gertrude would be annoyed because lunch was late.

By the time she got home and unloaded the groceries, she realized that Joe apparently had left. His winter jacket was gone from the peg in the back hallway. Judith knew he'd planned to study Bill's information regarding the patient's background and his harassment complaints, but he hadn't told her what was on his schedule for the rest of the day. Maybe he'd learned enough to meet his new client.

After putting away the perishables, she hurriedly prepared Gertrude's lunch. It was going on one when she went out through the falling rain to the toolshed.

"Well!" Gertrude exclaimed, looking up from the game of solitaire she'd been playing. "It's about time. I thought you were dead."

"I went to the grocery store," Judith said, moving some of the clutter around on the card table to make way for the lunch tray. "Pot roast sandwich, canned pears, some of those sour-cream-and-onion potato chips you like, and oatmeal cookies."

Gertrude scowled at the items on the tray. "Store-bought cookies? What's wrong with you? Did the oven blow up?"

"I haven't had time to bake," Judith admitted. "Don't you still have some of the spritz cookies left? I made four batches."

"When? In 2002? The last ones I ate were like hockey pucks. I almost busted my dentures." She returned her gaze to the tray. "Where's the horseradish? You know I like horseradish with pot roast. You gave me some last night for supper."

"I forgot," Judith confessed. "I'll go get it." She started for the door. "Oh," she said, turning around, "do you know where Joe went?"

Gertrude was about to bite into a sour-cream-and-onion chip. "Yeah, I know. He went to jail." She popped the chip into her mouth and chewed with gusto.

Judith sighed. "Never mind. I'll be right back."

She had one foot on the path between the toolshed and the house when Gertrude spoke again. "Aren't you going to bail him out?"

Judith stepped back inside to get out of the rain. "Of course not. I . . ." The serious expression on her mother's face made her pause. "You're kidding, right?"

Gertrude shook her head. "I wouldn't kid about that. Serves him right for being such a knucklehead. Didn't I always tell you that when it came to men, you should've been born wearing a dunce cap?"

"Mother!" Judith marched back to the card table, leaving the door open behind her. "What are you talking about?"

Gertrude's faded blue eyes met her daughter's anxious stare. "I saw it happen. I went to let Sweetums out a half hour or so ago and there was Dumbbell being hauled off by the cops, handcuffs and all. I haven't had so much fun since Dan's funeral."

Chapter Four

J udith didn't know what to think. Maybe her mother really was gaga. Sometimes when the old lady dozed off, she'd wake up and insist what she'd dreamed had actually happened. To give herself a moment to recover, Judith went back inside the toolshed.

"Tell me again what you saw," she said, trying to remain calm.

Gertrude nibbled at her sandwich before replying. "I looked into the driveway and sure enough, there was a squad car where your old clunk is parked now. See for yourself. Dimwit's fancy sports car must still be in the garage."

Judith had closed the double garage when she'd pulled out to go grocery shopping. It was a long-standing habit to prevent Sweetums from getting himself trapped inside if the doors were left open. His eventual release always made him even more fractious and destructive than usual. Without another word, Judith started out of the toolshed.

"Hey," Gertrude called after her, "don't forget the horse—"

The slamming of the door cut off the rest of the old lady's words. Judith rushed to the garage keypad. It took her four tries before her trembling fingers could enter the correct combination. The door seemed to open in slow motion, but when she saw the lower part of Joe's classic MG, she knew her mother wasn't hallucinating.

The rain was coming down harder. Hurrying into the house, she pulled the hood up over her already wet hair. Phyliss met her in the hallway by the back stairs.

"Where's Noah and his ark when we really need him?" she demanded. "This is a real downpour."

"Never mind Noah," Judith snapped. "What happened to Joe?"

"Joe?" Phyliss's prunelike face was blank. "Has he fallen into Satan's clutches again?"

"The police," Judith said impatiently. "Were the police here?"

Phyliss blinked two or three times. "To arrest Satan?"

"Stop it!" Judith shrieked. "Yes or no?"

Phyliss gave a start. "Yes or no what?"

"Oooh . . ." Judith leaned against the wall and took several deep breaths. "Did you see Joe leave the house?" she finally asked, trying to keep her voice and manner under control.

"No. I've been doing laundry in the basement." Phyliss seemed to realize that Judith was distressed. "I haven't seen Mr. F. since he came down to the kitchen to get some coffee around eleven. If there were any policemen around here, I wouldn't know unless they had their sirens on. That's what they usually do when they come here, isn't it?"

"They wouldn't," Judith murmured. "Excuse me, Phyliss. I have to make a phone call."

"Shall I pray on it?" Phyliss called as Judith went into the kitchen.

"Yes." For once, prayers from Phyliss didn't seem so outrageous. Judith had Woody's work number on her bulletin board by the entrance to the dining room. She carefully dialed the number, and didn't realize she'd been holding her breath until she heard a recording saying that Captain Woodrow Price could now be reached at 206-555-7441.

After jotting down the new number, she dialed again. A female voice with a slight Hispanic accent answered. "I am so sorry," she said after Judith had asked to speak to Woody, "but Captain Price is working a case. Would you care to leave a message or may I help you?"

"Ah . . . maybe," Judith replied. "Is he on the Towne homicide?"

The silence at the other end was further unsettling. "Captain Price is out of the office," the woman said at last, sounding a trifle shaken as well. "I can leave him your name and number."

"No," Judith said. "I'll call back later. Thanks anyway."

She sat down at the kitchen table, considering her options. Three of the city's five precincts surrounded the lake. If Delemetrios reported to Woody, then it must be the West Precinct, which included her own neighborhood. The station's headquarters was located between the south end of the hill and downtown. Judith's watch informed her it was only a few minutes after one o'clock. Guests wouldn't be arriving until four, the official check-in time at Hillside Manor. Maybe she should go to the station and find out what was happening.

As often as Judith had been involved with the police department over the years, both officially and unofficially, she didn't relish the idea of going alone. Renie was the logical choice, but she was busy. Arlene would be glad to help and Carl was the Block Watch captain. Judith dialed the Rankerses' number, but got their recorded message. Frustrated, she tried to think who else might be willing to join her. It suddenly dawned on her that Bill would be an ideal choice. He was smart, focused, and had a knack for going straight to the heart of any problem. He could be as pig-headed as Renie, but that wasn't always a drawback. The only problem was that he never answered the phone.

Judith took a chance and dialed the Joneses' house on the other side of the hill.

"What now?" Renie demanded.

"Hi, coz," Judith said meekly. "Is Bill around?"

"He's rounder than he used to be," Renie snapped. "And you're obtuse. Why are you calling when you know I'm up to my ears in work?"

"I'm not calling you," Judith said, trying to keep her nerves and her impatience in check. "I'm calling Bill."

"Are you crazy? You know he hates the telephone even more than your mother does. If you want to reach Bill, send him a letter. He doesn't open his mail very often, but you might get lucky. Just mark the envelope 'Attention Oscar.' "

"Even Oscar would be nicer than you're being," Judith shot back. "I really need to talk to your husband. This is serious."

"It is?" Renie's voice changed. "What's wrong?"

"Joe's been arrested."

"*What?*" Renie's shriek stung Judith's ear.

"You heard me," Judith snapped. "I want Bill to go with me to the police station."

A sudden silence followed. "You're not joking," Renie finally said, suddenly serious. "Bill's not here. He just left to get his hairs cut. All eight of them. What's going on?"

"It's that insurance case murder," Judith began. "I don't know what's happening with Joe, but Mother told me—"

"Skip it. I'll be right there. Bill walked to the barbershop. I'll leave him a note." She hung up.

Judith put the phone down. She was shaking, but didn't know if it was from fear or relief—or both. Seven minutes later, Renie pulled up in front of the B&B and honked. Judith had already told Phyliss she was going out and to please let

Gertrude know. For once, the cleaning woman didn't grumble about having to confront Judith's mother.

"I figured you'd be ready to roll," Renie said as Judith got into the car. "Where to? Our precinct station?"

Judith nodded.

Renie turned to exit the cul-de-sac. "Dare I ask why your husband got collared? Not soliciting, I hope."

"He's a homicide suspect."

"Oh. That's a change."

Judith nodded again.

"Why," Renie inquired as she headed for Heraldsgate Avenue, "would he kill the subject of his surveillance? That means he gets paid for only what? A couple of days?"

Judith kept nodding.

"Why did you ask for Bill? Did you want him to give his professional opinion that Joe is nuts so he can enter an insanity plea?"

Judith scowled at Renie. "Of course not. I knew you were busy, and Bill is never daunted by any situation. He has a very rational mind, not to mention that he never digresses from the matter at hand."

"True," Renie conceded, starting down the steep street known as the Counterbalance from the era when a cable car ran from top to bottom. "A bit of the bulldog in Bill, but if Joe shot the guy, why not wait until the end of the week so he could collect more money from SANECO?"

"Coz!" Judith cried. "This is serious!"

"It's also absurd," Renie said. "We know he didn't shoot him, and if Woody's on the job, he knows it, too. This is a mere inconvenience. I figure Joe will confess so he won't have you trying to solve the case, and for once, your husband can have some peace and quiet in a nice cell for a few days until the real detectives find the perp whodunit."

In Judith's current frazzled state, her cousin's rationale

almost made sense. "You don't really think . . . ? Or do you?"

Renie shrugged as she stopped for a red light at the bottom of the hill. "You have to admit it's not the worst idea I've ever had—looking at it from Joe's standpoint."

Judith was thoughtful for a moment. "Do you think he's set this whole thing up to help do just that?"

Renie grimaced as she drove away from Heraldsgate Hill toward the city center. "That idea crossed my mind."

"So maybe he *is* helping them," Judith said as much to herself as to her cousin. "Maybe Mother didn't see him in handcuffs."

"Handcuffs?" Renie almost rear-ended the car that had stopped in front of her at the crosswalk. "That . . . um . . . sounds like an unnecessary touch. I mean, unless Joe and the cops think Arlene and Carl or the Porters or the Steins—"

"I get it," Judith interrupted. "I don't think our neighbors are suspects. At least not this time around."

"True," Renie allowed, driving more slowly as traffic increased. "You've already had your share of victims and perps in the cul-de-sac." She made the turn onto the street that led to the precinct station. "Are you sure this is where they've taken Joe?"

"You mean instead of to headquarters further downtown?"

"Right."

"I . . . I don't know," Judith admitted. "It's where Woody is located since his promotion. I wonder why he's 'acting' captain?"

"Maybe he needs to rehearse," Renie said, though the lightness in her voice was forced. "You know how much Woody likes opera. A dress rehearsal would probably suit him." She slowed to a crawl as the station came into view. "Where do we park? The lot's full. So are all the parking places on the street."

"Drive around the block," Judith said, rummaging in her

purse to find the new cell phone her son, Mike, and his wife, Kristin, had given her for Christmas. "I'm calling the main headquarters."

"Okay." Renie turned the corner—and found herself facing a detour sign in front of what was obviously a construction project. "Dammit! I'd like to go someplace in this stupid city where the streets weren't closed or some giant crane wasn't looming over my head." She put the Camry into reverse—and realized that a cement mixer was blocking her exit. "Oh, crap! Now we're stuck! What am I supposed to do?" Swearing under her breath, she began honking the horn.

"Hey," Judith said, having dialed the downtown police-department number she'd memorized long ago. "I can't hear."

Renie ignored her and got out of the car, leaving the motor running. A faint voice answered. "Homicide, please," Judith said, a finger in her other ear to block out her cousin's shouts at the cement mixer's driver. She winced when a jackhammer began pounding away at the construction site. A second voice spoke into the phone, but Judith couldn't make out what was being said. Frustrated, she disconnected—just as Renie approached with a man in a hard hat.

"Hey, coz," Renie called, "it's Kevin Rankers. He'll back up."

Judith recognized the Rankerses' elder son immediately. "Hi, Kevin. What are you doing here?"

Kevin grinned at Judith. "Supervising." He had to raise his voice to be heard above the din. "I followed your example and got a hip replacement a couple of months ago. I can't do any of the grunt work for my construction company, so I decided to drive one of the trucks to keep my hand in. Office work bores me stiff."

To Judith's relief, the jackhammer stopped. "I heard you'd had the surgery," she said. "How's it going?"

Kevin shrugged. "Okay, I guess. Hey—is it true you've

got a bunch of Paines spending the night tomorrow? I went through school with Andy. Watch that guy—he's a big eater."

Lactose-intolerant, Judith remembered. "Is he the oldest Paine?"

"Right," Kevin replied, stepping aside so Renie could get back in the driver's seat. "His wife's Paulina. Hey, I better move the truck. Good luck with the Paines."

Renie was wiping rain from her face. "Did you call headquarters?"

"Yes," Judith said, "but I couldn't hear a damned thing. I still think that's where Joe must be. I was so upset that I wasn't thinking straight, but at least that's how it worked with a homicide suspect when Joe was on the force." She leaned back in the seat. "I can hardly believe he's been arrested. I keep thinking I'm having a very bad dream."

Renie was looking into the rearview mirror, watching Kevin reverse the cement mixer. "Tell me more about the actual incident. You sort of breezed through it earlier."

As the cousins drove farther into downtown, Judith tried to recall the details of what had happened while Joe was on surveillance. She finished just as they reached the city's police headquarters.

"Parking may be hard to find, so I'll drop you off," Renie said, pulling up by the main entrance.

"Thanks." Judith smiled wanly at Renie before getting out of the car. Her jaw dropped as she paused in front of the building. Even though Joe had mentioned that a new headquarters had been built recently, and she had probably driven by it several times, Judith hadn't realized how imposing the gleaming new glass-and-steel edifice was up close. The steps to the main doors seemed daunting, but there was also a handicapped-accessible walkway. Braving the rain, she decided to take her time and use the ramp instead of the stairs.

A husky security guard who looked as if he might be Samoan was posted in the lobby by the elevators. A bald man wearing a trench coat was opening his briefcase; a woman whose sari fell in graceful folds beneath her rain-coat was showing the contents of her purse. Judith tried to remember how long it had been since her last visit to the old headquarters. Four or five years, maybe? Time passed so quickly. Unable to recall when or why, she moved toward the security guard as the man and woman headed for the elevators.

"Here," Judith said, handing her wallet to the guard whose name tag identified him as Jonathan Tupali. "Should I take out my driver's license?"

"Yes, please," he said in a soft voice.

She fumbled a bit, trying to remove the license out of its slot. "Sorry," she murmured. "Here. Do you want me to take everything out of my purse or—"

"That's fine," the young man said, handing back the license. "Go ahead." He nodded toward the elevators. "Fifth floor, Mrs. Flynn."

"Thank you." Judith was pressing the button when it dawned on her that she hadn't asked for directions. She turned around to ask how he knew where she was going, but he was checking through another visitor's items. The eleva-tor arrived. Judith got in and poked the fifth-floor button. According to the list of departments, Booking was one of the sections on five. As the car rose, her heart sank. *This can't be real,* she told herself—but it was. The elevator slid open to reveal an area that—despite its cleanliness and fresh paint—felt like the entrance to Dante's Inferno. Listings, arrows, a directory of the floor's various departments in a dozen different languages overwhelmed her. Frustrated by what struck her as a criminal-justice maze, she approached a young dark-skinned woman at the reception desk.

"Yes?" the young woman said with a faint smile. "May I help you?"

Not in the way I want, Judith thought, *unless you can rouse me from this nightmare.* She glanced at the woman's name tag. "Yes, Darcy. I'm looking for my husband, Joe Flynn," Judith said, trying to make her request discreet. She cleared her throat. "He's a retired homicide detective with the department."

"Oh," Darcy said, seemingly enlightened. "So you think he may be visiting some of his old friends here?"

"Well . . . maybe. His longtime partner was Woodrow Price."

Darcy smiled. "Oh, *Captain* Price. He's assigned to the West Precinct. Mr. Flynn may be at the uptown station."

"Actually," Judith began, "I believe Captain Price may be—"

"Hold it." Renie suddenly appeared next to her cousin. "Why are you standing here like the Statue of Liberty? Or is that a poor simile?"

"I was trying to find Joe, but . . ." Judith turned away from Darcy, making a face at Renie. "It's not easy to find the right words."

Renie shrugged. "Sounds easy enough to me." She elbowed Judith out of the way and leaned on the counter that separated visitors from the hired help. "It's like this, Darcy. Mrs. Flynn's husband has had his butt hauled in as a murder suspect. Any idea where we might find the alleged killer or do I have to start a prison riot next door to get some info out of you? If you think I hate hospital food, you ought to see how I react to chain-gang chow."

As she backed away from the counter, Darcy's dark eyes had grown huge. Three of her coworkers were on their feet. Renie beckoned to the oldest of the trio. "You," she said, pointing to the gray-haired man. "Two words. Don't be scared. I won't hurt you. But I have to whisper them."

Reluctantly, the man approached the counter. He looked wary, but bent down so that Renie could speak into his ear. Judith, Darcy, and everybody else in the area stared as the man listened. After a moment, he stood up, nodded at Renie, and grinned at Judith.

"Let me check," he said, turning to Darcy's computer. "Take a left past the water fountain, then a right beyond the restrooms. Third door down just before the staff elevators. I'll buzz you through."

"Thanks," Renie said, grabbing Judith's arm. "We appreciate it."

The automatic door swung open. The cousins were halfway down the first hallway before Judith could find her voice. "What on earth did you say to that guy?"

"Two words," Renie replied. "Al Grover."

"Oh, for . . . !" Judith had to stop and lean against the wall. "How did you know Uncle Al's name would have that kind of clout?"

"Because I recognized the older guy," Renie replied. "He's the spitting image of his dad, Pete 'Shuffle Up and Deal' Petersen. Uncle Al used to sneak young Pete into all kinds of events, including the racetrack and the cathouse owned by one of the ex-sheriffs."

Judith put a hand to her head. "And I thought I had a good memory for faces. I didn't make the connection."

"You were too upset to make anything," Renie said as the cousins continued on their way. "Your mother could've been behind that counter and you wouldn't have noticed her."

"You're right," Judith admitted as they turned the first corner. "I was having a horrible time telling poor Darcy what I wanted. And how did you find a parking place so fast?"

Renie shrugged. "I used the mayor's. He's out of town this week. Or don't you read the newspaper?"

"You could still get a ticket or be towed away."

"Then Uncle Al will have to fix that, too."

"Maybe Uncle Al should've come with us."

Renie frowned as they passed the restrooms. "Did you forget he's in Vegas? He and Tess of the Timbervilles flew down Monday night."

Judith sighed. "I did forget. I wonder why Uncle Al and Tess have never gotten married."

"Maybe they have," Renie said. "It's more exciting at their age if they pretend they didn't. Besides, he told me once he'd never marry Tess because she had too much money. Timber heiresses like to hang on to their loot in these days of curtailed logging, and Uncle Al would never want to be a kept man. It'd kill his incentive to make money in more exciting, if risky, ventures."

"Sounds like Uncle Al," Judith murmured, stopping at the door by the staff elevators. The door's small window appeared to be one-way glass, preventing outsiders from seeing inside. "It says this is an interrogation room. We can't just walk in."

"Why not? We can interrogate them about their interrogation."

"Coz . . ." Judith spotted a buzzer on the wall. "Let's try this."

It seemed like a long time before the door opened a few inches. A dark-haired young man in a pale blue shirt and loosened navy tie peered out at the cousins. "Yes?" he said, puzzled. "Who are you?"

"Mrs. Joe Flynn," Judith replied in what didn't sound like her usual confident voice. "Is my husband here?"

"Are you his attorney as well as his wife?" he asked.

"No, but . . ." Judith tried to peer over the young man but she couldn't see anything but a wall. "Are you Detective Delemetrios?"

He nodded. "I'm in charge here and you have no right to be in this area. Please leave the same way you came in."

He started to close the door, but Renie reached out and grabbed the detective's tie. "Not so fast. Where's Woody Price?"

Delemetrios tried to pull free, but Renie's feet were planted firmly against the baseboard. "He's . . . he's on his way," the detective replied. "Please. Go away before I call someone to—"

A voice called out from inside the room. "Hey! Is that my wife?"

Judith leaned closer to Renie. "Yes, Joe! Tell this guy to let me see you or Renie is going to strangle him with his own tie."

"Simmer down, Serena!" Joe shouted. "Del's just doing his job."

Renie yanked at the detective's tie. "He's doing a damned crappy job of it. Either he lets Coz in, or," she continued, her voice somewhat muffled as she leaned down and used her free hand to take a pair of nail scissors from her purse, "he loses his fifty-dollar tie."

"Hey!" Delemetrios yelled, his face flushed, "my girl-friend gave me that for Christmas. It's from Nordquist's."

Renie looked him in the eye. "Shirt, too?"

He seemed more worried than scared. "My parents gave me that."

"I think it needs shorter sleeves," Renie said, brandishing the scissors. "We're having an unusually warm January."

"Coz!" Judith cried. "Stop it! You're going to get arrested, too. I can't afford to bail both of you out."

"No," Renie said, her face set. She narrowed her eyes at the detective. "Well? Your new wardrobe or your suspect's wife?"

Judith was about to grab Renie when Woody Price exited from the staff elevator. He stopped in his tracks when he saw the cousins, but swiftly regained his composure. "Hello, Judith, Serena." His smile was a bit ragged around the edges as he approached them. "I don't know exactly what to say. This is awkward, isn't it?"

Judith kissed his cheek. "It's a mess. I'm so glad to see you."

Renie turned toward Woody and lowered the scissors, but held on to Delemetrios' tie. "Got *Manon Lescaut* tickets?" she asked with an eager expression.

"Oh yes," Woody replied. "Carol Vaness, opening night. Personally, I like the Puccini version better than Massenet's."

"Me, too," Renie said. "That 'in quelle trine morbide' aria is enough to make it a deal breaker."

Woody's dark-skinned face virtually glowed with pleasure. "Oh my, yes, and then the tenor sings that amazing—"

"Enough!" Judith screamed, stamping her foot—and was immediately relieved that it was the one that wasn't attached to the artificial hip. "Both of you stop talking about the damned opera and do something helpful! I'm about to have a nervous breakdown."

Woody looked chagrined; Renie merely shrugged; Delemetrios appeared confused; Joe could be heard muttering a few choice cusswords from inside the interrogation room.

"Right," Renie said, letting go of Delemetrios' tie and flipping it back into his face. "I'll back off now, Woody, and let you take over."

"Yes." Woody shook himself and assumed his usual serious professional expression. "If you don't mind, let me speak with both the detective and . . . his person of interest." He moved to the door. "May I?"

"Sure," Renie said, stepping aside. "Nice meeting you, Del," she added as the door closed behind both policemen.

"You," Judith declared, "are a moron. I knew Bill should've come with me. You're damned lucky that poor detective doesn't charge you with . . . something."

"He's kind of cute, actually." Renie put the nail scissors back in her purse. "Woody looks good. He's aging well."

"I've just aged ten years," Judith said. "About the only thing that can divert Woody's focus is opera, and you just *had* to mention it."

Renie had the grace to look faintly sheepish. "Well—the first performance is only a couple of weeks away. You don't often get to hear *Manon Lescaut*."

Judith didn't respond. Several minutes passed in silence. Renie paced a bit between the interrogation room and the stairwell at the end of the hall. It was impossible to hear anything through the door. Judith figured it was soundproofed. She leaned against the wall, trying to keep her anxiety at a manageable level. At least five minutes went by before Woody finally emerged, looking even more somber than usual.

"This is very strange," he said, putting a hand on Judith's shoulder. "Please try not to get unduly upset, but we've got a problem, which means we have to follow police procedure."

Judith stared at Woody. "What do you mean?"

He grimaced. "It's the weapon. The bullet matches Joe's .38, and the gun has been fired very recently. I'm so sorry, Judith, but we're going to have to file charges. Joe understands."

Judith didn't.

Chapter Five

T hat's crazy!" Judith cried, shaking off Woody's comforting hand. "How could his gun have been used to shoot . . . whoever the dead man is?"

"That's what we have to figure out," Woody said. "Joe realizes what's happening. I mean, as far as police work is concerned. We'll do our best to keep this quiet until we have some answers."

"And meanwhile?" Judith demanded, raising both hands in a helpless gesture. "Joe sits in a jail cell while I go insane?"

"Actually," Woody said in a tone that sounded reasonable yet forced, "he thought maybe you should take a vacation."

"A . . . ?" Judith stared in disbelief. "Are you nuts, too?"

Woody shifted from one foot to the other. "He told me about your trip back east and how you had a really busy fall, then the holidays coming right after you got back from Boston, and all the family doings and how worn-out you were"—customarily a man of fewer and more measured words, he paused to take a quick breath—"not to mention that January is your slowest month at the B&B, so it'd only make sense for you to take a break and maybe go—"

"Soak my head," Judith finally interrupted. "No. I'm not

taking time off. Joe's afraid I'll get mixed up in this whole insane homicide situation. He wants me to butt out, right?"

"Well . . ." Woody made a face. "He worries about you. Especially if he's not around to look after you."

"Why can't I bail him out?"

"Ah . . . that's kind of awkward."

"How so?" Judith demanded.

Woody rubbed at his walrus mustache, but couldn't quite meet Judith's fierce gaze. "We agreed it might be better if he stays in jail. Given the complexities of the situation, it's the safest place for him."

"Oh, great!" she cried. "You're afraid somebody's going to bump him off!"

"No, no, nothing like that," Woody protested. "It's more like . . . let's put it this way. If he's free on his own recognizance, Joe will try to solve the case himself. That's not smart if he's really been set up."

Judith was incredulous. *"If?"*

"I mean," Woody said, finally looking Judith in the eye, "if it's an intentional setup aimed at Joe, instead of a more random thing."

"Wait." Judith's brain had begun to function again. "If the bullet came from Joe's gun, somebody stole it. That sounds personal. Did or did not Joe have his weapon with him when he was arrested?"

Woody gazed at the ceiling, but said nothing.

Judith sighed. "Okay. I'll shut up for now. Can I at least see my husband or is he already in solitary confinement?"

"Of course not," Woody said. "As soon as Del finishes up in there," he went on, nodding toward the interrogation room door, "you can go in."

"Great," Renie said to Woody. "Then we can talk about Puccini."

His smile was off center. "Right. I'd like to do that. In fact," he said, turning to Judith, "I'd like to do just about anything but what I'm doing now. This captain's job is . . ." He glanced again at Renie. "'*Sola, perduta, abbandonata*' describes it best."

Renie nodded. "Manon's final aria. So moving. So apt."

Judith gave Woody a shove. "Skip the weepy opera stuff and do your job. I've got guests arriving in an hour or so."

With a heavy sigh, Woody entered the interrogation room and closed the door behind him.

"Why," Judith said, "do I feel like strangling you, Woody, *and* Joe?"

Renie was still looking wistful. "Maybe because you're upset?"

Judith shook her head and turned her back on Renie. Of all the strange, confusing, and even dangerous situations that she'd found herself in over the years, this was the worst. When Renie had been briefly considered a murder suspect, it had seemed more ridiculous than frightening. At least her nutty cousin had never been arrested. Even having Joe and Bill apparently get kidnapped in Scotland hadn't been as upsetting as the current crisis. The occasional face-off with desperate killers was a piece of cake by comparison. This time Judith felt as if she'd hit bottom.

"Helpless," she murmured, staring down the vacant hallway.

"Huh?" Renie said.

Judith didn't turn around. "Helpless," she repeated louder. "I feel helpless. And you're no help at all."

"Sorry." Renie sounded uncommonly meek. "Should I go home?"

"How," Judith responded, finally turning to look at her cousin, "do I get home? In a paddy wagon?"

"Oh. That's right. Joe's MG is in your garage. How about a cab?"

Five more minutes passed in silence. Renie had wandered down to one end of the hall and then back to the other. Judith wished she could sit down. The headache that had come on shortly after her departure from Hillside Manor was now impossible to ignore. Digging into her purse, she reached for the cache of medications she carried for emergencies. Just as she found the small plastic pillbox, Woody came out of the interrogation room.

"Judith," he said solemnly, putting his hands on her shoulders, "Joe and I think it's better if you don't talk to him right now. He's going to call you later after we've sorted through some things. You have to be patient. I'm sorry. Really."

Looking into Woody's dark eyes, she knew he was sincere. "I don't have any choice, do I?"

He shook his head.

"Okay." Her expression was resigned. "I guess Renie and I will go home. Say hi to Sondra for me." Moving away from Woody, she started back down the hall, paying no attention to Renie and Woody's brief farewell exchange.

Neither cousin spoke until they got to the elevators. To Judith's surprise, Renie kept going, past the reception counter and through the opposite corridor from the one that had led to the interrogation section.

"Why are you headed this way?" Judith asked.

"Because I'm parked on the east side of the building in the mayor's slot and it's on the fifth-floor side," Renie replied in a reasonable voice. "You came in on the ground floor on the west side of the block."

"Oh." Judith tromped along behind Renie, but stopped at a water fountain long enough to take the Excedrin that was beginning to dissolve in her hand. When Renie reached the parking area, she patiently waited for Judith to catch up.

"You okay?" she asked Judith with what sounded like real concern.

"I guess I have to be," Judith replied glumly. "I don't have much choice, with the Beard-Smythes showing up to spend the night."

"The . . ." Renie stopped just short of the Joneses' Camry. "You mean from church? Why are they coming?"

"They ran out of gas."

"Highly unlikely," Renie said, "unless they've been bragging more than usual about how they're so upper class and stinking rich. If they tithe at church, I'm Mother Teresa."

"Whatever." Judith waited for Renie to remove a piece of paper from the car's windshield.

"Hunh," Renie said. "It's a ticket." She stuffed it in her purse and unlocked the car. "Who *is* our mayor? They all look alike to me."

"Larry Apples," Judith said, getting into the car. "*Appel,* I mean."

"Whatever," Renie said, sliding into the driver's seat. "Apples, oranges, who cares? Our mayors rarely do anything except screw up." She patted the dashboard. "It's okay, Cammy. It's not your fault. You just took up the mayor's space, which is about all he does in his office. The ticket's not much more costly than a legal downtown parking spot."

Judith tried to ignore her cousin's jabbering. A glance at her watch told her it was exactly three-thirty. Unless some of her guests arrived early, she'd get home in time for the four P.M. check-in.

Apparently Renie had gotten the silent-treatment message and stopped talking. Downtown traffic was heavy, but not yet bogged down by rush hour. Judith barely noticed the ebb and flow of pedestrians or the near miss of a couple of jaywalkers who had the temerity to attempt crossing the street in front of the Camry.

Ten minutes later they arrived at Hillside Manor. Judith mumbled a thank-you to Renie and got out of the car. The rain was still falling when she entered the house through the back door. Phyliss was in the kitchen, scrubbing the sink.

"You back from the hoosegow?" she asked. "Is Mr. F. on a chain gang yet?"

"Not quite." Judith had hung her jacket on a peg in the hall before entering the kitchen. "But he won't be home right away," she added, putting her purse on the counter by the computer. "Any calls or other annoying interruptions?"

"Just your mother, the reincarnation of Queen Herodias," Phyliss replied. "I think she wants your husband's head on a platter."

"Sounds about right," Judith murmured.

The cleaning woman ran some water in the sink before looking at Judith. "This sounds serious. Has Mr. F. done something sinful?"

"No. It's just that the situation is very confusing. Joe's innocent."

Phyliss nodded, her sausage curls bobbing up and down. "That's what I said. Just like John the Baptist. Not that being innocent did him much good. Losing your head makes it hard to wear a hat."

"At least Saint John got a halo." Judith tried to square her shoulders, but lacked the energy and sat down at the kitchen table.

"All done," Phyliss announced. "Guess I'll head for home. It's a good thing I brought my bumbershoot today. My bunions told me it was going to rain. God works in wondrous ways."

As far as Judith was concerned, God wasn't working at

all. Neither was her brain. She simply sat and stared unsee-ingly until Phyliss had gone home and the house suddenly became uncommonly quiet. *Too quiet,* she finally realized, getting up and opening the refrigerator door. After staring at the interior for at least a full minute, she closed the door and opened the freezer compartment. There were still some frozen hors d'oeuvres left over from the holidays that Cousin Sue had brought from Gutbusters, the huge discount chain's flagship store east of the lake. The Beard-Smythes might not show up for the social hour. Judith removed two of the three packages, setting them on the counter to thaw.

The middle-aged couple from Indianapolis returned shortly after four, complaining about the rain, but pleased with their purchases at a local souvenir shop on the water-front. They went upstairs to take a nap before going to dinner at a seafood restaurant that overlooked the ship canal. Judith wondered how close the restaurant was to the house-boat where Joe had been doing his surveillance work. The only newspaper and TV reports about the condo shooting had been mercifully brief, overshadowed by what had so far had been an unusually warm—and dry—winter. Weather always was big news, often being unpredictable in Judith's part of the world. No doubt the rain would lead off the local TV broadcasts at five. Not that she ever had time to watch the early edition—Judith was always too busy welcoming guests and preparing for the social hour.

Shortly after four o'clock, the single woman arrived via taxi. She immediately began griping about the rain. "I was warned it'd be like this," she said, shaking out her navy-blue raincoat. "Luckily, I'm only in town for one night."

Judith wasn't in the mood to argue. She handed the guest register to the new arrival. "I'll need your other information, too. Jean Rogers, right?"

"Yes. Do you want to see my driver's license?"

"Please."

Jean Rogers removed a black leather wallet from her brown suede drawstring handbag. "Here. I'm from Phoenix and I'm used to decent weather, even in the winter."

The picture on the license wasn't flattering, but, Judith thought uncharitably, there wasn't much to work with. Jean was in her late thirties, plain as a post, and wore her dark hair pulled back into a careless knot that only accentuated her sharp features and pale skin. According to the license, she was five foot seven, weighed a hundred and thirty pounds, needed glasses for driving, but had no other restrictions—such as being unpleasant. Or so Judith thought to herself. The background on the license looked like the Grand Canyon and was far more attractive than the driver's picture.

"I paid in advance with my credit card," Jean said as Judith handed back the license. "Did you get it?"

"Yes. You're all set. I'll show you to your room."

Jean picked up her belongings. "How far away is the convention center? I was told it was walkable."

"That depends on how much you like to walk," Judith said, starting up the stairs. "It's downtown, about two miles from here."

"I was informed it was at the bottom of this hill."

"That's the civic center," Judith replied, reaching the second landing. "Whoever told you that was misinformed."

Jean harrumphed. "Typical."

"There's bus service just a block away on Heraldsgate Avenue," Judith said, pausing in the hallway by the love seat and table. "That's the guest phone. Most people have a cell these days, but you can use that phone if you need it. There's also a current supply of magazines and some books if you care to take advantage of them."

"I won't have time," Jean said. "I must prep for my presentation tomorrow. I like to put my best foot forward."

Haven't seen that third foot, Judith thought. *The other two haven't done it yet.* "Of course," she murmured, and moved on. The single room was at the front of the house, off a short corridor between Rooms One and Three. "Here are your two keys," she said, opening the door. "One for the room, the other for the front door, if you go out this evening and come back after ten."

Jean frowned as she studied her surroundings. "This room is very small."

"That's why it's a single."

Jean set her carry-on, a laptop case, and handbag on the bed before looking at the single window. "I suppose there's a view when you can see it."

"You can see downtown and the bay," Judith said, pulling the curtain aside. "There's a ferryboat pulling out. You can see another one coming in halfway across the bay."

Jean rolled her pale blue eyes. "Ferryboats! What a thrill. Maybe they'll sink. Or is that too much excitement for this city?" She peered impatiently at Judith. "Never mind. Are you done?"

"I sure am," Judith retorted. "The social hour is at six."

"No thanks. I'll be forced to mingle with strangers tomorrow at the convention center."

Lucky them, Judith thought as she left Room Two. Obnoxious guests were the exception, not the rule, at Hillside Manor. Fortunately, the young couple from Kamloops, British Columbia, were friendly and chipper. The widowed sisters were natives, but had lived away from the city for many years. They had come for a family reunion with their brother, and were scheduled to leave the next day to visit other relatives who lived in nearby towns. Having been away for so long, they both lamented many of the changes since their youth. At least the weather was the same, and they liked it that way. San Diego had too much sun for one sister and the other had never cared for the extremes in Green Bay, Wisconsin.

Shortly before six o'clock, Judith took dinner to Gertrude. For once, the old lady didn't grouse about not having received her "supper" earlier. Instead, she was chortling over Joe's misfortune. "Didn't I tell you he was a bum?" she demanded as Judith set down the tray of leftovers from the previous night's meal. "Crooked, like most cops. I'll bet he stole more apples than anybody else on his beat."

"Joe never walked a beat," Judith said, "at least not after he—"

Gertrude jabbed at the potatoes on her plate. "What is this? Mush? I don't eat mush for supper."

"You do now," Judith snapped—and was immediately sorry. She put an arm around her mother's hunched shoulders. "I don't mean to be nasty. I'm just worried."

"About what? Dim Bulb getting out on bail? Maybe he'll try to escape and they'll shoot him."

Judith removed her arm, but held her tongue. "I have to get back to my guests. I'll warm up some of the marionberry pie for your dessert." She fled the toolshed before her mother could do more than make a couple of grumbling noises.

It was just after six when Judith went back into the house. All of the regular guests—except Jean Rogers—had gathered in the living room to nibble on Gutbusters' appetizers and sip sherry or sparkling cider. Judith joined them, as was her custom when she had time. Chatting with the visitors was better than stewing about Joe's dilemma.

"So much construction!" the sister from Green Bay exclaimed. "Cranes everywhere! It's like a steel forest around here."

"You should come to Kamloops," the young wife said. "We're growing, but we're still small and the countryside is beautiful."

"We went to Banff and Lake Louise a few years ago," the middle-aged husband from Indianapolis said. "Better than Europe. Never saw such pretty lakes and mountains in my life."

"We've got plenty of lakes," the Green Bay sister declared, "but we also have plenty of bugs in the . . ."

Judith heard the doorbell chime and realized she'd forgotten about the Beard-Smythes. Excusing herself, she hurried to the front door. Alicia and Reggie Beard-Smythe stood on the porch. So did a large Irish wolfhound.

"Good evening, Judith," Alicia said with a flashing smile that never seemed to reach her sapphire-blue eyes. "It's so kind of you to give us shelter." Without waiting to be asked, the couple—and the dog—crossed the threshold into the entry hall. "My goodness," Alicia said, slipping back the hood on her chic crimson all-weather jacket, "I already feel warmer. It may not be freezing outside, but our house is a refrigerator. We kept at least three of the fireplaces going, but that's such a nuisance. This," she added, with a sweep of her elegant hand, "is bliss! So many old furnishings! So much well-worn decor! So archaically quaint!"

"Have you ever met my mother?" Judith's question had popped out almost involuntarily.

Alicia looked uncertain. "I'm not—" She stopped as the wolfhound looked as if he—or she or it—was about to pounce on the elephant-foot umbrella stand despite Reggie's attempt to tighten his hold on the animal's leash.

"Down, Mayo!" Reggie ordered in his high-pitched voice. "Down, boy!" He danced around the large hard-side spinner piece of luggage he'd hauled into the house.

Mayo backed off, but began sniffing the Persian carpet. *The well-worn Persian carpet,* Judith thought. No doubt the dog smelled cat. She hoped Sweetums was in the toolshed or outside. She decided against having the Beard-Smythes formally register. "Would you like a drink?"

Husband and wife exchanged glances. "Well . . . that would be awfully nice," Alicia said. "How soon is dinner?"

Judith couldn't conceal her surprise. "Dinner? I don't serve dinner for our guests." She gestured toward the living room. "This is the social hour. You know—time for visitors to get together and compare impressions of the city."

Reggie's pinched face looked puzzled. "But the Paines are coming for dinner tomorrow, are they not?"

"Yes," Judith replied, wincing as Mayo scratched at the powder room door just off the entry hall. "But that's part of the school auction package."

"Oh." Reggie seemed crestfallen, stroking his thin mustache with long, delicate fingers. "We naturally assumed . . ." He looked at his wife. "What *did* we assume, darling?"

Alicia looked discomfited. "There must be some misunderstanding. Martha Morelli told me you were serving dinner. Or was it Norma who mentioned that?" Before Judith could respond, she waved a hand. "That's unimportant. I took it for granted that we'd dine here. It's quite impossible to cook when one's teeth are chattering. I'm sure that we could just have some of what you and Jack are eating tonight."

"*Joe*," Judith stated firmly. "Joe Flynn. Actually, Joe isn't here this evening. He's in ja—jaywalking school. As a retired policeman, he signed up to teach people to cross streets only in crosswalks. Both marked and unmarked. You've probably noticed how so many people on top of the hill just pop out from between parked cars, risking life and limb. Very dangerous."

"Done it myself," Reggie admitted, tugging again at Mayo's leash. "The avenue is so busy these days." He glanced at his wife. "We can go to a restaurant on top of the hill. But we won't jaywalk. Heh heh."

Alicia, however, seemed disappointed. "Oh, not after all we've been through." She suddenly brightened. "I know! I'll whip up one of my favorite soufflés. Would you enjoy that, Judith?"

"Well . . . sure. That sounds fine. Would you like to take your luggage upstairs? You're in Room Three."

"Will do," Reggie volunteered, pulling on Mayo's leash. "Ta-ta."

Judith was trying to figure out a tactful way to deal with the dog's presence. "Did Martha—or Norma—mention that I have a cat?"

Alicia removed her jacket and handed it to Judith. "A cat? No, I don't think so." She frowned. "Is your cat well disciplined? Mayo is afraid of cats. Wolfhounds are very sensitive."

"Cats in general are difficult to discipline. Sweetums spends much of his time with my mother in the . . . her apartment. Usually, there's no problem, because I don't allow pets at the B&B."

Alicia looked shocked. "You don't? How . . . well, I shouldn't say 'inhospitable,' but it strikes me as arbitrary. Mayo is like family."

"It's not a lack of hospitality," Judith declared. "It's a courtesy to guests who have allergies to animals. It also safeguards against the kind of damage that untrained pets can incur." A vision of the savaged lace curtains in Room Five flashed through her mind's eye. "What," she continued, changing the subject, "shall I do with your jacket?"

"Oh." The query seemed to stump Alicia. "I suppose you could put it in your coat closet down here for now."

"We don't have one," Judith said. "The original coat closet

was replaced by the powder room when I converted the house into a B&B."

"How very odd," Alicia murmured. "Never mind. I should start making my soufflé. Where's the kitchen?"

Judith placed the jacket on the hat rack before leading the way through the dining room into the kitchen. "What do you need?" she asked while Alicia studied the high ceiling, the appliances, and the schoolhouse clock.

"So delectably old-fashioned!" Alicia seemed transfixed by the almost imperceptible movement of the minute hand. "Tick-tock, tick-tock . . . oh! Ingredients. Five eggs, flour, milk, butter, salt, cayenne pepper, two kinds of cheese, lobster, shrimp, or crab. Mayonnaise, too."

"I have some frozen shrimp," Judith said. "Will that do?"

Alicia grimaced. "It'll have to. Oh, well. What kind of cheeses do you keep on hand?"

"Swiss, Gruyère, Havarti, and two different Cheddars."

"No Parmesan?"

"Only in a shaker," Judith admitted.

"Dear me." Alicia gently scratched her cheek with a perfectly manicured and polished nail. "I suppose the Swiss and Gruyère will do. Oh! Mushrooms, of course."

Judith wasn't going to waste the fresh mushrooms she'd bought for the Paines' dinner. "Canned?"

Alicia winced. "What kind?"

"Button. Sliced and unsliced."

"I suppose the sliced ones might work if there isn't any other variety." She gestured at the stove. "Would you mind turning the oven on to three twenty-five?"

"No problem." Judith moved to the stove to set the temperature. "I'll get the other ingredients from the fridge."

"You have a KitchenAid mixer," Alicia noted. "Mine has seventeen attachments and a glass bowl. So much easier to monitor the mixing process than these old stainless-steel ones. They look as if they belong in a hospital. I also need a quart-and-a-half-size glass baking dish."

"Sure," Judith replied, removing cheese, mayo, butter, and milk from the fridge. "I'll get the shrimp from the freezer so it can thaw. How long does it take for the soufflé to bake?"

"Forty-five minutes," Alicia replied, checking the oven temperature. "That's less heat and a longer time than for the creamy kind, but Reggie is one for a firm soufflé. Where are your spatulas?"

"Second drawer on the left from the mixer," Judith said, searching for the shrimp in the freezer compartment. "How much—"

The ringing of the phone interrupted her.

"I'll get it," Alicia said. She grabbed the receiver from the cradle on the counter. "Yes?"

Judith found the shrimp just as a loud crash practically shook the house. Screams and shouts erupted from the living room. Dumping the shrimp on the counter, she raced as fast as she could through the dining room and into the entry hall.

All of the guests who'd been enjoying the social hour were crowding together in the archway of the living room entrance. Judith couldn't see anything amiss. She counted heads to make sure everyone was alive.

"Suitcase," the husband from Indianapolis said, pointing to the first landing on the stairs. "I think."

Sure enough, the heavy piece of luggage belonging to the Beard-Smythes had fallen from above and toppled the stand on which Judith kept her guest register and visitors' information.

"How on earth . . . ?" she murmured, looking up to the second landing. No one was in sight. The impact of the hard-side case had broken one of the stand's legs; the register was under the luggage and the visitor guides were scattered all over the bottom stairs and the entry-hall floor.

"Let me help," the young man from Kamloops offered.

He was joined by his wife and the husband from Indianapolis, whose first name Judith suddenly recalled was Edgar.

"Did anybody see what happened?" Judith asked, aware that she was trembling.

No one responded right away, until finally the San Diego sister spoke up. "We were all chatting and having such a nice time. Then there was that terrifying crash." She moved closer to the accident site. "Oh my! That stand looks like an antique. Can you get it fixed?"

"I hope so," Judith said. "It belonged to my great-aunt and great-uncle. It was originally a lectern in their parish church. It's solid oak."

"Not solid enough," Edgar said as he and the younger man set the offending piece of luggage on the entry-hall floor. "Anybody here lay claim to this thing?" he asked with a disparaging gesture at the suitcase.

"It belongs to some guests who arrived just fifteen or twenty minutes ago," Judith said. "The husband took the case upstairs and his wife is in the kitchen. I'll let her know."

Judith rescued the guest register and set it on the Bombay chest. The rest of the group had joined in to pick up the restaurant coupons, city maps, bus and tour schedules, pens, notepads, and other items scattered around the entry hall. Judith explained that she had an artificial hip, making it risky for her to bend down, and thanked them for their efforts before returning to the kitchen.

Alicia appeared oblivious to the commotion in the entry hall. She had the mixer going at full speed, whipping the egg whites into small peaks. She apparently didn't hear Judith's first two attempts to get her attention.

"*Stop!*" Judith finally shouted within a few inches of the other woman's ear.

Alicia looked at her hostess and held up a finger. "One minute."

Judith reached across the counter and yanked the mixer's plug out of the socket. "Who called?"

"Who called what?" Alicia demanded, her eyes snapping with anger. "Why did you shut off the mixer? I had almost perfect peaks."

"I'm expecting an important call," Judith said, working hard to keep her temper.

"Oh." Alicia shrugged. "It was a wrong number."

"Are you sure?" Judith asked, trying to ignore the egg-shells on the floor, the counter, and in one of the drawers that her guest had left open.

"Of course. It was someone with a foreign name, and though his English was quite good, he sounded very peculiar. A sex fiend, no doubt. He was rattling on about bondage and handcuffs and all that type of ridiculous behavior. I hung up on him. There's no point getting angry or sounding frightened. That's how those people get their thrills. Would you please plug in the mixer before I lose my peaks?"

"Did he give a name?"

"A name?" Alicia said crossly. "A name for what?"

"His name. My name. Any name!"

Alicia shook her head impatiently. "Certainly not. In fact, he started out saying something about sandwiches."

"Sandwiches?"

"*Yes.*" The sapphire eyes sparked. "You know—bread, butter, egg salad, bacon, lettuce—"

Judith interrupted the recital. "That makes no sense. What exactly did he say?"

"Judith . . ." Alicia seemed weary of what she apparently perceived as nuisance queries. "He mentioned a deli at first, and then . . . well, he went off on all those vulgar things that definitely were not connected to sandwiches. Or if they were, I certainly don't want to know how." She picked up the mixer cord and jammed it back into the socket.

Judith snatched up the phone and headed for the pantry. It wasn't Joe who'd called. Woody had promised she'd hear from her husband, but something must have gone wrong. Alicia was as addled as the eggs she was beating. "Deli" translated as something quite different from sandwiches. Detective "Del" Delemetrios sounded more like it.

Judith called the cops.

Chapter Six

After dialing police headquarters, Judith asked for the homicide division. The information on her caller ID had come up as a general City Hall number. She knew from experience that this was routine for law enforcement calls in order not to alarm or scare off the person they were trying to reach. When an operator came on the line, Judith asked for Detective Delemetrios. After a slight pause, the call was transferred. Del answered on the second ring. After identifying herself, and apologizing for the confusion at her end, Judith asked why he'd called earlier.

"No problem," Del replied. "It's all this paperwork. We're also trying to keep the media at bay. The newspaper's beat reporter is a City Hall veteran, one of the few older staffers who isn't being forced into retirement."

"Is that Addison Kirby, by any chance?"

"You know him?"

"Yes. So does Joe. Have you told my husband about Addison?"

"Ah . . ." Del paused. "I don't think I mentioned him by name. Should I?"

"Let me talk to Addison first," Judith said. "That is, I

know him from the multiple murder case several years ago at Good Cheer Hospital. His wife was one of the victims. I also had some contact with him later regarding another homicide investigation."

"I don't remember much about the hospital murders," Del said. "I was away at college back then. Joe Flynn worked that case?"

"It's complicated," Judith said. "In fact, Joe and Addison both ended up in the hospital, too."

"Wow. Sometimes I feel as if I have a lot of catching up to do. You must've gotten the real inside scoop on that one."

"As a matter of fact," Judith confessed with some reluctance, "I was in the hospital already, and so was my cousin Serena."

There was a longer pause. "The one who tried to cut off my tie?"

"Serena sometimes lets her temper get the best of her."

"I'd hate to see the worst."

"Yes, you really would," Judith said. "But about Joe . . ."

"Excuse me," Del said deferentially. "I'm confused. You mentioned another homicide investigation besides the hospital murders. Are you retired from the force, too?"

"Ah . . ." Judith grabbed a can of mushrooms from the pantry shelf. "No, no. I've just always taken an interest in my husband's work. Not that I ever pressed him for information he couldn't reveal, but eventually the facts came out. I think it's important for spouses to appreciate what goes on with each other's jobs. My job as an innkeeper keeps me so busy that I don't have much time for outside interests."

"I can understand why," Del said, "but you must meet some very fascinating people. Ever had movie or rock stars stay at your inn?"

Since Judith was staring at her current guest who wasn't

really a guest, she asked Del to hold on for a moment. "Here," she said, handing over the mushrooms.

Alicia studied them with a critical eye. "How long have you had them on the shelf?"

"A week," Judith lied. It could have been a year, for all she remembered. "Excuse me, I'm talking to someone."

"Not that sex fiend, I hope!"

"This is business," Judith snapped. "It's also private."

Looking annoyed, Alicia returned to the kitchen.

"Sorry," Judith said into the phone. "A guest had a question. Can you *please* tell me about Joe?"

"Uh . . . not much to tell. I think he's having something to eat."

"In a cell?"

"Not exactly."

Judith waited for Del to elaborate, but he didn't. "Where is he?"

"He's with Captain Price."

Joe and Woody, sitting in a tree, E-A-T-I-N-G; first comes the menu, then come the drinks, then wife wonders why this all stinks. Judith was fed up. "Are they even on the premises?"

"Why, yes, of course," Del said. "Hey—I realize this is an unusual situation. Since you're married to a retired police detective, you know that sometimes we have to keep investigations under wraps."

"Of course I do, but I deserve—no, I *demand* an explanation. You'd tell any anxious spouse where her other half is. For all I know, he and Woody are at a seedy cop bar getting soused and leering at some tart in a low-cut dress." Judith grimaced, recalling that this was the scenario that led to Joe's elopement with Herself.

"They're not doing anything like that," Del said, his own patience obviously strained. "They're both here, and they're

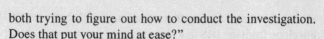

both trying to figure out how to conduct the investigation. Does that put your mind at ease?"

"I suppose it'll have to," Judith said grudgingly.

"Good," Del responded. "If Mr. Flynn—" He stopped, and Judith could hear faint voices in the background. "Hold on," the detective said. "Here's Joe now."

A moment later, Joe was on the line. "Hey—stop bugging poor Del. I'll make this quick. Can you get into my safe where I keep my guns?"

"I don't think you've ever given me the combination."

"Maybe not," Joe said, "but you have certain skills learned in Dan's School of Hard Knocks. This is an open line. I prefer not giving the combination over the phone. I doubt if anyone's listening in, but—"

"Joe," Judith interrupted, "stop trying to upset me even more. Are you insinuating—"

"Listen to me," he said sharply. "See if you can open the damned safe and take out the .38 Smith & Wesson. After you do that, call Del immediately and he'll have someone dispatched to collect it. Okay?"

"This all seems so cloak-and-dagger. Are you saying that your gun is in the safe? I thought you told me the police were holding it until the tests came back." Judith waited for a response, but heard nothing. "Joe? Joe!"

The phone had gone dead.

J udith exited the pantry, gazing at the back stairs across the hall. She wondered if she should try to open the safe immediately. It had been a while since she'd had to figure out the combination for a safe. Life with Dan McMonigle had been fraught with unpleasant surprises, including a foreclosure notice on the house they owned in the Wilmont district across the canal. On another occasion, Judith had seen an envelope from the IRS that she suspected was a notice about back taxes. Dan had foiled her when he grabbed the envelope, removed the letter . . . and ate it.

When her late and not always lamented husband installed a safe in their squalid rental house on Thurlow Street, he'd refused to give her the combination. After the repo man had towed away their car, Judith decided she had to find out what was going on with their finances—or lack thereof. Her early attempts to open the safe proved futile, but she finally figured it out. What she found—along with a pile of losing racetrack tickets—was all bad news, but at least she was prepared for the worst. And of course the worst always happened.

She was still mulling when a chipper Reggie Beard-Smythe bounded down the back stairs. "How's that soufflé coming?" he inquired with a toothsome smile.

"Ask your wife. It sounds as if she's still in the mixing process." Judith was about to go up the stairs, but stopped. "Where's Mayo?"

Reggie turned just before he reached the kitchen. "Asleep. He's very well behaved." He clapped a hand to his forehead. "I almost forgot. It would *appear* that the bathroom in Room Three is shared by the adjacent room. Is that possible?"

"Yes," Judith said.

"But . . ." Reggie moved back toward Judith. "Room Three is the most expensive? Without a private bath? Isn't that . . . peculiar?"

"No," Judith said. "Rooms Five and Six also share a bathroom, and there's another one in the middle of the hall on the other side of Room Four. We seldom have a problem. Most guests tend to be courteous about sharing. This is an inn, not a hotel."

Alicia's head appeared from around the open kitchen entrance. "No private bath? Oh, Judith, that simply won't do! We're going to give Mayo a bath tomorrow."

Judith was taken aback. "You mean in the bathtub?"

"Of course." Alicia came into the hallway, a cheese grater in one hand and a wooden spoon in the other. "We always do at home, but can't without any gas. Our furnace and hot-water tank both run on gas. Mayo does so enjoy a good soak."

"But doesn't dog hair clog the drain?" Judith asked. "Mayo's a rather shaggy sort of breed."

Reggie shook his head. "We cover the drain. It's never a problem."

"Make sure you do that here," Judith said, not wanting to get into an argument. "And please be mindful of the other guests. Granted, we're not at full capacity, but I wouldn't want the one bathroom that has a full tub off-limits for very long. The other bathrooms have only showers. And by the way," she went on, looking Reggie in the eye, "do you know how your luggage fell down the front stairs?"

Reggie looked surprised. "It did? I wondered what had happened to it. I could've sworn I brought it up to our room. Where is it now?"

"In the entry hall—along with the broken stand that it hit on the way down."

Reggie looked relieved. "Oh, thank you so much. I'll fetch it right now. It's not damaged, I hope?"

"No, but the antique stand has lost a leg," Judith said.

Alicia burst into laughter. "That is *too* funny!" She glanced at Reggie as he hurried through the kitchen, apparently to recover his suitcase. "Lost a leg! Oh my!" She turned away from Judith and began spooning grated cheese into a glass mixing bowl.

Judith shook her head in dismay. In the distance, she heard some of her paying guests wishing one another a pleasant evening. Apparently the social hour was over. She wished the entire evening were over as well. The Beard-Smythes were getting on her already frayed nerves.

Taking her time, she went up the back stairs, pausing to make sure Mayo wasn't marauding around the hallway, doing God only knew what to some of her other belongings. But everything seemed in order. She opened the door to the narrow stairway that led to the family quarters. By the time she entered Joe's office, she was worn-out.

Flipping on the light, she sat down in the desk chair and wheeled herself over to the small black safe by the bookcase. Would Joe use his birthday, address, or any other personal data as part of the combination? Probably not. That was too obvious. His favorite number was six, though she'd never known why. Several minutes passed without inspiration. The safe was set on zero. She reached for the dial to see if she could utilize her rusty skills. The door swung open. It had never been locked in the first place. Judith heaved a huge sigh of relief.

She saw a familiar black leather belt holster first, but it contained Joe's Glock 9mm. The tan shoulder holster held his Beretta. The Smith & Wesson was gone, along with the brown high-ride holster. The only other gun-related items in the safe were boxes of ammo. All of the other items were related to personal and business records.

Judith was stumped. Nothing made sense. She was certain that Joe's Smith & Wesson had been confiscated by the police. Why would he ask her to get it out of the safe? But why was the safe open? Joe would never have left it that way. Was it possible that the gun had been returned to him before he was hauled off to headquarters? That struck her as unlikely. But there was no logical explanation, and Judith clung to logic like a mountain climber clutches a dry rope.

Swiveling in the chair, she scoured the room for any sign of disturbance. Joe was reasonably tidy and remarkably organized, a lifelong habit from his police job. Everything looked perfectly normal.

Judith had no choice but to let Joe know that his Smith & Wesson was missing. She flipped through his Rolodex, hoping to find a direct line to Homicide. To her relief, it looked as if he had already written down Woody's new number. But Woody didn't answer. Instead, Judith got a standard recorded message. She hung up and tried the homicide listing on another Rolodex card.

A man with an unfamiliar voice answered. Judith was momentarily put off. "I'm trying to reach Captain Woodrow Price or Detective Delemetrios. His first name is . . . Keith, I think."

"Neither of them is available," the man at the other end said almost too quickly. "Would you like to leave a message?"

"Yes," Judith said, "and it's urgent. I'd prefer that Captain—"

"They're gone for the day," the voice interrupted. "If it's urgent, hang up and call 911."

"No! This isn't an emergency, but it *is* urgent. My husband—"

"Ma'am," the man said, obviously making an effort to be patient, "any domestic problems can be handled either by calling 911 or our nonemergency number at—"

Judith slammed the phone down. Fuming with frustration, she tired to think rationally. Was she purposely being stone-walled or merely dealing with somebody who thought she was a head case? Either way, she felt helpless. She finally picked up the phone again, made sure she hadn't broken it, and dialed Renie's number. To her dismay, the call went to the Joneses' voice mail. If her cousin was talking to her mother, it might take at least half an hour to get Aunt Deb off the line. Judith left a message anyway.

Feeling worn-out as well as discouraged, she got out of the chair to close the safe. A yellow Post-it note fluttered to the floor. Judith didn't want to risk bending down to pick it up, so she got back into the chair and moved closer to the safe. Being tall had definite advantages; long legs equaled long arms. She retrieved the scrap of paper and read what had been printed on it: *SF OR LA*. The initials meant nothing more to her than a reference to San Francisco and Los Angeles. The printing didn't tell her much either. Joe could've written it, though he usually printed in caps and lowercase. Unless the *OR* stood for Oregon, but that didn't make sense between allusions to two California cities. Apparently the note had been stuck to something in the safe. Maybe it was connected to his work or his private documents. She put the Post-it back in the safe, closed the door—and wondered if she should lock it. Maybe not. If Joe wanted her to search for anything else, she might not be able to open the safe. But she didn't like the idea of leaving the two remaining guns in an accessible place. She was trying to figure out another hiding spot when the phone rang.

"What's up?" Renie asked. "Why did you call from Joe's line?"

"Oh! I didn't think . . . never mind," Judith said, sitting back in the chair. "I've got a problem. I have to make this quick and please don't ask a lot of questions. Could you or Bill come over and get Joe's guns? Bill has two safes, right?"

"Three, in fact," Renie replied. "Bill is the safest man I know. Not always sane, but safe. I'll ask him. I'd rather not be driving around Heraldsgate Hill with an arsenal. Unlike my husband, I do not have a concealed-weapons carry permit."

"Thanks. How soon can he get here?"

"Let me find out."

Renie called to her husband—three times. Judith finally heard Bill bark a response. A muffled exchange ensued, with only a few audible, if unprintable, words from each of the Joneses.

"He'll be right over," Renie said into the phone before lowering her voice. "He has to leave the TV on for Oscar. The show they're watching has some Victoria's Secret commercials."

Judith ignored the remark about Oscar's alleged voyeurism. "Tell Bill to come in the back way and go up to the family quarters. I'm hanging up now."

"Okay. Bye." Renie clicked off first.

Judith figured it shouldn't take Bill more than five minutes to get from the north to the south side of the hill. The digital clock on Joe's filing cabinet informed her that it was 7:40. She wondered if Alicia had put the soufflé in the oven. It didn't really matter. Judith had lost her appetite. To kill time, she looked through some of the items on the desk. The SANECO file was peeking out from under an instruction brochure for the new fishing rod and reel Mike and Kristin had given Joe for Christmas. Judith couldn't resist taking a peek inside the file, but there wasn't much of interest: the alleged name of the now-deceased insurance claimant, his condo's address on the northwest side of the lake, his partially paralyzed but perhaps fraudulent condition resulting from an on-the-job accident while working for the city, and the address of the houseboat from which Joe would conduct his surveillance.

The house seemed very quiet on the third floor. Judith stood up, gazing out the window that looked over the garage, the toolshed, and the big white Dooley house on the other side of the cul-de-sac. It was still raining, but there wasn't much wind. Headlights appeared off to her left. A moment later, the Joneses' Camry pulled up just a few yards short of the Flynns' double garage. Judith went into the hall to wait for Bill.

Wearing his heavy-duty, all-purpose, all-ready-for-anything-short-of-the-Apocalypse jacket and snap-brim corduroy cap, Bill ascended the stairs without looking up until he got to the top. "Well?" he said in his usual no-nonsense manner. "Where are the guns?"

"Still in the safe." Judith led the way into Joe's office. "There are only two—the Beretta and the Glock."

"Are they loaded?"

"Yes."

Bill nodded. "Good answer. I'll check."

Judith left the guns in their holsters and handed them over. She knew, as Bill did, that the guns weren't loaded. But it was never smart to assume otherwise. She stood next to the safe, patiently watching Bill make sure there was no ammo in either weapon.

"Where *is* Joe?" Bill asked in his calm, midwestern voice.

"In jail."

"Still?"

"Well . . ." Judith wasn't sure what to say. "He's still at police headquarters. I think."

Bill frowned. "He's *somewhere*? Or not?" Before Judith could respond, he put the guns into a canvas bag and shook his head. "Never mind. Boppin'." Turning on his heel, he headed out of Joe's office.

"Thanks!" Judith called after him.

"Call if you need me," Bill said without turning around. He shut the door behind him.

Feeling relieved, not only in knowing the guns would be secure, but that Bill meant what he said, Judith took a deep breath. There was something reassuring about Renie's husband. Maybe it was all those years of listening to patients tell him their troubles and waiting to figure out if he could help them. Knowing, too, that most of the men and women who poured out their problems would be just as screwed up with or without his advice, but he'd still get paid. It was a living, and he needed that with three kids and Renie, all of whom believed money was good only for spending.

Making sure everything in the office was in place, Judith turned off the light and made her way downstairs. When she reached the kitchen, Alicia was taking the soufflé out of the oven.

"Shh," she warned Judith before speaking in a whisper. "We don't want this to fall, do we?" Cautiously carrying the soufflé, she went into the dining room, where Reggie was already sitting with a napkin tucked under his short chin.

"Ah," he said softly. *"Délicieux, eh, ma petite."*

Alicia gently put the glass baking dish on a ceramic tile. *"Voilà!"* she exclaimed under her breath. *"Bon appétit!"*

Judith felt obligated to at least try the soufflé. As she sat down at her grandparents' solid oak dining room table, she noted that not only had a place been set for her, but that there was also a Caesar salad in a large blue mixing bowl.

"It looks lovely," Judith said, aware that her voice lacked enthusiasm. "I'm sorry I didn't realize you'd be here for dinner. I would've prepared something. It's been kind of hectic here today."

"It's the least we can do," Alicia declared. "It's no trouble to make the soufflé. Reggie found the salad fixings, including the croutons. He also used your Caesar dressing, although it was the last of what was in the jar. You might want to make a note of that."

"I will," Judith responded, having filled her plate with some of the soufflé as well as the salad. "In fact, there may be an unopened jar toward the back of the—"

"Oh!" Alicia snapped her fingers. "Speaking of notes, I meant to jot down one for you. While you were gone wherever you went, Norma Paine stopped by to drop off a pillow for . . . Walter, I believe it was. I can't keep the Paine sons straight. Which one has the wart?"

"Ah . . . I'm not sure," Judith admitted. "I haven't seen the Paine children in years. Why did she bring a—"

"Must be Walter," Reggie broke in. "*W* for Walter, *w* for wart." He shrugged. "Wouldn't you think?"

Alicia looked thoughtful. "Perhaps. But not necessarily. It *could* be Andrew. Whoever it is, the wart's on his hand, and that would make me think of Handy Andy."

"True," Reggie agreed. "Oh, splendid soufflé, darling! Top-notch!"

Judith took a taste and deemed it edible, if gluelike. "Getting back to the pillow," she said, "why did Norma bring one here?"

"What?" Alicia looked puzzled. "Oh! The pillow. Yes, Norma told me that Walter—or Andrew—has neck problems and uses a therapeutic pillow. She keeps one for him at their house when he—whichever 'he' it is—visits. I gather Walter—or Andrew—is rather absentminded."

"He . . ." Judith paused. "Their son doesn't live around here?"

Alicia blinked several times at Judith. "Which one?"

"The one who needs the pillow," Judith replied patiently.

"Oh." Alicia tapped the table with her fork. "Let me

think . . . I don't know if either of the Paine sons lives in the city. One owns a ranch somewhere and another has a home in . . . I forgot . . . and one lives somewhere on the Eastside, but out near the hunt club. Which reminds me, have you and Jim thought about joining the club? It's very exciting."

Judith tried not to wince. "Jim? You mean Joe? My husband?"

Alicia laughed in her shrill, annoying manner. "Yes, yes, of course. How silly of me. Do you have pinks?"

Judith was beginning to think the grueling day had sucked her brain out of her head. "You mean . . . in the garden?" *Oh no, Alicia's going to laugh again . . . I can't stand it!*

But she was forced to endure another shrill round of mirth from her so-called guest. "I'm talking about hunting attire," Alicia said, the earsplitting hilarity subsiding. "The red—or *scarlet* jackets, to be precise, are called 'pinks.' " She looked at Reggie, who was devouring soufflé at a rapid rate. "Do you know why they're called that, darling?"

Reggie gazed up at the antique chandelier with its orange-flame-colored bulbs. "Some Brit tradition, I believe. Male riders and staff wear pinks, even though the coats are scarlet. Probably something to do with whoever was king at the time being color-blind. With equal rights, women can probably wear them, too."

"*I* do," Alicia huffed, "as you well know."

"Yes, darling, but you're an *American*." He shoveled another forkful of soufflé into his mouth.

"True," Alicia allowed, "and I intend to stay that way."

Judith decided to change the subject before she lost whatever grip on sanity she had left. "Where did Norma put her son's pillow?"

Alicia shrugged. "I'm not sure. She took it upstairs. Maybe in one of the bedrooms? I was focused on making the soufflé and I didn't pay much attention. Norma can be so overbearing."

Judith stood up. The soufflé was sticking to the roof of her mouth; she couldn't speak without lisping. "I bedder find where thee pud it. Excuthe me."

Using the front stairs, she glanced at the broken registry stand that was propped against the opposite wall. Maybe wood glue was the answer. The big suitcase was gone, no doubt removed to Room Three by Reggie. Reaching the second floor, she braced herself in case Mayo was on the loose. To her relief, there was neither sight nor sound of the dog. Judith noticed a plastic-covered package on the settee by the stairs. Peeking inside, she saw that it contained what looked like a modular-shaped foam-rubber pillow. Judith didn't know which room the son with the bad neck would be staying in, so she put the pillow in the linen closet between Rooms Three and Four. To save herself a trip to the third floor, she went into the vacant Room Four and entered the shared bathroom to dislodge the soufflé gunk before it drove her crazy.

She gave a start when she saw Mayo asleep in the bathtub. The animal didn't stir while she cleaned her mouth with a tissue, but Judith was not pleased that the dog had turned the tub into his sleeping quarters. His owners should have brought the animal's bed with them. It was possible that Jean Rogers might want to use the tub instead of the shower.

Judith went back through the hall and down the narrow corridor to Room Two. She knocked twice. No one responded. Maybe Jean was asleep. Judith knocked again, but heard nothing. Jean had indicated that she was staying in to prepare for her conference. Judith called her name. There was no answer. She turned the knob. The door opened. The room was empty. Jean must have changed her mind. Judith decided to leave a note about the dog in the bathtub. As she looked for something to write on, it dawned on her that the room was not just empty—it was devoid of any signs of occupancy. No handbag, no laptop, no carry-on bag. It was as if Jean had never been in the room.

But she had been there earlier to make her acerbic remarks about the accommodations. Judith wondered if, for some unforeseeable reason, Jean had suddenly checked out. Given the B&B's track record, Judith could only hope that yet another Hillside Manor guest hadn't checked out permanently.

Chapter Seven

Judith went back downstairs to the dining room. The Beard-Smythes were almost finished with dinner. Reggie, in fact, was just getting to his feet. "Time to take Mayo for a walk," he announced. "I wonder if it's still raining."

Any reproof about the dog sleeping in the tub had slipped down on Judith's priority list. "Did either of you see a woman in her thirties leave the house in the past hour or so?"

The couple exchanged puzzled glances. "Do you mean," Reggie inquired, "someone who was in the living room during the get-together?"

"No," Judith replied. "I don't think Ms. Rogers joined them. She's a professional woman. Not particularly striking, but she would have been carrying her belongings."

They both shook their heads. Alicia stood up. "I didn't come out to the dining room until we were ready to serve. Reggie set the table."

Reggie shrugged. "I didn't hear or see anything. Quiet around here after those guests went on their way."

"Good." Judith started to pick up the blue bowl and the salad tongs. "By any chance, do you know how—"

"No, no!" Alicia cried, snatching the bowl away from

Judith. "We can clean up after ourselves. It's the least we can do to repay your . . . oops!" The bowl slipped out of her hands, fell onto the hardwood floor just beyond the Persian carpet, and broke into a half-dozen pieces. "Oh no!" she exclaimed. "I'm so sorry. Do you think it can be mended?"

"Probably not," Judith said bleakly. "It's my grandmother's Depression-era LuRay mixing bowl." On a whim, she'd recently checked the bowl's price on eBay. The minimum bid was a hundred dollars.

"Just as well, then," Alicia said, picking up the broken pieces. "Who needs depressing cookware? I buy all my everyday china from Williams-Sonoma. I save the Sèvres and Limoges services for entertaining." She elbowed her way through the swinging half doors between the dining room and kitchen.

Judith cringed as she heard what was left of Grandma Grover's beloved bowl clatter into the garbage can under the sink. Reggie, meanwhile, was clearing the rest of the table. By something akin to a miracle, he didn't drop, spill, or break anything. Judith followed him into the kitchen.

"I must ask how your big suitcase crashed down the stairs," Judith said in what she hoped was a conversational tone. "I don't mean to pressure you, but it may have something to do with Ms. Rogers's early checkout. She may've been in a rush."

Reggie placed the dishes and cutlery into the sink. "Hmm," he murmured, stroking his thin mustache. "Can't think of any possible explanation. Sorry."

"Sure." Judith opened the dishwasher. "One other thing," she continued, still trying to sound pleasant. "Would you mind not letting Mayo sleep in the bathtub?"

Alicia, who had been gazing at the schoolhouse clock, whirled around. "Have you been snooping in our room?"

"I haven't been in your room," Judith replied quietly. "I

had to use the adjoining bathroom. That's how I happened to see your dog. Of course, the room actually belongs to me, doesn't it?"

A look of dismay came over Alicia's face. "Well . . . now that you mention it . . . but still . . ."

A banging at the back door stopped the argument. Startled, Judith muttered, "Now what?" before hurrying to see who wanted in. Only family members and the Rankerses came in that way.

"Where's my pie?" Gertrude demanded, rolling along the hall in her motorized wheelchair. "I've been waiting since Hector was a pup." She stopped halfway through the kitchen. "Who are you?" the old lady rasped. "The hired help?" She turned to Judith. "Since when could you afford to pay a couple of stiffs like these two? Or did you finally fire that Bible-beating nut job with the funny hair?"

"We are not the hired help," Alicia asserted haughtily.

"Could've fooled me," Gertrude grumbled. "Where's my pie? This pair better not have eaten it." She glared first at Alicia and then at Reggie, who was again stroking his sparse mustache. "Say, buster, what's with that fuzzy stuff on your upper lip? You trying to rub it into sprouting some real whiskers or make it disappear? Either way, it'd be an improvement."

"Mother!" Judith cried. "Please! This is Mr. and Mrs. Beard-Smythe from church."

Gertrude shot her daughter a puzzled glance. "Beard? Bad name for Buster. He must be Mr. *Smythe*." She stared up at Alicia. "You could use some tweezing on that chin of yours, Mrs. *Beard*. Or maybe you got piecrust crumbs stuck to it."

"I think," Alicia said stiltedly, "Reggie and I should retire now."

"Retire?" Gertrude shot back. "From what? If Dummy

here is paying you, it doesn't look as if you've finished clean-ing up. Get cracking." She stared at Judith. "Okay, Toots, let's see that marionberry pie. As Grandpa Grover used to say, my mouth's been set for it since six o'clock." The old lady maneuvered the wheelchair up to the kitchen table. "Well? What's with the two blockheads standing around? Fish or cut bait, chumps. You got to earn your keep around here."

Alicia grabbed her husband's sleeve. "We're going upstairs. I refuse to be insulted by such a . . . a *person*. Really, Judith, don't you have any control over this . . . *relic*?"

"Not really," Judith said placidly. "She's the house's legal owner."

"Oh my God!" Alicia cried, hauling Reggie out of the kitchen and into the dining room. "I've never been treated so shabbily in my life. I rescind my invitation asking you to join the hunt club. In fact, maybe we should have stayed at a . . ."

The rant trailed off as the Beard-Smythes stomped up the front stairs. Judith shook her head and removed the pie from the fridge.

Gertrude looked puzzled. "Hunt club? Hunt for what? Another job? They sure didn't do a very good one here."

Judith leaned down to kiss the top of her mother's head. "I've never loved you more than I do at this moment."

"Good," Gertrude said, patting her daughter's hand. "I took one look at those two and figured them for would-bes, as your aunt Deb would say. I don't know what they would want to be if they weren't stuck being themselves, but I didn't figure them for guests. Too pushy."

"You're right," Judith said, cutting a generous slice of pie for Gertrude and a smaller one for herself. "They're SOTS who have no heat at their house. In a weak moment, I let them spend the night here."

"They got coats, don't they? How about blankets?" Gertrude gazed reverently at the pie. "Are you going to warm it up? I wouldn't mind some vanilla ice cream on top."

"Sure," Judith replied. She put the pieces of pie on a larger, single plate, slid them into the microwave, and pressed the timer. "How much did you see today when Joe was . . . arrested?"

Gertrude chortled. "Enough to give me a good laugh. I haven't had one of those since Auntie Vance tried to shove Uncle Vince under the U-Haul in the cul-de-sac last summer."

Judith got a scoop out of the drawer and removed a quart of ice cream from the freezer. "So how did you find out he was arrested?"

"Uncle Vince? You mean after he got in the U-Haul and drove it off down the Counterbalance? Couldn't blame him. He thought it was the milk truck he used to drive before he retired. Your auntie Vance can make anybody go crazy. But she means well."

"I meant Joe," Judith said, her benign mood toward Gertrude beginning to fray.

"Oh. Him." Gertrude cocked her head to one side. "Because Knucklehead came to tell me he'd finally gotten caught for all his evil ways. I told him it was about fifteen years too late."

The microwave timer went off. "Joe came to the toolshed?" Judith asked, taking out the pie.

"Where else? Since when did I move to Buckingham Palace?"

"What did he say?"

Gertrude didn't answer immediately. She was distracted by the scoopful of ice cream her daughter was dumping on top of the pie. "Mmm-mm! Did you make this?"

"No," Judith replied, "it was on sale at Falstaff's last summer. I froze two of them for a rainy day."

"It is that," Gertrude said. She took her first taste and chewed happily.

Judith had sat down across from her mother. "What did Joe say?"

Gertrude shook her head and pointed to her mouth. "Bewwy theedth. Thuck in my denturth. Waid . . ." Dislodging the berry seeds, the old lady shrugged. "That he was going to jail. There was a police car in the driveway with two nice-looking young officers standing by. That kind of surprised me. Whatever happened to paddy wagons?"

"Was Joe in handcuffs?"

Gertrude shook her head. "Not then. Lunkhead went over to the car and they put the cuffs on him before he got inside. I waited until they drove away." She ate more pie and ice cream. "Say, do they still cart criminals around to work on a chain gang? I'd like to see Dunderhead out there on the highway under a hot sun with a shovel." She frowned. "Too bad it's winter."

Judith couldn't respond. She'd just taken her first bite of pie when the phone rang. Swallowing without choking to death, she got up and retrieved the phone from its cradle on the counter.

"Judith?" a faintly familiar voice said. "This is Addison Kirby. Do you have a reservation for tonight?"

"Tonight?" Judith asked in surprise. "For you?"

"Yes." He paused. "I know it's short notice, but I have some problems with the condo I bought after Joan died. I live at the bottom of the hill and thought maybe if you—"

"Yes, definitely," Judith broke in, sensing that this was no ordinary request. "What a coincidence. I was going to call you this evening."

"Mental telepathy," Addison replied. "I'll see you shortly."

Gertrude eyed Judith suspiciously. "You already got a boyfriend? What if Dumbhead escapes from jail?"

"That was Addison Kirby, the newspaper reporter," Judith explained. "He needs somewhere to stay tonight because there's something wrong at his condo. Apparently a lot of people are having problems with . . . gas."

Gertrude shook her head. "They should do what I do. Take some Pepto-Dismal or whatever it's called and rub their stomachs. Works for me every time."

"I mean gas as in heating," Judith said crossly, aware that her mother knew exactly what she was talking about. "You may recall that Addison's wife died at Good Cheer Hospital shortly before Renie and I had our surgeries there years ago."

Gertrude gave her daughter a sour look. "That's a pretty drastic way to get out of being stuck with you two goofballs."

"Never mind. I wonder if Addison would like some pie."

Gertrude shrugged. "Might give him gas."

"I'd better check out Room Four to make sure the dog isn't in the bathtub," Judith murmured, heading for the back stairs.

"I heard that!" Gertrude called after her. "I'm not *stone*-deaf. Come back here and tell me why there's a—"

"No, Mother," Judith said, continuing down the hall. "Later."

"What?" Gertrude shouted. "I'm *kind of* deaf, you know."

Judith went up the stairs. At least the other guns were now in a secure place, but she couldn't figure out why the Smith & Wesson was missing—or was *she* missing something? Was her husband trying to convey some other message that he couldn't say out loud?

First, she checked the shared bathroom between Rooms Three and Four. Mayo was gone. The tub had been cleaned except for a few stray hairs. She ran some water and made sure everything looked pristine. Then she went from the bathroom into Room Four.

And swore out loud. Mayo was asleep on the double bed. He stirred only slightly at the sound of Judith's irate voice. If the Beard-Smythes were using two rooms, they could pay for both of them. Besides, she was too tired to confront the couple again. Addison could just as well sleep in Room One, the only vacant accommodation left. It was slightly larger anyway.

Pausing in the hall, Judith listened for any sound from Room Three. All was quiet. If Alicia was still angry, she didn't seem to be taking it out on Reggie. Thankful for small blessings, Judith went down the front stairs just as the doorbell rang.

Addison Kirby still had his graying beard and looked a little older. He had lost more hair and added a few pounds in the five years since she'd last seen him. He smiled and shook Judith's hand.

"Good to see you," he said, stepping inside after making sure his boots were free of rain and wet leaves. "Anybody else around?"

"Just Mother. She's eating pie in the kitchen. Are you hungry?"

Addison took off his backpack and shook his head. "I already ate." His hazel eyes gazed meaningfully at Judith.

"Oh," she said, taking the backpack from him while he shrugged out of his all-weather hooded jacket. "I suppose you newspaper types get some free meals. On your beat, I assume the city picks up the tab."

"True," he agreed. "It's against the rules, but if it's a source we poor reporters can't afford to offend, we humbly eat *their* pie—not yours. In fact, my City Hall beat has expanded to cover everything and anything, due to our staff shrinking along with the size of the newspaper."

"I think I understand," Judith said. "How about a drink?"

"That sounds more like it," Addison said. "Should I take my wee bit of luggage upstairs?"

"Go ahead. You're in Room One, on your left nearest the stairs." She handed him the two keys. "The big one's for your room, the other is for the front door. The bathroom is between Rooms Five and Six. I'll see if Mother's finished her pie before I ship her back to the toolshed."

"I've never met your mother," Addison said.

"You want to meet her?"

"Why not? I like little old ladies."

"Uh . . . okay, sure. Why not?" Judith figured that as a beat reporter in a big city, he'd seen just about everything. Except Gertrude. "We'll be in the kitchen."

The old lady had almost finished her pie. "What did you do?" she asked. "Hide your new fella in the downstairs so-called powder room until you shove me out of here? And how come there's no powder in there? Or did he figure out I'm here and took a powder? Hey!" she cried as Judith took a bottle of Scotch from the kitchen cupboard. "You two are going to get drunk first? He can't be *that* homely compared to Whatsisname. Just put a bag over his head."

"Mother, please stop. Addison wants to meet you."

"Addison! What is he, part of a train, like the Addison, the Topeka, and the Santa Fe? Sounds about right—he's probably the caboose. Your first two looked like somebody's rear end. In fact, Jumbo Dumbo Dan looked like *two* people's rear—"

"Stop!" Judith glared at Gertrude. "He's a newspaper reporter and a very nice man. He may be working on a story involving . . . well, I'm not sure, but it may have something to do with Joe."

"I hope so," Gertrude said. "Make sure he interviews me. I'll give him an earful."

Addison strolled into the kitchen just as Judith set two

cocktail glasses on the counter. "Mother, this is Addison Kirby. Addison, this is my mother, Gertrude Grover." She held her breath, apprehensive of what the old lady would say.

"How do you do, Mr. Kirby," Gertrude said, offering her hand. "I've read a lot of your stories over the years. I enjoy the way you call Mayor Apples a numbskull without spelling it out."

Kirby gently shook hands. Judith's jaw dropped.

"A pleasure," Addison said. "Please call me Ad, Mrs. Grover."

Gertrude beamed. "Then you can call me Gert. And I know the mayor's name is really Appel, but I always call him that for fun. Just like I always call George Stuart, the police chief, Stoople, and the one before that, Dopey. It's my little way of having fun." She turned somber. "Life is hard when you're old. I was very sorry when your wife died. Joan Fremont was such a fine actress and a real lady. The last time I saw her onstage was many years ago." She paused, patting her wheelchair. "I don't get out much these days. The play was . . . Ibsen, I think. Yes, *A Doll's House*. Your wife was Nora. She had that part nailed down perfectly."

Addison seemed transfixed. "That was nineteen years ago," he said. "It was the first time she'd done the role."

"You'd never know that," Gertrude asserted. "She seemed to disappear into the role as soon as she stepped onstage."

Judith was so floored by her mother's recollection—if in fact it was even true—that she had to lean against the counter. Addison had sat down across from Gertrude. "Did you see her in other works?"

The old lady looked thoughtful. "Let me think. *The Beggar's Opera*—she had quite a nice singing voice. *The Crucible*—so compelling, especially for those of us who lived through the McCarthy era. My husband would've enjoyed it. He was very political."

That much was true, Judith thought. Donald Grover had been a high school history teacher with a passionate belief in individual freedom. Out of curiosity, he had attended a few Communist meetings as a college student, but never bought the party line. Still, at a time when anyone who'd ever rubbed shoulders with them risked retribution, Judith's father had been afraid that the Cold War witch hunt for so-called Reds and their sympathizers might cost him his job. Donald's fears had proved groundless, but his interest in politics remained. Gertrude gave her husband unreserved support, denouncing any threat to the American way of life—especially by Republicans.

"Scotch?" Judith said, as the memories of a half-century ago raced through her mind.

"Sure," Addison said. "That's my beverage of choice."

"Don't make mine too strong, dear," Gertrude said in a meek voice that was hardly recognizable.

"Ah . . . okay," Judith responded, getting out a third glass. "Are you sure you're not too tired?"

"Why, no," her mother replied. "It's only a quarter after eight." She smiled at Addison. "My little girl takes such good care of me. I even have my own little dollhouse in the backyard. We old folks need our privacy, too, and I'd never want to get in the way of Judith's business."

Good God, Judith thought as she poured the drinks, *what is she up to?* The old lady hadn't sweet-talked anybody since she'd conned Father Hoyle into giving parishioners over seventy-five a handicap of two free bingo numbers.

"Now," Gertrude said as Judith delivered the cocktails and sat down next to Addison, "tell me what you're working on these days, Ad. Is it true that the city is going to put in more of those handicap-accessible crosswalks at street corners? We have some up here on the hill, but I don't get out much in bad weather. My arthritis, you know." Her wrinkled face assumed an expression of resigned martyrdom that only Saint Agnes—or Aunt Deb—could have surpassed.

Before Addison replied, the phone rang. Judith got up to answer the call and moved into the dining room so her mother and Addison could continue their cozy chat.

"Is this Mrs. Flynn?" a woman's soft voice inquired.

"Yes. How can I help you?"

"Well . . . this is difficult to explain, but yesterday my purse was stolen while I was in the dressing room at Nordquist's downtown store. It was found about a half hour ago in a garbage bin outside of Moonbeam's on Heraldsgate Hill. I live only two blocks away from there, so I went to get it. Nothing had been taken, but there was a receipt and two keys in it from your B&B. Do you want me to come by with them?"

"Yes, I . . . what does your purse look like?"

"It's brown suede, a drawstring type."

Judith frowned. "Yes, maybe you should give me the keys and the receipt. We're in the cul-de-sac just off the avenue on your right as you head down the hill. Are you coming soon?"

"I'd better," the woman replied. "I haven't put my car in the garage yet and I'm leaving town on business tomorrow."

"Okay. I'll be waiting at the door. Oh—what's your name?"

"I should've introduced myself right away," she said in an apologetic tone. "Sorry about that. I was kind of rattled by this whole thing, especially since nothing was taken. My name is Jean Rogers."

Chapter Eight

After hanging up, Judith went straight to the phone book in the kitchen. Gertrude and Addison had moved on to discussing if the city was going to repair or tear down the viaduct that ran along the downtown waterfront. Both seemed engrossed in their conversation as Judith perused the directory. There were at least two pages of people named Rogers. Finally she found a J. M. Rogers who lived near Moonbeam's. Apparently the caller was legit. It was the other Jean Rogers who was the suspicious character.

As if he could sniff out anything that might suggest news, Addison interrupted his tête-à-tête with Gertrude long enough to inquire if all was well with Judith.

"I'm not sure," she said cryptically. "But ignore me and enjoy your drinks." After putting the directory back in the cupboard, she went to the front hall to wait for her visitor. If Jean Rogers had left for Hillside Manor right away, she'd show up momentarily.

Sure enough, headlights gleamed on the cul-de-sac's wet pavement. A small car pulled in behind what Judith assumed was the Beard-Smythes' Humvee. A young woman in a white rain slicker got out of the compact and hurried up the porch steps.

Judith had already opened the door. "Jean?" she said. "Come in. It's a nasty night."

"In more ways than one," Jean replied, entering the house and flipping off the hood of her slicker. "This is really weird."

Judith quickly studied the young woman's appearance. She was about the same size and coloring as the other Jean Rogers, but younger and better looking. Her dark hair was pulled back in a ponytail instead of scrunched into a knot. She reached into a suede drawstring handbag that was identical to the one the other Jean had carried.

"Here are your keys and the receipt," she said.

"Thanks." Judith put the items on the Bombay chest by the stairs. "Would you mind if I looked at your driver's license?"

Jean seemed taken aback. "Do you have to? It's awful!"

"Humor me," Judith said, hoping she sounded humble. "I err on the side of caution because I run a business out of my home. I have some concerns about the guest who signed the receipt and how her keys got into your stolen purse. Did you look at her name and signature?"

"Uh . . . no." Jean's tanned face fell. "I was so glad my purse was found. Then I was surprised that nothing was taken. When I saw the keys and the receipt from your B&B, I felt I should tell you. Lots of hotels and motels have keys saying if they're found, put them in the nearest mailbox. The least I could do since you live so close was to drop the stuff off."

The more Jean spoke, the more she seemed defensive. "Hey," Judith said kindly, "I'm very grateful. But something may have happened to the person who checked in to my

B&B." She picked up the receipt. "Take a look at the name and the credit-card number."

Jean warily accepted the receipt. "I can't read the signature, but . . . oh my God! It *is* my credit card!"

"Right. How long have you lived here?"

Jean was still staring at the receipt. "What? Oh—I moved here from Phoenix in June. I work for a chain of upscale retirement communities and I got transferred. The company's starting some new developments over on the Eastside, but they have an office downtown. In fact, I'm flying back to the Phoenix headquarters tomorrow for a seminar. That's why I was so relieved to get my wallet back with my driver's license and all the other information that I need for airport security."

Judith nodded. "I understand. But I'd still like to see your driver's license, if only to find out if I'm going blind. The woman who called herself Jean Rogers looks like you, except not nearly as pretty."

The real Jean looked shocked. "You mean she stole my identity?"

"Only temporarily. She's disappeared."

"Oh no!" Jean clutched her purse tightly. "Should I call the police? Someone at Nordquist's notified them yesterday, but they don't know my purse turned up at Moonbeam's."

"Yes, you should call both the store and the police," Judith advised. "I'll notify the cops about the woman who had your purse, but I still need to look at your license."

"Okay," Jean said reluctantly. "But it's an awful picture."

The black wallet also looked familiar. So did the driver's license. Judith had only glanced at the alleged owner's age, weight, and height the first time around, but now she scrutinized the details. The young woman standing beside her was thirty-one, but the photo made her look not only older, but much less attractive.

"There's a passing resemblance between you and the other woman," Judith said, handing the wallet back. "But you're ten times better looking than the impostor—or the photo."

"Thanks." Jean smiled for the first time, looking even prettier. "I suppose I got charged for the stay here."

"I didn't run the card through yet," Judith admitted. "It's been a hectic day."

Jean looked relieved. "Good. I already called about a couple of my other credit cards, but I didn't have time for the rest. The one that awful woman used is only a backup in case there's a glitch with my AmEx personal and business cards."

Good for you, Judith thought, *bad for me.* "That's fortunate. By the way, did you see anybody at Nordquist's who looked even vaguely like you when your purse went missing?"

Jean grimaced. "I was doing the winter sale and totally focused on clothes. That's why I left my purse in the dressing room. I needed a size eight, but I'd picked up a ten by mistake, so I nipped back out to the floor to get the right size. The clerks were so busy that I didn't want to bother them. It was hard enough to find a vacant dressing room right after work. As soon as it was five o'clock, it seemed like most of the working women downtown took off for the sale."

"Sure. That happens." Judith wondered how long the other Jean Rogers had waited to find a look-alike. Maybe she'd been browsing for some time. Someone who worked at Nordquist's might remember her. The store's clerks were very good about recognizing people. "Which department were you in?"

"Third floor, Free Spirit." Jean looked intrigued. "Are you going to try to find this person?"

"I'd like to," Judith replied. "But she may be gone."

"You mean you think she left town?"

"Ah . . . possibly." *Or,* Judith thought, *gone as in permanently.*

As soon as Jean Rogers left, Judith closed the front door and went back to the kitchen. Gertrude and Addison were still jabbering away.

"Well," her mother said, sounding more like her usual captious self, "what happened to you? We thought you'd moved out."

Judith noticed that though her own drink was untouched, the other two glasses were empty. "There's been a mix-up about one of the guests. A credit-card problem. It's straightened out now."

Addison nodded. "Hard to tell the innocent from the guilty these days. Say, Gert, would you like to show me your dollhouse?"

"Why not," the old lady said, releasing the brake on her wheelchair. "Seems like the barmaid's about to call time. Kind of an ornery wench, don't you think, Addy? Gimpy, too."

Addison chuckled. "Not saucy like you, eh?"

"Not much. Back in *my* day, I could've taught her a thing or two about men. She's less Polly Peachum and more Suky Tawdry, if you . . ."

Dumbfounded by her mother's uncharacteristic behavior and almost unbelievable knowledge of classical theater, Judith downed two quick swigs of Scotch. Her stomach growled; it dawned on her that she hadn't eaten much since lunch. The gluelike soufflé had stuck to the roof of her mouth, but not to her ribs. She'd barely touched her own slice of pie. Although her appetite was still missing, she had to nibble on something to offset the liquor.

Judith was making an egg-salad sandwich when Addison

came back into the house. "So how did the tour go?" she asked—and realized that she sounded cross.

"Fine. Your mother's an amazing woman."

"She sure is." Judith jammed the knife she'd been using into the cutting board. "Suddenly she's a theater buff? Where did that come from?"

Addison looked puzzled. "She told me that several years ago she and some of her friends from your church had season tickets to the Rep. You didn't know that?"

Judith felt like an idiot. "I'd forgotten." She leaned against the counter and hung her head. "Get yourself a refill. I'm sorry. Back then I didn't see Mother very often, or anybody else in my family when I was married to my first husband. He didn't want to . . . share me with anyone else. Besides, I had to hold down two jobs to keep a roof over our heads. A dirty four-letter word to him was spelled w-o-r-k."

Addison's smile was bittersweet. "It sounds like you've had some rough times." He picked up his empty glass. "Life's a bitch."

Judith carried her sandwich to the table. "You've had your share. Dare I ask about Amalia? The last time you and I spoke, you told me she was helping you mend."

"Amalia is doing the tango with some other guy these days," Addison said, pouring out an inch of Scotch. "It was fun while it lasted. My broken leg mended fine after Joan's killer tried to run me down in the hospital parking lot, but the broken heart won't ever get over my late wife. She was special."

Judith nodded. "How are your kids and grandkids?"

"Fine." He added a couple of ice cubes and a dash of water to his drink before sitting down across from Judith. "Let's cut to the chase. What do you know about your husband's last assignment?"

Judith swallowed her first bite of sandwich. "Not as much as I wish I did. He'd only been on the job for a little over a day."

"Really?" Addison seemed skeptical. "You sure about that?"

Judith looked straight into his penetrating eyes. "Why would I be evasive? I trust you."

He chuckled softly. "Because you're FASTO, and you've probably solved more murders in the past fifteen years than anybody in this town except your husband."

The reference to the fan-created Web site of Female Amateur Sleuth Tracking Offenders made Judith cringe. At least he hadn't referred to the site as FATSO—the more easily remembered, if inaccurate, acronym she found so irritating. Despite being tall enough to add a few pounds without detection, Judith had spent her life watching the scales.

"That's dubious," she said. "I haven't solved any murders since . . . uh . . . last summer." That wasn't true, but Judith had never acknowledged her role in fingering the killer of two people on the Empire Builder when she and Renie had headed to Boston to join their husbands. The arrest had been made in North Dakota and her involvement had been kept secret—even from Joe.

"Doesn't matter," Addison said. "Have you talked to Joe since he was arrested?"

"Briefly," Judith replied. "But you have."

Addison nodded. "So I did. I'm sure you realize what's going on."

"I'm sure I don't," Judith snapped. "Unless," she went on when there was no immediate response from Addison, "it's a blind to flush out the real killer."

"It's more than that." He took a sip of his drink. "There's some serious stuff going on behind the scenes. I'm not sure what it is either, but I have a feeling it involves some very important people on my beat."

Judith was taken aback. "City Hall?"

"That's right. No names, though I can make a few guesses. What I don't know is who the murder vic really was. My initial reaction is that he was an undercover cop, but I'm not sure."

"Was he paralyzed while on the job?"

"I don't know," Addison replied, frowning. "Ordinarily, the autopsy report would include that, but it hasn't yet been released, and I'm not convinced it won't be doctored when it is. This whole thing could even go higher than City Hall, up to the state level."

"Why not?" Judith murmured. "These days, party affiliations should stand for Dissolute and Rapacious, not Democrats and Republicans. Greed and sleaze, cupidity and stupidity, at every government level. I assume Joe realizes what he's gotten into by now."

"I gather that's a given."

"Which reminds me," Judith said, getting up. "I have to call the cops. A woman who checked in late this afternoon has gone AWOL. She stole somebody else's ID to register. The victim was the person I was talking to in the front hall while you and Mother were chatting out here."

"Whoa!" Addison put out a hand to stop Judith from reaching the phone. "What woman?"

Judith knew from past experience that she could trust Addison Kirby. But she often kept some speculations to herself. There had been many occasions when she didn't share her thoughts even with Renie.

"I don't know who she is," Judith finally said. "She claimed to be someone named Jean Rogers, who was in town for a conference at the convention center. She was a late arrival, checked in, and went up to her room to prepare for a presentation she's giving tomorrow. Then she disappeared into thin air."

Addison frowned. "Did she say what kind of conference or convention?"

"No, but I can look it up," Judith said. "I keep all the big events in my scheduling book. She did mention that it was at the downtown convention center. Now that I think about it, she's the only guest I've had who's involved in whatever's being held this week." Just as she started to get up from the sofa, she smacked a hand to her head. "Oh, good grief! It's the annual wedding show. That's usually aimed at mostly a local crowd. The B&B association sometimes has a booth for wedding parties who expect out-of-town guests. I don't think that formal presentations are part of the mix. It's more of a user-friendly event."

"Sounds like the first Ms. Rogers should've done her homework," Addison remarked. "So who showed up at the door while your mother was charming the socks off of me?"

"The real Jean Rogers, or so I assume." Judith explained that Jean's purse had been stolen from a Nordquist's dressing room yesterday, but recovered from a Moonbeam's trash bin in the past hour or so. "Which," she went on, "means the Jean who was in her room earlier this evening must've put it there not long before it was found."

Addison nodded. "That makes sense. Dump and run. The purse would be right on top and visible to whoever used the bin next. You ought to call Moonbeam's, too."

"You're right." Judith stood in the middle of the kitchen, pondering. "I wish I'd made a copy of that driver's license. It was a bad picture of . . ." She brightened. "Do you have a camera?"

"In my phone," Addison replied. "I'm no photographer,

but I have to equip myself with all the latest bells and whistles on the job."

"Be right back." Judith hurried into the front hall and grabbed the receipt and the keys. She was almost into the dining room when the couple from Indianapolis entered the house. "Oh! How was your dinner?" she asked, hoping they wouldn't go into details.

"Wonderful," the wife replied. "I had salmon and it was the best I've ever eaten. The view was lovely, too. All those ferryboats going back and forth. If it hadn't been raining, they said we could have seen the mountains in the distance beyond the ocean."

Judith recalled that the wife's name was Marcia. "We're not on the ocean," she explained for perhaps the five-hundredth time since opening the B&B. "The bay is part of the sound. The ocean is almost a hundred miles from here."

The couple exchanged perplexed—and possibly incredulous—glances. "Huh," the husband said. "That seems kind of odd."

"Blame it on the Ice Age," Judith said, forcing a smile. "Excuse me, I have to make a phone call."

Back in the kitchen, she showed the receipt to Addison. "Here's the real Jean Rogers's address."

He frowned. "In Phoenix?"

"Oh no!" Judith cried. "What was I thinking? She moved here last June from Phoenix. She's listed in the phone book, though. It's two blocks from Moonbeam's, 2455 Rosebud North."

"Good memory," he said admiringly.

Judith shook her head. "Not really. You met my cousin and her husband at the hospital. They live just two blocks down on the same street. Jean's address will be on the west side."

"You want me to talk to her?"

"Well . . . I'd like you to take a picture of her driver's license and show it around at Moonbeam's to see if anyone remembers the other Jean Rogers. They bear a slight resemblance, but the real Jean is younger, better looking, and has brown eyes. The phony Jean's eyes are blue."

"Okay," Addison agreed. "Maybe you should call her first. If she lives alone, she might not be too keen on having a strange man show up at her door on a dark night."

"Good idea," Judith said. "I'll do that before I call the cops and Nordquist's."

Addison was out the door by the time Judith had checked Jean's number on her caller ID. The phone was answered on the second ring. "Hi, Jean. It's Judith Flynn. I hate to be a pest, but would you mind letting a friend of mine take a picture of your license?"

Jean didn't respond right away. "Why would he want to do that?"

"To help find whoever stole your purse," Judith said. "Did you call the police and Nordquist's to tell them you found it?"

"Not yet," Jean replied. "I didn't know if anyone would be in the office this late at Nordquist's. I wasn't sure who to call at police headquarters. Anyway, as soon as I got back from your B&B, I started packing for tomorrow's trip." She paused. "Well . . . okay, but this kind of creeps me out. Are you sure the guy's somebody you trust?"

"Definitely," Judith assured her. "His name is Addison Kirby. I've known him for years."

Jean's sigh was audible. "If you say so. I'll be here."

Judith thanked her and disconnected, then called the police theft number. After four rings, she was put on hold. Five minutes passed before a live voice responded. Judith explained the problem. The woman taking the report said that recovery of the stolen property would be duly noted, thanked Judith, and hung up.

It was well after nine o'clock. Jean was probably right about Nordquist's not answering their phones. The store and the offices were closed. There might be a number for the security department, but she was tired of repeating the tale of the stolen brown suede drawstring bag. She was, in fact, just plain tired.

What little appetite she'd had seemed to have vanished. She put the uneaten half of her egg-salad sandwich into the fridge, carried the rest of her drink into the living room, and collapsed on the sofa. The fire she'd set off for the guests' social hour had almost burned out. Taking another sip of Scotch, she tried to relax and didn't realize she'd nodded off until the sound of the front door opening woke her up.

"Joe?" Her voice sounded foggy in her ears. No. Joe always came in through the back door. She was struggling to get to her feet when Addison entered the living room.

"Were you asleep?" he asked, taking off his jacket.

Judith felt sheepish. "I guess I was." She peered at the grandfather clock by the door to the front parlor. "My God, it's almost ten. Did you have any luck?"

"Sit back down," Addison said. "You look kind of shaky."

Judith didn't argue. "It's been a long day."

"It's about to get longer," Addison said, sitting down on the matching sofa by the fireplace hearth. "I got zip. Nobody at Moonbeam's remembered a woman who looked like the first Jean Rogers. The trash bin where the purse was found is outside of the store."

Judith groaned. "I should've thought about that. Joe and I always go there for the annual Halloween costume parade and sit outside with Renie and Bill. We use that trash can when we're finished. What about the real Jean? Did you get a decent picture of her driver's license?"

Addison shook his head and looked bleakly at Judith. "The real Jean Rogers doesn't live at 2455 Rosebud Avenue North and never did. Mr. James Michael Rogers told me so in person. No relation, never heard of her, and thought I was nuts. The phone number you used is for a cell he got rid of last month when he upgraded. For all we know, the real Jean Rogers is at the bottom of the Grand Canyon."

Chapter Nine

Judith was dumbfounded. "You mean . . . *both* Jean Rogers are fakes?"

"Maybe fakes, maybe crooks." Addison put his hands behind his head and leaned back on the sofa. "I don't know. Can you think of any way to tie in the two women with whatever Joe has gotten involved in at police headquarters?"

"No," Judith replied. "Unless . . ." She paused, wondering if her tired brain was playing tricks on her. "Unless the Jean Rogers who stayed here so briefly was the one who managed to open the safe. Joe would never leave it unlocked, not with his guns in there."

"Maybe there *is* a connection," Addison mused. "If so, there are some very clever people involved. Why would they want to get you and Joe mixed up in whatever is going on? Or is it just a coincidence because he's the PI assigned to the possible insurance-fraud case?"

Judith made a helpless gesture. "You mean it was part of an ongoing investigation, so they called on Joe because he's a former police detective—and a damned good one? But whose idea was that? SANECO? The cops? And has Joe been aware of this from the start?"

Addison smiled, but he looked more ironic than amused.

"I don't know. I may have gotten an inside track because I'm on the City Hall beat, but nobody's telling me everything. Did Joe approach this assignment any differently than he usually does?"

Judith considered the question carefully. "Not really. But when it ended so abruptly, he didn't seem concerned over the loss of income."

"That might indicate he knew the job wasn't finished," Addison suggested. "But he can't tell you—"

Judith held up her hand. "Wait—I think I know why he asked me to look for the gun that wasn't there. It was his way of letting me know something else was going on and that . . ." She took a deep breath. "That it has something to do with the B&B."

"Gun?" Addison looked puzzled. "What gun?"

"The Smith & Wesson he'd carried during the surveillance," Judith replied, then explained why Joe's request had been so odd. "He couldn't say too much because he thought someone might be listening in."

"At which end?"

The question startled Judith. "At the time, I thought he meant where he was, not here. But now I have to wonder."

"Maybe the safe holds more than the other guns," Addison murmured. "What else does Joe keep there?"

"I looked," Judith said. "Just personal stuff. Nothing to do with specific PI assignments. He keeps those in a filing cabinet."

"Okay." Addison stared at the embers in the fireplace grate. "If the safe was open, it might be that there *was* something in it that's also gone," he said after a long pause. "It could be background on someone, including the guy who got killed."

"Joe wasn't sure the vic was using his real name."

"So I gathered. But he must've been told how the on-the-job accident had happened."

Judith considered the idea. "Over the years, I've seen some of the forms he's gotten from his clients, especially the ones involving insurance fraud. They give the basics—name of suspected fraud perp, occupation, type of accident, and a copy of the original policy. Cheating spouses, missing persons—all that sort of thing is more detailed and there's usually no form involved. If a crime has been committed, there's a copy of a police report. Frankly, Joe doesn't like taking missing-persons cases, especially when children are involved. I can double-check to see if I missed anything pertinent to the current—I should say *former*—case."

"It's not really closed, is it?"

"No." Judith gazed at the plate rail that lined the living room's walls. "I'm trying to think of any suspicious guests—other than Jean Rogers—who've been here this week. Frankly, they seem like a pretty tame group. This is the B&B's slowest time of year. Are you really going to spend the night or was that just a ruse to grill me about what's going on downtown?"

Addison sighed. "I hadn't decided—until now. My condo's fine. I was reluctant to call you, but I had to find out how much you knew about what's happening with your husband. Now I think I should stay."

"You're welcome to," Judith said, "but why?"

He grimaced. "Because you need somebody you can trust."

In spite of herself, Judith shivered. Addison's keen blue eyes seemed to hold some kind of wisdom—or maybe portent—that she lacked. "If you're trying to scare me," she said quietly, "you've done it."

"Good." He stood up and stretched. "What time do you lock up?"

"Ten." She glanced at the grandfather clock. "Five minutes from now. All of the guests aren't back yet, but like you, they have a front door key."

"Where do you sleep?"

"The family quarters are on the third floor. I can lock the door behind me."

"Do that." Addison walked over to the bay window. "Still raining. I'm wondering if I should stay down here or go up to my room."

"You want to grill the guests? You already missed the middle-aged couple from Indianapolis."

"I'll catch that pair at breakfast."

Judith couldn't help but laugh. "I wouldn't worry about them. They think we're on the Pacific Ocean."

"So do most other people who aren't from around here. I don't think they ever look at a map."

"Bill calls it a 'bunker' mentality. The world moves so fast these days that people just hunker down and practice self-preservation. It's not only being self-centered, it's being centered on self."

Addison nodded. "If I ever go crazy, I'll have to make an appointment with Bill. Does he make house calls? Or does he practice what he preaches and never leaves his own house?"

"He prefers not to, but sometimes it's necessary—if only to escape from Renie." Judith picked up her unfinished cocktail and rose from the sofa. "I'm going to clean up the kitchen. If you want anything to eat, feel free to forage."

"Should I check on your mother?"

"You think she's in danger? Get real. Jack the Ripper would've set an unbeatable hundred-meter dash record if he'd come up against her."

"But . . ." Addison looked flummoxed. "She seems so . . . sweet."

"So did Lizzie Borden." Judith peered at Addison. "You've been reading people for as long as I have. You really aren't taken in, are you?"

Addison sighed. "No. But it was fun while it lasted. Your mother does know a lot about theater."

Judith nodded. "I'd forgotten that part of her life. It's strange. My father died when I was very young. There's so much I don't know about him. I've cursed myself a thousand times for not asking more questions about what he did when he was young, his courtship of Mother, how he felt about teaching."

Addison nodded. "Children—even adult children—don't seem to twig to the fact that their parents had a life before they were born. My own three only ask about my job if something I've written impacts them."

"Bunker mentality," Judith murmured. "Maybe it's been around a lot longer than Bill thinks. It's just gotten worse."

"My job is asking questions. That's why I wanted to talk to your mother privately when I went out to her apartment."

Judith frowned. "What did you want to ask her?"

"About what she saw or heard when Joe was arrested. There was a second vehicle in the driveway behind the squad car."

"Yes, she told me that, but couldn't see what kind of car it was."

"I pressed her a bit," Addison said. "It wasn't a car. What she described sounded more like a truck, dark color. What do you make of that?"

"Nothing," Judith said after a pause, "but maybe my neighbor Arlene Rankers saw something. She has what we call abS—Arlene's Broadcasting System. She knows everything that goes on around this neighborhood, especially in the cul-de-sac. Arlene's indispensable. I can't begin to tell you how many times she's helped me find out . . . things I've needed to know. Unfortunately, she and Carl go to bed early. I'll have to wait until tomorrow to talk to her."

"Wow. She sounds like a treasure trove of a source."

"She's all that and more. Both Arlene and Carl are amazing neighbors. They've taken over the B&B—and Mother—for me on several occasions."

"Do you think I should put them on the newspaper payroll?"

Judith smiled. "Is there such a thing anymore?"

Addison shook his head. "No. But I would if I could. You look beat. It's after ten. Go to bed. I'll be in charge."

Judith felt obligated to argue—but didn't. Addison was right. She was beat. But not beaten.

T he two widowed sisters were up early, despite coming in late from the family reunion dinner. They wanted to get a head start on their visit to other relatives who lived outside of the city. Traffic, the sister from San Diego said, might not be as bad as in Southern California, but it was still daunting—especially to the other sister from Green Bay.

The couple from Indianapolis had arrived in the dining room a quarter of an hour later, still talking about their waterfront experience—and apparently still convinced they had been on the ocean.

Addison had joined Judith in the kitchen just as she was about to take Gertrude's breakfast out to the toolshed. He insisted on delivering the tray in person. Judith protested, but only in a halfhearted manner. Despite being tired, she'd had trouble getting to sleep without Joe beside her. She kept picturing him lying in a dank cell on a cot with only a small, barred window so high up in the concrete wall that he couldn't see anything outside except dark nights and gray days. She knew better, having seen the local jail, but the image haunted her anyway. Instead of a grim cell, Joe might be sleeping in the spare bedroom at Woody and Sondra Price's Tudor brick house on the Eastside.

By 8:20, Addison had returned from the toolshed and was adroitly quizzing the widows between mouthfuls of buttermilk pancakes, ham, sausage, eggs, and freshly squeezed orange juice. Apparently they didn't strike him as master criminals, so he moved on to Edgar and Marcia from Indianapolis. The young couple hadn't yet come downstairs. Nor had the Beard-Smythes, which was just fine with Judith. She hoped they'd have breakfast elsewhere, anywhere except under Hillside Manor's roof. All she wanted was to take their money and let them run.

It was going on nine when Edgar and Marcia headed back upstairs. Judith sat down at the dining room table. "Any luck?"

Addison drank the last of his orange juice. "No. I couldn't even convince them they aren't on the ocean and I had trouble trying to tell them they couldn't drive to Alaska for lunch. Who's left?"

"Just the young couple from British Columbia, last name Owens."

"First names?"

"Geoff—spelled as in Chaucer, Cindy with an *i* and a *y*— in that order. I looked them up in the register. You can't be too sure how anybody spells anything these days, including Smith. Oh!" Judith made a face. "I completely forgot to tell you about the nonguests, Alicia and Reggie Beard-*Smythe*."

Addison looked perplexed. "You mean there are some other people here I didn't know about?"

Embarrassed, Judith nodded. "I forgot. I *wanted* to forget. The Beard-Smythes are a stinking-rich couple from our parish. Their gas furnace and hot-water heater went out and are supposed to be fixed today. I got conned into letting them stay here last night. They were in Room Three. Still are—if I can be that unlucky."

Addison scowled. "Do they have a dog?"

"Yes, an Irish wolfhound named Mayo. How did you know?"

"I heard a dog bark just before I got up," Addison replied. "At first, I thought it was outside, but when I went down the hall to the shower, I heard it again and thought it sounded closer. You allow pets?"

"Not as a rule, but I had no idea they were bringing Mayo along." Judith stood up. "Damn. That means they're still here."

"Want to give me a quick rundown?"

Judith sighed. "I don't know them well," she admitted, lowering her voice in case the Beard-Smythes were on their way downstairs. "They moved to Heraldsgate Hill several years ago. They had two children, both teenagers, who spent a couple of years at our parochial school before going on to high school. I suppose they're grown by now. We see them sometimes at church on Sunday morning, but I think they usually go to the Saturday-evening vigil Mass. I gather they've been active in some of the fund-raisers, which is more than I can be, other than offering something that doesn't involve attending the events. I simply don't have the time."

"Understandable," Addison agreed. "So where does the Beard-Smythe money come from?"

Judith was stumped. "I've no idea." She gestured to the dining room window that looked out toward the mammoth laurel hedge and the Rankers house. "I'll get Arlene over here to talk to you. But not until the Beard-Smythes have—"

She was interrupted by the phone. After hurrying out to the kitchen, she looked at the screen before answering. To her puzzlement, the name showed up as R. J. Smythe. "Yes?" she said, feeling relieved that the couple must have left without being noticed.

"When is breakfast delivered?" Reggie inquired. "We've

been up for half an hour. Norma Paine said you started serving at eight."

Judith's temporarily lifted spirits plummeted. "I do. But I serve it in the dining room."

Reggie's next words were indistinct, apparently intended not for Judith but for his wife. A shriek was followed by a spate of not-quite-decipherable words from Alicia.

"I'm afraid that won't do," Reggie said stiltedly. "This is a bed-and-breakfast, correct? Doesn't that imply that breakfast is served in bed?"

"No," Judith snapped. "Have you ever stayed at a B&B before?"

"Certainly not," Reggie replied. "When we travel, we stay in five-star hotels unless we're stranded in a city that has only four-star accommodations. Everyone has to put up with certain inconveniences, especially when traveling abroad."

Judith tried to keep her temper in check. "I have a full breakfast waiting for you in the dining room. If you're hungry, come and get it. Otherwise, try the drive-through at Booger Barn." Despite her best intentions, she slammed the phone down.

Addison was leaning against one of the open half doors, coffee mug in hand. "Could that have been the B-S couple in Room Three?"

"'BS' is right," she raged. "I'll get stiffed for their room *and* the one they let the dog sleep in. Not to mention the cost of fixing the antique registry stand. I bet Mayo knocked their suitcase down the stairs."

"No Christian charity involved, I gather?"

The mild tone of Addison's voice didn't belie what may have been an unintentional barb. "Oh—I *thought* I was doing them a favor, but I never considered they might not pay me. It was implied that they would when I talked to Norma Paine."

Addison strolled into the kitchen. "And who is this Paine?"

"Another parishioner, whose entire family is staying here tonight—for free." Judith grimaced. "It was my school auction donation. Now we're really broke. Joe can't work while he's in jail, and I'm getting screwed by what seems like half of my fellow Catholics."

Addison chuckled. "Thank God I was raised Methodist. I haven't been to church in forty years. Except," he added wistfully, "for Joan's funeral. She was Episcopalian."

"Episcopalians pray for good manners," Judith stated. "We should adopt that concept. Not to mention more of the other virtues."

"Sounds like I'm going to have to stick around unless you can vouch for all those Paines."

"I don't know them," Judith said. "Norma and her husband, Wilbur, are old-timers, but since their kids grew up, I haven't a clue about them. You can't stay the night. They're taking up all the rooms."

"I could sleep with your mother."

"Addison!" In spite of herself, Judith laughed. "Are you serious?"

He nodded. "I want to check out Joe's office. Okay?"

"Sure." She was standing eyeball to eyeball with Addison, hoping he was as trustworthy as he seemed. "Do you think I'll hear from Joe?"

"Don't ask me. I may go down to City Hall later."

"I'm going to call Arlene," Judith said. "Early to bed, early to rise. She may be able to answer some of your questions. And mine."

Amid much laughter, Judith could hear Geoff and Cindy Owens coming downstairs.

"I'm on," Addison said, putting his coffee mug down on the kitchen counter. "Pretend I'm your waiter."

"Quick, check to make sure everything's still warm on

the buffet. I'll be right there." Judith reheated the griddle to make fresh pancakes.

If the British Columbia couple were surprised to see a bearded man welcoming them to breakfast, they didn't show it. Addison indicated the coffee urn, then asked if they'd prefer tea.

"Coffee," Geoff responded. "We're caffeine fiends."

"Got it," Addison said as Judith entered the dining room.

"How many eggs," she inquired, "and how do you like them?"

Geoff wanted two, sunny-side up; Cindy requested one, over easy. Judith went back to the kitchen, flipped the pancakes, and started frying eggs. Then she dialed the Rankerses' number and asked Arlene if she could stop in for a few minutes around nine-thirty.

"Of course," Arlene replied. "Is something wrong?"

"Yes," Judith admitted. "I'll tell you when you get here."

A pause followed at the other end of the phone. "Judith," Arlene said in an uncharacteristically stern tone, "have you taken a lover?"

"Huh? Oh! No, of course not. I'll explain that, too. It has to do with . . . several strange things."

"Ah. 'Strange' can be enjoyable. See you as soon as I can get Carl out from under the dining room table." She hung up.

Addison had come into the kitchen. "Connecting to abS for the morning report?" he asked Judith.

"It's due at nine-thirty. You never gave me the report on Mother. Is she still alive and reciting Molière in the original French?"

Addison grinned. "She's reverting to type," he said quietly. "She wanted to know if I was making unwanted advances on you. I told her I only advanced as far as Room One. She asked if that was like getting to first base. I told her it was more like going to sleep. She sort of snorted and told me that was more than the Seafarers have done the last couple of baseball seasons." He sobered. "I'll admit that the baseball team hasn't been the same since Joaquin Somoza was murdered at Good Cheer Hospital." His eyes closed briefly. "Neither have I."

"I know." Judith flipped Cindy's egg before placing half a dozen pancakes on a plate. She offered a sympathetic smile. "Over the years, I sometimes forget about the aftermath of the horrific carnage I've encountered. If I stopped to think about it for very long, I'd go crazy."

Addison bit his lip. "Wouldn't we all."

He took the plate into the dining room. Judith followed with the eggs and more butter. "Is everything okay?" she inquired of her guests.

"Great," Geoff replied.

"Yummy," Cindy declared. "Any chance we can stay tonight?"

"Oh," Judith said with regret, "I wish you could, but I have a charity event. I'm booked solid."

The couple exchanged glances. "Maybe it's just as well," Geoff said. "We're supposed to meet with some animal-rescue people later today, and they're located about thirty miles from the city. They offered to put us up for the night at some friends' farmhouse nearby."

Judith nodded. "Coming back this way in Friday commuter traffic would be a problem. I'm sorry, though. Next time you come to the city, don't forget Hillside Manor."

"We won't," Cindy vowed. "We may be here again in the early spring. We're working on a project for an animal safe haven outside of Kamloops. That's why we're taking this trip instead of going skiing. There's not a lot of snow yet this year, so we made this a working holiday. We've got ski slopes outside of Kamloops anyway."

"The haven sounds like a worthwhile project," Judith

said, noticing that Sweetums had entered the dining room. "Would you take in cats?"

"Maybe," Cindy answered with an uncertain look at Geoff. "We've been trying to decide the best way to go. Geoff wants to focus on larger animals, not just wild ones, but horses and other domesticated creatures. Small farms are disappearing and livestock owners can't afford feed. Or are you referring to feral cats?"

Sweetums appeared to be stalking Addison, who had moved away from the buffet to Grandma Grover's breakfront. Judith was about to answer when the cat rubbed his big yellow-and-white furry body against Addison's leg. "Um . . . never mind," she said, hearing Sweetums purr like a small-bore drill. *Traitor,* she thought as Addison reached down to pet the cat. *The perverse animal must've sensed I was having an evil fantasy.* She excused herself and returned to the kitchen.

Fifteen minutes after she'd started the first load of dishes for the day, Phyliss Rackley arrived. "I thought people eloped *before* they came here to honeymoon," she declared, removing her plastic rain bonnet. "Or are you painting the house in this wet weather?"

Judith stared at her cleaning woman. "What do you mean?"

"The ladder out in the driveway," Phyliss replied, bending over to remove her galoshes. "It's outside of Room Three. A dog is on it. The Hound of Hell, I figure."

"Oh no!" Judith cried. She started down the hallway past Phyliss, but before she could open the back door, a commotion erupted nearby.

"Told you so!" Phyliss called after Judith. "Satan's chasing the elopers! That's what happens to sinners who have carnal knowledge before they tie the knot!"

Turning the corner of the house, Judith heard angry voices and barking dogs. Almost slipping on the wet pavement, she grabbed a recycling bin to steady herself. Arlene was by the ladder, shouting at Alicia Beard-Smythe, who was four rungs up from the ground. Tulip, the Rankerses' Boston terrier, was chasing Mayo down the driveway. Reggie's rear end could be seen emerging from the second-floor window.

"Shame on you!" Arlene yelled, trying to shake the ladder. "You're frauds! Are you trying to sneak out without paying poor Judith?"

Alicia held on for dear life. "Go away, you busybody! We're trying to escape with our lives! This B&B is a house of horrors!"

"Nonsense!" Arlene retorted before noticing Judith. "Call the police!" She did a double take. "Wait—where's Joe?"

"Never mind," Judith said. "Let them go. I never want to see that pair again."

Arlene backed off. "I don't blame you. But what's going on here? They told Carl on the phone they were locked in their room and wanted to come down for breakfast."

"I'll explain later," Judith said under her breath, motioning for Arlene to step away from the ladder. "Go ahead, Alicia. Move your butt and take Reggie with you."

"I can't," she said, slowly descending to the ground. "Reggie's stuck in the window with the suitcase."

Judith felt like gnashing her teeth. "Okay, I'll get someone to fetch the damned suitcase so he can come down."

Arlene backed away as Alicia stepped onto the driveway. Reggie apparently hadn't heard that help was on the way. His legs were flailing away as his midsection writhed on the windowsill. Out of the corner of her eye, Judith saw Tulip still chasing Mayo around the cul-de-sac.

"Shall I get Carl?" Arlene whispered to Judith.

"No, I'll get Addison," she replied, watching Alicia stomp off to the Humvee. "I thought Carl was stuck under the dining room table."

"He is, but . . ." Arlene stared at Judith. "Addison?"

"Never mind," Judith said, heading for the rear of the house. "Come inside. You're getting wet."

Addison was at the back door. "What's going on out there?"

Judith explained as concisely as possible. "So please get that idiot out of the window and throw the damned suitcase after him."

"Will do." Addison nodded vaguely at a wide-eyed Arlene and went up the back stairs.

"Who," Arlene demanded, "is that?"

"He's a newspaper reporter," Judith replied. "And stop looking at me as if I'm Jezebel. Remember the actress Joan Fremont?"

"Yes, but . . . oh!" Arlene put a hand over her mouth.

Judith nodded, aware of what Arlene was thinking. "He's helping me sort through what's going on with Joe."

Before Arlene could respond, Geoff and Cindy Owens entered the kitchen. "Is something wrong?" Geoff inquired.

Judith tried to maintain a calm demeanor. "One of our guests had a problem with the window in Room Three. He's a fresh-air fiend."

"Can we help?" Cindy asked, tugging at Geoff's hand as if to offer her husband as a sacrificial lamb.

"No," Judith said, "we've got everything—"

A loud crash from outside interrupted her words of re-assurance.

Startled, Geoff dropped his wife's hand. "What was that?"

"Probably Carl," Arlene said, unperturbed. "He'll be fine. He always is. He should never have brought the ladder over here for the Beard-Smythes to use."

Judith played along with Arlene's deception. "Carl's so good-hearted."

"It's those Christmas lights," Arlene said. "He usually

takes them down right after New Year's, but he kept putting it off because of his war injury. He was in Tasmania."

The young couple glanced at each other. "Tasmania?" Geoff finally said. "That's . . . unusual."

Arlene waved a hand. "Tasmania, Romania, Albania—I always get those manias mixed up. I was never good at geography. It wasn't really a war kind of war, it was business, but things got out of hand." She turned around as Phyliss entered the kitchen from the hallway. "Oh, here's dear Mrs. Rackley! Excuse us, it's our Bible study time." Grabbing a goggle-eyed Phyliss by the wrist, Arlene hauled the cleaning woman back down the hall and into the pantry. *Good move,* Judith thought. The last thing she needed was Phyliss to further muddy the already murky waters.

"Maybe," Geoff said, "Cindy and I should go meet the animal-shelter people."

Figuring that the B.C. couple probably already thought they were at the zoo, Judith nodded. "It's wise to get a head start. The drive's almost an hour if there's traffic."

"We have directions," Cindy said hurriedly, following Geoff out of the kitchen. "Thanks again. It's been . . ." Her voice trailed off, apparently stumped for the right word.

Addison came down the back stairs just as a squawking Phyliss flew out of the pantry. "Don't try to tell *me* about Moses," she cried. "He never rejected anyone who worshipped the Golden Cat!"

Arlene entered the hall. "He didn't? I thought that would please you. You always say unkind things about Sweetums."

Phyliss paused at the top of the basement stairs. "It was the Golden *Calf*!"

"Oh." Arlene was unfazed. "Cat, calf, cart, whatever. Catholics prefer the Bible's sequel. The first part has so many peculiar names, and if you think I have trouble with Romania and—" She stopped as the cleaning woman flounced back down to the basement. "Really," she said, putting out a hand to Addison, "that woman is very peculiar. You must be from the newspaper. I'm next door."

"Arlene." Addison smiled and shook her hand. "You are the font of all knowledge."

"Not according to Phyliss," Arlene responded. "The Old Testament is so *long.* Isn't there a short version? You know—like the wrap-ups you do after a tiresome city council meeting. Those people go on and on."

"They do indeed," he agreed, accompanying Arlene into the kitchen. "Gasbags, most of them."

Judith kept going to the front door to make sure the Humvee had left. She caught only the rear end of the big vehicle as it turned out of the cul-de-sac, but that was enough. "Good riddance," she muttered, heading back to the kitchen.

Arlene had already begun to tell Addison what she knew about the Beard-Smythes. "He runs Smythe's Suppliers. Reggie inherited his father's business."

Judith was surprised. "I didn't know he was born into money."

"He wasn't," Arlene said. "Mr. Smythe owned a pawnshop."

"Indeed," Addison remarked. "Reggie parlayed it into a fortune?"

"In a way," Arlene said, accepting a mug of coffee from Judith. "It was a fluke, really. After Mr. Smythe died of drink, Reggie's mother had to sell the shop. But first she wanted to make sure she got her money's worth, so she asked a friend who was some sort of appraiser to go through the inventory. He—I think it was a he—discovered a first edition of Mark Twain's . . ." She made a face. "I forget which book, not *Huckleberry Finn* or *Tom Sawyer,* but something less well known. Anyway, it was still worth a great deal of money. Mrs. Smythe sold it for a huge sum. Then she went to the track, put it all on a long shot in a big race, and won over five million dollars."

"Good grief!" Judith cried. "Talk about luck!"

Arlene shook her head. "Not really. She got so excited that she had a heart attack and died on the spot, right by the paddock. Being an only child, Reggie inherited everything and went into business for himself by starting a supply company. He and Alicia had been married less than two years when that happened. Later, they moved from Reggie's modest home by Boring Field to a big house just a few blocks from here."

Addison had made a few notes. "What does Reggie supply?"

Arlene frowned. "I'm not sure. Equipment of some kind, I think. I know he recently got a big contract from a hotel chain. Alicia bragged about it after Mass one day. She insisted it was all because she made a novena to Saint Oddjack."

Judith and Addison both looked puzzled. "Who or what is that?" he asked. "I'm not Catholic."

Arlene waved a hand. "Oh, I've no idea, but Alicia insisted it was the saint her mother-in-law prayed to before that long shot came in. Some saints have obscure names, though the New Testament ones have nice, simple names like Mary and Joseph and John." She looked at Judith. "Just think what'll happen if this younger set is canonized. My grandchildren have names like Jade and Brooks and Parker and Tuba."

Judith was looking even more perplexed. "Tuba? Which of your kids named somebody Tuba?"

"None of them," Arlene replied, "but you think that won't happen?"

"Well . . . anything's possible," Judith said. "By the way, how is Brooks feeling after his stomach upset the other day?"

"He's fine." Arlene shrugged. "Corinne Dooley told me

that before school let out, ten more kiddies got sick, including one of their grandchildren, Carson. Now, what kind of name is that for a girl? That flu must be a twenty-four-hour type. At least none of the teachers came down with it."

"The flu comes in all kinds these days," Judith said, "and the vaccines don't guarantee immunity."

"I know," Arlene agreed. "Carl and I got our shots . . . oh! I forgot to ask you about that car I saw in your driveway yesterday afternoon. I can't tell what's parked closer to your garage unless I stand on the upstairs toilet."

Judith caught Addison's bemused expression. "I've no idea. I wasn't home at the time."

"I suppose Joe was at work," Arlene said, then suddenly looked in every direction. "Where *is* Joe? I haven't seen his MG since day before yesterday. Did he have to go out of town?"

Briefly debating with herself, Judith decided to come at least semiclean. "Joe's helping the police with their inquiries."

Arlene rocked in her chair. "*What?* Doesn't that usually mean someone's committed a crime and is tortured until there's a confession?"

Judith grimaced. "Not this time. Did you hear anything about a man who was shot in a condo at the north end of Lake Concord?"

Arlene looked stunned. "Joe was shot by the police? No wonder he's helping them! They obviously don't know what they're doing. Things haven't been the same since Chief Silver Fox retired. Now, there was a *real* policeman."

Judith had lived on Heraldsgate Hill for only a short time before learning of her neighbor's frequent encounters with a former police chief whose real name was Lloyd Volpe. Arlene always called him the Silver Fox because of his lush, prematurely white hair. They'd been on a first-name basis due to her frequent calls while the infamous Under-

wear Thief was on the loose. The burglar had a fetish for
women's lingerie, and his loot had included what Gertrude
called her "bloomers." But even before Carl had become the
Block Watch captain, Arlene's sharp eyes and keen instincts
had reported every possible crime or suspicious character in
the area directly to the police chief. It was only after Judith
had reunited with Joe that she'd met Volpe at his retirement
party some years later.

"No," Judith said, "Joe wasn't shot. He was on surveillance near the site when it happened." She didn't want to
go into details. "I haven't had a chance to watch TV or the
newspapers. I thought you might've seen or read something
about the shooting."

Arlene thought for a moment. "Oh, *that* shooting. There've
been so many of them lately. Yes, Mavis Lean-Brodie mentioned it briefly last night on KINE's five o'clock news." She
turned to Addison. "Are you writing a story about it?"

Addison seemed absorbed in the dregs of his coffee mug.
Judith could have sworn that he was trying to keep from
laughing. He turned his attention to Arlene. "I filed an
equally brief account. It's probably buried in the regional
catchall section. I only had the bare facts."

"Maybe," Judith said to Addison, changing the subject,
"you should ask Arlene about background for your City Hall
investigation."

"Of course." His expression was faintly puckish as he
posed a question. "How about those Paines?"

Arlene scowled. "*Why* are you asking me these questions?
None of these people, including the Beard-Smythes, have
anything to do with City Hall. The Paine children grew up
here, but I don't think most of them live in the city. Norma's
always complaining about not seeing them often enough."
She glanced at Judith. "Isn't that so?"

Judith shrugged. "That's why Addison is asking you.

Mike was only at SOTS for a short time before we had to move. I was working, so I wasn't able to get involved with the parents' club. Dan wouldn't bother, so I never knew the younger generation. I didn't meet the senior Paines until I moved back to Heraldsgate Hill. I think most of their kids were older than Mike. Norma mentioned having adult grandchildren."

Arlene looked thoughtful. "Yes—they probably do. Norma always insisted she and I were the same age. We were—but in different years."

Addison, who had started to nod, burst out laughing. "Oh, Arlene—if I may call you that?"

"Of course you may," she retorted. "It *is* my name. Go on."

Addison composed himself. "Here's the situation." He looked quickly at Judith as if for approval. "I'm covering a story that may touch upon corruption at City Hall. Joe got involved through his work as a PI. I'm trying to find out if there's a link between his last surveillance job and anyone who has recently stayed or is going to stay at the B&B."

Arlene frowned. "Such as the couple leaving this very minute?"

"Yes," Addison replied as the front door closed. He stared at Arlene. "How did you know that? You can't see the front hall from here."

"I can't see, but I can hear," Arlene said, pointing to the ceiling and looking at Judith. "Room Six, correct? I heard them coming out into the hall. When Carl and I take over the B&B for you, I make sure I'm attuned to whoever is about to come down for breakfast."

Judith smiled at Arlene. "You've always had very acute hearing."

"I've had to," Arlene declared. "Raising five children in a house that's almost identical to this one, I trained myself to hear them sneak back in when they broke curfew." She zeroed in on Addison. "I'm not sure I understand what you're talking about."

Addison grimaced. "That's the problem—neither do I. Right now I'm trying to connect the dots. The Beard-Smythes and the Paines who are coming tonight are local. Even if they don't live in town, they have a connection with the city because they were raised here. I can eliminate most of the other guests, like the B.C. couple who just left."

Arlene's pretty face was puzzled. "You can? I thought they'd be at the top of your list."

Judith and Addison stared at Arlene. "You mean," Judith said, "because they're Canadians?"

Arlene shrugged. "He might be, but his wife isn't. She was born and raised here. I doubt Cindy remembers me, but I certainly recognized her." She turned to Judith. "You know that years ago I worked at Donner & Blitzen department store during the holidays to make extra money and take advantage of their post-Christmas sales. The full-time employee in charge of the department was Cindy's mother. Surely you remember me talking about Jean Rogers."

Chapter Ten

Judith's jaw dropped. Addison froze in the kitchen chair. Arlene was taken aback by their reactions. "What did I say? For all I know, Cindy *is* a Canadian. Maybe she became a citizen when she married . . . Geoff, isn't it?"

Judith was the first to regain her voice. "It's not that. But there was another guest registered here last night, who gave her name as Jean Rogers. She checked in, but left without notice only a few hours after she arrived. Then another woman contacted me to say *she* was Jean Rogers. Except she wasn't. Where is the Jean Rogers you knew at Donner & Blitzen?"

"In Phoenix," Arlene replied. "She moved there a year or so ago. I heard from her at Christmas. Her husband, Clark, was quite a bit older. He retired and liked to winter in Arizona. I wanted to ask Cindy how her mother was doing, but Phyliss showed up. I knew you didn't want her creating a diversion trying to save people, so I dragged her into the pantry to save you from her. Frankly, I don't know if Cindy would recall who I was. I only saw her two or three times when she was still in grade school. Jean would bring her into the store to see Santa Claus. But why are there so many Jeans? That makes no sense."

Addison agreed. "But the fact that it makes no sense *is* important. We just don't know how to put it all together." He looked across the table at Judith. "Any ideas?"

Judith shook her head. "If anything, I'm more confused than I was in the beginning. Can we be sure that Geoff and Cindy are from B.C.?"

"We could check through Canadian and U.S. Customs and Immigration," Addison suggested. "They might know if they crossed the border in the past few days. Security is much tighter since 9/11."

"Don't bother," Arlene said. "Jean wrote to me about her daughter getting married and moving to Canada. Drat! I should have paid no attention to Phyliss and talked to Cindy instead. What was I thinking of?" Her blue eyes widened as she got out of her chair. "Carl! That's what I was thinking of! His back went out after he brought the ladder over here. The Beard-Smythes should've called *you* to let them out if their door wouldn't unlock." Arlene was halfway down the hall. "They may be rich, but they aren't smart," she called over her shoulder.

Addison stood up. "I'm going down to City Hall. To think I thought everybody working *there* was nuts." He shook his head.

"Good idea," Judith said. "I almost wish I were in jail with Joe."

Addison shot Judith an ironic glance. "Be careful what you wish for." He rinsed out his coffee mug. "How about marrying me instead?"

Judith thought she hadn't heard him correctly. "What?"

He waved a hand at her. "I don't mean for real—just for tonight."

"I . . ." Startled, Judith wondered if she really was gaga. "Uh . . ."

"Relax." He grinned. "These Paines don't know you,

right? Thus they don't know Joe. Like you, Arlene doesn't seem to know much about the second and third generations. I never got a chance to quiz her closely. I can pretend I'm your devoted spouse and help you entertain the guests while wheedling all sorts of information out of them and going through their wallets when they're not looking. Isn't that what Joe would do if he were here with a houseful of non-paying guests?"

Judith put a hand to her breast. "You scared me for a minute. No—Joe usually keeps clear of the guests. Especially this bunch. He'd hide upstairs in front of the TV and pretend we'd never met."

"The Paines don't know that," Addison said, heading out of the kitchen. "Besides, I'm in love with another woman."

"Huh? Who?"

"Let me know if Carl got out from under the dining room table. If he didn't, Arlene is mine."

L ook," Renie said into the phone, "I know it's ten-thirty and I'm supposed to be awake, but I have no idea what you're talking about. Either we have a bad connection or I need to go back to bed."

Judith sighed. "I realize it's confusing. I'm trying to convince you that I need your help for the dinner after all, if only to bounce ideas off of you and get your impression of the Paines. When do you think you could come? That is, if you can do it."

"Um . . . I suppose around four?"

"Not any sooner?"

"I have to finish some preliminary sketches," Renie said. "Bill's doing the Friday grocery run. Has that man ever used a *coupon*? Has he ever checked out a *sale*? What doesn't he understand about 'buy one, get one free'? Has he ever met a seven-dollar French pastry he didn't like? No wonder we spend two hundred bucks a week on groceries."

"Yes. I mean *no*." Judith paused. "Three?"

"Three what?"

"Three o'clock. The Paines arrive between five-thirty and six. We need time to talk. Besides, Addison is going to help."

"He's still hanging around? Doesn't he have a beat to cover?"

"That's what he's doing—and why I have to talk to you in person."

"I'll try," Renie said, sounding resigned. "Let me finish my sketches in peace. How the hell do I put a hula skirt on an energy-saving lightbulb?"

"Gee, I wish that was all I had worrying me." Her tone was wistful. "As Grandma Grover used to say, I'll look for you when I see you."

"Hey—what about Joe?" Renie asked. "Can Bill see him during visiting hours?"

"I'll know more when Addison gets back from City Hall," Judith said. "Maybe it's good that the Paines are coming. It'll keep me busy instead of driving myself crazy by having too much time to think."

"You know perfectly well that Joe's fine," Renie asserted. "In fact, I'll bet he's enjoying himself."

"That," Judith said, "is what worries me most."

Given what had gone on during the past twenty-four hours, the rest of the morning and early afternoon were quiet at Hillside Manor. Gertrude had been picked up by one of her bridge-playing friends and wouldn't return until four. Phyliss had complained only a half-dozen times about Arlene's biblical interpretations. Sweetums had been in and out of the house, either missing Gertrude's company or disliking the steady, if not heavy, rain.

Aside from forcing herself to keep from calling someone at the city jail and asking about Joe, Judith's biggest concern was accommodating the Paine family's dietary restrictions. She decided to stick with a buffet supper. Renie could make labels listing the ingredients of each dish—or she could staple signs to the guests, naming their personal poison.

By three-thirty, Phyliss had left for an appointment with her chiropodist, Addison hadn't reported back, and Renie called to say that she was on her way. If Judith needed anything, she could stop off on top of the hill and get it.

"No," Judith said, slicing tomatoes while holding the phone under her chin. "I think I'm good. Thanks, though. Oh! Wait. Maybe tofu?"

"Oh my God!" Renie cried. "You *have* gone crazy! What are you going to do with it? Wash the car?"

"I've got a vegan or two," Judith said. "Don't they eat tofu?"

"Gack. For all I know, you can make Popsicles out of the stuff. See you as soon as I overcome the gagging factor." Renie hung up.

Judith went online, searching for tofu recipes. By the time she'd found a couple that sounded easy to prepare, Renie arrived. "Here," she said, handing over a Falstaff's bag. "It looks like a sponge."

Judith removed the package. "It *is* a sponge!" she exclaimed. "That's not funny."

"Oops. Wrong bag. Be right back." Renie grabbed the sponge from Judith and went out the back door.

Judith collapsed into one of the kitchen chairs and held her head. The preparations were getting off to a bad start. Maybe asking Renie to help wasn't smart. Her cousin was a sport about doing things she didn't really want to do, but out of sheer perversity, she often managed to make everybody else miserable in the process. Judith returned to her task of figuring out how to make a tofu scramble for the breakfast included in the auction offering.

"Sorry about that," Renie said breathlessly. "Bill wanted a new sponge for the upstairs bathroom."

"Fine," Judith said unenthusiastically. "What's he doing for dinner before he goes to the basketball game with Uncle Al?"

Renie had hung her jacket on a peg in the hall. "They're getting hot dogs before they go to their seats."

Judith began spraying cooking oil on a big baking dish. "By the way, now that Joe's temporarily out of commission, what's going to happen with Bill's stalking-victim patient?"

"No idea," Renie said. "Want me to trim the asparagus? The ends are too thick for human consumption."

"Go ahead. I'm going to steam them." She took two large packages of chicken breasts out of the fridge. "I keep thinking Joe's either going to call me or walk through the back door. You've no idea how frustrated I am with this whole mess."

"I do, actually," Renie said, slicing off an inch or more of the asparagus spears. "But you know he's safe. He has the police for company, and probably Woody's there most of the time. I think you're more curious than worried."

Judith considered the suggestion. "Maybe. But it's still unnerving, especially with the weird stuff that's been going on here."

"As far as I can tell from what you told me on the phone, the only really weird thing is the Jean Rogers duplications. For all you know, somebody's writing an article on credit-card theft and experimenting to see how far you can go without getting caught."

"That doesn't explain why Joe told me to find a gun that wasn't supposed to be where he said it was."

"Obviously, you were supposed to find something else."

"No luck. Addison said he'd help look in case Joe has anything connected to his newspaper story. I wonder what's taking him so long."

Renie had gotten out the big steamer kettle and was filling it with water. "You mean Addison? They're short-staffed at the paper these days. I imagine he has other stories to cover besides the elusive corruption angle. He may have deadlines."

"True. I tend to focus only on what affects Joe." Judith had gone back to the computer. "Now that I've got tofu, I can't figure out what to do with it. Except for the breakfast scramble, so many of these recipes call for other ingredients that the dietary-challenged Paines can't eat."

"You could stick some artificial flowers in it and use it for a centerpiece," Renie suggested.

"Thanks. You're a big help. Oh, wait—here's something. Lemon-baked tofu. And another one, sweet and spicy tofu nuggets."

"Gack."

Judith glared at her cousin. "Have you ever eaten tofu?"

"No, nor have I eaten an S.O.S. Pad or a bar of soap. So what?"

"So I'll do the sweet and spicy one first. It has to marinate."

"In what? Pennzoil?"

"Stop. Fix us drinks. Do something to keep me from killing you."

"Good idea," Renie said cheerfully. "By the way, have you got a list of the Paines so we know who's who, or do I have to make name tags?"

Judith had her hands full of lemon juice, soy sauce, and olive-oil bottles. "That's a good idea. I put their names on the bulletin board by the swinging doors."

"Okay." Renie had gotten out the Scotch and the bourbon.

"By the way, did you find anything interesting when you were going through Joe's safe?"

Judith shook her head. "The only odd thing was a Post-it note with 'SF OR LA' printed on it. I assume it must've gotten stuck to something else. I'd never have seen it if it hadn't fallen on the floor."

"The letters don't mean anything to you?"

Judith shook her head. "Only the obvious—San Francisco or Los Angeles. Maybe Oregon, too. Places that pertain to some of his cases and could be from a long time ago. Often he gives me the bare bones, but," she went on, removing a jar of Dijon mustard from the fridge, "like Bill, he has to worry about client confidentiality."

Renie nodded. "And snoopy wives like us." She'd poured out the drinks and set Judith's down next to the marinade bowl. "What can I use to make name tags?"

"Look in that drawer to the right of the sink. I keep a bunch of blank clip-on tags in there from the days when Arlene and I used to cater events," Judith said, wielding a wire whisk. "Every so often, I get some guests who want to wear name tags for the social hour."

"Bill refuses to wear a name tag. So does Oscar. He doesn't like anything pinned to his fur. Oscar, I mean. Good grief," Renie said, making a face as she opened the drawer, "your junk pile is worse than mine. Have you cleaned this out since you moved back home? Here's a newspaper clipping about Nixon's resignation in 1974. Who drew the horns on his picture?"

"Mother," Judith said. "In 1974, I was working at the Thurlow Public Library by day and hustling drinks at the Meat & Mingle at night."

"Hustling drinks or hustling drunks?"

"Both. At least it felt like I was," Judith said, after taking a sip of her Scotch-rocks. "I spent most of my time keeping an eye on the cash register. Dan's hired help had a tendency to loot the premises."

"The bad old days," Renie remarked, sitting down at the kitchen table with the name tags and the list of Paine attendees. "Gosh, I don't remember any of the Paine bunch except Hannah, and now that I think about it, she was three or four years ahead of Tony. Big girl, like her Amazonian mother. She fell down on top of Mugs Rankers—I should say *Meagan* now that she's a wife and mother—and they practically had to use a forklift to get Hannah off of her before she suffocated."

"Hannah sounds like a match for Kristin," Judith said, and immediately regretted the unkind words about her daughter-in-law. "Sorry. I still haven't quite recovered from Kristin telling me I'm a doormat and need to improve my self-esteem."

"Not to worry," Renie said, taking a green pen out of her purse. "At Christmas, I told her if she ever mouthed off to you like that again, I'd rearrange her dental work. I may be small, but I'm cunning."

"You are, alas," Judith allowed, "but I wish you hadn't done that."

"Why not? What else is Christmas for? Family, friends, friction."

"So Hannah is married to somebody named Zachary Conrad," Renie said, studying the guest list. "I know that name. The gas company? No, Conrad works for the city's lighting department. In fact, that project I'm doing for their retired employees had his name attached as one of the execs who has to okay my final design." She made a face. "I've never met him. Quick, I need an assumed name. Want to call me Rita?"

"I really don't," Judith said. "Why do you care?"

"Because," Renie pointed out quite seriously, "the higher

the echelon of management, the bigger the ego and the smaller the brain. That's true of most corporations, and it may be worse with civil servants, which is what Zachary Conrad is. He played basketball at the University, went into the pros for a couple of years, but hardly ever got off the bench. Still, he was able to get on with the city and rose through the ranks, which may or may not mean he's competent. Even if he's a genius, he'll carp at every little thing that requires his approval to show he has input, and thus an actual intellect. I've never met him, but I may have to. I don't want him thinking of me as the middle-aged moron dishing up Tofu Doodoo in the kitchen. Besides, I'm not wearing my professional wardrobe, which is very different from what I have on now."

"It sure is," Judith murmured, gazing at her cousin's rumpled green sweatshirt from Lefty O'Doul's bar in San Francisco. "You might consider combing your hair."

Renie shot Judith a disgusted look. "Why? I'm not posing for a portrait. In fact, I'm not going to sort out these Paines either. They can slap their stupid tags on and we'll play it by ear. I wouldn't recognize any of these goofballs if they fell in my birdbath."

Judith shrugged. "Fine. I just want to get this over with." She glanced at the schoolhouse clock, which showed that it was two minutes after five. "When you finish those name tags, would you call Woody?"

Renie scrunched up a name tag that she'd lettered imperfectly. "Why me? It's your husband who's in the slammer."

"You bond with Woody. I don't want to be a pest."

"Ooh . . ." Renie finished the last two Paines and stood up. "Okay."

Judith nodded toward the bulletin board. "Woody's new work number is pinned up there."

Renie grabbed the phone, checked the scribbled notation,

and dialed. "He's not answering." she said, disconnecting. "I'm not leaving a message. He's probably gone home."

"Drat." Judith was placing puff-pastry shells on a baking sheet. "This is so wrong." She all but yanked the oven door off its hinges. "If Joe's sitting on his dead butt at city expense helping solve crimes, it's mean of him to leave me in the lurch."

Renie's face was bland. "Yes, it's odd that the police would ask for help from a retired detective who is also a licensed private investigator. What are they thinking of?" She made an inept attempt at snapping her fingers. "Wait! I've got it! They should hire a rank amateur instead!"

"Not funny," Judith huffed. "I don't mean that, I—" The doorbell interrupted her. "Damn," she muttered. "It can't be the guests."

"I'll answer it," Renie offered.

"No, I will," Judith said, nudging her cousin out of the way. "I'm not a walking advertisement for getting loaded."

The doorbell sounded a second time. "Hold your horses," she said under her breath, going into the entry hall. Before she could reach the door, it swung open. Judith stopped, staring in disbelief.

A horse was staring back at her.

Chapter Eleven

Judith stood stock-still and let out a little yip. She was about to slam the door shut, but heard a disembodied male voice speak her name.

"Mrs. Flynn?"

"What?" she croaked, bracing herself on the banister.

A youthful freckled face with a mop of red hair leaned into view on the other side of the storm door. "I'm Chase Paine. Where should I put Knickers?"

Trying to collect herself, Judith moved to the doorway. "You're . . ." She paused as the horse brushed its mane against the glass. "Never mind. Why did you bring a horse?"

Chase spoke softly to Knickers. "Hey, buddy, step aside." The animal obeyed. "My mom told me it'd be fine. You have a toolshed, right? Can Knickers stay there? I brought him into town because he has to be reshod tomorrow."

"Holy crap!" Renie called from the door between the dining room and the entry hall. "What the hell?"

Judith jumped. Knickers whinnied. Chase opened the storm door. A gust of wind blew into the house.

"Can I take Knickers to the toolshed now?" he asked.

"No!" Judith cried, grabbing the door to keep it from blowing shut. "Wait! Yes, take the horse down the driveway.

I'll open the garage." She closed the door and leaned against it. "My God! What now?"

"A horse, of course," Renie said, and frowned. "There's no room for a horse in your garage."

"I know that," Judith snapped, hurrying through the living room with Renie at her heels. "I'm going to put my Subaru in the driveway and hope Snickers or whatever its name is doesn't eat the MG."

"Do the reverse," Renie said. "Back Joe's car outside. Even if the horse nuzzles yours, the MG will be safe."

"Joe would kill me if I left the MG exposed to the elements," Judith said, opening the French doors that led to the back porch. She paused before heading outside. "You're right, though. I'll put the canvas cover on his car. Can you help me?"

"Sure," Renie said. "You got his keys?"

Judith winced. "No. I'll get the spare pair from the kitchen." Hearing the *clip-clop* of horse hooves on the wet cement, she turned to see Chase Paine leading Knickers down the drive. It was quicker for her to go along the porch and back through the kitchen hall than to retrace her steps. Glancing over her shoulder to see if Chase was holding the horse's reins, she almost collided with Arlene at the back door.

"Careful!" Arlene exclaimed, grabbing Judith's arm to steady her before she stared as Chase and Knickers approached the garage. "Oh—I'm not hallucinating. Dare I ask why I saw a horse on your porch?"

"Of course it was a . . ." Judith leaned again, this time against the back door. "Yes. It's a horse. And that's Chase Paine leading him."

Arlene looked relieved. "Good. Then I was only seeing double."

"Double?" Judith echoed weakly.

Wiping rain from her forehead, Arlene nodded. "Chad just got out of a truck with a small trailer in front of your house. He's Chase's twin."

"Oh." Judith caught her breath. "I have to get—"

"Move it!" Renie yelled, opening the back door and dangling a key ring. "Take these. I found them in the junk drawer."

Judith stepped aside so her cousin could hand over the MG's keys. "Thanks," she said feebly.

"Hi, Arlene," Renie said. "Come in. You're all wet."

"Oh?" Arlene looked surprised, but stayed put. "I'm fine. I want to watch this. I think Chad's on the front porch. You should let him in."

Before Judith could make a move, Gertrude called out from the toolshed doorway. "What's all the ruckus about? Where's my supper?"

Wearily, Judith went down the porch steps to make eye contact with her mother. "It's a long story. I'll tell you when I bring out your supper. I mean, your *dinner*. That won't be for another half hour."

Despite the rain, Gertrude rolled her wheelchair down the short ramp onto the sidewalk and past the patio. "Lord help us!" she cried, seeing the horse. "Didn't that pain of a Paine woman realize I was giving her a bad time?"

Judith met her mother by the statue of Saint Francis. Sweetums darted out of the toolshed and ran toward the house. Arlene and Renie stood together on the porch, giving way to the cat, who wanted in. Chase waited in the driveway, holding the horse's reins and looking impatient while raindrops bounced off of his uncovered shock of hair.

"What Paine?" Judith demanded of Gertrude.

"Somebody from SOTS," Gertrude replied, one hand shielding her face from the rain. "She called me the other day to ask if she could stable her horse in the toolshed. I figured she was one of your usual nutty friends and said sure, and bring along the lions, the tigers, the bears, and the oh-mys, too. Couldn't take a joke, I guess."

Judith sucked in her breath, lest she say something she'd regret. Then she realized that Gertrude wasn't the one at fault. "That must've been Norma—or one of her clan."

Gertrude looked momentarily puzzled. "They ride around town on a horse? What kind of mess have you gotten us into now, Toots?"

"Good question," Judith murmured. "Go back inside, Mother. You'll catch cold. Please."

Gertrude ran a hand through her white hair. "You're right. Guess I'll stick my head in the microwave to dry out." She paused. "Is that your new boyfriend in the driveway with . . . hold it. Whoever is with him is already here. Am I having a stroke?"

Judith turned around. Addison had joined Renie and Arlene on the porch. Her gaze darted to the driveway, where two redheaded young men stood by Knickers. "They're the Paine twins, Mother."

Gertrude looked disgusted. "That bunch! Never could stand 'em. Wilbur's mother cheated at Bingo. Wouldn't trust any of that crew an inch." She wheeled around and sailed back to the toolshed.

Trudging over to the porch, Judith greeted Addison. "I thought you'd been arrested, too," she said—and grimaced. "Never mind."

Arlene offered a hand to Judith. "Hang on to me. You look very tired. Serena told me about Joe. I'm sure he didn't shoot anyone. If he did, Carl and I will swear we were with him the whole time. Or would it help if Carl confessed to shooting . . . who got shot? I could use a vacation. Martha Morelli asked me to go to Hawaii with her."

"Oh?" Judith paused at the top step. "Oh, damn! I forgot to unlock the garage and put the MG in the driveway."

"I'll do it," Renie volunteered. "What's the code?"

"You can't," Judith said. "You've never driven the MG. It's not like a regular car, not even a standard gearshift. In fact, you don't drive your own car that well. I'm not entrusting Joe's precious MG to you."

"Jerk!" Renie yelled. "Go ahead, catch pneumonia. See if I care." She stomped into the house and banged the screen door behind her.

"Great," Judith grumbled, her fist tightening on the car keys as she started back down the steps.

"Hold it," Addison called from the porch. "You open the garage, I'll move the MG. I owned one in my salad days."

"Thanks," Judith said, handing over the keys, and trying to ignore the whinnying horse. She moved as fast as she could, punched in the code, and hurried back to the porch.

Arlene opened the screen for her and followed Judith inside. "I hate to be nosy, but why are you going to keep that horse in the garage? Shouldn't it be somewhere like a *farm*?"

"It should be on Jupiter, for all I care," Judith retorted. "Somehow this is all the Paines' doing. They'll have to get that animal out of here before Joe gets back from . . . down-town."

"I'm confused," Arlene said, wincing as they entered the kitchen to the cacophony of Renie banging pots and pans together in an apparent effort to work off her anger. "Alicia and Reggie used our ladder to escape from your house. Now the Paines' grandchildren . . ." She grimaced and put her hands over her ears as Renie dropped a large cast-iron lid in the steel sink. *"Can you make your cousin stop that?"* Arlene asked through clenched teeth.

"No," Judith replied. "She only stops when she—"

Renie whirled around, stubbed her toe on a skillet she'd dropped, and crashed against the dishwasher.

"—hurts herself." Judith paused, watching her cousin clutch her rib cage and moan with pain. "Like that."

Arlene nodded and glanced at her watch. "Oh—it's going on six. I must take Carl to the ER. Have fun." She started for the back door.

"Wait!" Judith called after her. "Is Carl worse?"

"In a way," Arlene said over her shoulder. "That's why he was under the table. I had to take the ladder back to our house. See you later."

Renie was still doubled over. "Take me with you!" she groaned. "I think I broke a rib."

Arlene had made her exit. Judith took a big swig of Scotch and eyed her cousin with disgust. "So? Even if she does take you with her, they can't do much for broken ribs."

Renie straightened up. "You're mean. I should go home and leave you with this mess."

"You won't," Judith said blithely as Addison came through the hallway. "You may be ornery, but you're a sport." She waited for Addison to hang up his jacket. "Did you see Joe?" she asked.

"Not exactly," Addison replied, noticing Renie for the first time. "Serena?" He reached out a hand. "I haven't seen you since you were at Good Cheer Hospital."

"Weren't we all?" Renie muttered, but shook his hand. "Hi. It's nice to see another Good Cheer patient who got out alive." Immediately realizing her gaffe, she put her free hand to her mouth. "Oops! Sorry. Really. That was an awful thing to say."

Addison shrugged. "Maybe. But it's true." He noticed the cousins' drinks. "Would you mind if I . . . ?"

"Sure," Judith said. "Alcohol is the only thing that might get us through the evening. Where are the twins?"

Addison was putting ice cubes in a glass. "In the garage with the horse. They have to feed and water him."

"Great," Judith said. "I trust they won't bring him inside for dinner. Before all the Paines arrive, did you find out anything while you were gone?" She noticed that Addison had cast a wary eye at Renie. "Hey—my cousin may be ornery and impossible, but she's utterly trustworthy. Surely you know that from the Good Cheer nightmare."

"I do," Addison replied. "I just wanted to make sure she hadn't . . . changed since then."

"Alas," Judith responded, "she hasn't. If anything, she's worse."

"Stick it," Renie snarled, arranging raw vegetables on a wooden tray. "What were you supposed to find out, Addison?"

"Anything I could about why Joe isn't here and I am," he replied, leaning against the counter. "They still haven't ID'd the dead guy. Or at least they haven't released his name to any survivors. That would indicate they don't know who he really is."

Judith was filling small white fluted china bowls with three kinds of dip. "Does that mean he might be who he was supposed to be?"

Addison shook his head. "That person doesn't exist. Not anymore, at least. The real James Edward Towne died five years ago in a car accident. I ran the name through the computer at work. He was from here but was on a trip to a livestock show east of the mountains."

Judith frowned. "ID theft?"

"Probably." Addison gazed at the wooden tray. "Do you mind? I haven't eaten since I grabbed a hot dog at the food court in the America Tower by City Hall."

"Be my guest," Judith said. "Everybody else is." She caught Addison's sudden chagrined expression and apologized. "I didn't mean it that way. I just want to get through this evening. Most of all, I want to get my husband back."

Addison put a hand on Judith's arm. "You will. Try thinking about his situation this way: He's working. I don't know
exactly what he and the rest of the police are up to, but it's
something big. You know I can't reveal my sources."

"I . . ." Judith made a feeble attempt to smile. "Okay. I'll
try . . ."

The front doorbell rang. Renie took a quick gulp of her
drink before hurrying out of the kitchen before Judith could
stop her. "Damn," Judith said softly. "I should at least greet
the Paines. I wouldn't put it past my cousin to tell them to
take a hike."

To her surprise, she heard something akin to cheerful
voices emanating from the entry hall. A young woman's
giggle tinkled like a glass bell. A deep male voice said,
"Delightful place. Good choice on Mama's part."

Judith looked at Addison and shook her head. "Surprise."

"Your cousin being civilized?" Addison said, after swallowing a black olive. "Or the Paines being cordial?"

"Both." Judith wiped her hands on a towel. "I'd better play
hostess. Could you take that vegetable tray into the living
room and put it on the buffet for me?"

"Sure," Addison replied. "But not until I polish off a
couple more of these crab wontons in that chafing dish."

"They're not crab," Judith said over her shoulder. "They're
chicken. One of the guests has a seafood allergy." She continued on into the entry hall, where she saw a smiling Renie
helping the new arrivals with their coats.

"Coz," Renie said, smile still in place, "let me introduce
you to some Paines. This is Walter and Sonya Paine," she
went on, indicating a husky, balding man and a slim, rather
plain blond woman. "And this is their daughter, Zoë."

Judith exchanged handshakes with the older couple first.

"Delighted to meet you," Walter said.

Judith recognized the hearty voice she'd heard from the

kitchen. "Welcome to Hillside Manor," she said, before turning to Zoë, a younger, prettier version of her mother. "Goodness, it doesn't seem possible that I don't really know any of you after all these years of seeing Norma and Wilbur at church."

The couple who'd come in behind the first three Paines laughed. "That's because most of us fled the nest," the man said. "I'm Andy, the Number One Son of a Paine." He reached out and crushed Judith's hand. "This is the little woman, my wife, Paulina."

The "little woman" shot her husband an arch glance. "Stick it, Andy. You're not twisting arms to peddle your wares to hardheaded civic and corporate consumers. We're here to have *fun*. If we don't, your gruesome mother will demand her money back."

Judith offered her limp hand to Paulina. "I hope you *do* enjoy yourselves. I rarely have a guest complain."

Paulina's arch expression fell on Judith. "Really? How about Alicia Beard-Smythe?"

Dropping her hand for lack of a response, Judith stood very straight, eyeball to eyeball with the woman whose coal-black hair was pulled back to accentuate her high cheekbones. "The Beard-Smythes weren't guests. I offered them a roof over their heads for one night because they had no heat. Neither Alicia nor Reggie behaved gratefully or graciously."

To Judith's surprise, Paulina flashed a big smile and gave her husband's expansive midsection a hard elbow. "See, Andy, I'm right. The Beard-Smythes are trouble. Don't say I didn't warn you."

Andy Paine, who was a shorter but stockier version of his brother, Walter, looked embarrassed. "It was your idea to join that hunt club," he muttered. "You know I'm scared to death of horses."

"Chicken," Paulina said, and made clucking sounds.

Apparently attempting to change the subject, Renie nudged a Louis Vuitton overnight bag with her toe. "Let's get your bags upstairs. Mrs. Flynn has your comfy rooms ready." She gave her cousin a saccharine smile that almost made Judith wince.

The Paine brothers started collecting their luggage, but Addison suddenly appeared in the entry hall. "Allow me," he said with a little bow. "I'll be your valet and butler"— Judith heard Paulina utter a small gasp just as Addison hesitated—"this evening," he went on, lacking his usual panache.

"Thanks a lot," Walter said. "Got a bad back. Have to be careful with the heavy lifting."

"No problem," Addison assured the other man, picking up the Louis Vuitton bag and a couple of other pieces of luggage. "I'll return for those other two."

"No, no," Paulina said. "They're light. I'll take them up. One of them is mine anyway." She turned to Judith. "Which rooms?"

"Here," Judith said, handing Paulina a page from the registration book. "These are the assignments I made, but if any of you would like to switch places, go ahead."

"Thanks." Paulina followed Addison up the stairs.

"How about some appetizers?" Renie said in an unnaturally chipper voice. She gestured at the living room. "Come, enjoy. I haven't quite finished setting up the bar. I'll do that now."

The guests migrated to the living room. Judith grabbed Renie and propelled her into the dining room. "Since when did you turn into me?"

"Hey—you were out in the kitchen playing house with Mr. Kirby," Renie said, stumbling slightly before going through the swinging doors. "What's going on with him? And why did he do a double take when he saw Paulina Paine?"

"Good question," Judith murmured. "Maybe she can tango."

Renie frowned. "Huh?"

"Never mind. Finish with the bar on the buffet. I'm going to take care of the dinner while you set the table."

"Okay." Renie gulped down the last of her drink just as the doorbell chimed again. "Want me to get it?"

"No," Judith said emphatically. "Do the bar. Let's get the guests loaded and then we'll roll 'em."

"Good idea."

Judith hurried to greet the newcomers. A sour-looking trio of mismatched strangers stood before her. "Is this the bed-and-whatever place?" a rawboned thirtysomething woman asked in a testy voice.

"Yes," Judith replied, forcing a smile. "You must be . . . ?"

"Sarah Blair," the woman answered. "A Paine by birth."

"I'm sure you were," Judith said. "I mean," she went on quickly, "you *are*. Do come in."

Upon closer inspection, Judith could see a resemblance between Sarah and Norma. Both were big-boned women, though the daughter had not yet added as many pounds. Sarah, however, evoked at least a tinge of her mother's overbearing demeanor. The small, fair-haired man Judith assumed was Dennis Blair resembled a gremlin. Maybe it was the bright green bow tie or the pointed ears. He barely glanced at Judith as he carried in three pieces of luggage and placed them carefully by the credenza. The third member of the trio was a young woman who looked like neither of her parents. She had short curly red hair, a curvaceous figure, and would've been pretty if her expression wasn't so disagreeable.

"This must be Octavia," Judith said to break the awkward silence.

"You were expecting someone else?" Sarah inquired archly.

"Yes," Judith replied, struggling to remain polite. "Hannah and Zachary. It's well after six and they haven't shown up yet."

"So?" Sarah said, her hard-eyed gaze following Renie, who was trying to manage a tray full of bottles and glasses as she entered the living room. "Good. I could use a stiff drink." She dumped her leather satchel on the floor and followed the liquor.

"'Scuse me," said Dennis Blair, trailing behind his wife like a small caboose.

Judith was left with Octavia, who didn't seem inclined to budge from the entry hall. "This doesn't look like an inn to me," the younger woman said, scrutinizing her surroundings. "It looks like a . . . *house.*"

"Is this your first stay at a B&B?" Judith inquired.

"Yes. I've always thought there was something far too twee about a hostelry called a *bed* and a *breakfast.* Inadequate, as well. So why are we having drinks and dinner?"

"Because," Judith said, giving the liquor bottles Renie was placing on the buffet a longing glance, "this is a special occasion. I offered my *bed-and-breakfast inn* for the parish school auction. I assumed your grandmother informed you of that."

Octavia waved a perfectly manicured hand. "Grandame! Or that's what she insists I call her. She talks so much that I stop listening." Her jade-green eyes also strayed to the buffet. "Have you any coconut rum?"

"No," Judith replied. "Only dark and light rum."

"What about grenadine syrup?"

"Sorry. What did you have in mind?"

"A Big Pink Dink," Octavia replied. "Which reminds me, where are the twins?"

"Uh—I'm not sure," Judith replied, getting so frazzled that she couldn't remember if Chad and Chase belonged to the Walter or the Andrew Paines. "Why don't you ask your uncle and aunt?"

Octavia shrugged. "Why bother? Excuse me. I'll drink the dark rum. I assume you have hot-toddy mix left over from the holidays."

"I do," Judith said. "I'll get it and heat some water."

"Fine." Octavia stalked off to the living room.

Judith went back to the kitchen, where her cousin was juggling plates and silverware. "Well?" Renie said. "You look like you could use another drink. I already made refills." She gestured with her head at the counter by the sink. "Move. I don't want to break your second-best china."

"I'd rather break it over the guests' heads," Judith muttered, stepping aside. "They're *real* pains. Two of them aren't even here yet."

"What would you expect from a bunch of Paines?" Renie said over her shoulder. "If you hear a big crash, you'll know I didn't make it to the dining room table."

But Renie navigated the swinging doors without mishap. As she reached for the hot-toddy mix in the fridge, Judith heard only the sound of the guests talking in rather loud voices, and closer by, the rattle of plates and silverware as her cousin set the table.

She took a deep breath before sipping from the newly poured Scotch-rocks and gazed through the rain-spattered window over the sink. That was when she heard the shots outside.

Chapter Twelve

Judith almost collided with Renie at the swinging doors. The cousins stared at each other.

"Impossible," Judith said under her breath.

"Firecracker. Backfire. Anything but . . ." Renie's voice trailed off.

Walter Paine sauntered into the dining room. "You hear those shots?" he asked, swirling his drink around in his hand.

"Shots?" Judith echoed. "What shots?"

Walter shrugged his broad shoulders. "Fireworks, probably. Left over from New Year's. Kids these days." He shook his head and ambled back to the living room.

"Where did they come from?" Judith whispered.

"I'm not sure," Renie said. "Toward the back of the house?"

Before Judith could respond, she heard the gunning of an engine from somewhere in the vicinity of the cul-de-sac. "Hold on," she said, hurrying to the front door. By the time she got there, all she could see were taillights disappearing onto the cross street.

"Well?" Renie said softly, joining Judith in the hall. "See anything?"

Judith had opened the door a scant inch or two. "No. But the horse trailer Arlene mentioned is gone. I wonder what happened to the twins? Do you suppose they went home to change? I don't think they were dressed for dinner."

Renie leaned around Judith to look outside. "Maybe your answer is about to arrive. Here comes a car."

A Cadillac Escalade pulled up in a space by the Ericksons' house on the other side of the driveway. "Fancy," Judith murmured. "Not the kind of wheels for a couple of young guys."

"Oh, crap!" Renie exclaimed softly. "I'll bet it's Hannah with Zachary Conrad from the lighting department. I'm outta here." She rushed back down the hall.

When two very tall people emerged from the Escalade, Judith opened the door wider. Renie was right. Hannah Paine Conrad was a good six feet tall and almost half as wide. Her husband was even taller, but rail thin. As he lurched toward the steps, Judith figured that if his wife ever fell on top of him, he'd snap like a dry twig.

"He's sick," the woman said, trying to prop up her faltering spouse. "Where can we put him?"

"Hannah?"

"Yes, yes." Hannah managed to haul Zachary up the steps. "Help me out here. Our luggage is still in the car."

Offering a hand, Judith nodded in the front parlor's direction. "I have a settee in there." She tried to gauge Zachary's height—no easy task, since his thin frame was contorted in apparent misery, but figured he must be close to six four. "He'd be better off in a bed upstairs."

"The settee will do for now," Hannah said. "I'm starving."

The two women were lugging Zachary's dead weight to the parlor door when Paulina Paine came down the stairs. "Hannah?" she said in a startled voice. "Is that Zachary? What's wrong with him?"

Hannah turned sharply to look at her sister-in-law. "He's come down with something. Leave him alone."

Paulina had descended into the entry hall. "Gladly," she said, tucking in a few stray tendrils of black hair before heading into the living room. "I need a drink."

"Selfish woman," Hannah muttered. "No sense of family. Ooof!" she exclaimed, dumping her husband on the settee. "There you go. Will you be all right now?"

Zachary's head moved slightly, but Judith couldn't tell whether he meant yes or no. One long leg was bent at the knee; the other dangled awkwardly over the armrest. He winced as he tried to resettle himself. "Thirsty," he said in a thick voice. "Water."

Hannah turned to Judith. "Could you fetch a glass?"

"Water and glasses are around the corner on the buffet in the living room," Judith said, backpedaling. "I really must check on . . . dinner." She was out the door before Hannah could respond.

There was no one in the kitchen. Judith took a quick look at the two kinds of lasagna in the oven and turned off the heat. Not bothering to grab a jacket, she hurried out the back door. Renie and Addison were just going into the toolshed.

"Wait!" Judith cried. "What's happening?"

Renie went inside, but Addison paused. "We don't know," he said. "I'd just come down the back stairs when your cousin was running out the door. She told me you'd both heard something that sounded like shots. But everything around here seems quiet."

Judith had joined him at the toolshed. She went inside, where Renie was sitting on the arm of Gertrude's small couch. The old lady looked fit to spit.

"I'm deaf, you know," she declared. "Starving me won't work. It's going on seven. Where's my supper?" Seeing Addison behind her daughter, she suddenly brightened. "Well,

well, here's somebody who can help me instead of asking a bunch of dopey questions about shoot-outs by the birdbath."

Renie slid off the couch and shook her head. "You're a fraud, Aunt Gert. If you didn't hear those shots, I'll bring you a can of Sweetums' Toxic Tuna Treat for your supper."

Gertrude gestured at the TV, which had been muted. "How could I *not* hear a bunch of shots? I'm watching the news. All those wacky Eye-Rackies and Afghaniacs or whatever they call themselves are always shooting everybody. Why don't they just shoot each other and get it over with? President Truman wouldn't have put up with all those cuckoos." She made a fist and shook it at Renie. "Give 'em hell, Harry! That's what we'd say in *my* day—and he'd do it."

Addison had exchanged places with Renie. "You have a wonderful sense of history, Mrs. G. Tell me more about Truman. I was only a boy when he was in the White House."

Seeing that Addison was settling in, Judith and Renie made their exit and hurried into the house. "So Mother really didn't hear anything?"

Renie shook her head. "Of course the blasted TV was blaring—as usual. But no sign of anybody around outside. Maybe it *was* fireworks."

"Maybe," Judith conceded as they went inside. "Your lighting-department exec is sick."

"Aren't they all," Renie remarked. "It comes from hiding in their fancy offices. Out of contact with the real world."

"I mean sick as in ill," Judith said, taking the lasagna pans from the oven. "He had to be practically carried inside to the parlor."

"Sick?" Renie's brown eyes sparkled. "As in near death?"

Judith grimaced. "Don't say that. Not at my B&B anyway."

"Gosh," Renie said innocently, "I was so hoping that his arrival here would up the odds that he'd croak."

"Stop! You're making me even more nervous. See how

the guests are doing and ask when those twins are supposed to arrive. We're ten minutes away from serving dinner. I'll check on Hannah and Zachary. I hope he's not contagious. That flu's going around, you know."

Renie swigged down more of her cocktail before leaving the kitchen. Judith made sure the asparagus wasn't overdone, then returned to the parlor, where Hannah was trying to get Zachary to drink some water.

"Is he feeling any better?" Judith inquired from the doorway.

"No," Hannah snapped. "But at least he's not throwing up."

"That's . . . good," Judith said. "Should we get some help to put him in bed?"

Hannah shook her head. "I'm not going to let him spoil my evening. He picked a poor time to be ill." She paused to glare at her ashen-faced spouse. "Mama went to a great deal of trouble and expense to buy this event at the auction." She shook a finger at her husband. "Try to pull yourself together. I'm going to have *fun* for a change."

Zachary groaned, but closed his eyes. He looked so uncomfortable that Judith felt sorry for him. "We should put him to bed."

"Nonsense," Hannah said sharply. She looked toward the other side of the parlor. "Where does that second door go? Somebody left it ajar, but I've been too busy being a nursemaid to check it out."

"Into the living room," Judith replied.

Without another word, Hannah tromped out of the parlor.

Frustrated, Judith moved closer to the settee. "I'm worried about you, Mr. Conrad. Is there anyone in the family with medical expertise?"

Zachary made an effort to get more comfortable, but shook his head. "Only . . ." He winced. Judith grabbed a pillow that had fallen off the settee and put it behind his head. "Thanks." A very faint smile appeared on his thin face. "Zoë's studying to be a vet."

"Walter and Sonya's daughter?" She saw Zachary nod. "Do you think she could help you?"

He shook his head again. "Only first year. On winter break now."

"Do you need to be seen by a doctor?"

Zachary didn't answer right away. "Just flu." He sighed. "I guess."

"You should be in a bed. Do you want to go home?"

Before Zachary could reply, Judith heard a faint rap at the open door to the hall. Turning, she saw Addison looking grim. She motioned for him to come into the parlor, but he shook his head. Suddenly feeling uneasy, Judith joined him at the doorway. "What's wrong?"

Addison stepped back beyond the parlor door and the living room archway. "We've got a problem," he said in a low voice. "After chatting up your mother, I noticed the garage door was open. I didn't see any sign of those twins, so I went over to take a look. I assumed the horse was tethered, but it seemed odd that the twins had left without closing the door behind them." His expression grew distressed. "I hate to tell you this, but you've got a dead horse in the garage."

J udith leaned against the dining room doorjamb. It took her a few seconds to find her voice. "How could a horse die that suddenly?"

Addison led her to the dining room table. "Sit. You look pale."

"I feel pale." Judith sat in the captain's chair where her grandfather had exerted his benevolent rule over four generations of Grovers. "So?"

"I assume he was shot," Addison said, also sitting down.

"I closed the door. A dead animal is never a pleasant sight."

Judith felt uncharacteristically helpless. "What should we do?"

Addison shrugged. "Nothing right now. We'll deal with it after the guests leave tomorrow. You were right about hearing gunshots. I must've been at the front of the house with the luggage at the time."

Fleetingly, Judith wondered what else Addison had been doing upstairs while in the company of Paulina Paine. But that was none of her business and certainly not a priority. With some difficulty, she stood up. "I can't lose focus. Maybe once the guests sit down to eat, I can sort through some of the other things that are driving me insane."

Addison was also on his feet. "Did the twins show up for dinner?"

"I assume they had to change," Judith replied, going into the kitchen. "Meanwhile, I've got a sick man in the front parlor. I wish his wife would take him home."

"Do you want me to offer?" Addison asked.

"No," Judith said, watching Renie sprinkle bread crumbs on the asparagus. "I'm not giving advice to the Paines. That ill-bred bunch would resent it. They're very strong-minded."

Renie snorted. "They haven't got minds at all, if you ask me. Which one's the vegan? Maybe he or she shot the damned horse."

Judith sighed. "A vegan would never hurt an animal."

Renie shook her head. "That's all a front. Vegans hate animals. That's why they don't eat them. They believe animals were put here to eat humans—which is true. It's nature in its rawest form—eat or be eaten. I'm not fooled by their hypocrisy. They eat vegetables and fruit, don't they? So do animals, which means vegans are robbing the flora to feed the fauna. Or something like that." She blinked several times. "Where'd I put my drink? I just poured another one . . ."

"Good grief, coz," Judith cried, "you're drunk!"

"Pretty much," Renie agreed, "but I've still got a ways to go."

Judith held her head. "Oh God! Can we get through this evening without any more disasters?"

"No," Renie said, still scanning the cluttered kitchen for any sign of her drink. "Ha ha. I spy a Paine."

Judith turned around. "Hannah!" she exclaimed as the big woman loomed over the swinging half doors. "Can I help you?"

"I'm taking that wretched man home after all," Hannah said. "Don't set out dinner until I come back. I despise cold food."

"But—" Judith stopped. It was pointless to argue. She'd serve the food and warm up Hannah's portion. "How far away do you live?"

"We live over on the bluff. We always have." She turned around so fast that her large rear bumped the swinging doors, making them creak on their hinges.

"Good," Judith said. "I hope she never comes back."

"I'll drink to that," Renie said. "If I could find my damned drink. Now I can stop hiding from Zachary."

Judith sipped more Scotch. "We aren't twaiting for the wins. I mean *waiting for the twins*." She shook herself before getting her tofu concoction ready to serve.

Five minutes later, Judith heard the front door open and voices in the hall. She wiped off her hands on a towel, went to the dining room, and peeked into the hall. Hannah had somehow managed to get Zachary on his feet and was half carrying him out of the house. "Good riddance," Judith said under her breath. Waiting for the door to close behind the departing couple, she continued into the living room.

"Ahem," she said in a loud voice.

The guests, who had been engaged in what sounded like contentious conversation, turned in her direction. The only exception was Zoë Paine, who was sitting alone on the window seat and appeared to be brooding. Whatever had made her giggle upon her arrival apparently was no longer amusing.

"Dinner will be ready in less than five minutes," Judith announced. "Everything will be on the sideboard or the table. I've marked all the dishes to indicate the ones that are nonallergenic, vegetarian, lactose- or gluten-tolerant. Or intolerant." She grimaced. "You know what I mean. I hope."

Her announcement was met with less than enthusiasm. Apparently liquor hadn't improved the Paines' dispositions. Judith hadn't seen so many surly drinkers since the Meat & Mingle's Wednesday Whopper Whiskey Nights.

"Screw it," she muttered under her breath as she went down the hall. And immediately felt a twinge of guilt. It was followed by a voice in her head saying, *Hey—you have a right to be upset with these jerks. Your husband is AWOL, someone apparently has broken into his safe, you got stiffed by the Beard-Smythes, you've worked your butt off preparing for this event, there's a dead horse in your garage, and it's possible that one of your current guests may be involved in something shady. Give yourself a break.*

Renie, holding a big wooden salad bowl, was blocking Judith's way into the kitchen. "You look like bird crap," Renie said. "Why do I have the feeling you're mentally beating yourself up?"

"How do you know?" Judith snapped. "You're supposed to be drunk."

"I'm never so drunk that I can't tell when you're beating up on yourself," Renie replied, moving out of her cousin's way. "What now?"

"I should be relieved," Judith said, entering the kitchen, but holding the half doors open for Renie. "Hannah took Zachary home."

"*I'm* relieved," Renie said. "Now I won't have to avoid him."

Addison was dishing up the rice pilaf. "Zachary Conrad . . ." he murmured. "Lighting department, right?"

Judith nodded. "Renie's doing a project for them. She didn't want Zachary to see her slaving in the kitchen. It'd ruin her professional image."

"Conrad's a bit of a stuffed shirt," Addison remarked. "I've interviewed him two, three times over the years about power outages and rate increases. He was a pretty fair basketball player back in the day, and was a third-round draft pick, but only spent a couple of years in the pros. He went to fat. Good shot, but slow as mold."

"Fat?" Judith said in surprise. "The guy's a beanpole."

Addison's expression was puzzled. "The guy was six three, one-eighty—two-twenty before he was cut. He'd gained another fifteen the last time I saw him almost a year ago."

Judith was shocked. "Then he's got more than the flu wrong with him. I doubt Zachary weighs more than one-fifty. He's as thin as a rail."

"My God." Addison shook his head. "That's terrible. I should ask around City Hall to see what's wrong with him."

Renie had returned from setting out the salad bowl. "What's wrong with who?"

"Zachary Conrad," Judith said.

Renie shrugged. "He's an executive. Let me count the ways . . ."

"Never mind." Judith put a big serving spoon in the bowl of rice. "Did you say you've never met him?"

"That's right," Renie responded, "and I'd like to keep it that way. Why? Is he even worse than I expected?"

"He's very ill," Judith said. "I don't think it's mere flu."

Renie looked affronted. "You think I poisoned him?"

Judith sighed. "Of course not. I'm just stating a fact."

"Stick to feeding the herd that's here," Renie said. "Some of the Paines are gathering around the trough."

Judith peered over the half doors. Andy and Paulina Paine were picking up their plates. "You're right. And here come the three Blairs. Let's get the rest of the food out there pronto."

In less than five minutes, Judith, Renie, and Addison had finished setting out all of the dishes except for the desserts. The guests spent a long time reading the posted signs on each item before picking and choosing what suited their various dietary requirements. Judith, who had remained on the kitchen side of the half doors, motioned to Paulina and asked if the twins were still planning on coming to dinner.

"Who knows?" Paulina said with a careless shrug. "Kids!" She moved on along the sideboard.

Renie poked Judith. "Ask her if she likes horse meat."

"Keep it down," Judith warned between clenched teeth. "We're short four settings at the table. Hannah, Zachary, the twins . . . no, *five*." She moved farther into the kitchen to avoid being overheard. "Where's Zoë? She was moping on the window seat the last time I saw her."

"Which eating disorder does she have?" Renie inquired. "Starvation?"

Judith shook her head. "She's the vegan. And future vet."

Addison had started down the hall to the back door. "I'll check to see if I can spot her through the French doors."

"Good," Judith said. She polished off her Scotch and sighed. "I can't tell—are they enjoying themselves at all?"

"Maybe," Renie said slowly, "they have a different way of enjoying themselves. It could be genetics. Did you ever see Norma and Wilbur actually having a good time?"

"No, now that you mention it," Judith admitted. "It's so different from our own family. We always had such a wonderful time at that dining room table. Lots of laughter, heated but never hurtful arguments, uncles and aunts playing tricks on each other . . . it was the way we grew up. Lots of love, plenty of good times, and amazing memories to cherish. This bunch is . . . *painful* to behold."

Renie gave a start. "I hear a phone. It sounds like mine." She hurried over to the counter, where she'd left her purse.

Judith began loading the dirty cookware into the dishwasher. The drone of desultory conversation, interrupted only by an occasional caustic remark, made her feel as if all her hard work had gone for naught. She wondered if Norma Paine had forced her family to accept the auction item. It wouldn't surprise Judith. Norma's sheer willpower wasn't easy to fend off. Judith almost felt sorry for her cheerless guests.

A shriek from Renie broke into her gloomy thoughts. "Are you sure?" her cousin was saying into the phone. "He can't just disappear into thin air! He's too tall to miss." She paused, listening to whoever was on the other end of the line. "Keep looking, or go back to your seat and wait for him to show up." Another pause followed as Judith kept her eye on Renie, who was now shaking her head. "Okay, okay. Just call me back and let me . . . yes, I know you hate using the phone . . . fine, g'bye." Clicking off the cell, she leaned against the counter. "Bill's lost Uncle Al."

Before Judith could respond, Addison returned to the kitchen. "No sign of Zoë. Maybe she's in the bathroom."

"Maybe," Renie snapped, "she's run off with Uncle Al."

Addison looked puzzled. "Uncle Al? Who's—"

"Skip it," Judith interrupted. "What happened?" she asked Renie.

"Bill and Uncle Al got their hot dogs and ate them on the concourse." Renie moved away from the counter and started pacing around the kitchen. "Uncle Al ran into one of his many sports-loving chums. The game was about to start, so Bill told Uncle Al he was going to their seats, which, as you might guess, are practically on the floor at midcourt. Uncle Al told Bill he'd be right there. But by the middle half of the first quarter, Uncle Al never showed up. Bill went out to look for him and couldn't find him anywhere, including the men's room. He didn't see any sign of whoever Uncle Al was talking to either."

"Did Bill know who it was?" Judith asked.

"No. Bill didn't wait to be introduced. He always likes to see the very start of a game, even the warm-ups. Bill thought the guy looked familiar. He has a good eye for faces, but couldn't come up with a name. Tall, more Bill's age or younger. Bill thought the guy had prematurely gray hair. And before you ask, it seemed like a friendly conversation."

Judith thought for a moment. "Uncle Al probably knows at least half the nonstudent section. Maybe he went with this old pal to meet and greet some other mutual friends."

Renie made a face. "It's not impossible, but Bill would've seen him. Uncle Al's six four. He stands out even in a basketball crowd, especially if whoever he's talking to is already seated."

"True," Judith conceded. "But if anything happened to Uncle Al—like suddenly getting ill—someone would've noticed. I assume Bill asked the ushers or some other people working at the game."

"He did," Renie said. "Nothing to report."

"Damn." Judith had an urge to bite her fingernails, a lifelong habit. "I don't know what to say." She turned to Addison. "I should ask Walter and Sonya what happened to Zoë."

Addison's expression suddenly grew taut. "No. Let's wait."

"For what?" Judith demanded. "The entire guest list and

the rest of my family members to evaporate into thin air? If
you don't ask them, I will." She turned around and headed
into the dining room.

The group at the dining room table seemed to be arguing
over whether or not their particular dishes met their dietary
needs, or if some of the offerings had been mislabeled.

"This can't be real tofu," Dennis squeaked. "It tastes like
soap."

"I hate asparagus," Sonya declared. "Since Hannah isn't
here, why couldn't we have something else for a vegetable?"

Octavia laughed harshly. "You *are* a vegetable, Sonya."

"Watch your mouth!" Walter roared. "You and your father
are slow learners. Our family doesn't put up with insults
from ill-bred people. We take great pride in being Paines."

Octavia tossed a radish at Walter. "I can't think why. Stick
it, Wally. Don't ever criticize my dad."

"I will when he deserves it," Walter retorted, picking the
radish off of his tie. "And don't call me Wally!"

Dennis Blair bridled. "Leave my little girl alone. Can't
you tell when she's teasing?"

"She's not teasing," Sonya insisted, lips pursing.

Judith had heard enough. "Excuse me," she said, trying to
sound pleasant. "Is there anything you need?" *Like a group
kick in the butt?*

Most of the eyes that turned toward their hostess looked
hostile or angry. The eldest Paine, Andrew, answered first.
"We're managing. Did Mama send over my special pillow?"

"Oh!" Judith exclaimed, having forgotten about the
delivery Norma had made the previous day. "Yes. I wasn't
here, but it's upstairs." *I think. For all I care it could be in
Rankerses' hedge.* "I understand," she went on, glancing at
Walter, "that one of you lives on a ranch."

The Paine brothers frowned at Judith. "A ranch?" Andrew

said. "No. Paulina and I live over on the Eastside. Gated community. Very nice."

Paulina rolled her eyes. "The gates keep the rest of the population safe from the residents. They can only be unlocked from the outside."

Andrew stared angrily at his wife. "I bought that house for you! It's five thousand square feet of utter comfort."

"You bought it to show off," Paulina snarled. "I never wanted to live in a monstrous place like that. I was perfectly satisfied with our nice house in town. You're the one who complains about the commute to your damned food factory."

Andrew turned glum. "I thought it'd make you happy. I guess I was wrong. Again."

Walter reached around Sonya to put a hand on his brother's shoulder. "We shouldn't bicker like this. Mama wouldn't approve. She paid for us to have a nice time together."

"Together!" Sarah Blair cried. "I hate together!" She jumped out of her chair, knocked the salad bowl's wooden spoon onto the floor, shoved her way past Judith, and fled from the dining room.

"Touchy," Walter muttered. "Baby sister's always been the weak link. Hannah's made of sterner stuff."

Paulina sniffed. "Are you referring to the loose nuts and bolts inside Hannah's head?"

"Now, Paulina . . ." Andrew began, but caught his wife's warning glance and shut up.

Judith noted that there were now six empty chairs at the table. The auction event was a fiasco. Norma Paine had wasted Wilbur's hard-earned money. *But it's not my fault,* she thought. And yet she felt guilty. Not every guest at Hillside Manor had been happy. Some of them had ended up dead. *Not my fault, either,* she told herself. *They had brought their victim status with them.*

But Judith couldn't let the sense of guilt subside. It was in her nature to make people feel good. That was the reason she'd become an innkeeper. Failure clung to her like a damp shirt.

"I'm sorry you're not enjoying yourselves," she blurted. "Some of your family members seem to have left. The twins never actually arrived." She turned to Sonya. "Do you know where Zoë went?"

Sonya looked away; Walter fidgeted with his linen napkin. The silence in the dining room seemed filled with foreboding. Judith felt a shiver creep up her spine.

It was Sonya who finally spoke. "For all we know, she's dead!" She burst into tears and collapsed against Walter's shoulder.

Chapter Thirteen

Judith was momentarily speechless. Sonya's body shook as the tears flowed and she made little mewing noises. Walter awkwardly patted her back. "Now, now, sweetheart, you know Zoë's fine. Moody, that's our girl. I guess she wasn't feeling festive tonight."

Paulina looked pale, Dennis hung his head, and Octavia seemed perturbed. Judith moved closer to the table. "Can I help in any way?"

Walter waved a hand. "Just nerves. Postholiday blues."

"Has Zoë actually left?" Judith inquired.

"Uh . . ." Walter stopped patting his wife and rubbed his balding head. "Well . . . she's not here, is she?"

Andrew, who was seated in front of Judith, turned in his chair. "Didn't you poison a guest a few years ago?"

Judith was aghast. "Of course not! A guest poisoned a fortune-teller. I didn't even know those people. Did Norma—I mean, your mother—tell you that?"

Sonya sniffled before looking up at Judith. "It was in the newspapers and on TV." She sniffled again. "A couple of years later a gangster was shot by your mother."

"What about that movie big shot?" Walter demanded, all

but shoving his wife away from him. "Didn't he drown in your kitchen sink?"

"Hey!" Renie, wielding a carving knife, had come up behind Judith, startling not only her cousin but everyone at the table. "Knock it off! Don't any of you idiots remember that your father—or father-in-law or whatever that wimp Wilbur is to you—was a prime suspect in a stabbing death at *church*?"

Andrew had grown red in the face. "Papa wasn't a killer! He was the Easter Bunny!"

Paulina had stood up. "May I say something before the kitchen help goes samurai with that knife?"

Andrew put a hand on his wife's arm. "Don't, darling, please. You'll only make things worse."

"Get stuffed!" Paulina snapped, shaking off Andrew's hand. "In the interest of common decency, I say we end this farce right now. It isn't fair to Mrs. Flynn. It isn't fair to any of us, really. Be honest—we don't like or trust each other much. Not without reason, but I won't go into—"

"Stop!" Walter bellowed. "Don't you dare hang our dirty laundry out to dry here!"

Paulina narrowed her eyes at her brother-in-law. "I didn't intend to. That's why I think we should adjourn." She pushed her chair back, moved around behind Andrew, and offered her hand to Judith. "Thank you. It's not your fault these Paines are such . . . pains."

Sonya was still sniffling, but her tears had dried. "She's right. Let's go."

Andrew seemed reluctant. "Mama paid for . . ."

Sonya shook her head, but said nothing more. She, too, got to her feet and left the table. Octavia tugged at Dennis's sleeve. "Come on, Dad. You never should've let Sarah con you into this . . . whatever it was supposed to be."

Dennis gave his daughter a bleak look. "Sarah insisted

that her mama thought it would be an opportunity for us to iron things out as a family. I guess she was wrong." He scowled and scrunched up his napkin. "Where *is* Sarah? Did she leave without us?"

The question was answered by Sarah herself, who stood in the doorway between the dining room and hall. "Mama *was* wrong," she said, her voice quivering. "Even she can't fix our problems. Get our luggage. I can't wait to leave town."

Dennis reluctantly stood up. Octavia took his arm as they joined Sarah and disappeared into the hall. Paulina had already shaken hands with Judith and made her exit. The Paine brothers had little choice but to follow their wives. As the room emptied, Judith's guilt subsided, but was replaced with melancholy.

As often happened, Renie could read her cousin's mind. She put a hand on Judith's shoulder. "Where's Grandpa doing the after-dinner jig? Where's my dad asking what kind of apple pie Grandma made? Where's Auntie Vance pouring ice water down Uncle Corky's neck? Where's Cousin Sue wondering what happened to their portable bar?" She had spoken softly, but suddenly raised her voice. "And where the hell is Uncle Al? He should be doing card tricks for the kids and making football bets with Uncle Win!"

"Good question," Judith murmured, realizing that her eyes had grown moist. "Oh, coz, we had such fun! And these miserable people can't get through a free dinner without practically going down to the mat. Why are they so unhappy?"

Addison had joined the cousins. "If I may intrude, my pat answer would be the way they were raised. That's probably part of it, but there's more to it. I think something serious is going on with the Paines. They strike me as running scared, a lot like the bulls of Pamplona."

"Really? Why?" Judith said, dabbing at her eyes with a tissue she'd taken out of her slacks pocket.

Addison sighed. "We'll sit down and talk about it. But we should clean up the mess they left. It reminds me of wire photos I've seen after the bulls are chased to the ring. And often, somebody besides the animals gets gored."

Judith shook her head. "Don't say things like that. You scare me. Let's go to work."

They had barely gotten started when noises from the front hall caught their attention. "Good Lord," Judith said under her breath. "I forgot they'd gone upstairs to get their luggage. I hope they didn't hear us talking about them."

"Who cares if they did?" Renie said, loaded down with dinner plates. "Want me to give them a real send-off?"

"No!" Judith winced. "Let them go—quietly."

Just as she was about to follow Renie and Addison into the kitchen, Andrew Paine came into the dining room. "Excuse me," he said in a querulous tone. "I can't find my special pillow."

"Oh." Judith kept a tight hold on the serving dishes she'd removed from the table. "I put it away . . ." The exact location eluded her. "Let me take care of these dirty dishes first."

"Mama will be mad if you lost it," Andrew said from behind Judith as she entered the kitchen. "They're very expensive and have to be special-ordered."

Renie, who'd piled the dinner plates into the sink, shot Andrew a disparaging look. "My husband uses one. He has a chronic bad neck. Try Brookstone, costs a hunsky." She retrieved the carving knife she'd wielded earlier. "No reason to lose any . . . sleep over a pillow, is there?" She licked her lips and ran a finger along the blade. "Good-bye, Andrew."

He turned tail and rushed from the kitchen. Judith made a face at Renie before going back into the dining room. "Try the linen closet!" she shouted after Andrew. "I just remembered—" The front door banged shut before she could finish.

During the next few minutes, the sounds of footsteps and

the closings of the door that followed seemed to indicate that the rest of the Paines had finally departed. Just before nine, Judith, Renie, and Addison had cleared everything away, the dishwasher had been emptied and reloaded, and the living room was restored to order. Judith poured herself a glass of ice water, Renie got a can of Pepsi from the fridge, and Addison found a Diet Coke in the pantry. The trio retreated to the living room and collapsed on the matching sofas by the fireplace.

"I should've built a fire," Judith remarked, glancing at the empty grate. "I'm used to Joe doing it."

Addison moved as if to get up. "Do you want me to start one?"

"No," Judith said as the grandfather clock chimed nine. "It's too late." She let out a little gasp. "I forgot Mother's dinner!"

Renie, who was sitting next to her cousin, waved a hand. "I didn't. I took it out to her between rounds three and four of the Paine-filled smackdown. Don't worry. It wasn't tofu, it was the nonvegan lasagna with a salad and French bread."

Judith leaned back on the sofa. "Thanks, coz. I'm a mess."

"I don't blame you." Renie gazed across the coffee table to Addison. "Well? Are we going to do a postmortem or what? Make it snappy. I should go home and get some work done. The later it gets, the more creative I seem to be. I might wind up one project before two A.M. So start dishing, Addison. You're the one in the know."

"I need more information on the cast of characters," Addison replied. "I realize neither of you knows these people, but you do have some family background. Any chance I can get something to write on?"

Judith started to get up, but Renie nudged her back onto the sofa. "Sit. I know where you keep your notebooks and tablets. Be right back." She hurried out of the living room.

"I owe you a huge thanks for all the help you've given me tonight," Judith said to Addison. "I don't think Renie and I could've coped alone."

"You probably would've been just fine," he replied, putting his feet up on a small stack of magazines atop the coffee table. "Your cousin might've dispatched some of those ghastly people with that carving knife, though. For a little squirt, she's kind of feisty."

"She's never suffered fools gladly," Judith responded. "Renie's especially dangerous when armed."

"Hey," Renie said, returning to the room and tossing a spiral notebook and a ballpoint pen at Addison, "please don't talk about me when I'm gone. I'm not deaf. Even I heard those gunshots. Scoot over, coz. I need room for my giant purse. If Bill hasn't called me in the next twenty minutes, I'm calling him. The basketball game should be over by then. Knowing how Bill hates to use the phone, I assume Uncle Al showed up, and there's no way either of them would leave courtside to make a call."

"You're probably right," Judith allowed. "I hope so." She turned to Addison. "Should we notify the SPCA or whichever agency can haul away that poor dead horse?"

Addison grimaced. "I doubt they'd come out this late. Calling the police might be a better idea. Let them handle it."

Judith bit her lip. "I don't know . . . I'd like to get through this latest guest debacle without the cops showing up. The not infrequent arrival of emergency vehicles isn't good for Hillside Manor's reputation."

Addison shrugged. "Then wait. The horse isn't going anywhere." He flipped open the notebook. "Okay, let's take it from the top. Norma and Wilbur Paine, parents. Wilbur's an attorney, right?"

Judith nodded. "Norma was a legal secretary—that's

how she and Wilbur met—but she hasn't worked since I've known her."

Addison made a note. "Eldest son is . . . Andrew?"

"Also right. Married to Paulina. They strike me as ill-matched." She watched Addison closely, but he seemed to have no obvious reaction.

"The twins' parents?"

"Yes. I don't know if it's a first or second marriage." She kept her gaze on Addison, but there was still no sign that he already knew Paulina. "Chad and Chase look about twenty," she continued. "Paulina alluded to Andrew's business being in town because he has to commute. She also mentioned that he sells food to big companies." She looked at Renie. "Any idea what business he's in?"

Renie shook her head. "I didn't even know he existed. Both the Paine sons would've been several years ahead of our kids at SOTS. We know Andrew and Paulina live in a gated community on the Eastside. Other than that, I flunk."

"Okay, one couple down," Addison murmured. "Let's move on to Walter and Sonya. Anything you know about them except that they don't live on a ranch? And is Zoë their only child?"

The cousins exchanged blank looks. "Never knew about Zoë," Renie said.

"I never knew much about Walter," Judith added. "When the adult Paine children were growing up, I didn't live on the hill." She slipped off her shoes and wiggled her toes. "According to Zachary, Zoë is studying to be a vet. First year, on winter break. If Walter mentioned his job, I didn't hear it. All I can add is that Zoë seemed happy when she arrived. I don't recall actually speaking to Zoë, but I heard her giggle when she came in. Then she apparently turned glum during the cocktail hour."

Renie nodded. "I met them at the door. Zoë was smiling and seemed pleasant. Walter acted . . . hearty? I thought maybe things were going to turn out fairly well, but looking back, maybe it was all an act."

"Or they wanted to make a good impression?" Addison suggested.

Renie looked thoughtful. "Possibly. He was praising his mother for buying the auction event. Come to think of it, Sonya didn't say much, either. Walter did all the talking."

"Okay," Addison said, clicking the ballpoint a few times. "I know something about Zachary. He's in charge of the commercial and industrial department, reporting directly to the superintendent. That's the capacity in which I interviewed him, anyway. He struck me as a fairly smart guy, no sense of humor, no imagination, a go-by-the-manual type."

"Aargh," Renie groaned. "In other words, just what I expected."

Addison chuckled. "There was one thing, though, that humanized him. Besides having been a pretty good basketball player, that is. He tended to elude certain questions. Not unusual for his type when they know they're going to be quoted, but somehow it was different with him, as if he thought I was going to spring something on him that he wasn't expecting. Wary, as if there was something I *should* ask him, but didn't."

"Interesting," Judith murmured.

Renie shot her cousin a droll look. "Interesting that that type is interesting at all. They're usually soporifically dull."

"Not a totally unwarranted comment," Addison said, turning to Judith. "The other interesting thing is that you said he was very thin. That makes me wonder if he's seriously ill. It's been almost a year since I last saw him."

Judith stifled a yawn. "Hannah is certainly overbearing. If

Zachary is seriously ill, she seems lacking in sympathy. Not that any of the Paines struck me as compassionate."

Renie frowned. "You really are worn-out. Your keen insight into human nature is slipping. Octavia started out as a twit, but she made one of the evening's few charitable contributions in defending her father."

"That," Judith said with a wry expression, "is because Octavia's not a Paine. Walter's crack about her not knowing much about the family's pride made that pretty clear. And Octavia referred to Sarah by name—not as her mother. There's no resemblance between them either. To clinch my case, Sarah is the youngest of the Paines—she can't be more than early forties. Octavia is midtwenties, maybe older."

"You're right," Renie said. "I should've caught that. I guess I was concentrating too hard on which Paine I'd stab first."

Addison had been taking more notes. "But we don't know what most of them do for a living. We can check the Internet. Want to do that now or are you two exhausted?"

"Well . . ." Judith was torn. She was definitely tired and her brain wasn't up to full speed. For once, exhaustion trumped curiosity.

Renie was rummaging in her purse. "Tomorrow is another day," she said. "It's after nine-thirty. I'm going to call and see if Bill's home yet. It shouldn't take him long to get from the pavilion. Uncle Al has a special VIP parking permit." Finding her cell, she got up and went out into the hall.

"I should head home," Addison said. "I'm beginning to feel like a nonpaying guest."

"Oh no," Judith declared. "You've more than earned your keep."

His expression was ironic. "Only by fetching and carrying." He sighed. "I owe you an explanation. I was hoping to find out something about the elusive story I'm trying to break. From what I gathered about Joe's . . . let's call it willing detention at police headquarters, I assumed some of the answers might be here. Or that you'd know more than you actually do. Your reputation as FASTO has grown over the years."

Judith shook her head. "A reputation I never sought. But thanks for not calling me FATSO. I'm not holding anything back. Joe has kept me in the dark about this whole mess."

"That was the other thing," Addison said. "When I realized you didn't know much about it, I wondered if he thought you were in danger."

"You mean from my guests?"

"Possibly," Addison hedged. "Even though the Paine bunch has taken off, I still think they've got something to hide. It may be only some typical skeletons in the family closet. But I keep thinking back to that last meeting with Zachary Conrad. For all his apparent composure, he was definitely suspicious of my motives during what was a routine interview. Maybe I'm imagining it, but in retrospect, he seemed relieved when I left."

"You're a good judge of character," Judith said. "That's a useful trait for a journalist." She stopped as Renie came back into the living room. "Well? Did you run down Bill?"

"No," Renie said, leaning on the back of the sofa where she'd been sitting. "I called four times. Bill has been known to ignore the phone, but I've always told him that if I really needed to get hold of him, I'd keep trying until he picked up."

Judith checked the grandfather clock. It was about to chime the quarter hour at nine forty-five. "Overtime?"

Renie shook her head. "I called the *Times'* sports hotline. We lost, sixty-four to fifty-one. That doesn't sound like OT." She reached down to pick up her purse from the sofa. "I'm going home. For all I know, Bill turned off the ringer.

Except," she added in a woebegone voice, "I don't think he knows how to do it. Maybe he finally carried out his threat to throw the phone into the street."

Addison stood up. "Do you want me to go with you?"

Renie stiffened. "Why? Do you think I'm in danger, too? I couldn't help but overhear some of your conversation while I was waiting for Bill to answer the phone."

"Well . . ." Addison glanced at Judith and shifted from one foot to the other. "Maybe we should all go."

"Oh, for . . ." Renie slung her purse over her shoulder. "Never mind. This is dumb. I'll call as soon as I get home. Okay?"

"Coz . . ." Judith began, but Renie was already out of the room. "She's probably right. Bill simply isn't answering. He's worse than my mother when it comes to the telephone."

Addison sat back down again. "I'd better stick around, at least until we hear from Renie."

"Okay. I'll empty the dishwasher. I think that last load is done." She walked more slowly than usual back through the hall, the dining room, and into the kitchen. She'd just opened the dishwasher when Addison joined her.

"Got any garbage to take out?" he asked.

"Look under the sink. Didn't you already take out some bags?"

"Yes, but there was a lot of stuff—the actual garbage, recycling, glass—"

"Stop. I get dizzy remembering what goes where. The city keeps changing the rules. Why don't you write an article about that? We may've pioneered recycling around here, but it's getting out of control." She touched some silverware and realized it was too hot to handle. After Addison had collected two plastic bins from under the sink and headed outside, she went to the kitchen window to see what the weather was doing. It appeared to have stopped raining, though it was hard to tell. The night was pitch-black dark. Too dark, she realized, noticing that none of the Rankerses' lights were on. Although they were usually early to bed and early to rise, they generally watched TV upstairs until around ten. Maybe Arlene wasn't joking about taking Carl to the ER. The more she thought about it, the more she realized that her neighbor had sounded serious. Judith picked up the phone and dialed their number, but got their recorded message. She was wondering what to do next when Addison came back inside.

"What's wrong?" he asked. "You look worried."

Judith stepped aside so he could replace the garbage bins. "I can't get hold of the Rankerses," she said, and explained that she thought Carl must be sicker than she'd realized. "Occasionally it's hard to tell with Arlene. I love her dearly, but every so often she says something that isn't quite . . . accurate."

Addison looked concerned. "Should I go see if they're home? What does their car look like?"

"Cars," Judith said. "An older Mercedes coupe and a black SUV."

"Are they in the garage?" he asked, heading for the back door.

"No. They use the garage for storage. One of their daughters is in real estate and keeps her staging furniture and decor in there. Go the other way. If they're home, both vehicles should be in the driveway."

"Okay. Be right back."

The phone rang just as Judith heard the front door close. She snatched the receiver from the counter. "Coz?" she said, seeing her cousin's home number on the screen. "Are you okay?"

"Yes—and no," Renie replied, not sounding like her usual bristly self. "I'm home, but Bill isn't. That's so strange. My husband is the most responsible, predictable person in the world, midwestern to the core. I'm worried sick."

"If he's with Uncle Al, they may've gone somewhere with one of his buddies. Bill's at Uncle Al's whim, since he drove them to the game."

Renie was silent for a moment. "True—except we don't know if Bill ever found Uncle Al."

"Even if he didn't," Judith pointed out, "he wouldn't have stuck around this long. He probably had to call a cab and that could take a while after the game."

"You're talking bilge," Renie snapped. "I checked—the game was over at nine-twenty. That's almost forty-five minutes ago. Furthermore, I've rarely seen taxis pulling up by the pavilion. It only holds around ten, eleven thousand, and the parking lot is enormous."

"How about a bus?"

"You really are out of it tonight," Renie snarled. "I'm hanging up and calling the cops." She disconnected.

Judith's shoulders sagged. Her cousin was right. In her own defense, it had been a long day—a long week, too. She simply couldn't cope with another crisis.

Or so she thought until Addison entered the kitchen. "The rest of the house is dark and the SUV is gone," he said. "What do think has happened to the Rankerses?"

Chapter Fourteen

Judith reeled against the refrigerator. "Good God! I can't stand it! Bill's missing in action, too. Along with Uncle Al. What . . . should . . ." She staggered over to a kitchen chair and collapsed.

"Hey," Addison said quietly, "if Carl had to go to the ER, he may have a long wait. It's Friday night. Casualties pile up. I know, I used to cover the police beat in my younger years." He eased into a chair opposite Judith. "Where would they have gone?"

For a moment, she couldn't remember. "Norway General," she finally recalled. "Not the one on Pill Hill, but across the ship canal. That's where Carl was taken years ago when he was painting the house and fell off the scaffolding. He broke his arm and his leg."

"Hmm," Addison mused, "guess he shouldn't have stepped back to admire his work. Do you want me to call the ER? I can use my reporter's credentials."

Judith tried to get her brain in order. "Let's wait. You're right. They probably didn't leave until after six. We should focus on Bill and Uncle Al."

Addison glanced at his watch. "It's just ten. They may've

gotten stuck in traffic. Maybe one of the bridges was up. I assume Renie is upset. Is she an alarmist by nature?"

"No." Judith paused, still collecting her thoughts. "Renie's a lot of things, but not an alarmist. Under that somewhat fiery nature, she's rather coolheaded. It sounds like a paradox, but it really isn't."

A sudden silence fell between them. It seemed to Judith that the *tick-tock* of the old schoolhouse clock was unusually loud. It also seemed that Renie was right—her brain wasn't working properly. It was scattered, like Grandma Grover's broken bowl: fragments of Joe exiled at police headquarters; pieces of Uncle Al and Bill missing in action; shards of Renie pacing the floor; chunks of dead horse in the garage.

Addison finally spoke. "Tell me more about Uncle Al."

It took a moment for Judith to focus on the query. "Uncle Al? Does the name 'Al Grover' mean anything to you?"

After a brief pause, Addison grinned. "Al Grover—a name from my youth. I didn't realize he was *that* Al. I guess I never heard you mention his last name. Big high school and college basketball star. Quite a reputation as hotheaded and scrappy. Played football and baseball, too. Coached both college and semipro in the pre-NBA era. Became a referee for college and high school basketball games. Owned a watering hole or two downtown. Active in the Teamsters. Chummy with at least a couple of sheriffs and several cops. I actually saw him ride with the sheriff's posse in a parade once when I was a kid. Good-looking guy, too. Did he ever get married?"

Judith shook her head. "He's had a longtime girlfriend, Tess of the Timbervilles, we call her. Really a lovely woman, and an heiress to one of the timber companies around here. Over the years, Uncle Al had women chasing him everywhere he went, but he liked to play the field—in every sense of the word."

"Interesting," Addison said thoughtfully. "Maybe this isn't a coincidence after all."

Judith stared at him. "I don't understand."

Addison made a face. "It's hard to explain. There's been a rumor going around City Hall that some strange things have been happening at a fairly high level. Certain records disappear. Personnel changes for no apparent reason. A couple of usually reliable sources clamming up. There's an aura of unease that raises my reporter's hackles. I've been around long enough to know when something's brewing. But I can't nail it down. It's like catching snowflakes to study before they melt."

"So where would Uncle Al come in?"

"I don't know," Addison admitted, "except he's always been . . . connected. So to speak."

Judith took offense at the remark. "Uncle Al has never gotten so much as a traffic ticket!"

"No," Addison said. "He wouldn't, would he?"

She lowered her eyes, remembering her uncle telling the other relatives about being stopped for speeding. The patrolman had taken one look at his driver's license—and apologized. Another time a game warden had discovered an over-the-limit salmon catch in Uncle Al's boat. He recognized the would-be perp—and winked, adding that it was incredible how fast the other two guys had gotten back to shore. There were more such incidents stored in her memory bank, but Judith didn't care to retrieve them. Addison had made his point.

"Restaurants," he said quietly, almost as if he were talking to himself. "Bars. Taverns." His gaze fixed on Judith. "Do you know anything about the food-and-beverage business?"

Somehow, Judith's brain seemed to revive. "Are you kidding? I was part of it for a long time—too long. My first husband, Dan McMonigle, owned the Meat & Mingle out in the Thurlow area."

Addison looked startled. "You're kidding!"

"Believe me, that's not a topic I kid about," she said bitterly. "Dan lost both the business and our house. Then he stopped working altogether and died at forty-nine, leaving Mike and me virtually destitute. Why don't you just pour a glass of gall and I'll drink it?"

"God," Addison said, rubbing his forehead. "I didn't mean to upset you. I was just . . . surprised. I had no idea."

Judith leaned forward, one arm resting on the table. "Do you want to tell me that Dan was mixed up in something crooked I didn't know about? Am I about to get arrested, too?"

"No, no," he protested. "I mean, even if your late husband had done anything dodgy, the statute of limitations would've run out by now."

"I worked nights tending bar at the Meat & Mingle," Judith said. "I was never aware of Dan doing anything illegal."

"You wouldn't be. I mean," Addison went on hastily, "it wouldn't have anything to do with the bar. Not directly, that is. I have to ask, though: Did any cops hang out at your husband's restaurant?"

Addison's query annoyed Judith so much that she couldn't think clearly. "Not in uniform. There may've been some county police. We were officially outside of the city. Are you saying there's a history of corruption on the force?"

"Did Joe ever talk about it?"

"Well . . . nothing that you might call scandalous. He knew certain cops who weren't above accepting what he'd term more of a thank-you from grateful citizens. Some got caught, some didn't. I always assumed it was easier for the top dogs to turn a blind eye. Joe never did. Neither did Woody. I'd take an oath on that. There were also a few disciplinary actions taken over the years. Maybe some dismissals. I ran into members of the force who were lazy, stupid, self-aggrandizing, even borderline criminals." Judith paused, recalling at least two or three incompetent, even bad cops she'd met along the way. "Every so often there'd be a shooting that was questionable in terms of the danger an alleged suspect posed. They always seemed to result in an investigation and in a couple of cases the cops were either suspended or fired. Joe wasn't one to bad-mouth his fellow law enforcement coworkers, even to me. Of course he held them in contempt, but that didn't mean he'd rat them out. I suppose there were incidents he never—"

The phone rang. Judith had to get up to retrieve the handset from the counter. Once again, Renie's number appeared on the screen.

"Yes?" she said, her voice raised.

"I found Bill and Uncle Al," Renie shouted angrily. "They're being held at police headquarters. I'm going there now. G'bye." She hung up before Judith could say another word.

Addison had stood up. "I heard that. Renie didn't need to use the phone. We could've heard her without it. Shall we join her?"

Judith heaved a huge sigh. "Why not? I can't stay here and walk the floor all night." She set the phone back in its cradle. "I should tell Mother we're leaving. But I don't know what to say. She'll have a fit."

"I'll tell her," Addison volunteered, already headed for the back hall. "We can take my car."

"Okay. Wait—what kind of car is it? I've never noticed."

"An aging Land Rover, tan in color. It's out front. Meet you there." He grabbed his jacket and left.

Judith made sure everything in the kitchen was turned off and that the back door was locked. She took two Excedrin for the recurring headache, realized she hadn't eaten in hours, and grabbed some of the leftover carrots and celery from the platter she'd served to the guests. Finally, she put on her jacket, went out the front door, and took her time walking to the Land Rover. The doors were locked. Judith nibbled on some celery. The air was chilly, but the rain had stopped. A few moments passed before she saw Addison hurrying in her direction.

He unlocked the car without saying anything until they were both inside and he'd turned the ignition key. "I can park in the press area, but I'll drop you off so you don't have to walk so far. You can meet me by the elevators."

"Okay," Judith said, gripping her purse tightly in her lap. "I suppose Renie's already there."

"Probably." He pulled out of the cul-de-sac and turned onto the cross street leading to Heraldsgate Avenue. "I'm not sure what we can do except find Renie and see what's up with Bill and Uncle Al."

"What about Joe?"

"One thing at a time," he said, waiting for an opening in traffic at the intersection. "We don't want your cousin to get arrested for assaulting an officer, do we?"

"No." She paused as Addison turned onto the steep avenue. "What did you tell Mother?"

"That we were going dancing."

Judith looked at Addison to see if he was kidding, but he was concentrating on the red light three cars ahead of him. "How did she react to that?" she finally asked as the light changed and they continued toward downtown.

"She thought it was great," he replied. "She started to tell me about how she used to go dancing with your father at that old ballroom down on Second Avenue. Unfortunately, I had to tactfully cut her off. Your mother's a real treasure trove of local lore."

Judith considered asking if he'd ever seen the movie that had been loosely based on Gertrude's life. The old lady had made some money from the moderately successful film, but she'd been rightfully horrified by some of her alleged adventures as "Dirty Gertie." A different thought sprang into Judith's mind. "Are you writing a book about the city?"

Addison chuckled. "Not yet. But someday I will. You can't hang around City Hall for as long as I've done and not want to write a book about it, especially what went on around here before I was on the beat. Oh, I've done quite a bit of research off and on, but I'll wait for retirement before I devote the time it'll take to actually start writing." As they stopped at another red light, he shot Judith a grim look. "That might come sooner than later. With newspapers losing readers by the cartload, they'll cut staff—early and forced retirements."

"That's sad," Judith declared. "I can't imagine life without a newspaper."

"There are plenty of people who can—and do," he said. "Newspapers, alas, are dinosaurs."

They had reached the city's commercial core, where mannequins in resort clothes stood in the display windows at Donner & Blitzen, Nordquist's, and I. Magnifique. Judith shivered, but wasn't sure if it was from anxiety or looking at the skimpy bikinis. With or without snow on the ground, they seemed out of place in early January.

"Say," she said suddenly, "did the police track down the supposedly paralyzed man's caregivers?"

"The male one had yet to show up. He replaced a guy who was going off to Chile for a summer vacation. The woman vanished without a trace. Apparently, she never came back from her errands."

"Good grief!" Judith cried in disbelief. "Doesn't that make her suspect number one?"

"Possibly," Addison replied, braking for a midblock red

light by a converted movie house where theatergoers were exiting from a stage show. "It's hard to trace somebody named Beth Johnson, the only name the cops found in the condo, without an address or phone number. The neighbor who heard the shots saw her only once and described her the same way Joe did."

"That is beyond suspicious," Judith said. "I don't suppose the male caregiver knew anything about her."

"No," Addison replied, continuing up the avenue. "He came from an agency and had never heard of any Beth Johnson working there. It's possible she was someone the vic knew, but since nobody knows who the dead man really is, it's hard to track down."

Judith sighed. "Somebody has worked very hard to cover their tracks. It's more than frustrating." She paused, shaking her head as they continued toward the new courthouse and the refurbished City Hall. "I assume Renie went where I did—directly to the police department."

"Unless she planted a bomb in the lobby as a distraction."

"All things are possible," Judith murmured, glancing out at the gray granite elegance of the Cascadia Hotel, where she and Joe had spent many an evening of formal dress— and informal undress—in the days of their courtship some forty years earlier. "Maybe," she said, even more softly, "they still are."

"What?" Addison asked, stopping at the next red light.

Judith couldn't answer the question. Instead, she blurted one of her own. "How long have you known Paulina Paine?"

"Oh. I should've known you'd figure that out, FASTO." The light changed and he drove the next two blocks in silence before taking a right and then a left to get to City Hall's main entrance, where he pulled up in a no parking zone. "I met her right after Amalia dumped me," he said, not looking at Judith but staring straight ahead. "She and

Andrew had separated. That was two years ago. She was against buying that big, expensive house in the gated community on the Eastside. They were having money problems as it was, and she wanted to stay in town. Then somehow Andrew managed to get his head above water. He begged her to come back. She reluctantly gave in, mainly because of the twins. Our fling was fairly brief, but it was . . . nice. I swear I didn't know she was coming to your B&B. While she was separated, she used her maiden name of Markov, probably to show her distance from Andrew and the other Paines." He finally looked at Judith. "No matter how big this city gets, if you've lived here all your life, it's still a small town."

"True," Judith agreed. "I was best friends with a girl in junior high and we didn't know we were related until I went to her house. I saw a picture of my maternal grandfather on a table in the living room. We were first cousins. I never knew my grandfather because he died fairly young, but Mother had the same picture."

Addison looked in the rearview mirror. "I'd better move before I get a ticket. We media types have to park in the garage, but it's closer for you to walk from the front. I'll meet you in the police department."

"Got it," Judith said. She hung on to her purse and made her way into the lobby, where a guard was on duty. She showed him her ID and explained that she was going to find her uncle who had been arrested, and help bail him out. The guard, who was middle-aged and looked bored, nodded, but said nothing. Judith stepped into a waiting elevator and headed up to the fifth floor.

It was still a bit of a trek to her destination, but she remembered the way. The Excedrin had begun to work, but the glare of the overhead lighting bothered her eyes. *I'm really tired,* she thought, *but I have to do this. I can't let Renie down.*

She heard her cousin before she saw her.

"Listen," Renie yelled, "you poor excuse for a civil servant, if you don't tell me where my husband and my uncle are, I'll call Bub!"

"Bub?" the young uniformed officer said. "What's a bub?"

"Bub's my brother-in-law! He's gone one-on-one with those nine senile and stupid Supremes, that's what Bub is! I mean, *who*. One phone call and . . . urkk!"

Judith had come behind and put an arm around Renie's neck. "Calm down, coz. Do you want to get arrested, too?"

"Why not?" Renie demanded, whirling around as Judith let go of her. "We could have a whole damned family reunion if they can find a big enough cell!" She suddenly stopped, blinking several times. "Why are you here?"

Judith glanced at the young officer, who was adjusting his tie and shaking his head. She noticed that his name tag identified him as DOMINGUEZ but she couldn't make out the rest of it. "To keep you from killing somebody," Judith replied, giving Renie her most severe stare. "It seems I arrived just in time."

"Oh, for heaven's sake!" Renie, with an almost imperceptible sheepish expression, turned back to Dominguez. "Sorry about that. Next time I'll try seduction."

Dominguez didn't say anything, but looked as if he thought the alternative might be as horrific as the temper outburst. Judith stepped up to the young man. "My cousin, Mrs. Jones—Mrs. William Jones—is trying to find her husband whose name is—"

"William Jones?" the officer said, blinking several times.

"Yes. Of course." Judith made a face. "Sorry. I get rattled when I have to subdue the animal. We also want to find out what's happening to our uncle, Al Grover. He was with Bill Jones."

Officer Dominguez picked up a phone, but turned away

while he spoke softly to whoever was at the other end. Renie glared at Judith; Judith glared back. Addison appeared just as the officer hung up.

"Mr. Jones and Mr. Grover are being interviewed," Dominguez said. "If you care to wait, there's a—"

Addison had pulled out his press credentials. "These ladies are with me. We're all here to see Captain Price."

Dominguez cleared his throat. "I'm not sure if Captain Price is here. He works out of the—"

"I know where he works," Addison said calmly. "I also know that when he's involved in a homicide, he comes to headquarters. Be a good sport and tell us where we'll find him."

"I'll have to check that out," the officer said, his dark skin even darker. "Excuse me." He walked quickly away from his post, went out through a side door, and disappeared.

Renie and Judith had stopped glaring at each other. Instead, they were exchanging puzzled gazes. "Where . . ." They'd both spoken at the same time. Renie deferred to Judith. "Go ahead, coz. Maybe Addison knows the answer."

"As a matter of fact," Addison said, pocketing his press credentials, "I do. Follow me."

He led the way back down the corridor from which he'd emerged and stopped in front of a door that was marked PRIVATE—SPD STAFF ONLY. He knocked twice. Judith and Renie exchanged puzzled glances again. Addison stood patiently for what seemed like a long time. Finally, the door opened a crack, but neither of the cousins could see anything from behind their escort.

"Yes?" said a familiar voice.

"Joe!" Judith shouted, clumsily trying to get around Addison.

"Damn!" Joe exclaimed, opening the door wider.

Judith practically fell into his arms. "Oh, Joe! I'm so—"

"Stupid!" he snapped, pushing her out the door. Joe glowered at Addison. "Why in hell did you do such a thing, Kirby? Are you nuts? You know damned well I don't want my wife mixed up in this."

Judith started to protest, but Addison retained his aplomb and responded to Joe. "She already is," he said somberly. "Furthermore, I know the identity of your homicide victim."

Joe gaped at Addison, but recovered quickly. "You *are* nuts. How could you know if we don't?"

"Because," Addison replied calmly, "of Mrs. Flynn's insight."

Judith stared at Addison in disbelief, but kept her mouth shut. Renie, however, punched her cousin in the arm. "Nobody told me anything!" She shook her fist at Joe. "I don't give a rat's ass about who killed who—or do you want to be the next vic? Cut the crap and tell me where Bill is!"

Joe had come out in the hall to stand chest to chest with Addison. "I'm not saying anything until this guy IDs the vic."

Addison shrugged. "No problem. The dead man is Zachary Conrad."

Chapter Fifteen

Joe stared incredulously at Addison. "Zachary Conrad? Who the hell is Zachary Conrad?"

Woody Price appeared in the doorway. "I can tell you that, Joe," he said, his usual composure strained. "I've never met him, but he's the deputy superintendent of the city's lighting department." He offered Judith and Renie a tight smile. "Hello, there. I'm sorry you've been put through all this . . . mess."

"*You're* sorry—" Renie began, but stopped when Woody held up a hand. "Never mind," she mumbled, looking at her shoes.

Another voice resonated from inside the room. "Have you got a Percocet with you? My neck's freaking killing me!"

"Bill!" Renie cried, her brown eyes lighting up. She lowered her head and charged toward the door.

Woody stepped aside, realizing there was no stopping Renie short of wrestling her to the floor. He sighed as she rushed past him. "We'd better all sit down and talk about this vic."

By the time they got inside, Judith realized that this was no simple employee coffee room, but a luxurious lounge reserved for city VIPs and visitors—at taxpayers' expense.

The aubergine leather chairs and sofas, the oak cupboards with leaded-glass doors, and the plush burgundy carpeting gave off an aura of an exclusive men's club. Indeed, the air smelled of cigars. It was no wonder. Bill and Uncle Al were smoking what looked to Judith like the Cuban variety. Two other cigars rested in ashtrays by the vacant chairs. Only Keith Delemetrios wasn't smoking—instead, he held a large Italian deli sandwich in one hand and a big glass of dark ale in the other. Judith knew Guinness when she saw it.

"Good grief!" she shrieked, whirling around to glare at Joe. "So this is what you've been doing the past few days? Drinking fine beer and eating fancy food? When do the hookers show up?"

"Calm down," Joe said, resorting to his usual mellow tones. "This isn't what it seems. We need to refuel after a hard day's work."

Uncle Al expelled a puff of smoke. "Take a seat, doll. I'll give even odds you'll like the pastrami. You, too, Runt," he said to Renie, using his childhood nickname for her. "That fruit salad's pretty swell, too."

Renie, who had been trying to keep Bill from grabbing her purse, ignored her uncle. "I don't have any Percocet, you moron! I'm here to post bail for you and Uncle Fidel over there. What's going on?" She spotted a plate of pastrami and snatched up two slices. "Furthermore, I'm starving! You know how grumpy I get when that happens."

Bill looked unfazed. "Got any weird pop? They don't have my favorite flavors here—not even Beriberi Berry."

"Ladies," Woody said, sounding tense, "please have a seat. As long as you're here . . ." He paused, trying to ignore Joe's expression of displeasure. "I suppose we should try to explain . . . something."

The long cherrywood table could seat at least a dozen people. Delemetrios put down his sandwich and rose to fetch two elegant matching chairs that were sitting by the paneled wall. Addison got one for himself. Still fuming, Judith sat down. Renie snatched another slice of pastrami before taking a seat between her husband and her cousin.

"Got an IcyHot compress?" Bill murmured to his wife.

Renie shot him a dirty look and somehow managed to spew a bit of pastrami on her Lefty O'Doul's sweatshirt. "Dwilluklakafrekinurth?" she said with her mouth full.

"You look like a freaking mess," Bill retorted, brushing the residue off the tipsy leprechaun on Renie's bosom. "As usual. Hold it!" he cried, backing away and holding up his hands as his wife continued to chew lustily. "Don't get any of that stuff on me!"

Woody had also sat down. He cleared his throat after a surreptitious glance at Judith and Joe, who were both staring straight ahead. "Mr. Kirby," Woody finally said, "how can you be sure the victim is Zachary Conrad?"

Addison, who was sitting next to Woody, grimaced. "I have a confession to make. Before I came here I went to the morgue on a hunch." His expression was self-deprecating. "We reporters get hunches, and often they're correct. Or at least they lead us in the right direction. Anyway, I took one look at the vic and recognized Conrad. I've interviewed him a few times over the past five, six years."

Joe leaned forward, green eyes narrowed. "So how did my wife lead you to this so-called hunch?"

Addison wasn't put off by the question. "Innocently, as a matter of fact. Zachary Conrad was supposedly at the B&B tonight. He's related by marriage to the Paine family, who were taking part in the parish auction item that your wife donated. The alleged Mr. and Mrs. Zachary Conrad arrived late. Mrs. Conrad announced at once that Mr. Conrad was sick." He turned to Judith. "I wasn't there. Would you mind telling the others what happened next?"

Judith hesitated, certain that Joe was giving her the evil eye. "Zachary—or whoever he was—could hardly walk. I told Hannah—Mrs. Conrad, Norma Paine's older daughter—that her husband should be in a real bed, but she insisted on leaving him in the parlor on the settee. He's quite tall and obviously was uncomfortable. Hannah declined, saying she needed a drink and he could stay put. After she went into the living room, I tried to get him settled into a better position, but it wasn't easy. Then—" She stopped, her gaze fixed on Addison. "You had to tell me something . . . important, and I left the parlor to deal with the . . . latest problem. The next thing I knew, Hannah came out to the kitchen and told me they were leaving after all. And they did. I saw them out."

Joe's already rubicund complexion had turned very red. He shook a finger at Judith. "Are you telling me that none of the other Paines realized this wasn't Hannah's husband?"

"They didn't see him," Judith replied. "Nobody did, not even Addison. Paulina Paine came downstairs and spoke to Hannah but didn't come in the parlor." She paused for a brief moment before going on the offensive. "Excuse me," she continued, looking first at Woody and then at Delemetrios, "don't either of you know Zachary Conrad? He's a big wheel with the lighting department."

Woody looked faintly embarrassed. "I know the name, that's all. As you're aware, the lighting department is in a separate building. I've never met the man. I've never had reason to." He looked at his subordinate. "What about you, Del?"

The young detective shook his head. "I haven't been on the force that long and I've never even been in the lighting department. Gosh, it's two, three blocks away."

Uncle Al blew a couple of smoke rings and chuckled. "Typical. When it comes to City Hall, the right hand doesn't know what the left hand's doing—except putting both hands in the citizenry's pockets. I'll lay down a couple of Franklins that my niece will figure this out before the rest of you do. Any takers?"

"No," Woody said firmly. "I mean . . ." He rubbed at his graying walrus mustache and avoided Joe's angry look. "We've got enough loose ends to deal with as it is. This case is very complicated. We should stay focused." He turned his soulful dark eyes on Addison. "I don't understand how Judith—Mrs. Flynn—led you—however unknowingly—to the conclusion that the real Zachary Conrad was the homicide victim?"

Addison's shrewd gaze met Woody's. "I know Zachary Conrad. I interviewed him in recent months. He was hale, if not exactly hearty. He's a big guy, former basketball player, was in the pro—"

"Slower than a hippo," Uncle Al muttered in disgust. "Hands like hams. Prone to useless fouls. He was a bum."

"Uh . . . yes," Woody said. "I . . . I prefer baseball. I don't remember Zachary Conrad."

"You're lucky," Uncle Al said. "If he'd played for me, I'd have cut him the first time he put one of those big, clumsy feet on the hardwood."

Woody nodded slightly. "He sounds . . . terrible. Go on, Kirby."

"Not as terrible as my neck," Bill said, turning his head every which way.

Renie scowled at her husband. "Stop that, Mr. Bobble-Head! You're driving me crazy."

"You *are* crazy," Bill shot back, still turning his head.

"Please," Woody begged, "could we stick to the subject? Kirby?"

Addison nodded assent. "Zachary was big, not only tall, but close to two-forty when I last saw him. When Judith—Mrs. Flynn—said he was ill and described him as rail thin, my first reaction was that he must be suffering from some terrible disease. Then it occurred to me that maybe the man in the parlor wasn't Zachary Conrad." He paused. "I can't exactly say why this occurred to me. I've already told you I can't reveal my sources. But that's the reason I wanted to see the body. The corpse was Zachary Conrad."

Woody glanced at Joe. "You never knew Conrad either?"

"No," he said with a touch of regret. "I don't recognize the name. He may've been promoted after I retired."

Uncle Al shrugged, stretched his long arms, and yawned. "Are we done here? This old sport has to get up tomorrow to head for the track. Florida's on Eastern Standard Time."

"We're not," Woody said. "I'd like you and Kirby to stick around. Bill, you can go home with your wife. Can you give Judith a ride?"

"Yes," Bill replied. "Let's not do this again, Woody. Couldn't you just have asked Uncle Al to come down on his free time? I don't like staying up this late either."

Woody's expression was typically stolid. "We have to do things our way. We've been trying to talk to Mr. Grover all week, but he's been out of town. We received word that he was at the basketball game. We let him drive his own car down here. It's not our fault that he was your ride, Bill. I already explained that."

Bill snorted, but didn't say anything more to Woody. He grabbed Renie's arm, virtually dragging her from the chair. "Boppin'!"

The Joneses headed for the door. Judith didn't budge. Bill kept going, but Renie turned around to look at her cousin. "Aren't you coming with us?"

"No," Judith said.

Renie shrugged. "Okay. G'night." She and Bill made their exit.

An uneasy silence settled over the room's plush surroundings. Only Uncle Al seemed not to notice. He puffed his cigar and blew smoke rings. Del squirmed in his chair; Woody flipped through his notebook; Addison checked his cell phone; Judith sat as if she were carved in marble.

It was Joe who broke the silence. "I knew," he said quietly to Judith, "I couldn't keep you out of this. I'd blame Kirby, but I can't. One way or the other, you were bound to get mixed up in a murder case, especially if it involved me."

"Put your ego aside," Judith snapped. "You knew from the very start I was involved. Your stupid phone call about the missing gun gave that away. What did you expect me to find in that open safe?"

Joe stared at Judith. "What do you mean, 'open safe'?"

"It wasn't locked."

"I locked it myself. I figured you'd pick it like you did with Dan, and find the other gun."

"You mean the Glock or the Beretta?"

"Neither of those. I mean the other Smith & Wesson, the one that was used to shoot . . . this Conrad guy. Somebody had to substitute a similar weapon for mine. I should have noticed, but I almost never have to use my weapon on a damned surveillance."

"Oh my God!" Judith exclaimed. "Then somebody came into our house and . . ."

Joe sighed and leaned back in his chair. "Not necessarily. I looked into the safe Monday to find some of the tax information we'll need. I never would have left it unlocked. Who had access before I left the house that morning?"

"Nobody," Judith said. "I mean . . . nobody but the guests and Phyliss and Mother."

For the first time, Joe showed a glint of humor. "That's it—your mother set me up."

"Hey," Uncle Al snapped, "don't talk that way about my sister-in-law. She's a good sport. Damned good cardplayer, too. And when we played baseball up at the cabin, Gert could catch a ball with her knees."

Joe winced. "Sorry. I don't want to think about that last part."

"How," Judith said, equally eager to change the subject, "are you sure the gun wasn't taken before you started the surveillance?"

"Good point." Joe fiddled with his cigar, tapping off ash and examining the tip to see if it was still lighted. "I guess I don't."

"That's it," Uncle Al declared, standing up to his full six-foot-four height. "If we're going out in left field, I'm calling the game on account of pain. I've got bad basketball knees and I'm going home. I've given you plenty already, but I'm no rat. You know where to find me—window seven by the Jockey Club bar." He grabbed his leather jacket and didn't break stride when he patted Judith's back as he headed for the door.

Woody shook his head. "We can't make him stay here. But we still need more of his help." He got to his feet. "I think we should all take a" —he cringed as Judith accidentally knocked over a half-filled Guinness glass—"break."

"Oops!" Judith exclaimed. The glass had broken when it struck the pewter platter of deli meats. Dark ale trickled toward the table's edge. She grabbed a linen napkin to mop up the liquid before it overflowed onto the plush carpet. "Sorry," she murmured, making sure the pieces of glass were all collected into a little pile on a dirty plate.

"That's okay," Woody said wearily. "Maybe Del and I should check our notes. Or something." He glanced at Addison, who looked as if he'd like to hide under the table. "Why don't you join us, Kirby? Maybe we can compare some of our information?"

"Glad to," Addison said, almost upending his chair in his effort to stand up.

The policemen and the reporter made their hurried way out of the room. Joe gazed at the paneled ceiling. Judith folded her hands in her lap. The elegant room struck her as a stage setting, more suited to a drawing room farce than a homicide investigation.

"What is this?" she suddenly asked, though the question was more to herself than to Joe.

After a pause, he answered anyway. "This room? It's the previous mayor's idea of class. Sid Fahlman thought it'd impress big shots to move their companies here. Or not move them out of town. Larry Appel can't make up his mind whether to keep it. Of course he has to find his mind before he can decide anything."

Slowly, Judith turned to her husband. "Your color's better. I thought you were going to stroke out on me."

"Oh . . ." He picked up her hand. "I'd rather stroke you—all over."

She was surprised that it wasn't easy to smile at him. But she did. "All of this can't be easy for you."

"Or you either." His green eyes narrowed. "Unless, of course, Addison Kirby's been an adequate replacement."

"Oh, Joe!" She laughed, equally surprised to find that this was easy. "He's a nice guy and I trust him. But he's not you. Nobody is."

Joe leaned forward so that their foreheads touched. "I'd like to say it's been worth it. But it's not." He pulled her closer and kissed her softly on the lips. With obvious reluctance, he leaned back in the chair. "They plan to announce tomorrow that I'm a suspect in the murder of whoever the hell that guy in the morgue is."

"Oh no! Why? You can't let them do that. It'll ruin your reputation. Are they crazy?"

Joe shrugged. "You'd prefer they arrested Uncle Al? Or Bill?"

"Why do they have to arrest anybody who's innocent?" Judith demanded. "It makes no sense."

"That's because this whole case—and the investigation that started even before the homicide—makes no sense." He shook his head. "No, that's not accurate. It probably makes perfect sense, if we could only put the other pieces together. I just happened to find myself caught in the middle. A coincidence, I figured. But it turns out that it was no such thing. I was, in effect, set up. The problem is, I've no idea who made sure I was in the right place at the wrong time."

"Does Woody have any leads?"

"No," Joe said ruefully. "The murder site was in his precinct and he's only been on the job a short time, so he has to start from scratch. Woody's as baffled as I am."

"None of that makes you the fall guy. You've earned your reputation. Don't let this case tarnish it."

"Hey," Joe said, putting his thumb and forefinger on his wife's chin and staring into her eyes, "once we solve this, I'll be a hero, not a bum."

"No, you won't," she retorted. "Most people will only remember that a retired cop was charged with murder. That's what will stick in their minds. They won't recall what happened beyond that bald fact."

Joe's hand dropped to his side. "I'm doing this for Woody. And," he went on, the gold flecks in his green eyes sparking, "to flush out the real killer before he—or she—strikes again."

Judith tensed. "Do you really think that will happen?"

"It's very possible," Joe said quietly. "If the guilty party figures the setup worked, it could make him—or her—reckless. I've seen it happen. Then we have a better chance of catching this crafty bastard."

Judith stared at what was left of the pastrami. "I can't help you if you won't let me."

"I won't. I can't." He sounded helpless. "Keep Addison around. I want to make sure you've got somebody you can trust with you."

Alarmed, she looked at Joe. "You think *I'm* the next victim?"

"No," he insisted. "I just worry when I'm not with you."

Judith didn't believe him, but she kept that thought to herself. "Then I might as well go home." She stood up. So did Joe. "This is the worst fix we've ever been in," she said, feeling depressed. "What a horrible way to start the new year. I feel like crawling into a hole like the groundhog and never coming out."

"Hey," Joe said, putting his arm around her, "I know it seems pretty bad, but we'll figure it out." He steered Judith toward the door. "I'll try to keep in touch, though I can't tell you much about what's going on. If there's some kind of badass at City Hall, I have to avoid being overheard on a wire."

"You can spare me the details," Judith said as Joe reached for the doorknob. "You may be right about another murder. But it won't be me."

Chapter Sixteen

There had been no chance for Joe to ask Judith what she meant. In fact, the doorknob had turned in his hand. Joe stepped aside to let Woody in. Del and Addison remained in the corridor.

Judith offered Woody a peck on the cheek. "I'm leaving. I know you'll figure all this out and make a lawful arrest. Good luck. Give my love to Sondra. Bye, now."

She only glimpsed Woody's startled face. "You coming, Addison?" she said over her shoulder. "Or should I call a cab?"

"He's leaving, too," Joe called out to his wife. "Take it easy, Kirby."

Once they'd exited the side hall, Judith was surprised that Addison led her to the elevators. "I thought you parked in the garage," she said as he poked the down button. "Isn't that in the other direction?"

"I parked where I left you off," he replied, keeping his voice down. "It's okay for media types to do that after hours. I didn't want to mention going to the morgue." The doors slid open. He didn't continue until the car started its descent. "I knew you'd ask a lot of questions." He paused to offer Judith an apologetic smile. "I couldn't take you with me and I didn't want to waste time. Besides, it was better that you didn't know what I was doing in case somebody made a ruckus."

"Like the corpse?" Judith said drily.

Addison sighed. "It was definitely Zachary. What do you make of that?"

"Wait until we get to the car," Judith said as they exited the elevator.

A soft drizzle was falling when they left the building. Ever the gentleman, Addison opened the passenger door for Judith and waited for her to put on her seat belt. A moment later, he was behind the wheel.

"Well?" he said, turning the ignition key.

Judith didn't answer until they stopped at a red light three blocks later. "I'm trying to think this through logically. The man living in the condo was supposedly paralyzed or at least unable to walk after a serious accident. My first question for the medical examiner would be did the vic have such a disability? I assume they've done an autopsy."

"Iggy couldn't tell me anything," Addison replied. "He works nighttime security and used to be a truck driver for the newspaper. I was lucky he let me see the body. I could look, but not touch. And I only had about five seconds to do that. Given that, they may be waiting for official ID and next of kin to be notified before they cut him up."

"But it's a homicide case," Judith pointed out. "They've already waited three full days. That's too long."

"True, but they know cause of death," Addison said as the light changed. "Two bullets at the base of the skull. Time of death is verified by the neighbor who heard the shots. SANECO won't worry too much at this point about whether or not the deceased was a fraud. It's a moot point unless his heirs follow up on the insurance claim."

"His heir would be Hannah Paine Conrad," Judith said.

"So why does Hannah show up at the B&B with a bogus Zachary?"

"That's what I wonder, too. Are you thinking what I'm thinking?"

"Of course," Judith agreed. "Hannah is in on whatever hoax was perpetrated. But isn't that kind of obvious? And why would she do it?"

"It's *too* obvious. But that doesn't mean it isn't true."

Judith shook her head. "No. We're missing something. A lot of somethings. I need more time to think about this. If Zachary Conrad had suffered a bad accident that put him in a wheelchair, it'd have made the news. That's your beat, right?"

"Basically," Addison agreed, "but I was out of town visiting our son and his family in L.A. at Christmastime. Before that, I took a few days off to go see our daughter and her gang in Dallas. Sure, the story would be handled by whoever took on my beat, but I was updated on major coverage. I don't recall anything newsworthy about Zachary after I got back." He made a face. "On the other hand, we're so squeezed for space and staff that some things fall through the cracks. Since we went to a morning edition, our deadline is ten P.M.—eleven for a big story and sports scores. Once in a while we miss an otherwise usable piece of news, but with our rival out of business, it's been on TV or the Internet and grown cold by the time we go to press. It's hard enough to keep updating our online version."

"I understand," Judith murmured. "Every so often something happens on the hill that seems like news to me, but I never see it in the paper. Our last power outage in November was an example of that. I never saw a word about it."

"Right. Some drunk hit a pole around midnight, so it was pointless to run it thirty-six hours later. I didn't even bother calling Zachary."

"The other big question is why would he be living in a condo on the lake when the Conrads have a house on the Bluff?"

Addison chuckled. "To escape Hannah? She sounds like a virago."

"You should meet her mother," Judith remarked. "Norma's even worse. More years of practice." She frowned. "I wonder if she has any answers. I'd hate to have to talk to her, especially after the whole family walked out on me. But she must know *something*."

"Want me to do it?" Addison volunteered as they reached the steep ascent of Heraldsgate Avenue.

"Would you?" Judith couldn't keep the relief out of her voice. "I mean, you'd have to wait until there's a formal ID of the body. Hannah will have to be notified as next of kin."

"That should prove interesting," Addison murmured. "She'll have to explain why she showed up with her dead husband at Hillside Manor."

"No she won't. She'll figure the cops won't know what she did. Hannah is unaware that I have a connection to the police."

"Oh?" Addison responded, taking a left onto the street that led to the cul-de-sac. "You don't think she knows about FASTO?"

"I doubt it," Judith said. "She doesn't strike me as the type who'd be curious about anything that didn't affect her directly."

"You're probably right," he allowed, slowing down to make the next turn. "It seems as if I'm your guest again tonight."

"That's fine with me," Judith said. "You can take your choice of the rooms. They're all vacant."

"I'll stay where I did last night . . ." He hit the brake by the driveway. "The garage doors were closed, right?"

Judith leaned forward. "Yes. What . . . ?" In the headlights, she saw Joe's MG parked outside and her Subaru inside, but otherwise, the garage seemed empty. "Pull up behind the MG. I don't see any sign of a horse . . . carcass."

"Just as well," Addison said, reversing just enough to go straight ahead into the driveway. "Stay here. I'll check." He turned off the engine and got out of the car.

From her viewpoint, Judith still couldn't see beyond the void where the dead animal should have been lying. Addison flipped on the lights. The horse had disappeared. Judith got out of the Rover.

"I don't know what to say," she murmured, joining Addison in the garage. Even the water and the feed were gone. "I wonder how anybody got in. You locked the door, didn't you?"

"I thought I did," Addison replied, "but maybe I screwed up with the code. There's no sign of a break-in."

Judith nodded absently. "I'll ask Mother if she heard anything."

"It's going on midnight. Won't she be asleep?"

Judith shook her head. "She's a night owl. Her light's still on."

Addison followed Judith out of the garage and down the walk to the toolshed. As predicted, Gertrude was sitting in her chair, watching Jay Leno. The volume was unbearably loud. "Well," the old lady said when she saw her visitors come inside, "did you wear out your shoes with all that dancing? I could make some pretty good moves in my day, you know." Her gaze fixed on Addison. "Slue Foot there likes to think she can dance, but with a partner like Flat Foot, she hasn't got a prayer."

Judith waved an impatient hand at her mother. "Did you hear anything outside while we were gone?"

Gertrude put a hand behind her left ear. "Eh? I'm deaf, you know. Speak up!"

Judith snatched up the remote and hit the mute button. "No wonder. You make yourself deaf when you . . . never mind. Did you hear a noise outside—"

"I heard you the first time," Gertrude interrupted. "Do you think I'm *that* deaf? No, it's been quiet as a grave around here. Now go away and let me watch my show." She smiled coyly at Addison. "You can stick around. You like Leno?"

"Yes," Addison said, "but I should go. It's almost midnight."

"You young people," Gertrude said with a disgusted wave of her hand. "No stamina. Tsk tsk. That's fine. I've had enough company for one night. Get your beauty sleep. That daughter of mine sure needs it."

Addison smiled politely. "She's had a long day. Good night . . . Gert."

Judith started to hand the remote back to her mother, but paused. "What company, Mother?"

"The Doublegangers," Gertrude said. "Nice boys. Or *boy*. You better make an appointment with the eye doctor. I need new glasses."

"You mean the twins?" Judith asked.

"Twins?" The old lady frowned. "Isn't that the same as Doublegangers?"

"It's *doppelgängers*," Judith said, trying to hang on to her shredding patience. "Andrew and Paulina Paine have twin boys."

Gertrude looked surprised. "Those Paines doubled themselves? Aren't there too many of them already?"

"Yes, but never mind that," Judith persisted. "Why did they come to see you?"

"Why shouldn't they?" Gertrude snapped. "Some youngsters like old people."

Addison smiled. "So do I—and I'm no youngster."

"Oh," Gertrude said, "you're young to me. 'Younger Than

Springtime'—didn't your wife play Nellie Forbush in *South Pacific*?"

"She was the understudy for the lead years ago," Addison replied. "She did three performances when the star got a cold."

"I thought so," Gertrude said. "I missed her in that. I saw the road show years ago when it came to town at the amphitheater on Teal Lake."

"Mother," Judith said, leaning on the card table, "I don't believe the twins just dropped by to say hello. What did they want?"

"Oh . . ." Gertrude made a face. "They wanted to get into the garage. One of them left his wallet in there. I told them to take my house key and look for the secret code in your drawer by the computer machine. They found the wallet, came back, and returned the key. Took 'em long enough, but they were real polite. Can't believe they're related to that Paine pair from church. Maybe they're adopted."

Judith's shoulders sagged. "You gave a key to a couple of strangers and let them go into my private drawer? Are you crazy?"

"Probably," Gertrude said complacently, then glanced at Addison. "Dementia—isn't that the correct term?"

"And," Judith shouted, "stop talking in different voices! You're driving *me* crazy!"

"Short trip," Gertrude murmured. "Pull yourself together, Toots," she went on in her normal tone. "How many times have you run off someplace and told me to let in workmen like that old coot, Skjoval Tolvang, or those other folks who have to fix something you busted?"

Judith was forced to admit her mother had a point. "Okay, okay. At least I know who the Paine twins are. I'm sorry." She moved to the chair and kissed the top of the old lady's head. "Have a good night."

"The same to you," Gertrude muttered. "And don't take any wooden nickels."

Moments later, Judith was in the kitchen. The first thing she did was check the drawer where she kept the garage and other household codes. Sure enough, the garage-door information had been returned. She was checking her registration list for Saturday night when Addison came through the back door.

"You lingered," Judith said. "Was Mother spouting Shakespeare?"

Addison shook his head. "I only stayed a couple of minutes, but I had to park the car and close the garage. I remembered the code." He held out a small scrap of paper. "I found this next to your Subaru. Mean anything?"

Judith stared at the printed words on the soiled scrap:

and MIXED SALES
Tuesday, September 6

"Not offhand," she said. " 'Mixed sales . . .' of what? Bulbs, maybe? It'd be the right time of year."

"But it's not yours?"

She shook her head. "No. Whatever it is was torn off of a printed notice or from a magazine. It's not stationery or newsprint."

Addison smiled wryly. "Yes, I figured out that last part, sometimes being an investigative reporter. I assume the Paine twins dropped it. Or whoever shot the horse. Unless they're one and the same. Or two and the same." He shook himself. "I'm starting to talk like your mother."

"Be careful," Judith warned. "She's contagious."

For a few seconds, she stared at the paper scrap. "It's dirty, as if maybe someone stepped on it. I wonder if a print could be taken from it?"

"You think it's important?"

Judith leaned against the counter. "Probably not. But . . ." She shrugged. "The least little piece can fit into a puzzle."

"You ought to know. You've had more experience than I have with murder. This is only my second foray into homicide." His face grew bleak. "I wasn't much help, despite my wife being one of the victims."

"You had a broken leg," she reminded him. "Courtesy of the killer. You're lucky you weren't a victim, too."

He was staring out the kitchen window into the rain that was coming down harder. "Was I? Lucky, I mean."

Judith put a hand on his arm. "Don't talk like that. Someday you'll find someone to spend the rest of your life with. I know. I did."

Addison turned to look at her. "You didn't *find* Joe—he was always there. You just got him back."

"I got lucky," Judith said. "Maybe you will, too."

"I appreciate the thought." He squared his shoulders and moved toward the swinging doors. "I'm beat. I think I'll head upstairs. Is there anything you need for me to do before I go to sleep on my feet?"

Briefly, Judith studied Addison's face. He had aged more than she realized. Or maybe the deep lines and the lack of sparkle in his usually shrewd eyes were caused by fatigue. And yet he seemed to have changed since his arrival on her doorstep the previous day. An unexpected thought occurred to her, but she dismissed it. Instead, she merely smiled faintly and shook her head. "I'm fine. I'm turning in very soon, too. At least I don't have to get up early to fix breakfast for the guests."

Addison nodded and made his exit. Judith returned to her guest register, checking through the past few days to find anyone who might've opened the safe. Only Jean Rogers struck her as suspicious, but she'd arrived after the murder. The trail had seemingly gone cold.

She moved on to her incoming guests. It didn't take long. The lack of availability on Friday night had forced her to turn down parties who'd wanted to stay through the weekend. Thus she was left with only three of the rooms occupied by paying guests: a pair of middle-aged women from the Chicago area, a married couple from Savannah, and two young men from Lexington, Kentucky, who planned to check out early Sunday morning for a flight to the Middle East. Despite herself, she frowned at the Lexington duo's names: Qani Rahman and Darab Abdel.

Why, she asked herself, *do I have to even pause for a second to wonder about people with Muslim names? It's so unfair. And yet I do it, all because of a bunch of crazed fanatics who slaughter innocent people and, in the process, tarnish millions of decent Muslims?* She shook her head. And then it struck her that within hours, her own husband was going to be accused of a murder he hadn't committed.

What's wrong with me? Why didn't I ask—even beg— Addison if he could somehow stop the story from being released? But he could only keep the news out of the paper. The rest of the media wouldn't hesitate to tell the world that retired police detective Joseph Flynn was accused of killing a helpless man in a wheelchair.

Judith looked out the kitchen window. The Rankers house was still dark. One more thing to worry about, she thought, and picked up the phone to dial Renie's number.

"You're late," her cousin growled into the phone. "Don't tell me you're calling from jail, too."

"You've got caller ID," Judith retorted. "You know I'm home."

"Huh? Oh yeah—right. Didn't look. Assumed it was one of our children calling for money. So what's going on? You need money, too? I haven't got any."

"I need help," Judith said, and explained her delayed reaction to the ruse of Joe's arrest in the hope of ferreting out the real killer. "How can I stop this? It's outrageous."

"It's stupid," Renie said. "There's no guarantee that'll happen. What are those idiots thinking? Has Woody lost his mind?" Her voice kept rising with every question. "Why is Joe going along with it? Why doesn't he call Bub? *Has everybody gone nuts except thee and me?*"

Judith had to hold the phone away from her ear to keep her cousin's voice from piercing an eardrum. "Hey, keep it down, coz! You'll wake up Bill."

"Bill wears earplugs to bed," Renie said in her normal voice. "He says I snore. Is that true?"

"Not that I know of," Judith said. "It's that gum-chewing in bed that drives me nuts when we travel together. Don't get sidetracked. I need some sensible advice."

"Spring Joe," Renie said. "Kidnap him. Whatever. Just get him out of the cops' clutches. They don't know what they're doing. I'm surprised at Woody. He's very sharp. The only thing I can think of is that he's desperate." She paused for a couple of beats. "Or he's being pressured. How long has he been on this new job?"

"Two weeks," Judith said, realizing what Renie might be thinking. "Woody and Joe—*both* in the wrong place at the wrong time. They've been set up for a reason. But what can it be? Something to do with the police department's internal affairs? Or, as Addison has hinted, even higher up?"

"That sounds more like it," Renie remarked. "I'll bet it's not just recent dirt, but something from the past. Why else drag Uncle Al into it? He hasn't been a serious player for at least fifteen, twenty years."

"But he knows where the bodies are buried—literally," Judith said, warming to the subject. "Remember those stories he and Uncle Vince used to tell about the Teamsters meetings they attended and how anyone who disagreed with the bosses was hustled off and never seen again?"

"Right. The only witnesses were bottom fish out in the bay. But," Renie went on, "that was fifty, sixty years ago and some of those union leaders went to the slammer. I doubt that whatever's going on now would go back that far."

"Maybe not," Judith allowed. "That doesn't make me feel any better about Joe being the fall guy."

"Well . . ." Renie paused again. "You could always solve the whole thing before they charge him."

"Coz! I don't even know the problem, let alone the solution."

"True." She paused again. "How about this? I confess and they put me in jail?"

"What?"

"Why not? My projects keep getting interrupted. If I were in jail, I'd have some peace and quiet. In fact, I was just getting started when you called."

"Sorry," Judith mumbled. "I shouldn't have bothered you."

"That's okay," Renie said. "Maybe there's no rush on this lighting-department project now that Zachary's . . . say, what if Sam Forrester knows something about this? He's the guy I'm working with. If Zachary was hanging out in a condo in a wheelchair, a lot of people who worked with him must know something."

"Of course! I forgot about your connection to lighting— excuse the bad joke," Judith said, revitalized. "Why didn't I think of that?"

"Why didn't *I*? It should've dawned on me sooner, but I got so distracted with all the Paines and then Bill and Uncle Al being hustled off by the cops. I know Sam fairly well. He's their PR guy and we've worked together before. I'll call him tomorrow, even if it's Saturday."

"Great!" Judith exclaimed. "Any chance you'll be up before ten?"

"Not in a thousand years, even for you," Renie replied, "but I'll call him before noon. I've got his home phone number. Wait—I just thought of something. My deadline is for mid-February, but originally it was set for the end of this month . . . hold on."

Judith sat down at the kitchen table, hearing shuffling noises at the other end of the line. A glance at the schoolhouse clock showed it was twelve-thirty. She had perked up when reminded that her cousin had an in at the lighting department, but was yawning when she heard Renie speak into her ear.

"This is really interesting," she said to Judith. "I was notified of the deadline change just before New Year's Eve. The reason for it, and I quote from the message Sam e-mailed to me, 'We have some leeway with your retired employee newsletter design. Both Francine Sloane-Marcos and Zachary Conrad will be out of the office for much of January. Francine is going skiing for ten days in Switzerland and Zachary is taking a paid leave of absence for two weeks to work on a special project. Hope this eases up your scheduled workload. Happy New Year!' What do you make of that?"

Judith didn't answer right away. "Not personal reasons . . . a 'special project' . . . doesn't that sound to you as if he'd either been given an unofficial assignment or at the very least had someone over him who could okay whatever he was going to do?"

"Definitely," Renie replied, "since he was getting paid for it."

"A very high price," Judith murmured. "He paid for it with his life. I wonder if he knew what he was getting . . ." She sucked in her breath. "Whoa! No mention of his health or lack thereof. Surely if he'd been crippled, it would've been a medical leave, right?"

"Yes," Renie agreed. "Does this mean Zachary was sitting in for someone else and the wrong man was killed?"

"It could," Judith said. "But it could also mean something else. Maybe Joe and Woody aren't the only ones who are the fall guys. It's beginning to sound as if Zachary Conrad was set up, too."

Chapter Seventeen

Despite being dog-tired, Judith had trouble going to sleep that night. Her brain couldn't stop asking questions she couldn't answer. She had to force herself to close her eyes. But she still saw Joe, adamantly resigned to his fate; Woody, grim and yet somehow helpless; Arlene and Carl, waiting tensely in the ER; Addison, wistful and worried; Zachary Conrad, dead in the city morgue; and, more vividly, a phantom horse galloping across the night sky high above Heraldsgate Hill.

It was the horse that woke her up. She'd been dreaming, and rolled over to reach for Joe. Feeling nothing but the smooth flannel sheet, she was jarred into reality. What was the dream and what was hard fact? Pummeling the vacant space in the bed with her fist, she was on the verge of tears—until she realized that the first streaks of light had appeared on the eastern horizon beyond the Rankerses' house. Propping herself up on one elbow, she looked at the clock on the nightstand. Its red numbers informed her it was 7:33.

I've overslept, she thought, panicking. And then remembered that there were no guests preparing to come downstairs at eight o'clock. Gertrude, of course, would be waiting for breakfast. *I must have slept, but I don't feel rested.* With a twinge of guilt, she lay back down, rolled over, and went back to sleep.

The telephone woke her up. Struggling out of a drowsy fog, she fumbled for the receiver and croaked a hello into the earpiece. A sharp voice at the other end made her realize the mistake.

"Sorry," she said thickly. "Yes?"

"Are you okay?" Renie demanded in an anxious voice.

"Yes," Judith said, awkwardly sitting up. The clock registered 10:25. "I was asleep."

"Good grief!" Renie exclaimed. "Did you use knockout drops?"

"No," Judith replied, adjusting to the dull morning light. "I was tired. What's going on?"

"Well . . ." Renie hesitated. "You'd better get yourself together. Then we'll talk. It's not a crisis. I have some things to run by you. Okay?"

"Uh . . . I guess. Give me twenty minutes."

"I'll make it thirty." Renie hung up.

Fifteen minutes later, Judith had showered, shampooed her hair, blown it almost dry, and gotten dressed. By 10:40, she was entering the kitchen, where Addison Kirby was sitting at the table drinking coffee and reading the newspaper.

"Hello there," he said, closing the sports section. "Relax. Nothing in this morning's edition about Joe being charged with homicide. I knew there wouldn't be—they were already past deadline last night. I doubt it'll be in tomorrow's paper either. The early edition of the front page has to go to press today to be delivered outside the metro area."

Judith took a deep breath. "That's a relief. But Mother must be having a cat fit."

"Mrs. G. is just fine," Addison assured her. "I made her ham and eggs with toast. In fact, we had breakfast together and discussed Tennessee Williams. She considers him a better American playwright than Arthur Miller, but admits she only saw one of August Wilson's, *Joe Turner's Come and Gone*."

"Good Lord," Judith murmured, bracing herself against the fridge. "How did I miss her penchant for theater? I've always thought she considered *Ozzie and Harriet* the epitome of American drama."

Addison's hazel eyes twinkled. "According to your mother, there was a long period during your first marriage when you had limited contact with her—or anyone in the family."

Steadying herself, Judith nodded. "True. Dan held me a virtual captive. Sometimes I could see Mother on Sundays. I hardly saw Renie at all." She paused to get a mug from the cupboard and pour herself some coffee. "I did talk to Renie at night occasionally after Dan had gone to sleep—or passed out." Judith sat down opposite Addison. "But when I did see or even talk to Mother, our conversation necessarily stayed on more vital topics than the arts. I had no idea what she was doing most of the time I was with Dan."

Addison's expression was sympathetic. "That's grim. I'm sorry."

Judith shrugged. "You needn't apologize. It's just the way things were. I was also working two jobs. That didn't give me much time for extracurricular activities, even if Dan hadn't been a jackass about cutting me off from my family."

"No," he said quietly. "I suppose it didn't." His smile was wry. "It's odd how nobody ever knows what really goes on between married people once the door is closed."

"How true." She paused, wondering if Addison was about to reveal some deep dark secret about his own marriage.

But he didn't. Instead, he stood up, refilled his coffee mug, and picked up a sheet of paper next to the computer. "Journalists have insatiable curiosity. I don't know much about gardening and bulbs, but I decided to put 'mixed sales' into the browser. A long shot, but maybe that term is appropriate." He slid the printed sheet across the table. "What do you think?"

Judith's eyes widened as she read the various Web sites, beginning with *Tattersalls* **Mixed Sale**|| *Quality Horses! 2005 January SELECT* **MIXED SALE** . . . *at the Meadowlands in New Jersey.* The sites that followed were for similar upcoming sales around the country. "Horses! Is that what this is all about?"

Addison lifted his shoulders. "Could be. At least a couple of former city and county types are on the state racing commission. What about Uncle Al? Isn't he a betting man when it comes to the ponies?"

"Oh, and then some," Judith said under her breath. "He's probably at the track right now watching simulcasts from the courses that are open this time of year. I always wondered when he had his restaurants open if . . ."

"Yes?" Addison's penetrating eyes seemed to be reading her mind.

She threw her hands up in the air. "Oh, you know what I mean. They were making book behind the closed door. Horses, ball games, prizefights, the tortoise and the hare, for all I know. Renie and I were never allowed to take so much as a peek, but even now—" She stopped abruptly. "Let's just say that Cousin Sue and her husband, Ken, along with their two sons, have carried on the family tradition in a more . . . legalized way. I think."

Addison looked puzzled. "But Sue isn't Uncle Al's daughter?"

"Right, Uncle Al never married," Judith replied. "She's Aunt Ellen and Uncle Win's girl. They live in Beatrice, Nebraska. Sue married Ken Dalton, who was already in the restaurant business over on the Eastside. She met him on one of Aunt Ellen and Uncle Win's annual visits out here. Sue and Ken run a big poker room in the county, such things being illegal in some of the towns around here, as you probably know."

Addison smiled. "Yes, I've heard some interesting tidbits about their seemingly innocent family-style restaurant. More like La Famiglia. Didn't somebody try to blow them up?"

"Yes, on Christmas Eve morning a few years ago," Judith said. "The timing upset all of us. We didn't think Sue and Ken would make it for Santa Claus's arrival behind the curtain. Fortunately, their archrival was caught and is now serving time in the state penitentiary. Doing fifteen to twenty, and he was eighty-five when he set the bomb in their truck, so he may never be eligible for parole. If it hadn't been for the long-lost relative who showed up with astounding news about Great-Uncle . . ." Seeing Addison's expression grow more and more quizzical, Judith clamped her mouth shut. "Never mind. We ended up having a wonderful Christmas, despite all the accidents." She winced. "Oh my God, if you're channeling Mother, I'm starting to sound like Arlene! Which reminds me," she said, getting up, "I must call about Carl."

"Their SUV is in the driveway," Addison said.

Judith had taken the phone from its cradle. "Good. That may mean it's not serious." She dialed the number hurriedly and was relieved to hear Carl's voice at the other end.

"Oh, Carl!" she exclaimed. "How do you feel?"

"Better," he replied, "except when I stand, sit, or lie down."

Judith frowned. "I thought you were . . . dying."

"Not quite," he said with a trace of his usual droll manner. "It just felt like it. My back went out. I shouldn't have carried the ladder over to your house. I had to virtually crawl back home and ended up under the table. I was headed for the sofa, but couldn't make it that far."

"You should sue the Beard-Smythes," Judith declared. "I may do that, too. They caused me a lot of actual and emotional grief."

"We should team up," Carl said. "Hold on—Arlene wants me to move the piano."

"You don't have a piano," Judith said, "and even if you did—"

"It's a dollhouse piano," Carl said. "One of the grandkids left it on the stove and Arlene's got her hands full of what looks like her Anything-Goes Casserole. Or Tulip's dog dish. Talk to you later."

Addison turned around as Judith hung up. "Positive news?"

"For a change," Judith said, sitting back down at the table. "It was Carl's back. Not that backs can't be a pain. I—" She stopped. "Speaking of pains, I wonder if Hannah has ID'd the body."

"I was just about to check on that," Addison said, putting the newspaper aside. "Let's see if I can find a friendly contact at City Hall." He got out his cell and tapped in a number.

Judith realized she was hungry, despite not having much appetite. Cold cereal was quick and easy. By the time she'd sat down again with a bowl of cornflakes, Addison was chatting up someone somewhere who somehow knew something. It occurred to her that his reporter's job was not unlike her own when she just happened to become involved in a murder investigation. Chatter, banter, clichés, and pleasantries—all aimed at wringing vital information out of a witness or suspect. The thought galvanized her into action. She got up and was about to grab her own phone when Addison clicked off.

"Hannah Paine Conrad is not at home," he announced. "They called her three times this morning, but no luck. Finally, they sent a squad car to her house on the Bluff, but no one came to the door."

"She's done a bunk?"

Addison shrugged. "They'll go back later. Check to see if her mail's been taken in. See if there are any Conrad cars parked in the garage or on the street." He snapped his fingers. "I wonder if the cops looked to see if the newspaper was on the porch. Circulation may have plummeted, but the Conrads are the type who'd still be subscribers. Zachary would want to keep track of any city lighting references that might not make it to the online version."

Judith had turned thoughtful. "I wonder if they have a second residence." She picked up the phone. "Maybe I can chat up somebody, too," she said, flipping through her Rolodex.

"I'm going to get my laptop," Addison said, rising from the chair. "I want to check our 'mixed sales' around here. The Internet listings were all for the next month or so in other parts of the country." He headed out of the kitchen to the main stairs.

Judith had found the senior Paines' home number. Norma answered on the third ring. She burst into full-throated throttle before Judith could even identify herself. "I am so eager for a full report on the family's evening! Have they finished breakfast? What did you serve? Did anyone have a problem with their dietary needs? Were they all pleased with my very generous gift? Please let them know that I must hear all about it as soon as they can get in touch. I'm so thrilled that they could all make it to your luxurious and expensive B&B! I had a feeling that perhaps—" Norma suddenly stopped, coughing into Judith's ear. "Oh! So . . . sorry . . . I . . ." She coughed some more.

Judith took advantage of Norma's interrupted discourse. "They left right after dinner. There was a bit of a dustup. I assumed you knew." She paused. Norma had stopped coughing, but was blowing her nose, a trumpeting sound that made Judith cringe. "I hate to tell you and Wilbur what happened.

I gather that you haven't spoken to anyone in the family this morning."

"No," Norma said between sniffs and snorts. "Why . . . what do you mean, they left?"

Judith wasn't prepared to break the bad, even tragic, news to Norma Paine. "I don't want to upset you, but you should talk to one of your children as soon as you can. There's been a serious problem that only they should tell you about. I'm just a bystander. Please. And if there's any way I can help, let me know. Good-bye, Norma." Judith hung up. There was nothing more she could do for the senior Paines.

"Awful," she said out loud, and was startled when the word seemed to echo from the kitchen hall. Swerving around, she saw Renie hurrying in her direction.

"Are you deaf?" her cousin demanded, putting a Tupperware container on the counter by the cupboards.

Judith did her best to regain her composure. "It seemed weird. I heard you say 'awful' just when I did."

Renie scowled. "I didn't say 'awful,' I said 'waffle.'" She pointed to the container. "You keep asking me to bring some of my secret-ingredient waffles to try. I figured this would be a good day to do it because you wouldn't have to serve your guests breakfast. I brought enough batter so you can make Aunt Gert . . . what's wrong? You look . . . awful."

"You already said that," Judith retorted, squaring her shoulders. "I'm . . . just a little off track. Having a pseudo-homicidal husband can do that to you. Not to mention that the man you thought was your guest is a corpse."

Renie waved a careless hand. "Like that's the first time. You should be used to the guest corpse. Want me to make you a waffle?"

"No, thanks. I was eating cornflakes before you came. At least I think I was." She glanced at the almost-full bowl on the table. "I guess I got distracted. By the way, Carl's fine.

I mean, he's not fine, but he's not almost dead. He hurt his back."

"Oh." Renie flopped into the chair Addison had vacated. "Eat. I was going to call you back, but I ran out of root beer and had to go to Falstaff's, so I decided to drop off the waffle batter I made for tomorrow morning so I wouldn't have to get up early to make them for Bill and I could sleep in and go to noon Mass at—"

"Stop." Judith stared at Renie over a spoonful of cornflakes. "You really shouldn't get up before ten. You're worthless for the rest of the day. You're like a windup toy, on autopilot. How many cars did you hit on your way to my house?"

"Two." Renie made a face. "And a truck. No serious damage and I fled the scene. *Scenes*. I always tell Bill somebody must've hit me in the parking lot. You're right. I have to collect my thoughts. Give me a couple of minutes. Eat." She ran a hand through her already unruly short chestnut hair. "Or did I say that already?"

Judith munched on some of the now-soggy cornflakes and tried to be patient. At least a couple of minutes passed before Renie seemed to have turned on her brain.

"Okay," she said, pulling herself closer to the table. "Let's start with the basketball game."

It took a couple of seconds for Judith to remember anything about a basketball game. "Oh—you mean the one that Bill and Uncle Al went to but somehow ended up in police custody?"

"Yes, *that* basketball game," Renie said. "The old chum Uncle Al ran into was Lloyd Volpe. He needed Uncle Al's help."

Judith put down her spoon. "Lloyd Volpe? That name's familiar."

"Being Arlene's next-door neighbor, you'd know him as

the Silver Fox, former police chief and captor of the dreaded Underwear Thief. It was possibly his greatest achievement while running the department."

"Not true," Judith said. "Volpe was a better police chief than some we've had. Joe thought he was okay."

"Whatever," Renie remarked with a shrug. "All I know is that when he was chief I got a ticket on my way back from dropping our kids off at SOTS school just because I didn't stop in an unmarked crosswalk. If it wasn't marked, why was that gimpy old lady walking across the street? I never did figure that one out. The cop who gave me the ticket told me that the next time I saw somebody jaywalking, I could run 'em down without so much as a 'ha ha, gotcha!'"

"Could we get to the point?"

"Oh, sure." Renie folded her hands on the table. "Lloyd wanted Uncle Al to unload about some of the gambling operations he knew around town. I'd forgotten that although Volpe is ten or fifteen years younger than Uncle Al, he used to coach high school basketball before he joined the force, so they go way back. Thus both Uncle Al and Bill had to go downtown to talk to Woody and Joe and the young guy, Del."

Judith frowned. "Why wasn't Lloyd there when we arrived?"

Renie grinned. "He wanted to stay and yak it up with the coaches after the postgame locker room session. That's why Uncle Al had to take his own car and why Bill had to go with him."

"So what beans did Uncle Al spill?"

Renie laughed. "You know how he is. Sometimes I call him Uncle Anecdote. He's got more stories—most of them true, all of them incredible—and he never answers a question directly. But by the time he's finished, you're so entertained that you've forgotten what you wanted to know in the first place."

Judith wasn't amused. "You mean Joe and Woody got zip?"

"No, but Bill had a lot of laughs."

Judith's stern gaze fixed on Renie's humorous expression. "You're holding back. You as much as told me so on the phone. Give, coz. Was Dan involved in something illegal when he owned the restaurant?"

Renie sobered at once. "Lord, no! Dan didn't have that much ambition."

"He also couldn't say no to his so-called chums, many of whom were on the seedy side."

"Yeah, right," Renie agreed, assuming a less cheerful expression. "Uncle Al talked about the Teamsters, not in the past, but more up-to-date stuff, especially truck drivers on city routes. He keeps up with his old buddy Oly Oldstrom, who's still working at union headquarters."

"Oly!" Judith said in mild surprise. "Longshoreman, strong as an ox, worked on the docks until he hit eighty. Former college football player."

Renie nodded. "Also a basketball ref, along with Mr. Locke, my high school geometry teacher, onetime SOTS PE teacher Tony Morelli, husband of Martha, cookbook maven. And, of course, our former sheriff, Sid Flaherty, who's been out of jail for ten years and lives in Arizona."

Judith frowned. "Was Sid the sheriff with the cathouse?"

"No, that was Freddy Ferguson, one county up. He was paroled at least ten, fifteen years ago and died about six months later. I don't think he was ever a basketball ref. Too tired from hustling his hookers up and down Highway 99."

Judith shook her head. "Why can't we elect honest public officials around here?"

"We do," Renie said, "but they're so boring. We have lots

of rain and gray skies. We need something to pep us up during October, November, December, January—"

"Stop! You like the rain and gray as much as I do. Stick to the point."

"Two points, actually," Renie said complacently. "Which is one of them, as in college basketball games. No three-point line back in the old days. How many games were fixed, with the refs in on it? If so, who were the fixers who did the fixing? And that brings us back to former sheriff Sid Flaherty, who was convicted of accepting bribes."

"On basketball games?"

"No, but he may have done. Uncle Al hedged a bit on that one, though he himself insisted he never did such a thing. Uncle Al, I mean. He was always on the square, as he told Joe and Woody. The bribes were of Teamster truck drivers who were given money to keep their mouths shut about illegal cargo and businesses along their routes."

"How far back?" Judith inquired—and jumped when she felt a hand on her shoulder. "Addison! Have you been eavesdropping?"

"Of course," he replied, moving behind Judith to sit down in the chair next to her. "Serena saw me come in from the dining room."

"Sorry," Renie said with an obvious lack of repentance. "I was fixated on answering Coz's questions. She seems to think I lack focus."

"Tell me more about illicit deliveries," Addison said. "We may be onto something."

Judith swiveled in her chair to look at Addison. "We may be? How? What did you find out about those mixed sales?"

Addison looked pleased with himself. "The scrap of paper refers to a horse sale in this state last September. All very much on the up-and-up. But I made some phone calls and found out that one of the biggest buyers was Reginald Beard-Smythe."

Judith was aghast. "Reggie? Why? For the hunt club?"

"Hey," Renie yipped. "What are you talking about?"

"Horses," Judith said abruptly. "Addison found a scrap of paper in the garage after we discovered the dead horse was gone."

Renie looked as if she was about to dive across the table. *"What?"*

"Never mind," Judith barked. "I'll explain later." She turned back to Addison. "Well?"

"I managed to track somebody on the Eastside who occasionally sends in news items to the paper about the hunt club," he said, his expression turning grim. "They rarely acquire new horses. The members have their own. In fact, that's a problem. Once the hunt season is over, the owners often dump their animals. Turns out that one of the dumping grounds is ARBS Food Processing, Incorporated. Guess who owns the company?"

"ARBS . . ." Judith's dark eyes lit up. "Alicia and Reggie? Are you saying that those horses are . . ." She gulped and couldn't go on.

Addison nodded. "Yes. Those horses are horse meat."

Chapter Eighteen

J udith was horrified. Renie looked disgusted. Addison remained grim. "It gets worse," he said after a long pause. "ARBS supplies some of the local take-out restaurants on and around Heraldsgate Hill. And while Reggie owns the company, it's actually run by Andrew Paine. Reggie is an airhead and thus a figurehead."

Judith was holding her head in her hands. "Wait. I can't take all this in at once. What does any of this have to do with Zachary Conrad getting murdered?"

Renie slumped in her chair. "Holy crap! You don't care about anything that isn't connected to a dead body! Lighten up! Isn't horse meat of at least some diabolical interest? Would you rather we all turned into cannibals?"

Judith went on the defensive. "You seem to forget Joe has indicated that whatever went on at the condo with the murdered man had some tie to the B&B. How could I *not* believe him or try to make a connection when he's been set up?"

"Oh." Renie straightened up in her chair. "Yes, you have a point. But could we please get back to the dead-horse disappearance?"

Before either Judith or Addison could respond, Gertrude burst into the hall, her motorized wheelchair at full speed.

"Stop me!" she cried, passing the pantry, the coatrack, and flying into the kitchen. "My brakes are busted!"

Renie leaped up to grab the nearest armrest. One of the wheels banged against a table leg and stopped moving. Gertrude's gnarled hands were pressed against her breast as she bent over and gasped for breath. Judith slid off her chair, risking her artificial hip as she reached down to put her arms around her mother.

"Are you okay?" she asked breathlessly. "Mother! Stop shaking! You're safe." Judith managed to turn the chair's motor off in the hope that it would ease the old lady's breathing. "Mother?"

Gertrude slowly lifted her head. To Judith's shock, the old lady was smiling as the gasps became a cackle. "Dummies!" she croaked, wiping her eyes with a rumpled handkerchief. "Scared you real good, didn't I?"

Renie was examining the wheelchair. "Aunt Gert, you're a fraud! You didn't put the brakes on." She flipped the switch back and forth. "Why did you try to scare us to death? Doesn't poor Judith have enough trouble already? Or are you trying to impress Addison with your derring-do so he'll write you up in the newspaper?"

"Put a sock in it," Gertrude rasped. "Just because Knucklehead's in the clink doesn't mean my little girl can't have some fun." She cast her watery eyes at Addison. "That one's a real improvement. He even makes the furniture look better. But that's not why I'm here." She frowned at her daughter. "Stand up, dopey. You've got foreigners to see you. Want me to send them in the back way or go around to the front?"

Judith couldn't help but give her mother a reproachful look before checking the time. It was a few minutes past noon. "The Kentuckians," she mumbled. "They must not realize check-in isn't until four. Damn!" Unceremoniously pushing the wheelchair aside, she headed down the hallway to the back door. "If they're in the yard, they might as well come in this way," she called over her shoulder.

The door was already open. Judith opened the screen and stared in astonishment at the two people standing by the birdbath.

"Hi," Geoff Owens said. "We were on our way out of town and wanted to thank you again for your hospitality."

Foreigners. Judith never thought of Canadians as *foreigners.* Next-door neighbors was more her style, living closer as she did to Canada than to either of the adjacent states. "That's very kind of you," she said with forced enthusiasm. "Won't you come in?"

"We really shouldn't," Cindy Owens said. "There's snow in the forecast and we want to get back over the border at Sumas before dark. We happened to see your mother coming out of her little cottage."

"Oh, dear," Judith said apologetically, "we must not have heard you ring the front doorbell." She glanced at Renie and Addison who, along with Gertrude, had come out to the porch. "Did either of you hear it?"

"No," Addison replied.

Renie shook her head. "Shall I go see if it works?"

"Good idea," Judith said.

"Uh . . . wait." Geoff looked embarrassed. "We didn't try the front door. It . . . it seemed wrong when we weren't official guests, so we decided to come around the other way."

"That's right," Cindy agreed. "We never got a chance to see your garden. It looked so nice in the front, even if it is winter. We wondered what the back was like. It's charming, with the birdbath and the statue of Saint Franklin."

"Saint Francis," Judith said softly.

"Oh!" Cindy exclaimed, pressing her hands against her cheeks. "Of course! I'm Presbyterian. We don't do saints so much."

Judith smiled. "He's the patron saint of animals. I thought you might know of him if you have friends who are into animal rescue."

The young couple exchanged quick glances. "Well," Geoff said, "we are, too, in a small way. Your mother told us she'd recently been asked to temporarily keep someone's horse."

Gertrude frowned. "I did? Hunh. Oh." She gazed into her lap and scrunched up her handkerchief. "That was a joke. How could I put a horse in that chicken coop where I live?" She reversed the wheelchair and zipped back into the house.

"It looks very cozy," Cindy said, taking her husband's arm. "We should be going now. Thanks again."

The couple was turning away when Arlene came into the backyard. Seeing the trio on the walk, she stopped. "Oh, Judith, I'm sorry. I was wondering if you had any tomato paste. I'm making a casserole . . ." Her blue eyes widened. "Cindy Rogers!" Arlene rushed forward. "I thought I'd missed you. How wonderful to see you all grown up!" She enveloped the young woman in a smothering embrace.

"Mrs. Rankers?" Cindy said in a muffled voice.

"Of course!" Arlene cried, loosening her hold. "Let me think . . . you were twelve or thirteen when I last saw you at Donner & Blitzen? You're lovely. But you had promise back then, despite the braces, the orthopedic shoes, and the corrective hat."

"Thanks," Cindy said uncertainly. "Do you live around here?"

"Next door," Arlene replied, keeping her arm around Cindy and drawing her up the porch steps. "Come, sit, tell me about your mother. She mentioned something about foot surgery in her Christmas letter, but I didn't know if . . ." They disappeared inside.

Geoff looked bewildered. "Who is that?"

"My neighbor," Judith said. "She worked with your

mother-in-law at one of our department stores several years ago. Let's go in. It's chilly out here."

Geoff seemed uneasy, but he trooped after Judith. "We really should be on our way."

"I already am," Renie said. "I'll catch up with you later, coz. Bye, Addison." She blew Gertrude a kiss. "The next time you pull a stunt like that, I'm going to let you crash and burn, you crazy old coot."

"Go ahead," Gertrude muttered. "I need to have some fun once in a while, Toots."

"Take a seat," Judith said to Geoff. "Your wife won't escape from Arlene for at least ten minutes. Now tell me the real reason why you came back here."

Geoff slipped into the place that Renie had occupied, warily eyeing Judith and Addison. Gertrude edged her wheelchair closer to the table. "This is fun, too," the old lady declared. "Are we playing grill the suspect? Can I pretend this good-looking foreigner is Lunkhead and give him a hot-foot?"

"Mother . . ." Judith began in a warning tone, "please."

Gertrude shrugged. "Please yourself." She adjusted her baggy cardigan around her shoulders and gave Addison her sweetest smile.

"See here, Mrs. Flynn," Geoff began earnestly, "I can't tell you why we came back. Word of honor." He glanced at Gertrude. "As a so-called foreigner, Queen Elizabeth couldn't make me tell her the reason. I might add that she'd approve wholeheartedly if I could."

"Off with his head," Gertrude murmured.

Judith ignored her mother. "Let me take a wild guess. You came to fetch the horse."

The color drained from Geoff's face. "I . . . we . . . how did you know?"

"It's not exactly nuclear physics," Judith said, trying not

to sound impatient. "You're involved with animal rescue people. Judging from the distance you mentioned between my B&B and where you were headed when you left, I assume you intended to collect the horse that was in our garage and take it to their sanctuary not far from the mountains, Pedro's Paradise. Someone got here before you could get the poor animal and shot it. Then someone carted it off last night—evening, I should say. The horse's carcass was gone when we . . . I returned from downtown shortly before midnight."

Geoff gaped at Judith. "You mean Son of Scarlet's . . . dead?"

Judith was bewildered. "The horse that was brought here was called Knickers."

"Oh," Geoff said, "that was the name the previous owner used, but the horse had been renamed." His voice was leaden. "This is awful. Son of Scarlet is a Thoroughbred."

"I'm so sorry," Judith said. "Do you have any idea who would want to destroy the poor animal?"

Geoff couldn't seem to answer right away. "No," he said at last. "Stealing, maybe. But there's no way anyone who knows anything about horseflesh would kill an animal like that one."

"Who told you about the horse in the first place?" Judith asked.

Once again, Geoff became reticent. "I won't say more." He spread his hands in a pleading gesture. "I can't involve innocent people. "Not even you and Mr. Flynn."

"Actually," Addison began, "I'm not . . ."

Judith dug her nails into Addison's arm under the table. "My husband and I are involved. Deeply so. But I understand. Go ahead, extract your wife from Mrs. Rankers's fond clutches and drive safely."

Geoff's whole body sagged with apparent relief. "Thank

you. After what you just told me about Son of Scarlet, I'm not sure we'll be heading home after all. In fact, do you have a vacancy for tonight?"

Judith considered the pros and cons of hosting the couple again. "I do. I had a special event last night and couldn't accept guests who wanted to stay over the weekend. You can take your previous room."

"Thanks," Geoff said, getting to his feet. "I'll talk to Cindy."

"Good luck," Judith said.

Geoff went through the swinging doors and almost collided with his wife. "We're staying here," he told her. "Mrs. Flynn has room for us because of last night's auction party."

"Oh!" Cindy looked uncertain. "Are you sure we should?"

"Yes," he replied. "Come on, we have work to do. It seems we don't need that horse trailer after all." He turned back to Judith. "We'll see you later. Okay?"

"Of course," Judith said with a tight little smile.

The Owenses took their leave as Arlene reentered the kitchen. "Well! Such fun catching up with Cindy now that she's all grown and married," she said, putting her arm around Gertrude's sloping shoulders. "Oh, the tomato paste! Judith, do you—"

"In the pantry," Judith interrupted. "Take two. I've got plenty."

"No, just one. I'll pay you back," Arlene insisted, hugging Gertrude before starting toward the back hall. "I always do." She disappeared into the pantry, but emerged within seconds. "Time for Carl's back massage." She paused to gaze at the can of tomato paste. "I wonder if this would help his . . . never mind." She hurried out of the house.

Gertrude had rolled as far as the fridge. "I should leave you two lovebirds alone. I'm taking my lunch with me—stuff I like, for a change." As good as her word, she stockpiled cheeses, lunch meats, and dill pickles into her lap. "It's time for my Saturday TV comedy show. There's a channel that has a recap of our state legislature not at work." She flipped the switch on her wheelchair and headed down the hall.

Judith awkwardly stood up. "It's not yet one o'clock and I slept in and I still feel worn-out." She poured a glass of water and took two Excedrin for the onset of another headache. "What do you make of the Owenses' attempted rescue of the dead horse?"

Addison had also risen from his chair. "What am I to make of you clawing me when Geoff Owens thought I was Mr. Flynn?"

"Sorry," Judith said, draining the water glass. "Did you want to get sidetracked about how and why the real Mr. Flynn is in police custody?"

"I'm not complaining," Addison said, wandering over to the counter under the cupboard. "You didn't draw blood. I was flattered."

"Don't say things like that," Judith snapped. "The last thing I need right now is . . . complications."

"I apologize." He leaned against the counter, looking embarrassed.

"Never mind," Judith said. "Did you notice that Geoff mentioned the school auction?"

Addison shrugged. "So?"

"I referred to last night's disaster as an event. So how did Geoff know it was connected to the SOTS auction?"

"Good point." Addison turned thoughtful. "I feel like a fool."

"Why?"

"For embarrassing both of us. I apologize. Widowerhood doesn't sit well with me." He gave Judith a crooked smile. "I'm calling Paulina."

Judith was so disconcerted that she couldn't immediately

remember who Paulina was. "Oh—you mean about the twins and the horse?"

"It's as good an excuse as any," he murmured, and left the kitchen via the dining room.

Fine, Judith thought. *I don't need an excuse to call Joe.* She picked up the phone and dialed police headquarters. Five minutes later, she finally got through to someone who seemed to know something. "Captain Price and Mr. Flynn have left the building," the faintly familiar male voice at the other end informed her.

"Del?" Judith said.

"Uh . . . yes?"

"In case you've forgotten, this is Joe's *wife,* Judith *Flynn.* Are you the only one holding down the fort on the condo homicide case?"

"As a matter of fact," he responded, "I was about to go home. If I can remember where I live at this point."

"Before you do that," she said, assuming a less antagonistic tone, "please tell me if you people have tracked down Hannah Conrad."

"We haven't," Del admitted. "We called her parents, but they refused to talk to us. Mrs. Paine was very rude and hung up on me."

Judith sighed. "Why don't you arrest her for impeding justice?"

"Under the circumstances, that would be unwise," Del said primly. "We can hardly do that when she hasn't yet been informed that her son-in-law has been murdered."

"I suppose not. Where have Joe and Woody gone?"

"I can't tell you," Del said.

"It should be a food supply company called ARBS on the southwest edge of Heraldsgate Hill," Judith said. "If not, tell them that's their next stop." She hung up the phone before the young tec could respond.

Originally, her next task had been to run down the twins. But Addison was going to get in touch with their mother, Paulina. Given his current state of lonely self-pity and Mrs. Andrew Paine's obvious disdain for her husband, *touch* might be the operative word. Chase and Chad looked about twenty years old. It was possible that they didn't live at home. She got out the phone book, but there was no listing for either of the twins. Thwarted, she shoved the directory back in the cupboard. Maybe it was time to put aside solving the mysteries that hovered over the Paines and the rest of what seemed to be a frustratingly complex homicide case that might or might not lead to someone at City Hall.

Without Phyliss, who rarely worked weekends, Judith had to make sure the rooms were ready for the incoming guests. She spent the next hour on the second floor. Since the Paines hadn't stayed overnight, there wasn't much to do except some light housekeeping. Assuming Addison wouldn't move out, she didn't bother with Room One.

A little after three o'clock, Judith was using some of her leftovers from the previous evening for the social hour when she realized she hadn't seen or heard Addison since he'd mentioned calling Paulina Paine. Going to the front door, she looked outside to see if his Rover was parked where he'd left it after they'd returned from downtown the previous night.

The car was nowhere in sight. She went to the end of the porch, thinking he might have pulled it into the driveway. The Rover wasn't there either. Maybe he'd gone to see Paulina. Or maybe he'd just gone. Maybe that was just as well.

Back inside, she heard the grandfather clock chime the quarter hour after three. Otherwise, the house was quiet. Too quiet. Despite being a social animal, Judith occasionally appreciated a respite from other human beings, but there was something unnatural about the silence that enveloped her.

On a whim, she went out the back door and opened the garage. Maybe there was something that Addison had overlooked when he'd checked the interior after discovering that the horse carcass had been removed. The first thing she realized was that the temperature was dropping. Though the rain was fairly light, the clouds were heavy and low. It felt as if it could snow. Judith decided that as soon as she had given the garage a once-over, she'd move Joe's MG back into its usual spot next to her Subaru.

The first thing that struck her about the garage was that it was relatively clean. The twins must've provided the horse with feed and water, but there was no sign of either necessity. Joe kept the garage reasonably tidy, though there were some dried leaves and oil stains on the cement floor. What wasn't there was more intriguing than what was: Judith saw no blood. Surely if the horse had been shot, the animal would have bled. It might also have thrashed around before dying. She'd heard the gunfire. At least she'd assumed it was a gun that had been discharged. But could she have been mistaken? So much else was going on inside the house at the time. For several minutes, she continued her inspection, but found nothing of interest. Stumped, she went back inside to get the MG's keys.

Fifteen minutes later, Joe's beloved sports car was in the garage and Judith was at the front door, admitting the couple from Savannah. Marvella and Roscoe Billingsley were middle-aged, pleasant, and portly. Fortunately, they'd reserved Room Three, the largest room, and the only one with a king-sized bed.

Virtually on their heels came the Lexington duo. They had been on the same connecting flight out of Detroit. Tall, dark, and handsome, Qani Rahman and Darab Abdel were dressed in what looked like expensive casual clothes. They had only one sleek leather suitcase, explaining that since they were flying to Dubai the following morning, the rest of their luggage had been stored at the airport.

"We are here only for a brief meeting," Qani—or maybe Darab—told her. Judith was so dazzled by their good looks that she couldn't remember which was which. "We expect the arrival soon of our business contact. Will you announce her to us?"

"Of course," Judith said. "You're in Room Six. Here are your keys. If you go out this evening, I lock the front door at ten."

The other young man nodded. "We shall decide later," he said.

"That's fine," Judith said, smiling. "You both speak beautiful English."

"Oxford," said Qani—or Darab.

"Cambridge," said Darab—or Qani, and both men laughed, showing brilliant white teeth.

"Either one works for me," Judith assured them. "The social hour is at six, by the way. That is, if you aren't in your meeting."

They both nodded, smiled some more, and went upstairs. An hour passed before the two older women from Chicago showed up looking frazzled. Their flight from O'Hare had been delayed for almost two hours, their luggage had been misplaced but finally found in a storage bin, and they were in desperate need of a nap. Judith did her best to soothe them, although when they started arguing with each other, she handed over their keys and excused herself.

Just before six, the front doorbell rang. Expecting Cindy and Geoff Owens, she was surprised to see Zoë Paine standing on the porch.

"Come in," Judith said. "Did you forget something?"

Entering the house, Zoë looked nonplussed. "No. Why?"

"Ah . . . I didn't know . . . I mean, I didn't expect to see you again."

"Oh." She undid a striped muffler and removed her woolen gloves. "I'm here to meet with the cousins."

"Cousins? What cousins?"

"The emir's dudes," Zoë said. "Don't tell me they haven't arrived."

"Oh! *Those* cousins. I didn't realize they were related. Yes, they're upstairs. I'll let them know you're here."

Before reaching the second landing, Judith encountered the Billingsleys of Savannah coming down the stairs. "I'll set the appetizers on the living room buffet as soon as I deliver a message," she informed them. "The sherry and sparkling cider are already there." She squeezed past the chubby couple and continued on her mission.

A single knock on Room Six's door brought an immediate response. Both young men appeared when the door opened. "Yes?" they said simultaneously.

"Zoë Paine is here to see you," Judith said. "I'll show you into the parlor. The other guests are gathering in the living room."

"Excellent," one of the young men murmured, following Judith down the hall. She didn't speak again until they reached the bottom of the stairs, where Zoë was waiting, an impatient expression on her face.

Apparently, the visitors had not met Zoë. Elaborate introductions followed, accompanied by bows on the men's part and an increasingly irritated look on Zoë's face. Judith finally interrupted by indicating the door to the parlor.

"If you wish," she said, ushering them into the cozy room, "there are beverages and appetizers on the buffet in the living room." She pointed to the second door by the far wall.

"You can go through there. If there's anything else you need, don't hesitate to ask."

"We're fine," Zoë said. "This won't take long."

Judith knew a tone of dismissal when she heard one. The Chicago women had arrived in the entry hall, looking slightly less harried. Judith informed them she was fetching the hors d'oeuvres and moved on to the kitchen. Adding a bowl of salmon pâté to the tray, she went into the living room, relieved to see the chatty couple from Savannah engaging the Chicago women in what seemed to be amiable conversation.

Coming back into the hall, she noted that the door to the parlor was still closed. There was no way she could eavesdrop. The house's original oak doors were too thick. Besides, Gertrude would be champing at the bit for her supper.

Before Judith could figure out what to serve her mother, she noticed that the red light was glowing on her phone's base, indicating that a call had come in while she'd been away from the kitchen. With a heavy sigh, she picked up the receiver and dialed her voice-mail code.

"I won't be back tonight," Addison said in a slightly strained voice. "I'll call you sometime tomorrow." The message ended abruptly.

Fine, Judith thought. *Men are all idiots.* She was tempted to call Renie and say as much, just to let off steam. Then she realized it was after six, and Bill didn't permit taking calls during the dinner hour. Bill was an idiot, too. So was Carl, for trying to carry a heavy ladder with his bad back, and Mike, for not calling his mother in the past week to see if she was alive. As for Joe and Woody and that young nincompoop, Del. . .

Judith continued to fume inwardly while she took Gertrude's dinner out to the toolshed. "Ham, creamed corn, french fries, and chocolate pudding," she said, placing the tray in front of her mother. "Like it or lump it."

"Well, well," the old lady said, "somebody's cross as two sticks. What's wrong? You got dumped by your new boyfriend?"

"Screw him," Judith snapped.

Gertrude scowled. "Don't talk like that! Can't you act like a lady?"

"Sorry." Judith's shoulders sagged as she sat on the arm of the sofa. "I'm mad at the world."

"No kidding," Gertrude said. "What happened to Romeo?"

Judith tried to be fair. "Addison has a job that's not always nine to five. He may be on the trail of whatever's going on at City Hall. Joe's still there, helping Woody Price with the same situation."

"I thought Woody got the training wheels off of his unmarked police car a long time ago," Gertrude said. "Can't he do his job without Dumbbell holding his hand?"

"I'd like to think so, but apparently not. Even Uncle Al got dragged into it last night."

"Al?" Gertrude looked surprised. "Do I want to know why?"

"Something to do with the Teamsters' truck drivers," Judith said. "Maybe basketball games and gambling, too. I'm just beginning to sort through all this mess."

Gertrude finished chewing a piece of ham. "What about the horse? That sounds like Al, too. Is he the buyer?"

The question startled Judith. "Uncle Al is buying a horse?"

"He's been talking about it for a long time," Gertrude said, forking two french fries at once. "These frozen?"

"Yes. I mean, they were. They're not now. You're right—I've heard him mention it at family gatherings, but I never know when he's serious."

"Oh, he's a kidder," Gertrude agreed. "But as much as he loves the ponies, why shouldn't he have one of his own?

Never had to raise a kid, did he? Might as well raise a horse instead. They mind better than kids. Cheaper in the long run, too."

"Did you see the horse when it was brought here?"

"Kind of. It was pretty dark outside." The old lady peered at her daughter. "Is it still in the garage?"

"No." Judith didn't want to tell her mother about the animal's demise. "It was moved last night."

"By Al?"

"No. I mean," Judith said, allowing that nothing was impossible, given the events of the past few days, "not that I know of."

"Remember old Doc Epstein?"

"Didn't he have a family practice on top of the hill?"

"No, no," Gertrude said, waving a hand. "That was Doc Feinstein. During the Depression and afterward he took eggs, berries, even canned goods as payment. Never went after a deadbeat patient." She shook her head. "The hill was different then, blue collar through and through. Better, to my way of thinking." She paused, just a bit misty-eyed. "Anyways, Doc Epstein was a vet. Silent partner in the old racetrack by that hovel you and your first mistake, the original Lardbutt, lived in. How do you think Uncle Al got that fancy ring with the big red ruby in it?"

"He said he won it in a seven-card-stud poker game."

Gertrude waved her hand again. "That's bunk. Doc Epstein gave it to him. Al loaned Doc money to put into the track when it opened while the Depression was still going on. Al was the silent partner's silent bank. And don't ask me where Al got that kind of money. He was coaching and playing semipro basketball back then. No big paychecks like the millionaires today, but he and Sid Flaherty did all right by themselves with the Mountain Spring Dairy team. They won an AAU title just before Pearl Harbor got bombed."

"I remember their dairy trucks," Judith said. "They went out of business when I was in high school. What happened? They seemed to be all over when I was growing up."

"They sold out to somebody who went sticks up a few years later. Ran both companies into the ground. Somebody . . . Aunt Deb, maybe, told me that the original building on the southwest side of the hill is there, but now it's some kind of food plant. I guess whoever owns it dumped the milk routes. Dairy farmers around here have been forced to sell their land with all these newcomers moving into what used to be pasture and forest. Now it's housing developments and a bunch of malls. Kind of sorry I've lived to see that happen."

Judith reached over to pat her mother's shoulder. "I'm not sorry about you living this long. In fact, you may have given me an idea."

Gertrude shot her daughter a dubious look. "It better be a good one. Some of yours have been pretty stupid."

Rising from the sofa arm, Judith smiled. "When I figure it out, I'll let you know."

"Never mind me," the old lady said. "If you're thinking what I'm thinking, ask Al. He has the answers. Just make sure you know what's true and what's false. Your uncle walks a thin line. One of these days, he's going to fall off that tightrope. Keep your distance. Al's working without a net."

Gertrude waved her hand again. That a book, two-bit … I don't know Al himself. Too moody to put up the track when it quietd while the Depression was still going on. Al was the silent partner … and uncle. And that's as far where Al got that … line of money. He was on his own and playing tennis basketball back then. He … No points … of the million-dollar day … back and Sid Dalam's old oil again by the money … with … Mountain Spring Dairy … Thy … for an AA … line … the … Paul Hatter … a bootleg

Chapter Nineteen

As soon as Judith got back inside the house, she dialed Uncle Al's number.

"Odds are ten to one this is my niece," Al said when he answered on the third ring. "Odds on the game I watched earlier turned out about right. Illinois looks tough this season. Ohio State is better than Purdue, but that's about it for the Big Ten. Doesn't matter—North Carolina will win it all and you can take that to the bank. What's up, kiddo?"

"Got a question for you," Judith said, lest Uncle Al give her a wrap-up of all the games he'd seen in recent days. "Have you heard of a horse named Son of Scarlet?"

"A Thoroughbred?"

"Maybe."

"Hang on," Uncle Al said. "Let me check something."

Judith waited patiently, hearing the TV in the background. From what she could tell, it was yet another college basketball game. Or maybe the pros. The only time the play-by-play announcer raised his voice was when somebody scored from beyond the three-point line.

"Okay," Uncle Al finally said. "I'm looking at a list of last year's state-breeders-association yearling sales. A lot of these horses weren't yet named, but if I can find . . . ah!

Hey—this colt was born on my birthday in '04, April nineteenth. 'Rogue's Gallery–Scarletohara'—that's the sire and dame—'Terrasilva Farms, twelve thousand dollars.' Do you know if this Son of Scarlet is any good or are you picking your futures by colors like you did when you were a kid?"

"I wanted to know because that horse spent part of last night in our garage."

"Don't kid a kidder, kiddo." Uncle Al sounded serious. "What are you talking about? You were down at police headquarters last night. I didn't hear you mention a horse, in or out of your garage. Don't tell me Gert bought herself a pony. Nice idea, though. Better than that crazy cat you've got."

"It's a long story," Judith said wearily. "Do you know anything about the seller?"

"Terrasilva Farms?" He paused briefly. "Vaguely. They're somewhere out in the valley, not too far from the racetrack. I think they've had maybe four, five horses that ran there in the past couple of years. Didn't do much. In racing terms, they're still a maiden. I don't think they've been in business more than a few years. It takes time to build up a winning stable."

"Do you know if the horse was bought at the sale?"

"I didn't attend that one," Uncle Al said. "That was around Labor Day and I was in Vegas, making my pro football bets. I'm going with the Patriots. If the horse you're talking about is the colt on the list, then I figure it was sold."

"I thought you wanted to buy one," Judith said.

Uncle Al chuckled. "Oh, that was just talk. Remember the donkey I had years ago? Pokey was more trouble than he was worth, and he wasn't worth much to start with. I won him in a bet. He bit your cousin Sue once. Animals take too much—"

The doorbell forced Judith to interrupt. "Hey—I've got guests arriving. I'll tell you more later, okay?"

Uncle Al rang off. Judith was already halfway through

the dining room, the phone still in her hand. Once again, she expected to see Cindy and Geoff Owens. Instead, the brawny man in overalls who was standing outside her front door was a stranger.

"Yes?" she said, noticing a large truck parked in the cul-de-sac.

"Got a bill for you," the man said in a gruff voice, and shoved a clipboard at her. "Sign at the bottom. The pink copy is yours. And I'll need your credit card."

Judith stared at the invoice. The heading was *Sound Cartage, Inc., Abe Burleson, owner.* The amount due was $1,300 and change. "Are you Abe?" she asked.

"Who else would I be? Elvis?"

"Not likely," Judith murmured. "What's this bill for?"

"The horse in your garage." He jerked his thumb in the direction of the truck. "Hey, it's a deal. I gave you half off on the sling. When the damned nag woke up and started thrashing around after we got to the barn, I didn't charge for my aggravation, which was pretty damned big."

Judith gaped at Abe. "It's not my horse. It's not my bill. It's . . ." She looked at the customer name on the line at the bottom of the page: *Zoë Paine.* "Oh! I'm not . . . I think Ms. Paine . . . the horse was *alive*?"

Abe's bushy eyebrows came together. "Well, why else would you have the damned thing moved? You told us on the phone that it got scared by some kids shooting off fireworks and started going crazy, so you had to use a tranquilizer dart on it. Come on, sign the bill and show me the money."

"Ms. Paine's in a meeting. Come in. She's right in here," Judith said, indicating the parlor as she knocked on the door.

There was no immediate response. She opened the door. The room was empty.

"Invisible, huh?" Abe said, his expression turning even more disgruntled. "Who's in that other room?"

Wordlessly, Judith went through the archway to take a head count in the living room. The Chicago sisters and the Savannah couple were still chatting away, apparently having sampled enough sherry to create a jovial atmosphere.

"She must've left with the Arabs," Judith said bleakly.

"Oh, for . . ." Abe shook his fist. "I'm not budging until this bill is covered. Go ahead, call the cops, do whatever, but I know my rights!"

"Hey—I'm not Zoë Paine!" Judith said angrily. "I'm Judith Flynn and I own this bed-and-breakfast. Don't you have a phone number for her? She was a guest here last night."

"Rode in on her horse, did she? Okay, I'll play this game," he said, and stomped off to the living room. "Anybody here got a horse?" he bellowed, pausing only to grab what was left of the appetizers. "Anybody here hiding some A-rabs?"

The happy chatter stopped. "Arabs?" Mr. Billingsley said. "Not so far. But we just flew in from Savannah and, boy, are my arms—"

"Cut the crap," Abe said sharply. "What about the Paine woman?"

"I'm a registered nurse," the taller of the sisters responded. "I specialize in wound care. Are you injured?"

Abe had stuffed two salmon-pâté-covered crackers into his mouth. "This isn't funny," he declared after hastily devouring the appetizers. "What's going on around here?"

"I told you," Judith said, trying to refrain from screaming at Abe. "These are my B&B guests. It would appear that Ms. Paine has left. She may have taken the Arabs . . . that is, two of my other guests with her. I suggest you try to contact her by phone. It's possible that they're headed for the barn where you took the horse. Would you mind telling me where that might be? I may be able to help you track her down."

Abe polished off a couple of smoked oysters before answering. "I got her number somewhere." He fumbled in the pockets of his overalls. "This better not be some kind of trick."

"Please," Judith said, stopping just short of grabbing Abe by the arm. "Come into the kitchen. If you can't find her number, I can put you in touch with her grandparents."

By the time they reached the kitchen, Abe admitted he couldn't find Zoë's number. The appetizers seemed to have taken the edge off of his ill humor. Judith wrote down the listing for Wilbur and Norma Paine's home phone, but held on to the piece of paper while she posed a question: "Where did you take that horse?"

"Why do you want to know, if it's not yours?" Abe demanded with a touch of his previous hostility.

"Because my uncle wants to buy it," Judith said. "I was on the phone with him when you rang the doorbell. I told him about Son of Scarlet because he's in the market for a Thoroughbred. I'd like to know if it's for sale. The Arabs, as you call them, may be buyers, too. They came here from Kentucky."

"Damned if I know anything about that," Abe said, simmering down. "I took it to a place on the Eastside that has a barn. They still can keep horses in the residential areas over there if they were grandfathered after a law was passed some years back banning horses inside the city limits. I don't know who owns the place. It's by the old railroad tracks off of the freeway near the shopping center on your right when you get across the floating bridge. It's all a jumble to me. I live in the south end of town."

Judith understood. Like Abe, she recognized the area, but only in the vague sort of way that city dwellers knew the ever-growing, ever-changing Eastside. "You had an address on that invoice, didn't you?"

"Yeah, but it was one hell of a place to find. I left my clipboard out in the hall."

Judith realized she'd left her phone there, too. "Here's the number for Zoë's grandparents," she said, leading the way back through the dining room. "Let me take down the barn's address."

As they entered the hall, the four guests were leaving. Mrs. Billingsley announced that they were all going to dinner together, having become fast friends with the Chicago sisters. The appearance of the blustering Abe apparently hadn't dampened their spirits. Judith made appropriate comments to the jocular quartet and saw them out.

Abe handed her the clipboard. "It's one of those crazy southeast-lane-avenue-northeast-upside-downside-street-and-avenue jumbles. Took half an hour to find the damned place. I should get me one of those GPS things, but I don't trust 'em. If I don't know where I'm going, how can somebody who isn't in the truck know?"

"I can't explain that either," Judith admitted, committing the address to memory. "I should warn you, Mrs. Paine may be rather rude. It's her nature."

Abe grunted. "I can out-rude the worst of 'em. G'night." He ambled out of the house.

Judith rushed back to the kitchen and wrote down the barn's address before she forgot it. Abe was right—it sounded like a typical Eastside conglomeration of streets, lanes, places, avenues, parkways, and roads. Maybe she could find the location on the Internet.

As she sat at the computer trying to zero in on the barn in the maze of streets that snaked around the Eastside, she realized that the house again seemed too quiet. Four of the guests had gone to dinner. Apparently the two young men from Kentucky had left with Zoë Paine. When Sweetums brushed against her leg, she jumped.

"You can't be hungry," she told the cat, feeling a need to speak to someone, even if it was Sweetums. "I know Mother fed you." She reached down to pet the thick orange-and-white fur. "How are you at solving puzzles? At the moment, you're all I've got."

Sweetums purred, rubbing her leg again. "Nice try, but—"

A sudden thought struck her. She looked up at the school-house clock. It was a quarter after seven. Judith reached for the phone. It rang in her hand.

"Just found out you called," Joe said in his usual mellow voice. "Everything okay at your end?"

"No," Judith replied, surprised by the anger in her voice. "It sucks. I feel like a widow. Been there, done that, and got the love of my life back, but now he's not around. *When are you coming home?*"

"Wow," Joe said softly. "Sounds like you can't live without me. Who knew?"

"You're a jerk," she shot back. "This disaster better be worth it."

"Look," he said earnestly, "I'm not nuts about hanging out at City Hall either. But this is big stuff. I've got an obliga-tion, not just to Woody but to the whole damned department. They send me a pension check, remember?"

"Yes. I remember that it's because you're retired. Besides, I've got plenty of weird stuff going on here, starting with a horse in the garage."

"Better than in the living room," Joe said. "Got to go. Just wanted to make sure you were doing okay without me. Is Addison still around?"

"No," Judith retorted. "He left. I'm all alone. Don't you dare hang up yet. Tell me what you're actually doing. You owe me that much."

"Can't," he said. "I'm a suspect, remember? I have to wait for legal counsel. Later, okay?" He hung up.

"Jackass," Judith grumbled, shoving the phone across the counter so hard that it bounced off the wall. For several minutes, she frowned at the monitor showing the rabbit warren of streets where the resurrected Son of Scarlet was probably bedding down for the night.

The faint chime of the grandfather clock striking the half hour snapped her out of the self-induced stupor. Judith reached for the phone, but thought better of it. Putting on her jacket and grabbing her purse, she went out the back door to the toolshed.

"I'm going over to Renie and Bill's," she informed her mother from the threshold. "I'm locking up the house, so if anybody has forgotten their keys, they can wait until I get back."

"What are you two goofballs up to now?" Gertrude demanded. "It better be playing cards or doing a jigsaw puzzle."

"It's a jigsaw puzzle," Judith said, telling only a partial lie.

The old lady nodded. "I'll look for you when I see you. Let me finish my jumble puzzle in the paper."

It was raining harder when Judith drove from the south side of the hill to the north side, where the Joneses lived in their Dutch Colonial cocoa-colored house. The front room drapes were drawn and Judith knew that Renie and Bill were probably watching TV. Or Renie was watching Bill watch TV while Oscar— She stopped herself, wondering if the chaotic past few days had unhinged her mind. Judith refused to buy into the Joneses' fantasy about a damned stuffed ape.

Through the window with its tulip stained-glass window, she saw her cousin come down the hall from the kitchen to the door. "You lost?" Renie said, letting Judith into the entry hall. Bill leaned slightly in his chair and said hi before turning to Oscar, who was sitting on the arm of the sofa. They were watching what looked to Judith like the siege of Leningrad, judging from the snow-covered wreckage and bodies against a background of ruined Russian architecture.

"No," Bill said, apparently to Oscar, "that's not the Falstaff parking lot after Renie drove up there to get more eggnog for Christmas."

"Very funny," Renie muttered, leading Judith into the kitchen. "I'm just finishing dinner cleanup. What's wrong? You look a bit odd."

"I feel a lot odd," Judith replied, slumping against the work counter that jutted out in the middle of the kitchen. "I need someone to bounce ideas off of and you're it."

"Then let's sit in the nook," Renie said, turning on the dishwasher.

Judith shrugged off her jacket and sat in the captain's chair staring out the window where heavy raindrops bounced off the deck railing. Renie was getting something out of the refrigerator. She appeared a moment later with a can of Diet 7-Up for Judith and the ubiquitous regular Pepsi for herself.

"Okay," her cousin said, plopping down into another captain's chair on the other side of the table. "Start your tale of woe."

"I don't know where to begin," Judith confessed. "What was happening when I last saw you?"

"Your mother tried to crash and burn in the kitchen," Renie said. "Then the B.C. couple arrived. Addison was looking sage when he wasn't looking uncomfortable. Then I made my exit."

Judith nodded. "I can go on from there," she said—and did, catching Renie up on everything that had happened in the past six hours. "I honestly don't know if Joe can tell me what's going on, but his attitude aggravated me. And then I had a sudden brainstorm."

"Which blew you in our direction?" Renie shrugged. "Let's hear it."

"I . . . I can't quite put it into words yet. You know it has to be logical and what occurred to me isn't. In fact, the more I think about it, the more I'm sure I'm crazy."

Renie looked disgusted. "You drove a mile to tell me what you *can't* tell me? Why didn't you send me a blank e-mail and save gas?"

"I know. It sounds stupid. But it also occurred to me that we should go over to the Eastside and try to find that barn where the horse is stabled."

" 'We'? Now? Yes, you *are* crazy."

Judith laughed nervously. "Okay, now that we've put my insanity on the table, I'll admit I'm afraid to stay alone tonight."

"Coz." Renie looked shocked. "Oh my. This is serious. You've faced off with hardened killers, you've stared down gun barrels, you've confronted strangers who were mad as hatters, you've even gone one-on-one with your mother . . . and yet you're afraid to stay alone in your own house? That really upsets me."

"I know. It's absurd." She gazed at the random stacks of notepads and other work-related items Renie kept at hand on the main floor. "If I put all of these puzzle pieces on paper and tried to connect them in some way, would that make sense?"

"I won't know until you try," Renie said, pushing a legal pad toward her cousin. "Go for it." Picking up a pen, Judith drew a house representing the B&B. Then she drew lines leading from the house that indicated all of the factors involved in the baffling occurrences of the past week. Renie sat quietly, sipping her Pepsi.

"What have I left out?" Judith mused. "Something's missing."

"Your artistic talent is one of them," Renie noted. "Your printing's not so hot either."

"Never mind the idiotic comments. Just try to figure out what *is* on my primitive diagram."

"Why did you include SANECO?" Renie asked. "Is that because you don't think Zachary Conrad was the original person who was supposed to be bilking the insurance company?"

"That's right," Judith said. "If something serious had happened to Zachary, it would've made the news. Not a big story, but at least a few inches, since he was a city employee of some stature. Remember that the body had phony ID. I assume—always a mistake to assume anything—that Joe and Woody had been in contact with SANECO. The question should be what happened to the real person who was possibly trying to defraud the company? Or did he ever exist? And if he did, is his body somewhere at the bottom of the lake?"

Renie nodded. "I get it. But we have to assume SANECO is on the up-and-up, right?"

"The company, yes. One person who works there may not be, but I have no way of knowing. That's something Joe and Woody would investigate. Which," Judith went on, tapping her fingers on the table, "may mean that the whole situation was a setup. Maybe there never was an insurance-fraud attempt. How long did Zachary live in that condo? Who owns it? That's what the police would know. And that's what Joe's not telling me. He says he can't."

Renie's round face brightened. "A sting operation with Zachary Conrad as bait? Why him?"

"Because," Judith said slowly, "he volunteered."

"Wow." Renie grinned at Judith. "That's brilliant. Of you, I mean. Not so smart of Zachary, being dead. So why would he do such a thing?"

"That's the problem," Judith said, frowning. "It had to be very important for him to do it in the first place. Some sort of connection to whatever lead Addison is following at City Hall. What do we know about Zachary except his job and his connection by marriage to the Paines?"

"Not much," Renie said.

"Same way with Addison." Judith stared at her crude diagram. "Connect the dots—or lines. Horses. Hunt club. Gambling. ARBS."

"You didn't put the truck drivers down," Renie pointed out.

"No, I didn't. In my mind, they come under 'Uncle Al.'" Judith made a face. "But I left out something else. 'Sick kids at SOTS.'"

"Doc's Burgers? We've been eating them for years," Renie said. "You think they get their meat from ARBS?"

"Maybe," Judith said. "Who'd know?"

"Ohhh . . . Martha Morelli, probably. She's been involved in the hamburger lunch program forever. Want me to call her?"

"Why not?"

Renie flipped through the Rolodex. "Gee, maybe I can con Martha into using my Shrimp Dump recipe after all." She tapped in the number. "She's a slow starter, but she does tend to run on once she— Hi, Martha, it's Serena Jones . . . Oh, really?" Renie shot Judith a beleaguered glance. "That's a shame . . ."

Judith saw Renie slump down in the chair. Recalling her own phone conversation with the woman, she wondered if maybe it hadn't taken Martha so long to get up to speed this time around.

"That doesn't sound like my cousin," Renie said, one hand to her head. "Judith is always . . . Yes, but I heard . . . No, of course, I wasn't there . . . Gosh, that isn't what Arlene told us about the ladder . . . Confused? I don't think . . . But why would Alicia and Reggie need the ladder in the first . . . No, I told you, I wasn't there when . . ."

Renie had slouched down so far in the chair that her chin

was almost on the table. Judith could only imagine what the Beard-Smythes had told Martha and the rest of the parishioners about their stay at Hillside Manor. Come morning, it might be wise to avoid Mass at SOTS and attend the adjacent parish near the city center instead.

"Yes, yes," Renie said, finally sounding testy as she pulled herself back up in the chair, "that's a shame, but that's not why I . . . Martha! Stop! This is important! Who poisoned the schoolchildren?"

Judith leaned forward, watching her cousin's expression change from annoyance to puzzlement.

"Martha?" Renie frowned. "Martha?" she repeated in a loud voice. After a long pause, she disconnected. "I got dead air, then the fast busy signal. I think Martha passed out. Does that answer your question?"

"Why am I not surprised?" Judith said. "It makes sense, I guess. The school would want to contract through a hamburger place that buys meat from a parishioner."

"It must've been a onetime-only occurrence," Renie remarked. "Doc's Burgers has never had a problem I know of before this. Maybe we're wrong. I wonder what went awry? Or could we be mistaken?"

"We may be jumping to conclusions," Judith allowed. "I'll call the health department Monday. Don't you know someone who works there?"

"Yes," Renie replied. "The son of a former neighbor when I was growing up. I keep in touch with the family. So does Mom. Rob's worked there for years. He must be pretty far up the food chain by now. So to speak. Smart, nice, and probably would be helpful." She began going through her Rolodex again. "I imagine Shrimp Dump won't make it into the SOTS cookbook now that Martha either fainted or hung up on me. I gather she's very tight with the Beard-Smythes."

Judith nodded. "That's how I got roped into having them

spend the night. Good Lord, it seems like a long time ago."

"I'm calling Rob now," Renie said. "If he's not home, I'll leave a cryptic message. That'll ensure— Rob? Hi. This is Serena. How are you?"

Judith stood up. She knew Renie would have to lay some groundwork before asking pertinent questions. Wandering through the dining and living rooms, she came to stand by the fireplace, where a single log was sending out a bit of extra warmth.

"Just in time," Bill said. "The Russians won."

"Again?" Judith responded.

"You bet." Bill leaned forward. "No, Oscar, they didn't cheat." He turned back to Judith. "Oscar swears he had a friend who was a Swedish spy at Leningrad."

"Oh? His friend must be quite elderly."

Bill shook his head. "Oscar has no sense of time passing," he said in a low voice. "He thinks all this happened today. Poor little fella."

"Say," Judith said, "what's going on with the client who was being stalked? Has anything happened to him while Joe's been out of action?"

"I don't know," Bill replied. "I won't see him again until Tuesday."

"And you wouldn't tell me if it had, right?"

"Right." Bill scanned the circled items on the TV listings. "Sorry, Oscar, we're stuck with a bunch of bad movies. Saturday's not much good for TV viewing. How about *The Godfather Part One*?"

"I like that," Judith said. "It's one of Joe's favorites, too."

"I know," Bill said, getting up to take a DVD out of the cupboard by the TV. "Oscar has a pal who works in Vegas. Renie and I saw Jack at the MGM Grand when were we there the last couple of times. Nice guy. He just sort of hangs around in a jungle setting at a restaurant."

"Does Jack get paid for . . . never mind, I think Renie's winding up her phone call." *Help me, Lord, I'm starting to sound as insane as the Joneses. They're contagious.*

Renie, however, was still talking to Rob. "That's awful," she was saying. "Did it make the news?"

Judith sat down and sipped her soda. Her cousin was looking more and more shocked by the second. "Yes, of course, I understand . . . No, I won't say a word. Maybe he'll still turn up . . . Okay. Thanks. I'm glad everything else is going so well for you and yours . . . I will. Bye." She put the phone down. "That was more than worthwhile. Rob sent one of his inspectors to ARBS right after Christmas. The guy had some kind of accident there that put him in the hospital for several days and then he went home in a wheelchair. You'll never guess where he lives. Or *lived,* since he's disappeared."

Judith stared at Renie. "The condo on the lake?"

"You got it. He hasn't been seen or heard from since last Sunday."

Chapter Twenty

After taking in the thunderbolt of news, Judith had several questions for Renie. "Do they think he's dead?"

"They don't know."

"Could he have been perpetrating an insurance fraud?"

"I've no idea."

"He must've been seriously injured or he wouldn't have ended up in the hospital, right?"

"Right."

"How did he get hurt?"

"Nobody's sure. Something apparently fell on him. He suffered severe damage to his pelvis."

"That doesn't sound like fraud, does it?"

"Not to me," Renie agreed. "I didn't mention anything about Joe and the surveillance. I just let Rob talk."

"Good thinking," Judith said. "So something fell on him . . . Do you suppose it was an accident?"

"That would be the job of the insurance investigators," Renie said. "Rob told me they were looking into it, of course, but no report had yet been filed. There was a very brief item under the local news in the paper, but no TV coverage. None of the parties involved want to talk until the investigation is over."

"Again, this would be something Joe and Woody would look into," Judith said. "Damn! I wish Joe could tell me what's going on. They must be way out ahead of what little we know."

"We need a spy," Renie declared. "Volunteers?"

"Us? How?"

"You're the queen of liars around here," Renie pointed out. "Think, coz. We couldn't do this incognito. We know some of the players, such as Andrew Paine and the Beard-Smythes. That leaves Addison. He doesn't need to be incognito. It's his job. Call him."

Judith grimaced. "I'm not sure that's a good idea."

Renie started to argue, but seemed to change her mind. "You look odd. What's going on with you two? I'm getting some strange vibes."

Judith went on the defensive. "Like what?" she snapped. "Are you joining forces with Mother and Arlene and insinuating that I've got a thing for Addison? That's crap and you know it. He's a nice guy, and I've been grateful for his help, but that's it."

Renie shook her head. "No, I don't taunt you like Aunt Gert does and I don't get peculiar notions like Arlene occasionally has. But I do know you and I kind of know Addison, or at least I can make some judgments about men like him. Widowed, lonely, not lucky in love since his wife died. You're sympathetic, good-hearted, open with people, always trying to please. Two frustrated adults, permanently or temporarily spouseless, living under the same roof for a couple of days. Danger. Excitement. Sharing your thoughts about the investigation and God knows what else. He's playing protector. You're in the role of possible victim. What could possibly go wrong?"

"Nothing!" Judith shouted—and immediately felt foolish. "Really. I understand what you're saying, but it's . . . not true."

"Bull. It's true." Renie smiled ironically. "I mean, the situation is. Obviously, you're suddenly backing off. How come?"

Judith tried to find the right words to explain herself. And Addison. Or both of them. She jumped when she realized Bill was standing in the doorway of the nook.

"You two okay?" he asked.

Renie's smile softened. "Sure. Just Coz here, trying to deny that she's really hot. Guess I shouldn't have sent that letter to AARP nominating her for the Bodalacious Babe Award."

Bill shrugged. "Oscar signed it." He turned and went through the other door to the kitchen. "Time for my snack. Got a napoleon from Begelman's Bakery for tonight. Seems appropriate after watching the siege of Leningrad, even if it's the wrong war." Bill moved on to the refrigerator.

"Sometimes," Judith murmured, "I'd really like to strangle you."

"Right." Renie stretched and yawned. "Bill feels the same way. Start with telling me why you won't call Addison."

"I think he may be onto something," Judith said after a short pause. "I told you he left that odd message on the phone."

"You didn't say why you thought it was odd."

"He sounded . . . odd. He'd gone to see Paulina Paine."

"Oh?"

"I didn't mention it, because it didn't seem important to . . . to the rest of the stuff that's been going on," Judith explained, feeling awkward. "She and Andrew separated a while back and during that time, Paulina and Addison had a fling. I realized there was something between them when they saw each other last night and later they disappeared upstairs for a while."

Renie couldn't help but laugh. "Gee, you really are a sleuth. But that's fairly intriguing, for more than obvious reasons. You think she'll rat out Andy to Addison?"

"If, in fact, there's any ratting out to be done," Judith replied. "Paulina and Andy didn't strike me as a very happy couple."

"Paulina started out bitchy," Renie said. "Maybe that's not really her, but living with Andy has made her brittle and sharp-tongued."

"Defense mechanism," Bill called out from in front of the microwave, where he was warming his Sleepytime Tea. "The opposite of my wife, who's treated like a queen and is ever cheerful and sweet."

Renie leaned out of her chair. "Why don't you stick your head in that thing and turn it on for two minutes? Your brain has stopped functioning, Dr. Bill."

Her husband didn't comment, but continued his nightly ritual.

"He's right, of course," Renie said as Bill exited the kitchen. "That's another thing about the Paines. Are any of them happily married? How on earth could Hannah pretend the man who came with her was Zachary Conrad? And who was he?"

"That," Judith said, "is a good question. Is it possible that she didn't know Zachary was dead?"

"She should by now," Renie pointed out, "even if the Paines have been avoiding calls from the police. Frankly, their attitude is beyond strange. It's as if the whole family is running scared."

Judith agreed. "That's what I've been thinking all day. The youngest of Norma and Wilbur's children, Sarah, isn't Octavia's mother. It was clear that Sarah and Dennis Blair haven't been married very long. Octavia obviously doesn't care for the rest of the Paines. If there's any ratting to be done, I wonder if she'd be our best source. The only problem is, I don't know where she works or even if she lives with her father and Sarah."

"We could go retro and see if she's in the phone book," Renie suggested. "So many people aren't these days, with all the cell phones. Let's see if I can get a number from Directory Assistance." She picked up her own phone and dialed.

Judith sipped at her soda while her cousin went through the paces of eliciting information from an operator. "Okay," Renie said, after making some notes. "There's an O. D. Blair who lives close to downtown, probably a condo or an apartment, judging from the address. I think I'll give her a call."

Judith was surprised. "And ask what?"

Renie was already dialing the number. "I got the impression she's some kind of professional. Don't ask me why, but—" She stopped, holding up a hand for silence. After a few moments, she spoke into the receiver. "Hi, Octavia. This is Serena Jones. I met you last night at my cousin's B&B. I'm sorry for your family's loss, but I'm a graphic designer and I understand you're involved with a small press. I need your input about a project I'm doing. If you could give me a call at . . ." Renie slowly uttered the number, offered her thanks, and rang off. "How was that?"

"Very neat and tidy," Judith said. "What if she doesn't know about her family's loss?"

"She may think I'm talking about their minds, which they all seem to have lost quite a while ago." Renie shrugged. "Doesn't matter. At least I established contact. We'll see if she responds."

Judith checked her watch. "It's nine-thirty. I should go home."

"You do have guests," Renie remarked. "Do any of them look like ax murderers?"

"They seem normal," Judith said, "at least the Chicago sisters and the Savannah couple. As I mentioned earlier, I suspect that Zoë Paine is selling Son of Scarlet to the Kentucky Arabs. Or Middle East guys. I think they may be buyers for some emir in Dubai."

"It was the twins who brought the horse, right?"

Judith nodded. "They must've been helping their cousin. Now I know why Zoë disappeared during the evening. She may've heard what we thought were shots, but were kids—probably the Dooley bunch in back of us—lighting off New Year's firecrackers. Zoë would've guessed they'd upset the horse and went out to check, tranquilized the poor animal, and had Abe Burleson haul him off to the barn."

"So Zoë had bought the horse? Why put it in your garage?"

Judith took a last drink of soda and stood up. "That's where my logic doesn't factor in, but I don't think she bought Son of Scarlet. I think she rescued the horse from whoever owned it."

Renie was also on her feet. "A rescue animal?"

"Yes. I have to guess what it was rescued from."

The cousins exchanged glances. "I can give that a shot, too."

Judith knew they were on the same wavelength. "Right. Zoë didn't want the horse to become horse meat."

After arriving home and collecting Gertrude's dinner tray, Judith found Geoff and Cindy Owens making sandwiches in the kitchen. The sight surprised her, yet was reassuring.

"We didn't get a chance to eat dinner," Cindy explained.

"I hope you don't mind. We'll pay extra for the ham and cheese and bread."

"Don't worry about it," Judith said. "You can make it up to me with some information."

Geoff gave a start, almost dropping the mustard jar he'd been putting back into the fridge. "Information? What about?"

"Animal rescue," Judith said. "That's why you came to town, isn't it? I'm interested in your work."

"Oh, that!" Cindy giggled, a false note in Judith's ear. "It's just something we feel is worthwhile to do when we have spare time."

"Kind of a hobby," Geoff added, closing the refrigerator door. "We don't have kids yet, so we volunteer a bit."

"Oh," Judith said. "That's generous of you."

Cindy gathered up the sandwiches and a couple of bottled waters. "Better than just sitting at the beach getting a tan in the winter. Cheaper, too. See you in the morning."

The couple headed out of the kitchen. Judith stood by the sink, wondering why they were lying. Or at the very least, being evasive. After she heard ten o'clock chime from the living room, she picked up the phone and dialed Addison's number.

She got his brief recording and decided to hang up without leaving a message. But she felt uneasy. He seemed dependable. Considerate, too. Judith admitted to herself that she was worried. She was startled by the ringing of her fax machine next to the computer. Only rarely did she receive guest information via fax, but sometimes the machine rang and nothing came through. Junk mail she'd been told, filtered by her carrier. But what appeared to be a message was printing out. Judith waited anxiously until it finished.

To her amazement, it was from Joe. "I only now got back the photos I took while on surveillance. One is of Zachary

Conrad in his wheelchair. The other is of the female care-
taker. Thought you and your co-conspirator, Addison, might
be interested. By the way, have I told you lately that I love
you? I do."

Judith was momentarily appeased. But it seemed to take
forever for the first photo to print out, and when it arrived,
the quality was somewhat grainy. The man in the wheelchair
didn't look familiar, but she'd never met Zachary, so it could
have been anybody. He was a fairly pleasant-looking sort
and she could tell that he was big in girth and probably tall
as well.

The second photo finally finished printing. Judith didn't
know what to expect of an untraceable woman known as
Beth Johnson, but she was stunned when she recognized her
immediately. Grainy or not, the face of Sonya Paine stared
back at her.

Sonya, Judith thought, aware that her heart was beating
faster. Sonya, Walter's wife, who had become hysterical
when their daughter, Zoë, disappeared at dinnertime. How
many of the Paines were involved in whatever was going on?
No wonder they were all running scared. She picked up the
phone to call Renie.

"Sonya was Zachary's caregiver?" her cousin exclaimed
after Judith relayed the news. "You say she never showed
up after going on her errands that day? Good God, did she
murder her brother-in-law?"

"She might have," Judith said wearily. "Though I can't
imagine why. If I'm thinking straight, it sounds more to me
as if Zachary and maybe Sonya and who knows how many
other Paines were setting a trap for someone or something.
Obviously, it backfired horribly."

"Have you told Joe who the woman is, or do you think he
knows?"

"He wouldn't recognize Sonya." Judith paused. "Woody

and Del wouldn't either. They think she's somebody who goes by the name of Beth Johnson, which is one of those common last names that's all but impossible to trace. But they would have taken prints, fibers, whatever. For all anybody knows, Sonya's never been fingerprinted."

"Zachary Conrad would've been," Renie said.

"He would? Why?"

"Because he worked for the lighting department. Don't you remember that's where I worked during the summers to put myself through college? I had to be fingerprinted, but it didn't take. Once again, I proved to be a freak of nature."

"Unarguable," Judith murmured. "Your hair doesn't turn gray, you can eat like a pig and not gain an ounce, you have no fingerprints. It'd be helpful if you had special powers. That's what it seems like it's going to take to figure this whole thing out."

"Ha! You're the one with those. Use 'em or lose 'em, coz."

"I'm *trying*," Judith asserted. "I'm going to see if I can get hold of Joe. He must still be at City Hall."

"Go ahead," Renie said. "How could he know who she is? This sounds important. Call me back and let me know how he reacts."

"Will do." Judith rang off and went through the process of trying to reach Joe, using the number that had shown up on the caller ID earlier in the evening. Hopefully, she wouldn't have to jump through hoops to get through. But it wasn't a direct number. After the second transfer, she got disconnected. Frustrated, she considered calling Woody's wife, Sondra, to see if she knew how to reach either of their husbands without a hassle. But first she should lock the front door. She was in the entry hall before she remembered that she'd locked the door before going to see Renie. Maybe she should make sure the Owenses had locked it behind them when they entered the house.

She had her hand on the knob when the doorbell chimed. Suddenly her hands were trembling. *Damn, I'm spooked just like that poor horse. What's wrong with me? It's probably a guest who forgot his or her key.* Steeling herself, she looked through the peephole. A woman stood on the porch, familiar, but not one of her current visitors. Judith cautiously opened the door.

"Yes?" she said, and stared in speechless shock.

"You don't remember me?" the newcomer said. "My name's Jean Rogers."

Chapter
Twenty-one

The woman who called herself Jean Rogers was the younger version who had come to the house with her reclaimed handbag and wallet. Judith hesitated before letting her inside. "How can I help you?" she asked, hiding her shaky hands behind her back.

"I need to talk to you," Jean said, sounding sheepish and yet more mature than Judith remembered.

"I thought you were leaving town," Judith said, still blocking the young woman's entry.

"I did." She held out her handbag, not the brown suede drawstring bag Judith remembered, but a marine-blue leather hobo style. "Take out my wallet. Check my ID."

Judith sighed. "Okay, come in. I'm a bit edgy this evening."

By the time she had led Jean into the living room and indicated she should sit opposite her on the matching sofa, her hands had stopped trembling. The hobo bag was on the coffee table. Judith picked it up. "Do I have to search or just take out your wallet?"

"The wallet's fine," Jean said. "You looked as if you

needed some reassurance. I didn't want you to think I had a gun in there."

"Nothing would surprise me right about now," Judith said. She found the wallet at once. It was the one Jean had carried on her previous visit and the Arizona driver's license was also identical.

"Look at the next card," the young woman suggested.

Judith obeyed. Her eyes grew wider as she first saw a different, better photo of Jean, and then noticed the heading of *The Department of the Interior, Bureau of Land Management.* "You're a federal agent," Judith said. "And you really are Jean Rogers."

"Yes, and I live in Tucson, but I move around on my job. I stay with an old college friend when I'm in town." She retrieved the wallet and the hobo bag. "There are at least a dozen other women named Jean Rogers living in the same part of Arizona. It's a common name. But I suspect whoever stole my wallet wasn't one of them."

"Do you know who she really is or why she stole it?" Judith asked.

"I lied about it being taken at Nordquist," Jean said, looking unperturbed by the admission. "I was at a restaurant meeting with a colleague in that big complex across the street from Nordquist. We were talking about the wild-horse-and-burro problem in Arizona and the similar problems you have in this state on the other side of the mountains, mainly with horses."

Judith nodded. "I've seen them once or twice on the cross-state highway. They look so beautiful—and free."

"Their freedom is the reason there's nothing beautiful about the situation," Jean said with a trace of bitterness. "The Native Americans also fall under the Department of the Interior. They've taken on the problem of the wild animals in some states, but the animals are getting out of control here. There are too many horse owners who find out that they're an expense. They let them loose and they multiply. Eventually they'll become so numerous that the grazing habitats will be destroyed. It's not reached epidemic proportions here, but it will if something isn't done. The Native Americans have a solution that could work—except that it's not palatable to most other Americans. I mean that literally."

Judith frowned. "You're saying . . . ?"

Jean nodded. "Horse meat. In other countries, it's perfectly acceptable, but not here. It'll take education to change public opinion."

"Yes, I think it would." Judith smiled weakly. "The concept doesn't appeal to me. My uncle Cliff insisted that muskrat was quite tasty. He'd eaten it in Alaska. He couldn't convince my aunt Deb and my cousin Serena that they should try it."

"A hard sell," Jean conceded, "as horse meat will be. That's why I'm in town. But getting back to what happened to my purse at the restaurant, I realized that a woman at the next table seemed to be checking us out," Jean said. "She was older than I am, so I thought maybe she was interested in my companion, who was more her own age. On her way out, she bumped my chair. I didn't think anything of it until later, when I tried to find my wallet. It was gone. She'd picked me clean." Jean shook her head. "Some officer of law enforcement, security, and emergency management, huh?"

"She didn't take your purse?"

Jean shook her head. "I had my hobo. That suede drawstring bag belonged to the thief who tossed it and the wallet into the garbage. I pretended it was mine when I was here just to avoid suspicion. Besides, I wanted to use it for evidence if she was ever tracked down. That's why I'm here."

Judith tried to take Jean at her word, but sensed that the younger woman was holding back. "All I can say is what you already know. She did a bunk, and since you canceled your credit cards, I didn't get paid."

"I can make amends," Jean said. "It's a legitimate work-related expense. Instead of ogling my companion, I think she was spying."

Judith's smile was more genuine. "Was he so unattractive?"

Jean laughed. "Not really. He's a big man, forties, balding, looks like a salesman and can act the part, but that's just a cover. He's one of our best security agents."

"You mean he actually uses a cover in his job?"

Jean's eyes twinkled. "Oh yes! Sometimes I do, too. You have to when you're investigating what may be criminal activity. It's a skill I've had to learn, but Walter's a natural. He could fool anybody with that hail-fellow-well-met act of his."

Judith hazarded a wild guess. "Walter Paine?"

Jean nodded, then apparently realized that something had struck Judith as odd. "What's the matter? You look . . . puzzled."

"Not really," Judith said, assuming a casual air to hide her deceit. "I didn't know what Walter does for a living, though he's the hearty type who could be a salesman. His parents belong to our church."

Jean was flabbergasted. "What a coincidence! It really is a small—" She stopped, frowning. "Have you seen Walter lately?"

"Last night, in fact," Judith replied. "He and the rest of the family were here for dinner."

"I see." Jean grew thoughtful. Judith waited for her to speak again. "That might explain it."

"Explain what?" Judith asked innocently.

"The phony Jean Rogers staying here. But how could she know that Walter would be at your house last night?"

"It was an auction event that Walter's mother bought at the parish school last May," Judith explained. "The date was set several months ago. I suppose there are any number of ways the phony Jean could have found out. But why would she want to come here? The only information I had about Walter was that he was a guest. In fact, they were supposed to spend the night, but," she went on, glossing over the truth, "they changed their minds at the last minute and left after dinner."

"I see," Jean said again, though she was still frowning.

Judith, however, couldn't figure out what, if anything, she saw. "I hardly think that the family's decision to leave had anything to do with your so-called spy," she said. "The other Jean was here only a few hours before she sneaked away."

"I don't know her motivation. I don't even know why she stole my wallet, unless she wanted to pass herself off as me."

"Who would she be spying for?"

"She's an industrial spy," Jean replied. "She could be working for any number of companies or individuals who want to determine what our agency is doing that might impact their livelihood. Follow the money, as they say." She leaned forward on the sofa. "I checked you out. You're FASTO. I didn't know that until today."

Judith heaved a big sigh. "That's a bunch of misguided people who somehow think I'm a supersleuth. Everything that's happened to me has just . . . happened. The only difference between me and other people is that maybe I have more curiosity. And I can't seem to stop running into bodies."

"You certainly do." Jean's tone was ironic. "What's the count up to? A couple of dozen?"

"I've no idea. It's not a contest. My husband was a police detective for a long time. After he retired from the force, he became a private investigator. It's only natural that I'd be interested in his work."

Jean laughed. "Nobody is *that* interested. I hear things. I know some of the cases you've been involved in have occurred when Mr. Flynn wasn't anywhere near you. Have you looked at your site lately? What about the train trip you were on last fall?"

"I never look at the site. Never." Judith was angry. "I've no idea who may have alluded to that incident. My cousin and I never even told our husbands what happened."

"Then," Jean said, sobering, "it's a good thing Mr. Flynn doesn't check your site either."

"No reason why he should," Judith said. "I've never told him about it. And I don't intend to. Which brings me to the present situation," she went on, taking the offensive. "What do you really know about Walter Paine and the rest of his family?"

"I haven't talked to Walter since my wallet was stolen," Jean replied. "I've been on the other side of the state, meeting people involved with the wild-horse situation. Why do you ask?"

Judith took a deep breath. "Maybe you should ask *him*."

Jean's face showed concern. "Has something happened to Walter?"

"Not directly. But ask him, not me."

"You're withholding information."

"Am I?" Judith shrugged. "Call him. Go see him. I assume you trust Walter."

"Yes," Jean said. "I've worked with him off and on for five years. He has integrity." She picked up her hobo bag. "You've got me worried."

"Join the club," Judith said as they both stood up. "But you have to promise me something."

"What?" Jean asked, pausing halfway out of the living room.

"That you'll let me know what he says."

"I can't do that."

"Then I won't tell you what I know—and it's plenty."

Jean stopped just short of the front door. "How do I know you have any information I need?"

"Because," Judith said, "I'm FASTO. I may never read what's on that site, but I can guess what's there. You would never have come back to see me if you didn't believe it." She opened the door. "I'll expect to hear from you tomorrow."

Five minutes later, Judith was on the phone, eager to discuss Jean's visit with Renie. But her cousin had qualms. "Hold it," she said after the first few words. "I know I told you to call me, but after you left I remembered you mentioned a call from Joe at City Hall and his inability to tell you anything over the phone because he was afraid of eavesdroppers. At which end did he think somebody was listening in?"

"I never found out," Judith admitted. "His end, I assumed. On the other hand, it could've been here. I'm trying to recall who was here that night. It seems so long ago." She went into the entry hall to check the guest register. "Oh—the Beard-Smythes," she said before looking at the entries. "I'd like to forget them entirely." She scanned the page for Thursday. "A middle-aged couple from Indianapolis, two sisters—one from Green Bay, the other from San Diego—the Kamloops, B.C., couple, and Jean Rogers."

"So the Kamloops duo is a repeat," Renie murmured. "Maybe we should hang up."

Judith was reluctant. "I feel like you're my lifeline. Keep talking. Anything, just so I don't have to think. I'm beyond tired and I'm crabby."

"Oh, for . . . what shall I say? That Auntie Vance and Uncle Vince are coming down from the island tomorrow? That Bill wishes Joe would get out of jail so they could go steelheading? That I need to get my hair cut? I was actually trying to get some work done."

"Okay," Judith said, "I'll shut up."

"Fine. See you at Mass tomorrow."

"No, you won't. I can't face any SOTS. I'm going to St. Rita's."

"Good thinking. Good night."

Feeling tired, glum, and ill at ease, Judith tried to focus on what she'd serve for breakfast in the morning. She'd keep it simple. Toast, eggs, sausage, bacon, fruit, and juice. Maybe she'd make regular toast and French toast. She scribbled some notes on the tablet she kept by the kitchen bulletin board. *FT & RT, S&B, F&J, EGGS?* Fried, scrambled, poached, whatever. She frowned at the letters. They reminded her of something. Another note, but not one she'd written. . .

SF OR LA. That was what she'd seen on the slip of paper in Joe's office. San Francisco or Los Angeles, she'd thought at the time. But why would Joe write down the initials for two cities? What if they stood for something else? Businesses? ARBS came to mind, along with SANECO. Both companies were known by acronyms. No help there. People, maybe. Was there anybody relevant to the current muddle of a mystery? She went over the Paine family members. None of them came close. Nor did any of the other recent newcomers in her life—not Jean Rogers or Cindy and Geoff Owens or Abe Burleson.

The newspaper was still on the counter. Judith picked it up to put in the recycling bin. A headline about Mayor Larry Appel's plan to fix the city's potholed streets caught her eye. She frowned. *LA*—for Larry Appel? The mayor was no whiz kid, but his reputation for honesty had never been questioned. He'd gotten elected because of his integrity, replacing the incumbent, who'd appointed unqualified friends and relatives to city jobs.

Judith wondered if she was going down a blind alley. It was almost eleven-thirty. She chucked the newspaper into the bin under the sink before turning off the computer. Just as she was about to shut it down, an e-mail notice popped up from Keith Delemetrios. Judith went to the message site and clicked on the detective's name.

A man named Sidney Foxe is coming to see you in the next fifteen minutes. Let him in. He'll offer you as much assistance as he'll require from you. Joe.

Sidney Foxe. *SF,* Judith thought, her heart suddenly racing. Before turning off the computer, she checked the other messages that had come in earlier. Hurriedly, she deleted the e-mails from catalog companies and stores, saving only three reservation requests. She printed them out, but would wait until morning to deal with the would-be guests. At least Joe had figured out a way to reach her without being overheard. Judith wondered why neither of them had thought of e-mail before. She considered responding, but that might be risky since he'd contacted her from the police department. Maybe she should get a cell phone that would text. The world moved so fast and she was so slow at keeping up with the maelstrom of new technology.

Judith had just finished her kitchen tasks when she heard the doorbell. Wiping her hands on a towel, she hurried to the entry hall. When she looked through the peephole, she couldn't see anyone on the porch. The only activity in the wet, dark cul-de-sac was a set of red taillights turning onto the cross street. The wind had come up, blowing the camellia bush against the house and making the Rankerses' porch chimes jangle like broken glass. Bracing herself, she opened the door. To her astonishment, a man in a wheelchair was seated a few feet away.

"I'm Sidney Foxe," he said in a vaguely familiar voice. "I believe you're expecting me?"

Judith tried not to gape. For the third time in the past few hours, she was startled by the sight of an unexpected visitor. Unlike Abe Burleson, who was a stranger, but like Jean Rogers, whom she'd recognized after the initial shock, the newcomer was known to her, not as Sidney Foxe, but as Zachary Conrad.

"Come in," she said, holding the storm door so that her guest could maneuver inside. "I assume you came by cab?"

"A cabulance," Sidney replied. Like Gertrude, he had a motorized scooter chair. "The parlor again?"

"No," she said. "The living room. There's more space. Come by the window seat. I'll sit there. May I get you something to drink?"

"No, thank you. I dined just a short time ago."

"You seem to have recovered from your illness," Judith said, indicating he should sit by the bay window.

Sidney stopped the wheelchair. "I'd overexerted myself by trying to walk too much." He gazed at the view of the bay, though it was blurred by the heavy rain. "A nasty night. Snow's in the air."

"It's January," Judith remarked absently, moving some of the pillows and cushions before sitting down. "I have to admit I'm anxious to hear your story. I did find out you weren't Zachary Conrad."

Sidney smiled, revealing uneven and slightly discolored teeth. "It's not a happy story."

"That doesn't bother me. I've heard plenty of sad stories."

"I've been homeless," Sidney said. "Do you know any homeless people's stories?"

"I do," Judith replied, thinking back to a homeless man who had become a murder victim.

If Sidney was surprised by her response, he didn't show it. "I'm an engineer with a degree from MIT. That sounds impressive, doesn't it?"

"I suppose it does," Judith allowed. She tried to ignore the wind blowing down the chimney and battering the shrubs outside the bay window. "Apparently it didn't spare you from hard times."

"True." Sidney folded his hands in his lap. He was dressed in a suit and tie under a black raincoat. The clothes looked worn, but of decent quality. "I'm not totally paralyzed, by the way."

"I assumed that," Judith said, feeling a draft through the window. "Otherwise, you couldn't have walked at all when you were here last night posing as Zachary Conrad."

"Yes." Sidney stared at his thin hands. "I had a good job for years with Northeast Utilities in Hartford, Connecticut. I got married, had two children, a boy and a girl. One night we were coming back from my son's hockey game. There was black ice on the road. I missed a turn and crashed into a utility pole. Ironic, eh?"

Judith hated to ask the obvious, but did. "What happened?"

"My wife and children were killed. Outright, not even a scream. I was seriously injured. I couldn't work for over a year. I lost my job. I lost my whole world." Sidney related the events as if by rote, staring past Judith into the rain-spattered window, as if he could see each horror unfolding like a slide show. "All I had was the memory of something I couldn't see—six feet of black ice. And the sound of those power lines snapping, snapping, snapping." He shook his head, as if the noise was still beating on his brain like a death knell.

Judith started to say something comforting, but for once nothing came to her. It was just as well. Sidney had taken up his tale again. "After many months in hospitals and rehabilitation centers, I made a partial recovery," he continued, speaking more naturally. "I had no close family in New

England, but my wife had a nephew attending college here. I thought he might be a source of comfort. He wasn't. He didn't have time for a crippled uncle he hardly knew. That was six years ago."

"He had no relatives in the area?"

Sidney shook his head. "He'd moved here from Los Angeles. His own family was a quarrelsome bunch. He was diligent about his studies. I was an unwanted distraction."

"The young can be selfish," Judith murmured.

"Indeed." Sidney took a deep breath. "I ran out of money very quickly. That's when I became homeless, living under the freeway at night, spending my days on the streets. One late Sunday afternoon I was sitting on the sidewalk by the football stadium. The game was just letting out. Hardly anybody noticed me. They were talking about the home team's victory. Then an older man stopped to ask when I'd last eaten. I told him I wasn't sure. He offered to take me to dinner. I was stunned. I didn't know what to say. He was a big fellow, and despite his age, he was strong. He got me on my feet and half carried me to a nearby café. I told him my story. He listened and promised to get me a job with the city. He had connections. His name was Al Grover."

"Uncle Al!" Judith gasped. "I've heard that story. But it was about a doctor, not an engineer."

The hint of a smile touched Sidney's lips. "I suspect there've been hapless doctors, lawyers, and Indian chiefs who've crossed his path."

"Yes," Judith agreed. "Uncle Al's generous. Did he get you a job?"

Sidney nodded. "He tried to get me on with the lighting department, but they didn't have any openings. I met Zachary Conrad then." He paused. "A true bureaucrat. I didn't like him. I don't think he liked me either. I had, at the time, what some might call an 'attitude.'" Sidney cleared his throat. "I had lost my respect for other human beings, despite your uncle's kindness."

"Understandable," Judith remarked, moving a bit to get out of the window's draft. "Did Uncle Al find other work for you?"

"Yes, with the health department. But I'm getting ahead of myself." His reproachful expression indicated that Judith was pressuring him. "I literally bumped into Conrad's wife on my way out of his office, being crippled. Hannah Conrad was supposed to have lunch with her husband, but he'd canceled. Too busy, he'd told her. She was angry. She berated me for my clumsiness before she realized I was handicapped. In her ire, she suddenly took my arm and said she would take me to lunch instead. And she did. During that meal, I discovered she was crippled, too—not on the outside, but the inside. An overbearing mother and a domineering husband had destroyed her self-confidence. We became lovers that very afternoon. That was two years ago. Three weeks later, I became an inspector for the health department."

Pieces were beginning to fall into place, but Judith didn't want to further rush Sidney. "You must've been relieved."

"I suppose I was," Sidney said vaguely. "It was not, of course, my forte. There was no challenge. Checking for past-due dates on food and making sure kitchen help wore hairnets was unsatisfying work. I wanted more. I have a curious mind. By chance, I came across my nephew, who was also working for the city. He's a police detective. You may know him. His name is Keith Delemetrios."

Judith tried to hide her surprise. "Really? Yes, I've met him."

"Oh? What do you think of him?"

Judith sensed she had to be careful. "As a person or a detective?"

"Either. Both."

"He seems conscientious about his job," Judith said truthfully. "I know almost nothing about him except that."

"He's driven," Sidney said simply.

"You mean to seek justice?"

"Yes. You could put it that way."

Judith caught something in Sidney's dark eyes that disturbed her. "That's all I can say. Could I ask you about your job?"

"Why? It's very boring."

"Were you sent to ARBS a week or two ago?"

Sidney laughed, a rather unpleasant sound. "Of course I was. That's how I was reinjured."

"It was termed an accident," Judith said, involuntarily moving farther away from her visitor on the window seat, draft or not. "Do you own the condo on Lake Concord?"

"No, no," Sidney replied, scooting a bit closer to Judith. "That's Hannah's pied-à-terre for our romantic rendezvous. She sometimes lends it to other family members when they need . . . to get away."

"I'm confused," Judith admitted. "I know that Zachary Conrad was there in a wheelchair and that he was shot to death. Can you explain how that happened? It makes no sense."

Sidney's smile was quirky. "You are too impatient. Of course I can explain. Zachary was a bureaucrat, but a conscientious one. He'd heard rumors of an investigation in the police department. When I had my accident—and I don't consider it an accident, but a deliberate attempt to keep me from investigating what was going on at ARBS regarding some of their meat products. In any event, Hannah told me he couldn't understand why the police didn't investigate my mishap. I was able to get around with a cane and sometimes, on bad days, crutches." He caressed the arm of his wheelchair. "But this was a setback. I couldn't stay in my apartment. There's no elevator and I'm on the second floor. Hannah suggested I move into the condo. Zachary knew it was a retreat of sorts for family members, but he had his suspicions about his wife. He wanted to be a hero in her eyes and those of the police department. He was also ambitious, having sat in the same job for too long. Hannah told me all this and I spoke to Keith—Del, he likes to be called—to ask about the lack of a police investigation. He insisted he wasn't fully informed, but it had something to do with a former chief before his time. Like most young people, if it hadn't happened to him, it hadn't happened."

"I understand," Judith said, "but why are you telling me all this?"

"Because," Sidney said, "it's all your fault." He smiled. "That," he went on, standing up, "is why I'm going to kill you."

Chapter
Twenty-two

Judith froze on the window seat. She opened her mouth, but no sound came out. Sidney had taken a lethal-looking hunting knife out from under his raincoat and released the blade.

"I have great upper-body strength," he said calmly. "You may scream, but I will slit your throat so fast that anyone who hears you will find only your corpse."

Judith shook her head, trying to find her voice. "Why?" The single word was a whisper, so soft that she wasn't sure she'd actually said it.

He stood only a foot away from where Judith sat. She'd forgotten how tall he was. "You ruined my life. The accident was your fault."

"No." Again, she didn't know if she'd spoken out loud.

"Yes. You meddled in police affairs. You besmirched my father's reputation."

"Your . . . ?" *This must be a nightmare. Nothing makes sense. I don't know anybody named Foxe. This man is insane. And I've got to wake up.*

"I changed my name when I moved here," Sidney said,

the light from the lamp on the cherrywood table glinting off of the steel blade. "Foxe is so close to his name, so clever of me. You recall Lloyd Volpe?"

Judith gasped. The Silver Fox—Volpe, vulpine, foxlike. "I never . . ."

The grandfather clock in the corner of the room struck midnight. The deep sound startled Sidney. He grimaced, clapped his free hand to his ear, and turned, just enough to lose his balance. Judith flung herself at him, heedless of her artificial hip, oblivious to what damage she might do to her own body, desperate to save her life.

He fell against the wheelchair, crumpling in pain. The knife was still in his hand. Judith was lying halfway on top of him, but she couldn't reach his arm. If only he lacked the strength to use his weapon, she might be able to stand.

The clock finished its twelve chimes for the hour. The sudden silence seemed to have a favorable effect on Sidney. He, too, was trying to move just enough to take aim with the knife.

The unearthly quiet was broken by what seemed like a disembodied voice from somewhere nearby.

"Yoo-hoo," Arlene called. "Where are you? I found my tomato paste. Judith?" She glanced into the living room. "Oh my goodness! I didn't realize you were . . . ah . . . entertaining. I'll go now."

"Arlene!" The name felt ripped out of Judith's throat. "Help!"

"What . . ." Arlene, who had momentarily disappeared, poked her head around the corner of the archway. "Oh, dear! Are you hurt? Is he . . . ?" She saw the knife and let out a little cry of shock. "What is this?"

Judith suddenly realized that Sidney had stopped moving. The knife lay on the carpet. "Oh my God!" she cried. "Help me up!"

Arlene was spurred into action. "I don't know what to think," she murmured, carefully getting Judith to her feet. "You're shaking like a leaf. You'd better sit." She looked at Sidney. "Who is this? Is he dead?"

"I don't think so," Judith said, still leaning against Arlene, "but we'd better call 911. Kick that knife out of the way, would you?"

Hanging on to Judith, Arlene kicked the knife so hard that it skidded all the way across the carpet to land by the piano at the other end of the living room. "Shall I call for you?" she asked, settling Judith back onto the window seat.

"I can do it," Judith said, reaching for the phone on the cherrywood table. But before she could steady her fingers to dial, she heard sirens. "Maybe we don't have to. Is the door still open?"

"No. I'll open it," Arlene said, with a last look at the unconscious man. "I don't know what to make of all this," she said, heading for the entry hall. "I thought the wheelchair was your mother's, but it's not . . ."

Her words faded as she went out of sight. The next voice Judith heard was Joe's.

"Oh my God!" he cried, rushing into the living room. "Oh no!" He awkwardly circumvented Sidney to get to the window seat and wrap Judith in his arms. "Damn, damn, damn! I knew this might happen!"

Judith barely heard him. She was still trembling, but all that mattered was that she was pressed against Joe and she was still alive.

"Brandy," he said to someone, though Judith wasn't sure who, as she could tell from the sounds of movement and lowered voices that several people were in the living room.

"Joe," she whimpered as he slowly pulled away. "Don't."

"I'm taking you into the parlor," he said softly. "Can you stand?"

Judith wriggled her toes, then planted both feet on the floor. "I think so, if you help me."

It was only a short distance to the door that led from the living room to the parlor. Judith glimpsed the activity, but didn't really take it in. She only noticed Arlene, who was apparently heading for the kitchen. "I have no idea," she was saying to a man whose back was turned. "I came here with tomato paste. I've never seen that man on the floor in my life. Maybe he's a traveling salesman. But that's not Mrs. Grover's wheelchair, I can tell you that much. Oh—there's a knife by the piano. You'd better take that as some sort of evidence, Woodrow."

Woody, Judith thought as Joe half carried her into the parlor. *Of course.* "I must be gaga," she murmured. "I didn't even recognize Woofy. I mean, *Woody.*"

"Doesn't matter." Joe eased her onto the settee. "I should take you up to bed, but I'm not sure I can carry you all the way to the third floor." He looked a bit sheepish. "I'm not as young as I used to be. We'll wait until you're steadier on your feet."

"I still don't understand what happened," Judith said in a querulous tone. "That man must be insane."

"Probably," Joe said, glancing out one of the windows. "It's starting to snow."

"It is?" The weather was the least of Judith's concerns. "Who is he? Sidney Foxe, I mean."

Joe leaned on the settee's arm. "Just take it easy. You've been through hell. I can see that." He sighed ruefully. "I'd hoped to keep you out of this. Maybe you should've been arrested instead of me. At least you'd have been out of harm's way."

"But," Judith persisted, "what does Volpe have to do with all this? He hasn't been chief for several years."

"Did you mention the Silver Fox?" Arlene asked, entering

from the hall door. "I poured the brandy into juice glasses. It seemed wrong to use your nice snifters with that man lying on the living room floor. Some of the guests heard the sirens and came into the kitchen. I reassured them it was merely a false alarm caused by Tulip tripping our security system."

Judith didn't bother reminding Arlene that she didn't have a security system. Instead, she looked at her neighbor with a grateful expression. "You saved my life—and you've come to my rescue before. In fact, the first time it was up at church. Thank you, thank you!"

"Well, what are neighbors for?" Arlene shrugged and raised her glass. "Cheers. Or something."

"You usually go to bed early," Judith said after taking the first strong sip of brandy. "Why were you up this late?"

Arlene waved a hand. "Oh, Carl! His back is bothering him when he lies down and he was all over the bed, so I decided if I couldn't sleep, I might as well clean out the kitchen cupboards. That's when I found my tomato paste. I saw your lights were still on, so I thought while I remembered I'd come over to repay you."

Judith smiled. "You certainly did."

"Is there anything else I can do?" Arlene inquired. "I can't tidy up the living room with all those people in there doing whatever it is they're doing, which I might add, seems rather unpleasant. I don't think that man on the floor is dead, though. Do you know him?"

"No," Judith said. "That is, not exactly."

"Some people are like that," Arlene remarked. "You think you know them, but you don't." She drained her glass in one gulp. "I'll sleep in Kevin's old room tonight. Call if you need me." Seemingly unfazed by the midnight terrors and the strong drink, Arlene left the parlor.

"Incredible," Judith said. "Arlene is utterly unflappable. Raising five kids has given her some kind of inner strength."

Joe rubbed her shoulder. "You're kind of a tough nut, too. It's a good thing Woody checked the outgoing e-mails. But I realized you'd know I'd never send such a stilted message."

Judith struggled for breath. "You . . . didn't? Who did?"

"Del's crazy uncle, I guess. He'd stopped by just as Del was about to leave. I'd never seen the guy before. How come you let him in?"

Judith grimaced. "I thought the e-mail *was* from you. It seemed like a good way to communicate so you could delete it immediately."

Joe held his head. "Jeez."

"I feel like an idiot!" Judith cried, clutching Joe's arm.

"No, no. I'm the idiot. I should have . . . I never thought much about the guy except that he seemed a little weird. Del didn't mention that his uncle sent an e-mail. Maybe he didn't know. Damn!" He shook his head. "I wouldn't have found out if Woody hadn't checked for messages and saw a new one had just gone to you. That's what made us race here with all systems on red alert." He sipped more brandy before putting the glass down on a tiered side table. "I'd better go see if the guy's really alive, and if so, what they'll charge him with. Attempted homicide, and maybe get him to confess to shooting Zachary Conrad. I gather he had some grudge against the guy."

"Don't," Judith said, her voice almost normal. "He didn't kill Conrad."

Joe stared at his wife. "How do you know that?"

"Sidney Foxe or Sidney Volpe or whoever he is has tinnitus. You know—ringing of the ears. Renie's uncle Balthazar had it. It's a recurring disease that, in his case, may have been caused by a car accident that . . . never mind. I'll tell you later. The grandfather clock chimes set him off. My point is, he would never fire a gun. That's why he carried a knife."

Joe leaned against the parlor door frame, his expression quizzical. "Spare me details. You wouldn't know who did kill Conrad, would you?"

"Well . . . I think so. The obvious first suspect in any homicide case. Mrs. Zachary Conrad, née Hannah Paine."

J udith slept until almost noon. Joe had seen to the guests, making his special egg dish that Martha Morelli had disdained as "unoriginal."

When Judith got out of bed, she was stiff and sore, but grateful to be alive. It was too late to make it to noon Mass. Maybe she'd try for an evening service at another nearby parish. She certainly had a lot to thank God for on this snowy Sunday in January.

By the time she got downstairs, all the guests had departed. Joe had cleaned up the kitchen and was in the living room watching a pro football game.

"Hungry?" he asked when she sat down on the arm of his side chair.

"Oddly enough, I'm not," she said. "I don't remember when I last ate. How's Mother?"

"Disgusted," Joe replied, muting the TV sound. "I thought she'd pass out when I brought her breakfast. She was sure I was gallows bait. In fact, she thought the sirens last night were the cops coming to arrest you as my accomplice."

"Maybe if I get a cup of coffee, I can focus on you explaining what was really going on with this nightmare."

Joe put a hand on her leg. "Sit. Go over to the sofa. I'll get your coffee." He turned off the TV. "Stupid game. The Giants are getting their butts kicked by the Panthers."

Judith didn't argue. She paused only to look outside, where a dusting of snow remained on the ground. *Pretty,* she thought, and shivered, despite the burning logs in the fireplace. Had it not been for the grandfather clock, she might be *in* the ground. On her way to the sofa, she blew the clock a kiss.

Joe had brought coffee for both of them. "Let's time-travel back to an occasion when you managed to take down a crooked cop," he said, sitting across from Judith on the other sofa. "Uncle Al was involved in that one, as I recall. After the cop was canned and went to prison, Chief Volpe got a lot of criticism for hiring him in the first place. Lloyd didn't like criticism. Not long after that he took early retirement—voluntarily. We knew he had kids, a couple of daughters, one in the Bay Area, the other in the Twin Cities, and a son back east, which is where Lloyd came from originally. He was hired, in fact, from the Boston Police Department, where he'd made a name for himself as a hard-nosed drug buster. He never talked about family much, being a private kind of guy. You met him a couple times, right?"

Judith nodded. "At least. He was pleasant, if not exactly warm. I did my best to be friendly, but he seemed immune. I suspect the only person who knows much about his private life is Arlene. She's relentless when it comes to eliciting information."

"Arlene." Joe shook his head. "Incredible woman. I talked to Woody this morning. Once they had the doctors check out Foxe—or Volpe or Nut Job—he talked and talked. The current departmental investigation of misdeeds triggered flashbacks for him and he was fixated on the idea that his father's career had been deliberately destroyed by some amateur." The green eyes sparked. "Guess who?"

Judith was stunned. "How did he find out about that old case with the bad cop?"

Joe leaned back on the sofa. "It seems you have a fan site. Why didn't you tell me?"

"It's stupid. I never look at it. They refer to me as FASTO

and half the people who look at it think I'm called FATSO. It's embarrassing."

"You should take a peek now and then," Joe said. "You might also have told me about it. There are at least two dozen references to the bad-cop incident—just in the past six weeks. That's what set Sidney off. He was sure you'd caused his father to leave the force. The guy's psycho, but that doesn't mean he isn't clever. Now Woody and Chief Stuart have to give the bad news to Lloyd, who is blissfully basking in the sun on Kaanapali Beach in Hawaii."

"Oh, dear!" Judith tried not to feel guilty. "But what about Hannah? Has she been found?"

Joe chuckled. "Yes. She was at the condo, waiting for Sidney."

"What?" Judith shrieked. "But it's a crime scene!"

"They took the tape down after my alleged arrest," Joe said. "We've had it under surveillance ever since. She confessed. She's as crazy as Sidney. Her biggest mistake was letting Sonya act like a caregiver. Sonya figured out that Hannah and Sidney had something going on there and confronted Zachary, who admitted he thought his wife was having an affair. Sonya was so disgusted with the whole bunch of Paines that she stomped off and never came back."

"Walter's not so bad, I guess," Judith remarked.

"Walter? Oh—the government agent. Maybe not, but he apparently carries out his jolly-good-fellow act too far."

"You know about Walter?"

"It's not a state secret to other law enforcement officers. He's been helping with the ARBS horsemeat violations. That whole family is screwed up. No love lost between the brothers Paine. Andy is going down. I'm guessing, but I figure he caused the so-called accident to Sidney at the food factory." Joe leaned forward to pick up his coffee mug. "No doubt about it, some of those truck drivers who had ARBS on their route were taking bribes to tote dead horses to Andy and that dink from the parish who owns the plant. Yes, a few of our uniforms were turning a blind eye—or worse."

" 'Our'?"

Joe's ruddy complexion darkened as he lowered his gaze. "Okay, so I've spent the last few days playing cop. It's a hard habit to break."

"You never will break it," Judith said. "It's your nature. How long did it take you to figure out you'd been set up?"

Slowly, he raised his eyes to look at Judith. "I knew from the start, as soon as Zachary Conrad insisted on setting a trap with himself as bait so he could be a hero. It also gave him a chance to find evidence that his wife was having an affair at the condo."

"You mean there was never any insurance fraud?"

Joe shook his head. "Only poor Sidney's so-called accident. But it gave Chief Stuart a chance to try a sting operation, figuring that it might bring out one of the departmental bad apples or at least somebody from ARBS. Maybe offering a payoff to the supposed victim. SANECO was told about it on the q.t., which is how we got to use the houseboat as a surveillance site. Then Zachary muddied the waters by volunteering to replace Sidney. Chief Stuart liked that idea, just in case whoever contacted the supposed victim wouldn't actually be incapacitated in case things got ugly. Zachary was a big, strong former athlete. Besides, the chief likes to keep the other city divisions happy. It just didn't work out so well for the would-be hero."

Judith was flummoxed. "That's . . . that's infuriating! I was worried sick! What about the gun? Who stole it?"

Joe winced. "Nobody. I had it all along. But it was the only way I could warn you that danger might be lurking somewhere. I knew my so-called arrest would send you into a sleuthing tizzy. I figured that if I sent you off on a false trail, you'd stay out of trouble. Or at least be on guard." A faint smile played at his mouth. "After all, it's your nature."

"Touché," Judith muttered. "But why did you leave the safe open when there were still guns in there? Wasn't that dangerous?"

Joe looked puzzled. "I didn't. I locked it, knowing you'd be able to figure out the combination, and even if you didn't, you'd be on your guard."

Judith grimaced. "I think I understand. I'm not the only person who can get into a safe without the combination. A crafty guest may have the same skills. She turned out to be an industrial spy and was probably trying to figure out what was going on with ARBS and the horses and the Paines coming for the auction event. But that's up to the Department of the Interior to resolve."

Joe was looking flummoxed. "The Department of the—"

"Skip it," Judith urged. "It's a long story and I'll save it for another time. The main thing about the safe is that my search for the gun offered clues about those initials so that I realized Sidney Foxe was involved."

Joe frowned. "Huh?"

"That slip of paper with 'LA OR SF' on it. Sidney Foxe or Larry Appel, the mayor."

Joe scratched his head. "I don't know what you're . . . oh!" He grinned at Judith. "That was a year ago when I was trying to figure out where we'd go on our vacation—Los Angeles, San Francisco, the Oregon Coast. Then I got the idea for the Scotland trip."

"Oooh . . ." Judith leaned her head against the back of the sofa. "I feel like an idiot!"

"But you're a live idiot," Joe pointed out, getting up from the sofa. "How much do you hurt?"

"I took some Excedrin," Judith said as he hovered over her. "I . . ." She saw the magic gold flecks in his eyes. "I feel great."

Joe slipped his hand inside her sweater. "Yes, you do."

The grandfather clock struck two before Judith remembered that Gertrude hadn't had lunch.

Hey," Renie said on the phone later that afternoon, "Bill and I just heard about what happened at your house last night. It was on the news, which we never listen to, but it came on after the ball game Bill was watching. I feel terrible. I should've kept talking to you on the phone or stayed with you."

"It all worked out," Judith said. "Come for dinner. I'm making stew and dumplings as penance for Mother missing lunch."

"Oh. Bill likes stew and dumplings. Maybe we will. Speaking of dump," Renie continued, "Bill dumped that client who was being stalked. I can tell you now who it was."

"Who?"

"Reggie Beard-Smythe. He stiffed Bill on his bill, and it sounds as if Reggie's in big trouble. He's been taking discarded animals from the hunt club and turning them into hamburger, which is why those kids at SOTS school got sick. Somebody at the club was onto him. The carnations were pinks, as in the colors of the coats, the leather belt was a horsehide reference, and . . . I forget the rest, but Bill can tell you at dinner. See you."

Judith had barely hung up when the phone rang again. "Big headlines," Uncle Al said. "Hey, kiddo, you've got to work harder at staying out of trouble. Why don't you take up another hobby, like toxic waste sites or getting shot out of a cannon? Nobody's luck lasts forever."

"I know," Judith said. "But you played a part in this one. What makes me sad is that this crazy man who tried to kill me was someone you helped. I guess that wasn't so lucky after all."

"No good deed goes unrewarded," Uncle Al said. "Sure, you can't win 'em all, but I made a bundle off that guy. Two days after I fed him, I made a Trifecta bet on three long shots at a California track and won over fifteen grand—I wheeled 'em. Foxy Loxy, Café Au Lait, and Downandout. Hey—got to go. Here comes a newspaper reporter to interview me. Whoa—he's got a looker with him. Talk to you . . ."

"What newspaper guy?"

"That Addison Kirby. You read his work?"

"I know *him*," Judith said. "What does the woman look like?"

"Hang on," Uncle Al said. "I have to let them in."

Judith heard the door being opened, followed by her uncle's greeting. Addison said something she couldn't quite hear. The woman's voice came through more clearly, but it was Uncle Al who made the positive ID. "Pleased to meet you, Paulina. Have a seat while I say good-bye to my niece."

Joe sauntered into the kitchen just as Judith hung up the phone. "What are you smiling about?" he asked.

She put her arms around his neck. "Earlier, I was thinking of how much pain the Paines had brought to so many people, themselves included. But I just realized that sometimes a Paine can be a pleasure."

Joe pulled back slightly, staring at his wife. "Huh? Have you been in the brandy again?"

"It's a long story," she replied, still smiling. "Move. I have to peel some potatoes."

"I can do that," Joe said, opening the utensil drawer. "I figure you may have a lot of stories to tell me about what happened while I was gone." He took out the vegetable peeler and suddenly clapped his hand on the counter. "Oh—I forgot to give you this." Reaching into his pocket, he pulled out a folded piece of notebook paper. "One of your guests left this for you."

Judith unfolded the handwritten message. *Mrs. Flynn— those men from Kentucky didn't want Son of Scarlet for their buyer in Dubai. Said the price was too cheap!!! The contact, Zoë something-or-other, is willing to give us the horse, so we're making arrangements to take it to Kamloops. We'll be coming back here in February to get SOS (!!!) and to meet again with the animal shelter people. Is it possible we could stay the weekend of Feb. 18–20? Thanks again for everything!!!*

The note was signed *Cindy Owens*, complete with a Happy Face.

"Well?" Joe said. "You're still smiling. What's that all about?"

"A horse."

Joe paused. "A horse?"

Judith nodded. "Of course."

Shrimp Dump

1 tbsp. butter
1 tbsp. flour
½ cup chicken broth (I recommend using Watkins
    Chicken Soup and Gravy Base, but any basic
    chicken bouillon will do)
Salt and white pepper to taste
½ cup milk
1 hard-boiled egg, cut up
3 cups small shrimp

Melt the butter and stir in flour in a quart-size pot over low heat. Blend in the broth, salt and white pepper, and milk. Turn up the heat just to boiling, while continuing to stir. Add the egg and shrimp.

Turn down the heat and simmer 3–5 minutes. If you're too impatient to wait, go ahead and pig out—I do recommend, however, removing it from the pot first.

Pour the mixture over toast or Pepperidge Farm Puff Pastry Shells. Toast takes only a minute or so; pastry puffs take much longer and should be heated in the oven before preparing the filling.

Serves one, but then that's just me—I really love this as a late-night snack.

Judith McMonigle Flynn is fed up with criticism from the state B&B association, which is threatening to yank her innkeeper's license over a few occasional corpses. Thus, when Judith—along with Cousin Renie—heads off for Little Bavaria to help man a state B&B booth during Oktoberfest, the last thing she needs is another homicide to sully her reputation.

But—being Judith—the first thing she finds is a dead body, right in the middle of an oompah band and a herd of German dancers. She flees the scene even before the cops arrive, telling Renie this is one time she will not get involved. Alas, her reputation has preceded her to the mountain village, and the local police chief seeks her help in solving the death of the beloved town patron, nonagenarian Dietrich Wessler. Judith finally agrees, but only if Renie poses as the sleuth. Little do the cousins know that . . .

THE WURST IS YET TO COME

Available July 2012 in hardcover

WILLIAM MORROW
An Imprint of HarperCollins*Publishers*

Judith McMonigle Flynn heard the knock at the back door of Hillside Manor, wondered which friend or family member had forgotten the key, and hurried to see who was on the back porch.

"Joe!" she cried, looking through the small window and turning the doorknob. "Why can't you . . ." The knob fell off in her hand. "Come around to the front," she said to her husband whose round face looked miffed—and wet—from the October rain.

Joe Flynn's green eyes narrowed at Judith as he held up the other half of the doorknob. "Warzdadamtolbag?" he shouted.

"I can't hear you," Judith replied, gesturing at the leaky downspout where the rainwater dripped with a noisy *plop-plop-plop* into a steel bowl by the porch steps.

Joe tossed the doorknob aside and stomped off the porch. Sighing, Judith went back down the hallway, through the kitchen, the dining room, and the entry hall. She opened the front door just as Joe appeared on the walkway.

"What did you say?" she asked, irritated by her husband's scowl.

"I said," Joe responded, dripping rainwater off of his navy blue raincoat, "where's that damned Tolvang? I thought your handyman was going to be here today."

"He couldn't come," Judith replied. "His truck broke down."

"No kidding," Joe muttered, heading straight for the kitchen. "Did the crank fall off so he couldn't start that old heap?"

Judith traipsed after him. "The crank is leaving mud on my clean floor. Bad day or did you stop off to see Mother first?"

Joe was in the back hallway, hanging up his raincoat. "Why would I want to see your ghastly mother? Wasn't it bad enough I had to go through about a million background checks for the police department all day? Why did I take on this job? It's not worth the money."

"Because we need the money? Because you like your former partner, Woody Price? Because you're still a cop at heart?"

"Hmm." A faint smile tugged at Joe's mouth. "All of the above?" He entered the kitchen and put his arms around Judith. Brushing her lips with a kiss, he sniffed. "You smell like a lemon."

"I've been squeezing lemons for a meringue pie," Judith said, leaning against Joe. "Renie gave me a whole bag of them."

Joe tipped Judith's chin to make eye contact. "Why would your goofy cousin do that? No," he said quickly, putting his finger on her parted lips. "I don't want to know. Let me guess. She's growing lemons in the basement instead of sweeping out the dirt she tracks in?"

Judith shook her head.

Joe frowned in concentration. "Somebody sent her a bag of lemons after trying her God-awful Shrimp Dump recipe in the parish cookbook?"

Judith shook her head again.

Joe sighed and released his wife. "I give up. And by the way, I hate lemon meringue pie."

"So does Bill," Judith said, referring to Renie's husband. "I'm making it for Arlene and Carl Rankers when they arrive tomorrow to take over the B&B while I'm in Little Bavaria."

"Damn, I forgot you were leaving so soon," he said, moving to the cupboard where the family liquor was kept. "I keep thinking this is Tuesday."

"You could've gone with me," she said accusingly.

Joe shook his head. "Not with this special assignment. I've got until Friday to wind it up. I feel as if I've still got another three, four million records to go through. No wonder I thought it was only Tuesday. Drink?" he asked, holding a fifth of Scotch.

"Yes, please," Judith said. "Renie thought they were onions."

"What?" Joe paused with the bottle in hand. "What onions?"

"The lemons," Judith said, checking the oven to see if the pie was done. "Renie was in a hurry at Falstaff's and she grabbed a bag of lemons, but she thought they were onions and didn't notice until she got home. She couldn't figure out why her grocery bill was at least ten bucks more than she thought it'd be. Lemons cost a lot more than onions. So she gave some of them to me."

"Why didn't she take them back to the store?" Joe asked, pouring their drinks.

"Because . . ." Judith frowned. "Renie doesn't like making exchanges. She gets all mixed up with numbers."

"She gets all mixed up with lemons and onions," Joe said, handing Judith her Scotch on the rocks.

"She has a deadline of today for designing a corporate web site," Judith explained, opening the oven and removing the pie. "I baked some meringues for the guests. I thought it'd be a nice change for the social hour." Glancing at the old schoolhouse clock, she saw it was ten to six. "I'd better get everything out to the buffet. We're full tonight, thank heavens. The economy is starting to hurt the entire hospitality industry. Ingrid Heffelman was chewing off my ear today, saying how everybody at the state B&B association is complaining about vacancies." She shot Joe a sharp glance. "As usual, she told me to give you her best."

"Wish I knew what it was," Joe said breezily. "Maybe I'll find out while you're gone."

Judith glared at Joe. "Don't even think about it. Have you ever seen Ingrid Heffelman up close? Renie calls her Inbred Heffalump."

"Renie's got a bad mouth," Joe said in his usual mellow tone. "I've seen Ingrid a couple of times when I picked you up after one of those state association meetings. I'd describe her as . . ." He took a sip of Scotch and gazed up into the high kitchen ceiling. "Rubenesque."

"You mean she looks like the painter? Maybe it's her beard."

"Hey," Joe said, swirling the liquor in his drink around the ice cubes, "when have I ever given you cause to be jealous?"

"How about the twenty years you were married to Herself instead of to your fiancée who happened to be me?"

"Good God," Joe muttered, "that was another twenty years ago. Now *we've* been married that long."

Judith removed a tray of crab and mushroom hors d'oeuvres from the oven. "Are you crazy? It's only been sixteen. You can't count any better than Renie. And don't you dare say it *seems* longer."

The gold flecks danced in Joe's green eyes. "It seems like only yesterday."

"Right." She transferred the hors d'oeuvres onto a serving platter. And berated herself for being waspish. Judith and Joe had managed to make unfortunate first marriages that had kept them apart for two decades. Fate had not been kind—until a homicide case at Hillside Manor brought them together again. "I'm sorry," she said, platter in hand. "I just wish you were going with me to Little Bavaria instead of Renie. In fact, I wish I'd never taken on the task of helping out at the state's B&B booth during the Oktoberfest. I'll be working and Renie will be bitching. She gets bored easily. And neither of us likes beer much."

"Nothing wrong with good beer," Joe remarked, swiping an hors d'oeuvre off the platter.

"Nothing right about this whole gig," Judith said. "Ingrid made it her own little project to get the B&B booth. I got the impression that the organizers weren't all that crazy about the idea, because they wanted to focus on tourism in their own part of the state. But Ingrid persevered, probably by being her usual obnoxious self."

"Gosh," Joe said in mock surprise, "I guess you really don't like her much."

"That," Judith responded as she headed for the living room, "is all too true. And the feeling is mutual."

Five minutes later, as she was setting out the meringues, the Wilsons and the Morgans from Omaha showed up for the social hour. They gushed appropriately and Judith chatted with them for a few minutes before the businessman from St. Paul arrived along with the newlyweds from Salem, Oregon. Blanking on any of their names, Judith returned to the kitchen just in time for yet another confrontation between Joe and her mother.

"Listen here, Buster," the old lady said, wagging a finger at her son-in-law, "just because you *claim* you had to work late doesn't mean my supper should be even later. Where is that useless daughter of mine?" Gertrude Grover leaned from her motorized wheelchair to see beyond Joe. "There you are. Well? Did you ruin whatever slop you were going to feed me?"

"Mother . . ." Judith began, dismayed that Gertrude hadn't bothered to put on any rain gear, but had merely thrown a sweater over her head, "you'll catch cold. Your hair's wet."

"*You're* all wet. What's for supper?"

"Beef Stroganoff," Judith replied, realizing that Joe had left the kitchen and Sweetums had entered it, trying to brush his wet, furry body against Judith's leg.

Gertrude glowered. "Like my niece Serena makes?"

"Renie uses about a gallon of sour cream," Judith said. "That's fine for her. She doesn't have to watch her weight, but I do. And it's not good for your cholesterol."

"My cholesterol is perfect," the old lady declared, "as you know."

Judith did know and couldn't understand how her mother, who considered grease a food group and smoked like a chimney, could have such a low—and healthy—reading. "I use a different recipe, and that's . . . ow!" Judith jumped as Sweetums clawed her leg. "Damnit, you've trained that wretched beast to attack upon silent command!"

Gertrude looked smug. "Okay, we're even. Dish it up and bring it out." She turned the wheelchair around and headed back to her converted toolshed apartment. With a last malevolent look at Judith, Sweetums followed, his big plume of a tail waving in triumph.

Judith rubbed at her leg, thankful that the cat hadn't torn her slacks or drawn blood. She was dishing up her mother's dinner portion when she realized that Joe was talking to someone in the entry hall. Whoever it was sounded as if he—and she, as a female voice joined in—knew Joe. Curious, she set her mother's plate down on the counter, went into the dining room, and peeked discreetly into the entry hall.

She didn't recognize what little she could see of the burly, middle-aged man and the willowy, ash-blond woman who were standing by the Bombay chest. Maybe Joe knew them from his days as a police detective. Or perhaps they were someone from his first marriage to Herself. Judith had missed all those years in her husband's life. Most of all, she'd missed Joe.

Ten minutes later, after delivering her mother's dinner, Judith was dishing up dinner in the kitchen. Joe strolled in with the dregs of his drink and sat down.

"Your mother's off-base," he said. "As usual. I like your version better than Renie's."

Judith avoided looking at Joe's slight paunch. "It's much less fattening and the wine adds some zing. In fact," she confessed, sitting down opposite her husband, "it's not beef Stroganoff. It's Beef Bourguignon. Mother doesn't trust food with French names."

"I figured as much," Joe said. "I know my way around a kitchen."

Judith smiled. "Yes, you do. You're as good a cook as I am. By the way, who were those guests you were talking to? Are they the Wainwrights?"

Joe shook his head. "No. Their last name is Lowman. Mel and Patrice were a couple doors down from where Vivian and I lived years ago. They moved to San Diego not long after Vi and I split."

"They look younger."

"Younger than what?"

"Younger than we do," Judith said.

Joe laughed. "That's because Mel wears a toupee, they've both had tummy tucks, and Patrice isn't a natural redhead."

"I color my hair," Judith said glumly.

"Sort of," Joe conceded, "but that's because you went gray about a month after marrying Dan McMonigle. It's a wonder my hair didn't fall out when I heard that news."

Judith gazed at her husband's receding—and graying—red hair. "At least you waited twenty-five years before that happened. What else could I do when you left me knocked up with Mike?"

Joe lowered his eyes. "Don't remind me. I haven't gotten drunk since the night Vivian hauled me off to the JP in Vegas."

Judith gave a start as she heard someone come through the back door. "Arlene! Are you here to get prepped for your stint taking over the B&B?"

"Not really," their neighbor replied. "I stopped by to see your mother. She's so excited about all the fun Carl and I will have with her while you're gone." Arlene's pretty face beamed. "Honestly, she's such a sweetie! You must exaggerate how she sometimes upsets you, Judith. I've never heard a harsh word tumble from her lips."

"That," Joe said, "is because she saves them up for us. Excuse me, I'm going upstairs to get some Tums. My stomach just turned sour."

Arlene shook her head. "Joe's such a card. Oh—I have to borrow a can of cream of chicken soup. Do you mind? I don't want Carl to have to go up to the store. He's worn out from painting the kitchen. Besides he has to fix the upstairs plumbing and check out the roof. That windstorm last week loosened some of the shingles."

Judith was used to Arlene's sometimes contradictory statements. "Sure, you know where to find the soup. Third shelf in the pantry."

Arlene started back down the hall but stopped. "By the way," she said, "someone stopped by this morning asking for you. He had the wrong house, of course, but I didn't let on that you lived next door. Couldn't he see your sign saying Hillside Manor? Anyway, I thought his bike was in need of repair. It made some very odd noises."

"He didn't come here," Judith said.

"Good. By the way, where will you be staying in Little Bavaria?"

"At a B&B called Hanover Haus," Judith replied. "I'll write it all down for you. Several of us who are manning the innkeeping booth will be staying there, too. I've never done anything like this before, but Ingrid Heffelman from the state B&B association talked me into it." *Cajoled, badgered, browbeat* were the words that rushed through Judith's mind. And *payback*, as Ingrid had stated, for not pulling her B&B license after so many dead bodies had shown up at or near Hillside Manor in the seventeen years that Judith had been an innkeeper.

"You'll have a wonderful time meeting so many new people," Arlene said. "I hope none of them are murderers. For your sake, of course." She kept on going down the hall.

Joe came back downstairs a few minutes later to get a beer out of the fridge. "I forgot to mention that I intend to put in some overtime tomorrow and maybe Friday to wind up this job for Woody. The last few months have been a real headache after he was appointed a precinct captain and the mayor ordered an investigation of the police department. Or have you already forgotten what happened to us last January?"

Judith sighed. "Hardly. Those few days that you were supposedly under arrest drove me to the brink. In fact, that whole episode almost got me killed."

"I figured you'd recall our nerve-wracking start to the new year." Joe polished off the last of his dinner and stood up. "What time does the train leave tomorrow?"

"Nine-thirty," Judith replied, before taking the last bite of broccoli.

"I'll drop you off on my way to headquarters."

Judith shook her head. "Bill volunteered."

"Bill can un-volunteer," Joe said. "The last time he took you and Renie to the train she had him so confused that you almost missed the damned Empire Builder. I'll call him. He'll thank me."

Judith didn't argue. Renie's weird rationale for changing clocks to and from daylight and standard time the previous October still was so confusing that she'd tried to forget it ever happened.

"One thing, though," Joe said, putting his plate and cutlery in the dishwasher, "promise me you won't get into trouble."

Judith smiled ingenuously. "Don't worry. I won't have time to do that. I'll be busy with the booth and making nice with potential guests."

Joe frowned. "What's Renie going to do?"

"God only knows," Judith admitted, "but I'll probably spend the rest of the time keeping her from antagonizing people that I'm making nice with."

Joe didn't look convinced. "You didn't promise."

"That's dumb," Judith said. "I already told you what I'd be doing. Isn't that good enough? We'll be coming back Sunday night."

Joe shrugged. Judith sensed what he was thinking. They both knew she never made promises she couldn't keep.